MAGGIE ALDERSON

Cents and Sensibility

PENGUIN BOOKS

PENGUIN BOOKS

Published by the Penguin Group
Penguin Group (Australia)
250 Camberwell Road, Camberwell, Victoria 3124, Australia
(a division of Pearson Australia Group Pty Ltd)
Penguin Group (USA) Inc.
375 Hudson Street, New York, New York 10014, USA
Penguin Group (Canada)
90 Eglinton Avenue East, Suite 700, Toronto, Canada ON M4P 2Y3
(a division of Pearson Penguin Canada Inc.)
Penguin Books Ltd
80 Strand, London WC2R 0RL England
Penguin Ireland
25 St Stephen's Green, Dublin 2, Ireland
(a division of Penguin Books Ltd)
Penguin Books India Pvt Ltd
11 Community Centre, Panchsheel Park, New Delhi – 110 017, India
Penguin Group (NZ)
67 Apollo Drive, Rosedale, North Shore 0632, New Zealand
(a division of Pearson New Zealand Ltd)
Penguin Books (South Africa) (Pty) Ltd
24 Sturdee Avenue, Rosebank, Johannesburg 2196, South Africa

Penguin Books Ltd, Registered Offices: 80 Strand, London, WC2R 0RL, England

First published by Penguin Books Ltd, 2006

3 5 7 9 10 8 6 4 2

Copyright © Maggie Alderson 2006

The moral right of the author has been asserted

Cover design by Marina Messiha © Penguin Group (Australia)
Cover illustration by Elizabeth Lamb
Author photograph by Adrian Peacock
Typeset in Monotype Garamond by Palimpsest Book Production Limited, Polmont, Stirlingshire
Printed and bound in Australia by McPherson's Printing Group, Maryborough, Victoria

National Library of Australia
Cataloguing-in-Publication data:

Alderson, Maggie.
Cents and sensibility.
ISBN 978 0 14 300606 0.
1. Finance, Personal – Fiction. 2. Interpersonal relations – Fiction.
I. Title.

A823.4

penguin.com.au

For Josephine Fairley

Acknowledgements

Thank you to:

My wonderful publishers – Julie Gibbs in Australia and Mari Evans in the UK. Thanks also to the entire teams in both locations. Penguin rules OK.

To my adored agent, Jonathan Lloyd, and all at Curtis Brown in London, particularly Camilla Goslet and Alice Lutyens. To Fiona Inglis, Pippa Masson and the gang at Curtis Brown in Sydney. And Christy Fletcher in New York.

Always to my treasured novelist gal pals, for advice, support and emails: Jessica Adams, Kathy Lette and Karen Moline.

To Stephanie Donaldson for help with what blooms where and when, Mark Connolly for his New York insider eye, and Chris Durlacher for Côte d'Azur savoir faire. Rose and Grace Eastell for their sage advice on pop music. Chris, Iain and Johnnie Alderson for the same on death metal.

To all the people who lent me havens to write in: Glenn and Kath Veness for Windy Corner; Jean Howell for Oxford Terrace; Lionel Copley for Trafalgar Cottages; Jane Scruton for Garden Cottage; Hilary Robertson and Alastair McCowan for the Old Brewery; Roland Shiers for the Old Printworks.

And always, always to Popi – for hiding books from me, among many other services – and to my darling Peggy, for being the light of my life and knowing *The Gruffalo* by heart.

HENRY ALEXANDER MONTECOURT-FAIN, THE LORD MONTECOURT OF CLIFFE

m

1 Delphine	2 Margot	3 Rose	4 Kristy	5 Nicola	6 Chloe
Stella	[no issue]	[Alex, Claudia, Rowan] Tabitha, Toby	[Archie] Venezia	Marcus, Freddie [Beatrice, Hattie]	Daisy

I

There's only one thing worse than having a boyfriend with no money – and that's having an incredibly rich one. But I didn't understand that until I had known Jay for quite a while.

I'd had no idea just how rich he was when I first met him, or perhaps I would have been more wary. I mean, I knew right away he wasn't exactly short of cash, because of where we met, at the Grand-Hotel du Cap Mimosa, on the Côte d'Azur. It's a seriously jet-set sort of place. You can't get a room there for less than £300 a night and I knew that he was there just for the hell of it, paying his own way – and in the middle of the week, too – whereas I was there strictly for work.

I was on a press freebie, to do an interview for the newspaper I worked for with the 'legendary international megastar' Jericho (that was her publicist's description, by the way; I would have said more 'singer-turned-actress-turned-nightmare'), about her new line of diamond jewellery.

She was launching the range there because 'the sparkling light and laughter of the South of France was a major inspiration for the Collection'. Or, at least, that's what it said in the press pack the PR had given us in the Business Class lounge at Heathrow, where we were waiting for our midday flight to Cannes.

'Listen to this bit,' I said to my friend Amy, the editor-at-large of society magazine *Pratler*, and my favourite partner in crime on such trips.

'"I have always loved Diamonds . . ."' I read out. '"To me, the spark of light in Diamonds is like the celestial flash of Brilliance that inspires my Work. Diamonds are nature's Music."'

We snorted with laughter.

'And what's with all those capital letters?' said Amy, looking at her own copy.

'Rampant ego?' I suggested. 'Extreme pretentiousness? Bullshit overload?'

'All of that,' said Amy, slamming the press pack shut, with a shudder. 'Reckon this could go one of two ways, don't you?' she continued, in confidential tones, as Tara – the PR who was organizing the trip – walked past us. 'Could be totally divine – spa treatments, poolside drinks, minimal shite about the product; or it could be two days of illustrated lectures in darkened rooms and a four-hour wait for a group interview with Miss Jericho, as they call her. What do you reckon?'

'No darkened rooms,' I said. 'I checked it out with Tara before I agreed to come.'

Amy laughed.

'You're hilarious,' she said.

'Just bitterly experienced,' I said. 'But there'll be no avoiding the wait. We all know how famously late Miss Jericho is. And it is a stupid group interview, you're right. Then they expect us each to write an original piece . . .'

Amy rolled her eyes. 'Oh well, at least we'll have each other – and we'll need some good company, look who's just walked in.'

She nodded towards the entrance, where Tara was effusively greeting a woman with a severe bob haircut and heavy-rimmed statement spectacles. It was Laura Birchwood. My equivalent from a rival broadsheet newspaper.

'Now that *is* annoying,' I said to Amy.

'Yes,' she agreed. 'She's so over-focused, that girl, I find it exhausting. She takes work much too seriously. Sense of humour: *nul points*.'

I agreed with Amy about all that, Laura was infuriatingly competitive, but I was annoyed for another reason: I'd made Tara tell me who else was going on the launch before I'd agreed to cover it and Laura's name had definitely not been mentioned – while the words 'British newspaper exclusive' definitely had been.

But with the prospect of two nights in my favourite hotel on the French Riviera and further larks with Amy, I decided to put such irritations aside and just enjoy myself, exclusive story or not.

The Cap Mimosa was certainly as gorgeous as I remembered it, when I was shown to my room later that afternoon. The white lawn curtains were blowing gently in the breeze, and when I stepped out on to the balcony, the Mediterranean was intensely blue and sparkling, just the way it's supposed to be – although even Jericho couldn't have arranged that in advance. Not even by yelling at it, as she was famous for doing to her personal assistants. Rumour had it, she'd had to pay one of them off, after attacking her with a Christian Louboutin stiletto heel.

Back in the room there was a huge vase of heady tuberoses, and six mini-bottles of Pommery 'Pop' in an ice bucket on the table, with a welcome note apparently signed by Jericho herself, although on close inspection I could see it was printed.

A few more little touches laid on to put us in the right frame of mind for her latest 'oeuvre' – as it said in that dreadful press release – included a large floppy hat (from her accessories line) and a pair of large black sunglasses (likewise), in a charming local basket. A particularly nice touch, I thought, the basket, a little low-key accent to counterpoint all the luxury.

And luxury was something I knew plenty about. I was a senior feature writer on the *Daily Journal* – which was considered London's most prestigious broadsheet newspaper – and luxury was my special area of expertise.

While my colleagues specialized in the Middle East, or crime, or parliament – for me it was crocodile-skin handbags, inlaid backgammon sets, bespoke shoes and couture fragrances. All those little areas that add up to the modern ideal of the luxury lifestyle.

And the Cap Mimosa pretty much summed that lifestyle up, I thought, as I looked around the exquisitely elegant cream and gold room. Then, after checking the schedule in the press pack, I saw I had time to enjoy a bit more of it, before the first official event, a welcome dinner for all the journalists, with Tara and the rest of Jericho's global publicity machine.

Eager to make the most of my stay, I headed straight down to the hotel's heavenly swimming pool to do some laps. There was only one other person in there, powering up and down, while I took it a little more gently, pausing each time I reached the end to gaze out over the Med, and the huge white boats bobbing in the hotel's private marina.

When I felt I'd swum enough, I sat at the top of the pool's elegant curving stone steps, with my feet in the water, just breathing in the garden-scented air and enjoying the feeling of sun on my skin.

The other swimmer stopped for a moment at the other end, to let the water out of his goggles, giving me a tantalizing glimpse of well-muscled brown shoulders. Then he resumed swimming and I stood up to leave the pool.

I headed off towards the steam room at the hotel spa, but before I got there I ran into Amy, who was en route to her idea of a rejuvenating Riviera afternoon: the outdoor bar.

The prospect of Amy's company was irresistible so, with my healthy intentions immediately abandoned, we were soon installed on the rattan sofas set among orange trees in pots, the wisteria in glorious full bloom along the loggia next to us, drinking champagne and roaring with laughter. That was where she introduced me to Jay.

I noticed him immediately when he walked on to the terrace. He was startlingly tanned in a white linen shirt, which was flapping open, a towel around his waist, his black hair wet and elegantly slicked back. He had very brown bare feet.

It was the guy from the pool, I realized. Class Eurotrash, I thought to myself, now I had a chance to look at him properly, and I saw his eyes – strikingly dark blue – rest on me for a moment as he walked over to the bar.

He didn't notice Amy immediately, as she had her back to him, and it wasn't until she shrieked with laughter – at a story I was telling her about my last, disastrous press trip to a Bavarian *schloss* for the launch of a solid silver pencil sharpener range – that he came over.

'Amy?' he said, standing behind her, but looking at me, making me suddenly aware of the wet T-shirt competition effect of my wet bikini through the kaftan's semi-sheer fabric.

She turned round and then jumped up to hug him, with her customary enthusiasm.

'Jay!' she squealed. 'Darling one, what a heavenly surprise, but of course you're here. This is your natural territory. Are you with anyone? Come and join us. This is my gorgeous friend, Stella Montecourt-Fain. She works for the *Journal*. She's terribly clever.'

So he did join us and, fuelled by more champagne which he insisted on buying, the chemistry between us was instant and vivid. Amy chatted on in her infectious way, telling long involved stories that somehow never got boring, with Jay and I interjecting the odd one-liner, our eyes meeting with increasing frequency.

I was just trying to stop mine sliding down to his chest and stomach, as he slowly did his shirt buttons up, with elegant fingers. I'd never seen anyone look so sexy putting their clothes on.

'So, Jay,' said Amy, having come to the end of a hilarious anecdote about a trip to the Arctic Circle, when she had been bounced out of a reindeer sleigh at high speed and no one had noticed for five minutes. 'We're here for a riveting jewellery launch with international megastar, Jericho. Are you here for any particular reason, or just because it's rather nice?'

'Well, I'm here for the launch too, actually,' he said in his strange accent, a weird mixture of Posh London Mockney and Cape Cod American. 'I ran into Jerry in Aspen and she said I should come hang out for the launch.'

Amy's eyebrows shot up.

'Jerry, is it?' she said, archly.

'That's just what people call her, Amy. Nothing more than that. She's kinda fun, so I thought I'd come and see what happens at these things.'

'Maybe you should launch a range of jewellery too, Jay,' said Amy and he pretended he was going to throw his drink over her.

'What do you do?' I asked innocently, having no idea that was the very worst question I could have asked a money bunny like him.

I knew I'd made a mistake, when I saw Amy's face freeze, but Jay kept his cool, in a way which would have amazed me when I knew him better.

'I'm an investment manager,' he said smoothly, shooting Amy a look which I didn't understand at the time. 'But mostly, I like to have a good time. Would you girls like to come out dancing with me tonight?'

'Not if you're driving,' said Amy, prompting another near miss from Jay's drink. And then she added, glancing quickly at me, 'And only if you've got a friend for me to play with.'

'Spotter?' said Jay.

'Oh, brilliant,' said Amy, delightedly, beaming at me, although I hadn't a clue what they were talking about.

'Who or what is Spotter?' I asked her, when Jay had gone back into the hotel, after arranging to meet us in the lobby at ten.

'Oh, he's really great,' said Amy. 'Such a funny guy. Great

friend of Jay's, ex-army boy, you'll love him. Shall we go in and change? We can bolt down the welcome dinner and then plead exhaustion and sneak out to meet Jay. Plan?'

'Plan,' I said, nodding.

'Er, Stells,' said Amy, with an unusually serious tone in her voice, as we stood up to leave the bar. She touched my arm gently. 'Wear something pretty tonight. We'll be going somewhere nice with Jay.'

She looked at me intently, and nodded quickly a couple of times, as though she was giving me some kind of coded message. I wished she would just come out and say it, whatever it was, but I sensed she wouldn't be comfortable to spell it out, so I just smiled and nodded back.

Fortunately, I did have something really pretty to wear. My years of press trips had taught me always to pack one killer dress, because you never knew where you might end up going.

And I knew I could go anywhere in the blue silk Lanvin number I had just slipped over my head. With my favourite gold Prada wedges and a nice tan left over from my January holiday in Goa, I was pretty happy with the way I looked.

When I stepped out of the lift into the hotel foyer, after a quick trip back up to my room to check my make-up after the hurried dinner, I could see that Jay was too.

His face broke into one of those spontaneous smiles that signals a man is relieved to find that you are no less attractive than he remembered. And I'm very good at reading men in that way – because with a father like mine, I'd had expert tuition.

So far my dad has had six wives. And his name is Henry, which is pretty funny. Unlike his royal namesake, though, he has no problem producing heirs. I think it was seven, the last time I totted us all up.

What makes it really confusing is that some of his wives already had children of their own when they arrived in his life, or have had more subsequently with new husbands. So as well as all my half-brothers and sisters, I have swathes of stepsiblings and semi-steps, which is what I call the ex-wives' subsequent children.

On top of that, Venezia, one of my half-sisters – the daughter of wife four – was born while my father was still married to wife three. Sometimes, I think even he loses track.

Henry Alexander Montecourt-Fain – I call him Ham – is an architect. He just likes to build things, whether it's a palace for a president, a major museum, affordable housing for the masses, a tree house for his children, or a dynasty. He's a true creative, physically incapable of not producing things.

I remember watching him once when he was talking on the phone in his London house. As he droned on – the sound of his own voice is the only thing Henry likes more than the glug of a newly opened bottle of claret – leaning against the stainless-steel countertop, his big strong hands were constantly fiddling with something.

When he eventually hung up the phone, having told the person on the other end that they were a wicked little flirt who needed a good spanking in the very near future, I saw what he had been fiddling with.

Propped against the digital scales was a tiny little man made out of about two inches of electrical cord and a matchstick. He'd pared back the cable so that the earth and live cables were the limbs, with the revealed copper wire bent to make hands and feet. The pink top of the match was the head.

I stood and gazed at it for a while, then I put it in my pocket.

I am the oldest of Henry's children, from his first marriage, although my mother was definitely more the Anne Boleyn type than a loyal Catherine of Aragon. She was a wild thing, by all accounts, but she died before I was two, so I really don't remember her.

I know what she looked like – rather beautiful, in a centre-parted kind of way, with long dark wavy hair and high cheekbones, which I am told I have inherited – but that's just from photographs and a few reels of cine film which Ham has occasionally shown me, but only when he's been between wives. And on the wrong side of a few bottles of claret.

If I sound casual about it, it's just because my mother never featured in my conscious life. She'd bolted away from us before my first birthday, to live in Marrakech with some painter she'd taken up with, where she'd caught the flu and died. Just like that.

'A very mundane death, she would have thought,' Ham had said about it once. 'She would have preferred to go like Isadora Duncan, or to have had a wasting disease that made her even more elegantly beautiful, ending in a heartrending deathbed scene, where I would have come and begged her forgiveness. Which I would have done, of course. Even though she left me, the cow.'

Then he'd look at me sadly. He never quite said it, but whenever he spoke about my mother – which was very infrequently – I had the strong impression that he still missed her.

Maybe I was kidding myself, because I wanted to feel special, rather than just abandoned, but I did wonder on those occasions whether she really had been the true love of his life and whether the procession of women since had just been a futile search to replicate what they'd had together.

But while that carousel of stepmothers and assorted siblings had made for a fairly unusual childhood, I'd always had my Ham, like a great immovable mountain at the heart of it all. He may have been flighty and fickle with his lovers, but he was solid as a rock for me. He was my dad and my buddy and my very best friend – and the most marvellous tutor in the ways of men.

'Men are appalling,' he'd told me from early childhood. 'We never really mature, not on the inside. It's all just an act. Don't ever trust men, Stella, my darling. We're dreadful. Enjoy us, use us, abuse us, but never ever trust us.'

'But you're not dreadful, Daddy,' I'd say, gazing up at my hero, all craggy six foot three of him.

'Not to you, my little duckling,' he'd reply. 'Not to you.'

Just before I'd left my hotel room that night at the Cap Mimosa, to meet the others downstairs, I had taken Ham's little electrical cable man out of my sponge bag – I never travelled without it – and given him a kiss. He was my get-lucky charm and after having a glimpse of Jay's chestnut-brown chest earlier on, I was definitely in the mood for it.

And right from the start of that night, the charm had seemed to be working its magic. As Jay kissed me on both cheeks in greeting, holding me with very attractive confidence by my bare upper arms, I was enveloped in a wonderful cloud of Acqua di Parma, my favourite male smell.

Then he had quite naturally taken my hand and led me out to a ridiculously long, white stretch limo that was idling by the entrance. Amy and a large red-haired person I assumed was Spotter, were already in it.

'I'm sorry it's so crass,' said Jay, as we got in. 'They couldn't get me a black one at short notice. But Amy doesn't care for my driving and it would have been too cramped in a town car.'

'Oh, I don't know,' boomed Spotter, who was clearly an Englishman of a central casting kind I had thought were dying out. 'Might have been fun.'

He leaned across and slapped me heartily on the leg, then shamelessly squeezed my thigh. Under my dress.

I forced myself to smile at him, and moved discreetly away as soon as I could.

'Settle down, Spotter,' said Jay, firmly.

I found his casually proprietary air thrilling and the evening went on in the same vein, as we seemed to go on a bar crawl of the Côte d'Azur's chicest private-member establishments, with me making every entrance on Jay's arm.

As we moved from venue to venue – he seemed to be a member of all of them, the way they let him in with no hassle – I gathered that we were somehow looking for the action, although the walking into each place always seemed to be the best part, as heads swivelled to check out the latest arrivals.

Jay seemed to know people wherever we went, as did Amy, and my head whirled with introductions, but we never stayed long enough anywhere to get attached to any other group. It suited me, as all the – universally ravishing – women who greeted Jay seemed to come particularly brightly alive when they saw him. I was not welcomed so warmly.

After we'd been to four different places I realized I was actually enjoying the rides between them more than the clubs themselves, particularly the corners, which threw me and Jay against each other, because none of us were wearing seat belts.

I had been about to put mine on when we got into the limo, but when the others didn't, I remembered that seasoned limo passengers were above such banalities. This was not real life and, for the elite few who inhabited that elevated realm, the normal rules did not apply. Or so they thought. I just wanted to fit in.

When we got back in for what turned out to be the last leg of our tour, I was particularly glad I wasn't wearing any kind of restraint, as the corners seemed to get so extreme I was practically sitting on Jay's knee half the time. I even wondered whether he had secretly told the driver to lurch around as much as possible.

It was just the kind of caper Ham would have come up with in his endlessly inventive seductions, and it worked, because after I had shot along the cream leather upholstery a few times like a speeding pinball, it seemed quite natural for Jay to put his arm around me and pull me close. I really didn't mind.

Amy thwacked Spotter with her handbag when he tried

to pull the same stunt with her, and braced herself by clinging on to the ceiling strap.

But all too soon, as far as I was concerned, we arrived
at our destination, an imposing white edifice with a large
crowd of people standing outside it, waiting on the wrong
side of a barrier patrolled by two enormous bouncers. They
all turned to gawp when we pulled up in what Jay had christened the Pimpmobile.

'Oooh,' said Amy, like an excited small child, looking up
at the huge neon sign on top of the building. 'Wonderland.
I've heard so much about this place. There was a big piece
in the mag about it when it opened. Is it as good as they say,
Jay?'

'I've no idea,' he replied. 'I've never been here before
either. It's not really my kind of a place, but I thought we
should check it out, as there's so much hype about it.'

He wasn't kidding. It was supposed to be 'the hottest club
in Europe', with so much publicity about its ridiculously
fearsome entrance vetting nonsense, I actually felt quite
nervous as we approached.

The initial two Incredible Hulks had taken one look at
the car and let us straight through their velvet rope to the
next checkpoint, which was policed by two more tuxedoed
Gigantors and a simply terrifying drag queen, who was
surveying the crowd through opera glasses from the top of
a small flight of steps.

She was wearing a one-shoulder dress made from what
appeared to be an entire crocodile skin, dyed emerald green
and complete with head. Combined with towering platform
shoes and vertical hair (well, wig), she must have been eight

feet tall. Her lips were like a couple of red patent-leather bananas.

'Scary Mary,' said Jay, taking my hand again. 'I thought King Kong killed Godzilla.'

She turned to look down at us imperiously through the opera glasses and then nodded at her guards. We were in. The crowd roared with approval.

As we approached her final silk rope, she smiled broadly.

'Hey, Jay, honey,' she said, in a voice as Southern as the Mississippi, and kissed him warmly on both cheeks. 'Good to see y'all. I'll radio ahead so you can go straight up to the private rooms.'

I was impressed – very impressed – but I still didn't twig that there might be rather more to Jay Fisher than just the charming, good-looking playboy I had taken him for.

2

From the moment we walked through the – huge, gold-leafed – door, I could see that Wonderland was more than appropriately named. In size, decor and sheer volume of music, it was the most over-the-top club I had ever been in – and I'd been to Moscow a few weeks before.

We had a quick look round, but the pounding beat from the main dance floor was so overwhelmingly loud, even by normal club standards, I was more than a little relieved when a man in a silver boiler suit and a headset approached Jay and asked if we would like to go straight to the VIP area.

He took us up there in a lift and we got out into what looked like the interior of a spaceship, with lines of giant rivets across the metallic walls and ceiling, the area around the dance floor interspersed with little white pods, like futuristic yurts with large porthole windows.

'This is all a bit weird,' said Spotter, looking around suspiciously as we settled into a pod. 'Makes me fancy a pint of bitter in a good old British pub, all this *Dr Who* nonsense. It's only an upmarket boozer, isn't it, this place, really?'

'Oh, Spotter,' said Amy, giving him a hard nudge. 'Just because it's not The Admiral Cod. This is cutting-edge stuff – Philippe Starck designed this bit of the club. You just concentrate on the pretty ladies and you'll have a lovely time.'

He already was. All the waitresses were wearing skintight

silver catsuits, with large panels cut out in crucial places. Spotter went all pink, as one went sashaying by, a large expanse of bare buttock visible at his face level.

'Bloody hell,' he said. 'I've always had a thing for Barbarella.'

Jay rolled his eyes.

'Not very subtle, the French, are they?' he said.

'Well, they did invent the cancan,' I said. 'That should have been a warning to us.'

'Let's have a drink,' said Amy, with customary pragmatism. 'That will make it all seem a bit more normal.'

She was right. After a couple of champagne cocktails, it seemed practically normal to have a waitress in a bare-bottom catsuit bending over next to me.

We'd been there for a while before it struck us what else was surreal about the place, apart from the decor and the staff uniforms: Jay and Spotter were by far the youngest men there.

It was Jay who pointed it out.

'Check him,' he said. 'The guy in the white jacket and the white shoes, dancing the frug with his great-grand-daughter's best friend. If she shakes her booty much more, he'll have a cardiac arrest. He looks like the grandpa from *The Simpsons*.'

Once you'd noticed, it was hilarious. The women were all young and beautiful, the men were all old and shrivelled. With their dark orange tans, they looked as though they'd been pickled.

'I can't stand this any more,' said Jay, after we'd laughed ourselves nearly sick at it all. 'Let's go and even things up, huh?'

He took my hand, Amy jumped up and grabbed Spotter's, and we hit the dance floor at a run.

From the first step I could tell that Jay was one of those men I could really dance with. We hardly broke eye contact as we shook and shimmied and did impersonations of the various ageing fruggers and babes on the dance floor. We were fooling around, but we both knew the real score. Sexual tension was hanging in the air between us so palpably we didn't need to overdo it.

I turned and danced with Spotter from time to time and we even swapped partners with some of the other couples. I liked dancing with old chaps, because it reminded me of happy times with Ham, and the girls were very happy to take a turn with Jay and Spotter. Happy to the point where Amy and I had to go and entertain ourselves back at the pod, before they could escape back to us.

'Bloody hell,' said Spotter, when they eventually returned, redder in the face than ever, flapping his collar and blowing down the front of his shirt. 'Thought we were going to be eaten alive out there. Men devoured on dance floor. Terrifying.'

But then something really scary happened. The lift where we had come in opened and standing there, fully striking a pose, in a sparkling sequinned minidress, with a full Barbarella hairdo, was Jericho.

Even though we were only there for her launch the next day, it was still a shock to see such a famous face when you weren't expecting it. Jericho was somehow more of a concept to me than a real person, but there she was, in all her glory.

She really did look amazing and even as I recovered from

the surprise, I was registering that she must have researched the venue before she got her look together for the evening, to make maximum impact. What an operator.

She stayed still for a few beats, her white fox-fur coat slipping down her shoulders, surrounded by four enormous men in the immaculate white suits her bodyguards always wore. She made sure everyone had noticed her entrance, and then she headed straight for our pod.

'Jay, darling!' she was yelling, before she even got to us.

I turned to Amy in dismay. I knew they were friends, but I hadn't realized we were going out on a double date. With me as the spare.

'Here comes Jerry,' Amy whispered to me. 'You can get a scoop for the paper.'

Jay stood up to greet Jericho and almost disappeared into those famous curves. I began to feel distinctly uncomfortable as he emerged.

'Jerry,' he was saying. 'Great to see you. I'd like you to meet my friends, Stella, Amy, Spotter . . .'

She couldn't have been less interested in meeting us. The crocodile on the door-bitch's dress had given us a more sincere smile, and then, just as suddenly as she had arrived, she had stolen Jay away.

Amy, Spotter and I were left just sitting there, while Jericho engaged him in what appeared, from what I could see through the portholes, to be a very intense conversation in a neighbouring pod, with her bodyguards stationed firmly between us.

So much for my get-lucky charm, I thought. But then, I told myself, Jay clearly was too good to be true, I should have known better. He'd just been toying with me to pass the time until his real date arrived.

I tried not to show how disappointed I was, but I felt really stupid for ever thinking that a smoothie like him could have been seriously interested in me – after all, he'd pretty much told us he was with Jericho when we'd first seen him at the pool bar.

'So is Jay schtupping Jericho?' Amy asked Spotter, with customary frankness.

'I didn't think so,' he replied, frowning like a puzzled gun dog. 'I thought he was just coming on this trip for laughs. I think he would have told me if he'd ridden that pony, don't you? Not a thoroughbred, but definitely a champion.'

I followed Spotter's gaze to see Jericho, now minus the fur, shimmying on to the dance floor, leading Jay by the hand.

'This will be worth seeing,' said Amy and she was right. It was quite a spectacle, to see the world's biggest pop diva strutting her stuff, just yards away from us. And she was a great dancer, damn it. Even with her security guards circling round her – like Stonehenge with rhythm, one of them holding her fur – she was a great dancer.

So, I thought miserably, slumping down on the white leather banquette, she was a brilliant dancer, she had the most famous figure in the world – her breasts were reputedly insured for $5 million each – she was wearing next-season Dolce & Gabbana (I recognized it, because I'd just interviewed them in Milan) and she was dancing with the gorgeous man I had foolishly thought might be interested in me. Great.

They stayed on the dance floor for what seemed like six

hours, but was probably only about three tracks, when the white suits abruptly walked off, with just a flash of silver sequins visible in front of them.

As I took that in, Jay reappeared and flopped down in the pod next to me. Amy and Spotter had gone off on missions of their own, so it was just the two of us and he was sitting very close to me.

'Oh, my,' he said quietly. 'I've made a big mistake.'

'What do you mean?' I practically squeaked.

'When she said "come and hang out" down here, I didn't realize quite how serious she was about the coming part.'

'She's cracking on to you?'

'Fully cracked,' he said.

'Isn't that good?' I said, because I thought I ought to. 'Isn't that what ninety-nine per cent of the world's hetero-sexual male population would dream of? And gay for that matter.'

'No,' he said, simply. 'Not me. Of course, she's got a great body, but so has that waitress over there. It's not enough.'

And he held my gaze for just that crucial extra beat. I swallowed. I couldn't help myself and his eyes twinkled in recognition. He'd seen it.

'Where are the others?' he said, looking round.

'Amy's gone to the loo and Spotter's over there dancing with the girl who was with Bart Simpson's granddad. He's left. Gone back to the rest home.'

Jay laughed.

'Let's go,' he said.

'What?' I said.

'Let's go,' said Jay again, standing up and putting his hand out to me. 'You and me. Now, before the Venus flytrap in furs comes back. She's only gone to check out the rest of the club – or to let the club check her out, more like.'

'But what about the others?' I asked.

'Spotter can look after Amy. We'll leave them a note. Tell them to take the Pimpmobile.'

He fished in his pocket.

'Here's the driver's card; we'll leave it for them.'

I was about to ask him some really pathetic questions along the lines of: 'But how will we get back to the hotel if we leave them the limo . . . ?' when sense took over. I scribbled a note for Amy on my business card and propped it with the driver's one, against her drink. I knew she'd find it there.

'OK,' I said, standing up. 'Let's go.'

That was our first challenge. We were heading towards the lift where we'd come in, when a commotion in that area revealed that Jericho was just re-entering by that route. We needed an alternative way out, and fast.

I was looking around for the fire exit, when Jay grabbed the nearest waitress and slipped a banknote into her hand. She looked momentarily surprised, as she glanced down at it, and then took us behind a partition wall to the service lift. We jumped in and down it went.

When the doors opened at the bottom we found ourselves in a dark and smelly back alley.

'Guess this is the true VIP exit,' said Jay, taking my hand as we squeezed past some rank industrial garbage bins.

I laughed.

'I'm not kidding,' he said. 'They often leave the real back way, like this, to escape the paps and crowds, but I can't see Jericho coming out this way. She actually likes to be followed by the paparazzi and mobbed by fans, which is lucky for us.'

After stepping over a pile of unsavoury-looking wet cardboard boxes, we finally emerged on to a scruffy four-lane road, nothing like the elegant avenue of plane trees at the entrance to the club.

'Hmmmm,' he said, looking around and rubbing his stomach thoughtfully. I envied his hand. 'Nothing. Not even a bus stop.'

He looked up and down the road a bit, then back at me. I was shivering in my flimsy dress. It was only mid-March and the night air had a biting chill in it.

'Are you cold?' he said, and taking off his jacket, he placed it gently round my shoulders. He pulled it closed across my chest, letting his hands rest on my shoulder blades, and then, as I breathed in the scent of Acqua di Parma, he leaned forwards and kissed me, very gently, on the lips.

'Pretty girl,' he said, his eyes roving over my face. 'Very pretty girl. Let's get you home.'

He took a coin out of his pocket and flipped it in the air, smacking it down on to the back of his hand and then looked up at me, with one raised eyebrow.

'Call,' he said.

'Heads,' I answered.

'Heads it is,' he said, taking his top hand away. 'Good. That means this way.' He started walking along the road, holding firmly on to my hand. 'And I'm glad about that, because this is the way I wanted to go all along.'

'So which way would we have gone if I'd called tails, Jay?' I asked him.

He turned to me and grinned. 'This way. I'd better watch you. You're on to me.'

We walked for what seemed like ages, until I could no longer hide how much my shoes were hurting me. Jay stopped and turning his back to me, stooped down a little.

'Hop on,' he said. 'I just want to get us to those shops along there. I'll carry you.'

So he did, with both of us, I'm sure, equally aware of my breasts pressing into his back and a similar scenario lower down. My heart was pounding and my mouth was dry by the time we got to what had looked like shops from further back.

But they weren't shops, they were apartments. Nasty little concrete bunkers of apartments. And outside them was a row of scruffy mopeds, chained to a line of metal posts.

Jay bent down and looked at one of the padlocks, and then he glanced up at me before producing a penknife from one of his jeans pockets. In what seemed like just a couple of little twists, the lock was open.

Then he pulled out a thick wad of banknotes, which I could see were American dollars. I'd never known a guy who carried so much cash. He peeled about ten notes off and after folding them carefully, wedged them under the chain and padlock. As he did it, I saw they were $100 bills.

He rocked the moped off its stand and wheeled it back along the road a few hundred metres, with me hobbling behind. Then he got out the penknife again and with a little more effort than it had taken to break the lock, and a little light swearing, the engine eventually spluttered into life.

He climbed on to the Vespa and put out his hand for me, smiling brightly.

'Misspent youth,' he said, smiling broadly. 'Picked up a few tricks.'

I jumped on the back and we whizzed off, my arms tightly around his waist, back in the direction we had come from.

'I'm just going to keep going until we get somewhere,' Jay shouted over his shoulder. 'And then we can figure out how to get somewhere else from there.'

We could have been on Mars for all I knew. We'd been riding around in that limo for hours – I had absolutely no idea where we were and I didn't care. I was grinning into the wind that was whipping the hair back from my head and making my eyes water.

Eventually we came to a big junction with a proper signpost. Jay pulled over and we stared up at it.

'Cagnes-sur-Mer,' he said, after a few moments. 'That's where we need to go. That'll get us back to Cap Mimosa, I think . . .'

He turned round and grinned at me. He had a truly beautiful smile, which lit up his whole face. I beamed back, then we set off again and after a few turns, we were on the coast road.

As we hummed along, passing hardly any other vehicles, the sky ahead of us gradually started to lighten. With that, and the sea being on our right, I knew we were going east, but I didn't get my bearings until we were zipping along the Promenade des Anglais, in Nice, which was eerily quiet at that time of the morning.

It was an exhilarating run, but by the time it was nearly fully light I was so cold I had practically no feeling in my bare legs, so I was relieved when Jay stopped by a small café, where the proprietor was just beginning to roll down his awnings.

'Let's have a break,' he said.

Speaking what sounded like pretty perfect French, he persuaded the man to make us some coffee, although he wasn't officially open yet, and then he popped over to a nearby bakery and brought back some *pains au chocolat* still hot from the oven.

We huddled together and ate them like the starving beasts we were – my rushed dinner seemed a lifetime ago – and then Jay gently rubbed my feet and legs until the feeling came back into them. It seemed the most natural thing in the world.

'Tell me about yourself,' he said suddenly, looking at me in that intense way he had, with his dark blue eyes moving around, like he was trying to put my face together.

'What do you want to know?' I asked, suddenly shy.

'Well, I know you're covering this trip for the *Journal*, so what do you write about? Pop stars? Jewellery? Motorcycle thieves?'

I hesitated before replying. Even though I took professional pride in my work, I always felt stupid telling people what I actually wrote about. My nickname on the paper was 'fluff correspondent' and it bothered me a lot more than I let on.

'It sounds really dumb,' I said, playing with a sachet of sugar on the table. 'But I write about luxury – about luxury goods, the big brands behind them, the artisans who make the things, the history and traditions, the business side of it, and of course, the shopping.'

Jay looked quite serious. There was a little frown line between his brows.

'Is that something you're really into?' he said quietly. 'Luxury shopping?'

I laughed.

'No. That's why it's so silly. I mean, I love shoes as much as the next girl, but I only ended up doing this by accident. I always wanted to work in newspapers and I did politics and economics at university because I wanted to be a foreign correspondent, covering wars and revolutions, and things like that. But then while I was a postgraduate trainee, working in features on the *Journal*, I did an interview with Henri Krug – you know, from the champagne family?'

Jay nodded.

'Well,' I continued. 'The editor of the paper really liked the piece and he offered me a permanent job on the strength of it and that's what I've been doing ever since.'

'Why do you think you have a feel for that kind of subject matter?' said Jay, still looking serious.

I was slightly beginning to feel like he was interviewing me for a job himself, but as long as I had his attention, I didn't mind.

'Well,' I said, slowly, thinking as I spoke. 'My father is an architect and he brought me up to think in terms of quality and design and to analyse why some things are somehow just right and others aren't. I'm certainly not into luxury brands for the status-symbol side of things, I actually don't really like that element of what I do, but I do love good things which are beautifully made. It's the integrity I like, not the status.'

Jay was smiling broadly at me again, his whole face was animated.

'What's your dad's name?' he said, enthusiastically. 'I'm

really interested in architecture, would I know him?'

'You might,' I said. 'Henry Montecourt . . .'

'Lord Montecourt?' said Jay, sitting up suddenly.

'Er, yeah,' I said.

Dad had been ennobled a few years earlier for his services to architecture – particularly for his work on low-cost public housing – but it wasn't something we ever talked about. I was really proud of him, and while he did take it seriously and go to the House of Lords and all that, it embarrassed him to have a fuss made about it.

He was a low-key kind of guy in some ways. He didn't use the Fain part of his double-barrelled name professionally, for the same reasons I didn't use the Montecourt bit. As far as the paper was concerned I was just Stella Fain and I'd been embarrassed the day before when Amy had used my full name to introduce me to Jay.

Montecourt-Fain was such a mouthful and made us sound much posher than we really were – like tenth-generation landowners, or something – but while maybe we had been quite grand around 1066, when our ancestor had paddled across the Channel with William the Conqueror, we certainly weren't any more.

Ham had made all his money himself, he hadn't inherited a bean of it and any property he owned, as he was fond of saying, was from the toil of his own head and hands, and he was fiercely proud of that. Very much a Labour peer, he wasn't a big fan of inherited wealth as a concept – to put it mildly – and he'd always told us kids not to expect anything when he popped off.

And I knew he wasn't kidding; after four divorces and with a tribe of younger children still to support, I knew

Ham didn't have much cash hanging around, even with the extremely high professional fees he commanded. I didn't mind, though; it was one of the reasons I was so serious about my career.

'I love his work,' Jay was saying, really enthusiastically. 'He did the museum in Boston for . . .'

Then he stopped suddenly and it wasn't until much later that I understood that the end of that sentence would have been 'for my family's arts foundation'.

At that point, though, I was still blissfully ignorant about the true nature of Jay's background – and he was loving it.

We finished our coffee and after a quick chat to the café owner and a look at a map, Jay said he knew exactly how to get us back to the hotel.

The sun was out as we set off again and it was a glorious run along the coast. I was almost disappointed when we pulled up on the circular driveway outside the hotel.

The porter ran forwards to park the Vespa for us and Jay turned and smiled at me as he tossed him the keys.

'Good thing he doesn't know how I got hold of it, huh?' he said. 'But don't worry, Stella. I know the concierge here pretty well and I will make sure the bike gets taken back to its owner later today.'

I was sure he would, but I had other worries. As we walked into the lobby I caught sight of myself in a mirror. I looked like a voodoo doll. My dress was all crushed, I had mascara smeared down my cheeks, and my hair had been blown into a fright wig. I was just taking in the full horror of it when my rival from the *Post* newspaper, Laura Birchwood – immaculately coiffed, as usual – walked out of the lift and saw me.

And then, just as she noticed me, Jay turned and called over to me from the reception desk.

'Stella, honey,' he said, in a most affectionate tone. 'What's your room number?'

'Hello, Stella,' said Laura, loudly, making it clear she wasn't going to save my embarrassment by just nodding and walking on. 'Looks like you've been out on the town. Or was it the gutter?'

Jay came over with the room keys and clearly not registering Laura's presence, he took my hand and brought it gently to his lips. But Laura had certainly noticed him; she was staring at him like a hungry dog looks at a sausage.

'Hi,' she croaked, as Jay finally glanced up and clocked her. I mean, Jay was good-looking and all that, but I couldn't understand why she was gazing at him as though he was a heavenly vision.

'Hi,' he said back, coldly.

'Oh, er, Laura,' I said, hating her for standing between me and Jay and the lift. 'This is Jay. Jay, this is Laura. She's here for the press trip too,' I added, not wanting Jay to think she was a friend of mine.

'Are you Jay Fisher?' said Laura, still staring at him.

'Are you Laura Ashley?' said Jay, in the iciest of tones, and stepped round her, into the lift, almost dragging me with him.

'The first presentation is in five minutes, Stella,' Laura practically shouted at me, as the lift doors closed.

'What was all that about?' I asked him.

'I thought she was quite rude, didn't you?' he said, with a look on his face I hadn't seen before. He looked all cross and pinched, with a deep frown line between his brows.

It was an expression I would get to know well, in the future, when I would call it his 'money-horror face'. It was always brought on by crass people making direct references to his family and his wealth. But back then, still in the innocent flush of our first attraction, I had no idea what was bugging him.

I was about to ask him how on earth Laura knew his name, but something in his expression stopped me and then, as he took my hand again and smiled, I simply forgot about it.

The lift stopped at my floor and Jay put his finger on the hold button and kept it there.

'I'll see you to your door, Miss Montecourt,' he said, then he smiled wickedly and moved closer to me. 'Unless you would like to come up with me and see what a really good room in this place is like . . .'

I replied by knocking his hand off the hold button and he pressed the one for the top floor. His 'room' covered about half of it. I'd noticed the plaque on the door as he opened it: Presidential Suite.

'Crikey,' I said, taking in the wall of glass and the vast deck looking out over the bay. 'It *is* a nice room, you weren't kidding.'

'Come out here,' said Jay, leading me to the deck, where there was a large spa tub, gurgling away. 'Feel like a bubble bath?'

I nodded and he slid the straps of my dress off my shoulders and then, torturously slowly, he nibbled and kissed his way round my neck, and gently behind my ears, his mouth finally meeting mine as his hands reached up and found my breasts through the fine fabric of the dress.

As his tongue slid into my mouth for the first time, I

felt as though my entire body had just gone into freefall on some kind of crazy theme-park ride.

Pulling away, I took a deep breath to recover myself, and then stepping back a little, I reached behind and pulled down the zip on my dress, so that it fell suddenly to my feet, and I was standing there in nothing but my yellow silk Myla knickers and my gold shoes.

Jay moaned slightly as his fingers grazed my bare nipples, which were standing to full attention through the combination of his stroking and the gentle sea breeze.

Then he dropped his hands suddenly and just stood looking at me, his eyes sliding slowly down my body. He wasn't even touching me and I felt like I was going to faint. I had never felt so sexually attracted to anyone in my life – and I wasn't an inexperienced girl in that area.

I could see Jay was similarly affected. His chest was rising and falling quickly beneath his shirt and I moved back towards him and slowly unbuttoned it, so I could run my fingers over the chest and stomach that had been tantalizing me since the first moment I had seen him.

I pulled his shirt down over his splendid shoulders, and he let it slide off his arms. Then, not taking his eyes from mine, he slowly unbuckled his belt, then pulled down his jeans and kicked them off, so he was standing there gloriously, splendidly naked.

I still wasn't and as I took his hand and led him over to the hot tub, I didn't take my knickers off. It was quite deliberate. I wasn't going to take them off – even though the chlorine in the spa would ruin them – because I wasn't going all the way with Jay.

I had never wanted to have sex with anybody so much

in my life, but it was a decision I had made much earlier in the evening. Round about the time we hit the dance floor at Wonderland. There was no way I was going to sleep with him that first night, because I wanted there to be a lot more nights than that.

Was I being deliberately manipulative? Yes, I most definitely was. Like I say, Ham had taught me everything about men, how their minds work, how to control them and how to keep them interested. And I knew that if I had sex with Jay now, however much he liked me, I would never see him again.

Although I didn't yet understand how he could get instantly into any night club on the Riviera, why he carried wads of cash in his pockets, or why Laura Birchwood thought she knew who he was and was struck dumb by it, I had figured out that Jay was a serious Alpha Male and Ham had told me exactly how to play them.

Make them wait.

'He was a Junior Alpha Male,' Ham had told me, years before, when I'd had my heart broken while I was at university, by a handsome lothario who had loved me and left me in a particularly callous way.

'What you have to understand, darling,' he had explained, 'is that these are men who can have anything they want. They can buy or demand whatever they want, when they want it, so you have to hold something back from them. Make them wait for it, and they'll be your slaves. Look at me – I still fall for it every time.'

So, calling on all my strength of will, I climbed into the spa with Jay, still wearing my silk knickers, and while we had a wonderful time, kissing and stroking, I never touched him where he most wanted me to, much as I longed to, and I didn't let him inside my pants either. That he would have to wait for.

After a while, when I knew I couldn't hold out much longer, I knew it was time to go. I pulled my head away from his and held his cheeks in my hands.

'I'm sorry, Jay,' I said. 'I'd love to stay here with you all day, but I have to go. God knows what I've already missed at the launch, I'm sure it was all rubbish, but I am here to work and I've got to go and do it. I'm really sorry.'

He opened his mouth like a goldfish. He really couldn't speak he was so surprised.

I kissed him one last time on the lips and climbed out of the tub. I saw him shake his head quickly, as if he was trying to make sense of it.

'I want to see you again,' he said, his voice croaky with frustration.

I nodded. 'Well, I'm not going until tomorrow,' I said.

'I might have to leave today,' he said, raking his wet hair back with his fingers and rubbing his face. 'Jericho might come after me again.'

I laughed. 'You better run for it then.'

'Where can I find you?' he said.

'I'm at the *Journal*,' I said blithely. 'The number's in the directory.'

It was textbook stuff. Ham would have been proud of me.

I dropped my dress over my head, zipped it up with one hand and then – in what I knew was a master stroke – I wriggled out of my wet knickers and left them there on the deck. Then I picked up my shoes, blew him a kiss and left quickly, before I changed my mind.

I knew I had to do it that way. If I wanted to see more of him later, he had to have less of me now. Was I as calculating as all the gold-diggers I would later witness pursuing him around the world? Yes, I was.

But the difference was that I was doing it because I really liked him.

3

After a record-breaking quick change in my hotel room, I'd arrived with wet hair and probably a red face, halfway through the morning's second slide presentation.

I groaned inwardly, as I saw that Jericho's personal diamond cutter was going step by step through the process of selecting the stones. A topic I had only sat through about five thousand times before at jewellery launches.

And I don't even like bloody diamonds. Too many associations with terrible African civil wars, forced child miners, and environmental devastation – all in pursuit of sparkly bits of carbon.

The whole diamond trade made me sick, actually, but it was my job to be there and to write about it and, by the time I'd got down to the conference room that morning after leaving Jay, I had been very late.

Tara Ryman, the PR, had given me a mystified 'what's going on?' look, when I'd crept in at the back, mouthing apologies to her. Mind you, I thought, as I scrabbled to find my notebook in my handbag, she could hardly come the moral high ground with me; she'd lied shamelessly when she'd promised there would be no darkened rooms and slide shows at the launch – and when she'd told me I had the story as a UK newspaper exclusive.

I could have used that as a counter-attack defence for my lateness, but she was the London representative for a lot of important luxury brands, as well as Jericho's ghastly trinkets, so I had to tread a bit carefully. Plus, I really liked Tara, and didn't want to piss her off totally with my poor showing at the launch. Not that Laura Birchwood didn't try to make maximum capital out of it.

'Wasn't that Jay Fisher I saw you arriving with in the hotel lobby late this morning?' she said in full and deliberate earshot of Tara, during a coffee break on the hotel terrace, before the next brain-numbing presentation. 'Looked like you'd been out all night.'

I saw Tara's head swivel slightly to listen better. I just smiled wearily at Laura and shrugged.

'Yeah,' I said. 'So what?'

'How do you know him?' she asked me, her eyes like a cunning little rat.

'How do *you* know him?' I said and walked over to Amy, who I could see was shaking with laughter.

'So do you know him?' she said, punching me on the arm. 'Carnally, I mean.'

'No,' I said. 'I like him, though.'

'I bet you do,' said Amy, although I didn't yet understand what she was getting at. I was still at the stage when I thought Jay was just a good-looking guy, with a certain savoir faire beyond the ordinary.

Looking back, it is hard now to see how I remained dumb about his true identity for so long, but the name Fisher is just not that unusual. It's not like Rockefeller, or Getty, or Onassis, or Rothschild, or Sultan of Brunei, or any of those names that instantly spell huge money. It's just a general sort of name that lots of people have.

If I'd met somebody called Jay Turner, or Jay Gates, I

wouldn't have instantly presumed he was closely related to CNN, or Microsoft, so I just didn't twig that someone called Fisher was necessarily part of the legendary American banking family with the equally famous art collection.

And I suppose I just didn't pay enough attention to the gossip columns and trash mags either, or I would have had an idea who he was, as quickly as loathsome Laura had – i.e. the extremely eligible and cute bachelor and major heir to the family fortune, who had been linked to so many beautiful women.

Speculation about his future wife was not quite as hot as it was for, say, Prince William, or Albert of Monaco, but he was somewhere up there, as I later discovered.

The fact was, even though I was a fluff correspondent and had to keep abreast of fashion and celebrity red-carpet gowns and stuff like that, the first part of the paper I turned to every morning was still foreign news. That was what really fascinated me.

When I was alone in a hotel room, it was CNN I turned on, not E!, let alone Fashion TV. As I'd told Jay, that was why I had become a journalist in the first place – hard news, world events – and even if I had ended up writing about haute couture, rather than coups d'état, my interest in current affairs hadn't waned.

And in all honesty, I actively avoided reading things like celebrity magazines, as they were too much of a reminder that I had strayed so far from my original career intentions.

I would mug up enthusiastically on interviews with the CEO of Louis Vuitton in the *Financial Times*, or analysis of trends in the luxury market in *The Economist*, but articles about film stars' facelifts in the trash weeklies, and even the tabloid gossip columns, were more than I could bear.

But it was a while yet before the full wisdom of journalists reading broadly around their subject, as I had been encouraged to do since my earliest days as a graduate trainee on the paper, would really come home to me.

As I stood chatting to Amy, on that sunny Riviera terrace, a warm buzz still between my legs from the long ride on the Vespa the night before – and what came after – I was still blissfully unaware of the shark-infested waters I was swimming into.

'I'm sorry we abandoned you last night, Amy,' I said. 'Jay just wanted to escape from "Jerry" . . . She wants his bones badly.'

'I'm sure she does,' said Amy. 'Don't worry about it. I was fine. I found your note, pulled Spotter off the dance floor and made him come back in the limo with me. Had to beat him around the head a bit and remind him I'm a happily married mother of two, but it was a good night, wasn't it? Wonder if Jerry will recognize us at the press conference this afternoon?'

She didn't appear to, when she was introduced to us later, after keeping us waiting a full two hours before making her entrance.

When she finally showed up, it was hard to see what had taken so long. Her hair was pulled back into a simple chignon and she was wearing a black cocktail dress of Audrey Hepburn simplicity, the better to show off her hideously flashy jewellery – which was even worse than we had braced ourselves for. It was amazing really, how she had managed to make things that were so expensive look so cheap.

While she clearly didn't recognize me and Amy, she

certainly paid us more attention than she had the night before, when we had been just irritating detritus around Jay.

Now in her full professional megastar mode – and with us in the role of temporarily useful journalists – she treated us to the ultra-wide, blinding smile we knew so well from music videos and movie posters, and even a modicum of eye contact.

But while she started off happily enough, as a woman from the US edition of *Glow* magazine asked her some astonishingly inane and sycophantic questions about the 'philosophy of the range' and 'her deep personal connection with the gemstones', I could see her mood start to darken.

She sighed her way through the rest of our questions, which were clearly not craven enough for her, getting visibly more restive – unless the queries were brazenly flattering.

Then, when I asked her – reasonably enough, I thought – if she was aware of 'the startling similarity between her diamond heart pendants and the famous heart design by Elsa Peretti for Tiffany . . .', she finally blew.

She glared at me like some kind of terrifying gorgon and then, after slamming her water glass down on the table with a mighty crash, so that the contents spilled all over the microphone and everyone within range, she turned and hissed something at her personal publicist, before standing up, kicking her chair over and stalking out of the room.

I had never heard a door slammed so hard. Then she reopened it – glared directly at me – and slammed it again, so the room shook.

Amy and I turned and gaped at each other, bug-eyed. In all our years of diva press conferences, we'd never seen anything like it: true prima donna-ish behaviour, with an added frisson of violence.

There was a moment of stunned silence and then it was Amy who started the laughter – and to my great relief, everyone joined in. Even Tara.

'Oh, you've done it now, Stella,' she said, coming over and punching me playfully on the shoulder. 'She's probably gone up to get her Christian Louboutins. You do make me laugh, though. Always the one with the tricky questions. Why do you do it to yourself?'

'I work for the *Journal*,' I said, with complete sincerity. 'It's my job to ask the tricky questions. And her stupid pendants *are* identical to the Elsa Peretti ones – they're a complete rip-off. Someone had to tell her. They'll probably sue her.'

'Do you know what, Stella?' said Tara, lowering her voice confidentially. 'I've been trying to tell her exactly that since the start of this bloody awful project – so thank you. Maybe she'll listen now.'

After that, the whole launch fell to bits. I was up in my hotel room emailing my news story back to the office for the next day's paper – a story which was much more interesting than it would have been, thanks to Miss Jericho's outburst – when Tara called.

The formal dinner planned for that evening had been cancelled, she told me, and we were all being shipped home right away.

Suited me. When I'd got back to my room after the press conference, I'd found a note under the door from Jay, saying he'd had to leave and promising to contact me in London. Result.

*

The next morning I was back at my desk at the *Journal*, my news story in the paper on the desk beside me – page two, an excellent position for a fluff report – working on ideas for a longer feature about Jericho's burgeoning fashion empire, on orders from the features editor, and bracing myself not to answer my phone.

Normally it wasn't an issue. I never answered it, because I'd never have got any writing done if I had. It rang all day long, with people trying to persuade me to put their products on my pages, so I just ignored it and checked the messages twice daily.

Everyone I wanted to speak to had my mobile number, or my email address – everyone, that is, apart from Jay. So every call that came through that morning on my office phone was potentially him and I had to steel myself not to grab the receiver every time it rang, and to limit checking my messages to once every hour.

By twelve noon I'd checked them three times and there was nothing yet. Between that and having to think more about Jericho and her hideous jewellery, I was feeling a bit edgy – and the twenty-four hours at the Cap Mimosa were starting to seem like a dream.

I was almost tempted to email Amy to ask her if it had all really happened. Had I really met someone called Jay Fisher?

I was just about to go to the kitchen to make yet another cup of tea to try and clear my head when I saw a very large bunch of flowers coming towards me. Behind them was the mahogany-haired head of my least favourite colleague, the features editor, Jeanette Foster.

'I found these in the delivery dock,' she was saying,

plonking the huge bouquet of beautiful pink roses rudely on my desk.

'Oh, thanks,' I said, my heart sinking. Jeanette took a dim view of *Journal* writers being sent flowers – or any other gifts – and as I got plenty of both, it was a source of friction between us. One of many.

I hoped if I didn't say anything else she'd go away and I wouldn't have to tell her who they were from, but she didn't. She just stood there, glaring at me.

'Well, who's this bribe from then?' she said. 'Aren't you going to look?'

I opened the card, but deliberately didn't read what it said. I knew I couldn't trust my face not to reveal anything if, maybe, possibly, they weren't from a PR.

'Oh, they're from that young milliner I did the piece about last week,' I lied, putting the card back into the envelope and throwing it into the bin. 'How sweet of her. It was the first bit of editorial she'd ever had.'

My heart was pounding, as a result of what I'd really just read on that card, but I wasn't going to share the secrets of my private life with Jeanette Foster. I stood up and reached for the flowers.

'I'll get Moira to send them to the women's refuge,' I said.

'Good,' said Jeanette. 'But before you go, I want to talk to you about this bigger Jericho piece. Have you come up with an idea yet?'

Jeanette was always telling us how she liked her writers to generate our own ideas, because it 'kept us active'. But I knew it was really because she was simply too arse-lazy and boring to come up with any ideas of her own. She was a

43

great one for taking credit where it was not due.

'Well,' I said. 'I thought we could broaden it out into a look at the whole concept of celebrity brands. You know, Kylie's undies, Liz Hurley's bikinis, Madonna's children's books, P Diddy's fashion ranges, Victoria Beckham's jeans and the like . . .'

Jeanette was smiling her anaconda smile. It was a good idea, she should have been smiling.

'George Forman's health grills . . .' I added, for my own amusement.

'Yes,' said Jeanette. 'I like that. Good photo possibilities, too. That's good for the layout, lighten the page . . .'

She got a look in her eye that I knew was advance satisfaction at the prospect of presenting the idea as her own. And from that I surmised she was responding to an order from the editor-in-chief, to have more of the 'quality fluff', as he called what I did – hence my office nickname – to lighten that week's papers, which were looking a bit 'bum heavy'.

Those were just a couple of characteristic phrases from our editor, Duncan McDonagh – or Doughnut, as we all called him for obvious reasons, although not to his face. Doughnut was a classic Glaswegian short-arse with an equally short temper, a huge personality, a massive ego and a seriously oversized intellect. You didn't mess with him.

A lot of people on the paper hated Doughnut, or were – like Jeanette – just plain terrified of him, but I understood men like him. I suppose they seemed normal to me. My beloved Ham was no slouch in the monster ego area himself.

And if you worked hard and were passionate about

your area, Doughnut would treat you with respect. More than once I had come back to my desk to find a bottle of champagne on it and a note saying he'd liked something I'd written. Probably one of the reasons Jeanette liked to give me a hard time.

'OK, I'll leave you to get on with it then,' she said, walking off with her usual lack of charm, then pausing to bark back at me over her shoulder. 'I want it by Monday.'

I waited a full minute to be sure she had really gone, before I pulled the little white card that had come with the flowers – Moyses Stevens, nice – back out of the bin.

'*Call me . . . Soon*,' it read, followed by a mobile number and one kiss. No name, just the kiss, but I knew exactly who it was from.

I pondered for a moment how I felt about the presumption of him not putting his name and decided I liked it. It was thrillingly cocky. Then I considered the significance of the one kiss, as opposed to, say, three, or three hundred, and came to the same conclusion. He was clearly a very confident guy. I liked that.

I was just checking the back of the card in case it had more clues on it, when the neat little frame of my friend Tim appeared at my desk.

'I saw Smiler bringing the flowers over,' he said, sinking his face into the deep pink roses. 'Want me to do a rescue mission on them?'

Tim and I had a system to save all the beautiful bouquets which Jeanette expected me to give away, outrageously in our opinion. He'd take them down to his – deliberately cultivated – pal in the delivery bay, on the pretence of having them sent on to a hospital, and then he'd take them home

45

later. He lived quite near me in Westbourne Grove and we'd take turns who got to keep them.

'These are really nice,' he was saying. 'Is that the card you're holding?'

He reached over to take it.

'Oy,' I said, snatching it away. 'That was addressed to me.'

'Spoilsport,' said Tim, but still he didn't offer me any privacy, getting comfortable on the edge of my desk, with his unusually short arms tightly folded, his face pink and perky with excitement. 'Go on, then, Princess Aurora, tell me. Which luxury brand are these from?'

I had to smile at him. Tim loved my world. It was one of the ironies of my life at the *Journal*; Tim had my job and I had his. This squitty little fellow – who adored luxury shopping with a fervour more normal in footballers' wives and other B-list celebrities, whose every move he followed with glee in the weekly trash mags – was a real-life war correspondent. Award-winning.

He was just back from his most recent stint in Iraq. And the first thing he had wanted to know when he got off the plane home were the latest plot twists in *Desperate Housewives*.

'Actually, Tim,' I said, 'these are personal. They're from a boy I met the other night.'

'Cute?' he said.

'Seriously cute,' I said.

'So you clearly haven't done him yet, if he's sending you flowers.'

'You've got it,' I said, laughing.

'Mmmm, I'd like to hear more. Lunch?' he said, making a

gesture as though he was raising a glass of wine to his lips.

'I can't do lunch today,' I said. 'I have to finish this Jericho thing.'

'Oh, my GOD,' he said, his hands flying up to his face. 'You went on that launch. I'd forgotten. What is she like? Nightmare? Fabulous? Did she hit anyone?'

'Ubernightmare,' I said. 'Nearly hit me. Drink later? Email you at six?'

He nodded enthusiastically and bustled off to his desk, where a bullet which had been gouged out of his thigh in a field hospital in Afghanistan was suspended in perspex and mounted on a silver plinth, alongside a small forest of award statuettes. For a little fella, who had been the mercilessly bullied school swot, he was quite a guy.

Once Tim had gone, I made myself tear that card up into very tiny pieces and throw it back into the bin. It was the only way I knew I could prevent myself from dialling that number. But by five thirty that afternoon I was punching a mobile number into my phone. It wasn't Jay's. I was ringing Jack.

Jack was my fallback guy. I didn't have what you would call a boyfriend – I didn't want one – but I did have men in my life. I had a little collection of them, to satisfy the various needs of a relatively young and healthy girl around town.

I had several pleasant, amusing and well-dressed chaps who were my human handbags for work events; one or two more intense ones I liked seeing movies, or exhibitions, with; and Tim, who was my work bestie. Jack supplied the sex side of things. That was the deal and we both respected it. We met for sex, nothing more, nothing less. It was great sex, but that was all it was.

I wasn't particularly proud of the way I had met Jack, but I was happy with the way it had worked out. He'd stepped into my life one day, getting into my carriage when I was on the train going down to Ham's country place, near Lewes.

It had been a couple of years earlier, when they still hadn't quite phased out all the old commuter trains and there were still some running which had the separate First Class compartments. Jack had stepped into mine at London Bridge.

From the moment he got into that carriage I had felt like a tuning fork, there was such an instant sexual chemistry between us. He was a big, strong-looking guy. Broad shoulders, big hands, big legs and, I couldn't help thinking, no doubt a great big . . . to match. And a very attractive face, in a slept-in kind of a way. But really, the most attractive thing about Jack, was his ease with himself.

He sat right opposite me in the empty carriage, his feet firmly planted in their dusty working boots, his knees wide apart. He owned the space he occupied in a very complete way. He grinned at me. I smiled back, I couldn't help it.

'That's one of mine,' he said, suddenly, jerking his head towards the window. I looked out. I had no idea what he meant.

'The church there,' he said. 'The steeple. I'm a steeplejack and I did that one.'

'It's very high,' I said.

He grinned at me. 'I like a challenge,' he said.

And that was it, we'd picked each other up. Like I say, I'm not proud of it and it's not something I would recommend doing, but sometimes life just seems to offer things up in such a way that you have to take them.

Either way, that was the start of a very satisfactory arrangement between us, where I would ring him whenever I felt like what he had to offer and if we could meet we did. He never rang me.

We always met at a hotel, the same one, near Victoria Station, not sleazy, not smart, just faceless and anonymous, and if the staff there ever recognized me as I checked in and connected me with the big bloke in dusty jeans who would arrive not long after, they never showed it.

This was definitely a night to see Jack. It was the only thing that would stop me obsessing about Jay and possibly spending the evening trying to piece the jigsaw of that shredded card back together. He answered straightaway.

'Jack?' I said.

'Allo, Posh Totty,' he replied. That was his name for me. He didn't know my real name and I didn't know if Jack was really his. Considering his occupation, I strongly suspected it wasn't.

'Can you make it tonight?'

'Sure can, Totty, darling. Six thirty suit ya?'

At five forty-five I sent a cowardly intraoffice email to Tim cancelling our drink date and promising to catch up with him the next day, then I raced out to get over to Victoria.

It was as good as always with Jack. Not much talking, down to business, great sex. And I fantasized about Jay all the way through it. By nine p.m., as I hailed a cab outside the hotel to take me home, I felt like I had the situation fully under control.

I was very much my father's daughter.

*

49

Physically weary – in the nicest possible way – and with my overactive brain blessedly calmed, it was wonderful to get back to the haven of my place. I had a tiny little mews house, which you entered down a cobbled side street in Notting Hill.

It was actually the original stable that went with Ham's very large house and I could get into his garden through a gate in the courtyard behind my place. It was the perfect arrangement. I was close to him, but there were three walls, a hedge and a stretch of lawn separating us.

When I needed solitude – which was often – I could always retreat into my little house. Hardly anyone ever came there, not my friends, certainly no boyfriends, or lovers, and not even Ham. When he'd given it to me, he'd said it was mine alone and he would always respect that, while I was always welcome in the big house.

So while I loved curling up in my own little world, happily reading in my big brass bed, or watching BBC World and the History Channel into the small hours, whenever I felt like a dose of family life, I would let myself through the gate, trot up the lawn and see what the latest generations of my half-siblings were up to.

The morning after I saw Jack, I woke up early – after a pleasantly dreamless night's sleep – had a quick shower, threw on jeans and a T-shirt, and ran up through the garden gate.

I stood on the lawn outside the glass doors for a moment before any of them saw me, and took in the scene. It was a typical morning in my father's house.

His youngest daughter, Daisy, who had recently turned three, was sitting on the kitchen table eating cereal dry, from the packet, wearing her Snow White outfit. As I watched she jumped off and pranced around the room a bit, waving a sparkly plastic magic wand. I could just make out the pink shape of Angelina Ballerina on the plasma TV screen on the wall.

Her mother, Chloe, Ham's current wife, was standing at the steel counter in an old silk kimono, studying a book and yawning. Freddie and Marcus, the six- and seven-year-old boys from his previous marriage – born so close together due to a contraceptive miscalculation by their mother – were playing a video game, squashed together on one big armchair in a corner. And Venezia, the fourteen-year-old glamour queen from the marriage before that, was mixing up some potion in the blender.

Daisy saw me first and came racing to the door.

'Stella, Stella, Stella,' she cried, jumping up and down. 'Look, Mummy! Look! It's Stella. Pick me up, Stella. I want you.'

I picked her up, burying my face in her fluffy little blonde head and blowing raspberries. She giggled wildly.

She looked up into my face. 'I like you, Stella,' she said, nodding earnestly. I kissed her little pink lips and set her down on the floor again.

'Show me your latest ballet steps,' I said to her.

'OK,' she said and set off round the room twirling on fat little bare feet, while I went to say hello to the others.

I gave Chloe a kiss on the cheek.

'I see your daughter is more gorgeous than ever,' I said.

Chloe smiled sweetly at me.

'She is rather adorable, isn't she? Would you like some food? I'm making pancakes.'

I nodded enthusiastically. Chloe was a great cook – she wrote cookery books – but even apart from that obvious attraction, I really liked her. She was Ham's best wife for ages, possibly ever, and I was always pleased to see her. OK, so it was a bit weird that she wasn't much older than me – only about eight years – but we got on really well and I was long past the stage of resenting my stepmothers.

Fourteen-year-old Venezia was more of a piece of work, which wasn't a surprise, when you knew her mum, who was really the only one of Ham's wives who had ever been actively unpleasant to me.

Kristy, as her mother was called, was your actual full-on gold-digger. She'd been Ham's mistress for years before she was his wife and Venezia had been born while Ham had still been married to the previous wife, Rose.

When Kristy did eventually get him to marry her, she deeply resented any of Ham's other children having any claim on his resources whatsoever, and she was always doing things like trying to make him take me out of the private girls' day school where I was in my last crucial year and so happy.

'If she's so brainy,' she used to say, 'why can't she just go to a normal school? It's my children who might need to have serious money spent on their education . . .'

Luckily for me, Ham had ignored her, but she used to take every opportunity to make me feel like I was only partly attached to the 'real' family. It was only Ham's dogged loyalty to me which had got me through that difficult time.

It was after the hideous Kristy finally ran off with a richer man – her cosmetic dentist – that Ham had given me the mews house.

'I just want you to know that you are a permanent fixture in this family,' he had said. 'Whoever else comes in or out of it . . .'

'What are you making, Venezia?' I asked, peering over her shoulder; her failure to greet me a reminder of her mother's poisonous manners.

'An oat and fruit face pack,' she said, glancing up at me. 'Want some? You look like shit.'

'No, thank you, dearest half-sister,' I said, pulling a face at her, as she bent back down over the blender. It was the kind of behaviour she brought out in me.

'How's Archie?' I asked her, sitting on one of the high stools by the counter.

'Boring, ugly, stupid, whingeing, just the usual,' she said, without looking up. 'And why should you care, anyway? He's not your brother.'

She was right. Archie – or Archimedes, to give the poor bugger his full name – was Venezia's sixteen-year-old half-brother by Kristy's husband before Ham. So he wasn't any kind of a relation to me, in actual fact, but I still really liked him.

I liked him a lot more than I liked her – my half-blood sister – and there was a connection between us, even if it wasn't blood. I was still very fond of Archie, and I worried about him, because I knew he didn't get on with Kristy's new husband at all. Or with Kristy.

'He's my ex-stepbrother,' I said. 'And I still care about him. Give him my love, will you?'

She just snorted and walked out of the room with her blender of foul gloop. I rather hoped it would bring her out in a rash.

Chloe was just dishing up the pancakes, when a loud thundering on the stairs indicated the imminent arrival of Ham. He was incapable of doing anything quietly. He could pretty much fill a room just with his personality, and his booming voice, heavy footfalls and frequent barks of laughter, would fill any little bits of space left over.

A journalist had once written that you could stand in the Tate Modern Turbine Hall with just Ham and feel it was crowded.

'Mmmmmm, vittles,' he was booming, as he strode down the hall. 'I can smell vittles. A man needs his fooooooood.'

I heard a loud thwack, followed by a squeal, which I strongly hoped was him whacking Venezia on her Diesel-jeaned bottom, as she slouched past him.

'Where are all my little ducklings?' he said, as he entered the room, scooping up Daisy with one hand and throwing her over his shoulder, to her shrieks of delighted laughter. 'Here's one . . . Now let me see.'

He padded round the corner to where the boys were engrossed in their ghastly game and, ignoring their protests, kicked the console out of their hands and on to the floor.

'Gotcha!' he said, scooping them up like piglets, one under each arm, and with Daisy still clinging on to his shoulders, he turned towards the kitchen. When he saw me he dropped them all on the floor and strode over with open arms.

'Duckling number one,' he said and folded me into his

cavernous embrace. He pulled away and had a good look at me. 'You look OK,' he said nodding. 'You'll do. Caught any fierce handbags lately?'

Before I could answer – he knew I'd rather be writing about terrorists than luxury brands – he had rounded the counter and was embracing Chloe from behind, with the lack of inhibition which I would never cease to find embarrassing, no matter how many wives he had.

'Hmmmmmm,' he was grunting, as he buried his face in her neck. I was glad I couldn't see where his hands were. 'Most excellent woman. And food as well, marvellous.'

With much booming and clapping from Ham, everyone – including Venezia, who had been summarily summoned back – sat down at the round dining table for breakfast.

Ham considered family meals the very bedrock of civilization and even Venezia knew she couldn't challenge him on it, although her response to that was to sit through them silently and eat as little as possible.

'So,' said Ham, with his mouth full, 'what's the plan for this weekend? How many ducklings will be in residence with me at Willow Barn, Chloe darling?'

It was Friday morning and Ham always left for the country straight after lunch, alone in his car – an ancient Morgan, which frequently broke down – so he could 'think'. It was Chloe's responsibility, as current wife, to marshal the various brigades of offspring, either returning them to their other parent, or collecting others who were due to be with Ham for the weekend.

As there were different custody arrangements for them all, it kept life pretty interesting for Chloe, but with an excellent system of flow charts on the kitchen wall, she coped.

It was these kind of expectations – and this was just one of many – which had eventually frightened most of Ham's other wives away, as they grew to understand the full extent of his charismatic selfishness, but Chloe, who came from a big family with a tyrannical father of her own, seemed to thrive on it.

Ham's previous wife, Nicola, was a high-flying publishing executive, but after producing two boys in such quick succession, she just couldn't cope with them, the job and Ham's demands, and had fled.

But apart from her cookery books and occasional contributions to magazines, Chloe devoted her entire life to Ham and his extended family, and it seemed to work for them both.

It certainly kept her skinny – I had never seen her sit through a full meal without getting up since she had arrived in our lives – which was another important factor in the stability of the marriage. If a woman showed any signs of letting herself go in the figure department, Ham would immediately lose interest. He's a total bastard, as he is the first to admit, just a very lovable one.

As usual, that morning, after just a couple of mouthfuls of pancake, Chloe got up from the breakfast table to consult the chart she had made on a magnetic whiteboard, with coloured pieces representing each child. Ham immediately helped himself to what was left on her plate.

'Well,' she said. 'It's quite an interesting one this weekend. Obviously Daisy is with us. The boys are going back to Nicola, who will send the au pair to pick them up from school. Venezia is coming with us and she wants to bring her friend, Chanel ... and Kristy has asked if we could possibly have Archie as well, this weekend, as she's just *got* to go to Paris . . .'

'Selfish bitch,' said Ham. 'Of course, we'll have him and ghastly Chanel. That it?'

'No,' continued Chloe. 'Toby and Tabitha want to come down, even though it's strictly a Rose weekend, because they missed out on their last visit because of her birthday, and Alex has offered to drive them. Is that OK?'

'Marvellous,' said Ham. 'The more the better, and Alex is a great chap, I'd like to see him. Haven't seen him for ages.'

He paused for a moment, chewing thoughtfully, then he looked at me.

'Why don't you come down too, Stella?' he said. 'You haven't been for a while. And you used to be quite close to Alex, didn't you?'

I nodded, suddenly a little uncomfortable. Alex was the eldest son of Ham's third wife, Rose. He'd come with her as part of the deal, along with two siblings, when she'd married Ham. I was embarrassed because I'd had the most monstrous crush on him, which had started the moment he'd arrived in our household, building to a crescendo when I was about thirteen.

There was nothing wrong with it – we weren't related, strictly speaking – but it was still a bit cringe-making for the whole family. Particularly as it had been obvious that he had never felt the same about me.

Mind you, perhaps it wasn't surprising I had been a bit overwhelmed by the situation. My mother had left before I was one, and Ham didn't have any children with his second wife, Margot, so I'd been an only child until I was eight.

Then, suddenly, I'd had three glamorous older siblings

all of my own, the oldest of them the amazingly handsome and dashing – it had seemed to me – Alex, then aged fourteen.

He had been a rower in his first year at Radley when he arrived in my life, with broad shoulders, a strong jaw and pink cheeks; the whole package. I was immediately smitten and he had to put up with me following him around like a little puppy every school holidays, until the years passed and he'd grown up and gone off to Cambridge and could escape me.

I'd run into him at parties over the years, but not for a while. I was a bit nervous at the idea of seeing him, really, but at the same time, with so many of us there, it would be good fun. And, I thought simultaneously, it would stop me thinking about Jay.

'I'd love to, Ham,' I said. 'Is that all right, Chloe?'

She gave me a big thumbs up and added another coloured piece to her whiteboard. Yellow, that was my colour.

4

It was the usual mayhem that weekend at Willow Barn, but before the chaos kicked off with the arrival of Chloe in her people mover, with Venezia, Chanel, Archie and Daisy on board, I had something very unusual – a couple of quiet hours alone there with Ham.

Due some time off in lieu, I'd left work after lunch and gone down on the train, arriving before he did. I got a taxi from the station and opened the front door with the key Ham had given me years before, another of his gestures to make me feel I was a permanent part of his life, whatever the changes in it.

For a moment I just stood and took it all in. Willow Barn was an amazing space, which he had created out of an old farm building, with a lot of glass and steel girders.

I had so many memories of that place – some happy, some not, all vivid – and it was good to have some time alone in it. A very rare experience in that house, which had been filled with shrieking children and equally voluble grown-ups, since Ham's team of builders had finished it some twenty years before.

He'd bought the barn when Rose had arrived in our lives, with the three children and several dogs, to create a space that would give us room to 'act out whatever psychodramas will get you all through it', as he had put it at the time.

He'd written a treatise about the project for an esteemed

international architecture journal – called 'Creating Domestic Spaces for the Emotional Journeys of the Modern Family' – and it was one of the things that had catapulted him to international fame.

His ideas about how you could positively foster relationships by manipulating the spaces in which people interact, were so radical and far-reaching, they were on the syllabus of architecture schools around the world.

Some schools had even created whole courses based around Ham's ideas, and he was always flying off to far-flung universities to give keynote lectures. The interplay of architecture and emotion was his big thing and he had the awards to show for it.

The same ideas applied to public housing had been shown to reduce radically the level of antisocial behaviour in some of the most desperate and deprived urban pockets in Britain.

It had all sprung from his years of postgraduate study in Los Angeles, in the early 1970s – where he had met my mother – when the personal development movement had been in full flow. Blissfully freed from the British tendency to repress all emotion, Ham had embraced it enthusiastically – primal screaming, rebirthing, he'd done it all – and the ideas had flowed into his architectural work and become one with it.

His theories certainly seemed to work at Willow Barn. The open spaces of the house – and equally importantly the gardens, orchards and woods surrounding it, and all the little gazebos, grottos and tree houses he had scattered through them – absorbed friction, with enough room to allow festering tensions to dissolve.

There was always somewhere private to go to plot, giggle or sulk, while the huge communal main living area – the kitchen, dining area, sitting room and library flowed into each other in one masterfully articulated space – would gently bring us all together again, like a mother hen gathering in her chicks.

So despite our disparate parentage and allegiances, our different personalities and hang-ups – and the problems they created – we were always a tight little unit again, before we went back to our London lives on Sunday nights. Willow Barn actively absorbed stress and promoted harmony. No wonder we all loved that house so much.

I unpacked my bag in one of the rooms in the guest wing – Chloe had told me that the kids' rooms where I usually slept would all be needed – put a large bunch of parrot tulips into a vase on the table in the sitting area, and a bottle of Jo Malone bath oil on Chloe's bedside table.

By the time Ham arrived, I had Joni Mitchell – another hangover from his LA days, when he had actually lived near her in Topanga Canyon – playing on the whole-house stereo system, the kettle steaming happily on the Aga, ready for his afternoon cup of tea, and some of Chloe's legendary cheese scones out of the freezer and warming in the oven.

I knew so well how my dad liked things to run and the beam on his face when he heard the music, smelled the scones and took in the other details, made my efforts worthwhile.

He made the tea – he was so finicky about it, it was easier just to let him make it and pour it himself – while I sat at the kitchen table happily doing nothing.

'So, number one duckling,' he said, pouring a stream

of his favourite Yorkshire tea – Resolution blend from Botham's in Whitby, and no other – into white Wedgwood cups. He wouldn't drink tea out of anything except white china, because he said it affected the taste. And the milk had to be organic semi-skimmed. Just some of his many micro-obsessions.

'How are things at the paper?' he asked me. 'Broken any major stories about corruption in the Hermès workrooms, eh? Black hearts at Boucheron? Boardroom coups at Gucci Gucci goo.'

I smiled weakly. Ham's constant teasing about the frivolity of my work sometimes went just over the edge with me.

'It's fine,' I said, tersely. 'I went to the South of France last week. Stayed at the Grand-Hotel du Cap Mimosa. Fluff has its benefits.'

'Jolly nice too – rather a pretty building, good gardens, marvellous pool. Had a memorable weekend there once myself, with a rather beautiful woman. One of the few I didn't marry.' He smiled sweetly at me and took a big, satisfied slurp of tea. 'How's your love life these days? Met anyone you might want to introduce to me, yet?'

I shook my head. It was another sticky point between us. I had never really brought a boyfriend home. I just hadn't ever met anyone with a strong enough personality to stand up to Ham, and it really wasn't worth putting someone through it just for the sake of it. And the real truth of the matter was, I didn't really do 'boyfriends', as such. The cosy couple thing just didn't appeal to me.

All my girlfriends seemed to want nothing more than a man they could stay in with, as far as I could tell, but I liked men I could go out with. I liked to live it up with someone

– people, movement, bright lights, fast cars, champagne, dancing. All the stuff I'd done with Jay really.

Nights at home together, watching videos and eating pasta, just didn't appeal to me. Those were the things I liked doing on my own, so why would I want someone else there, getting in the way, wanting to change the channel, or go to sleep early?

And whenever I did feel like a dose of domestic bliss, I could just nip through the garden gate into Ham's world and, while that was usually fun, I was always glad to get back into my own little solitary space again.

Really, after a life of watching the women on rotation in Ham's life, I didn't think it was very surprising I felt that way, but Ham was such a fan of married life himself – as he liked to joke, he loved being married so much he'd done it six times – he just couldn't quite understand why I didn't want it as well.

He'd get all misty-eyed and sentimental sometimes about walking me up the aisle. He had it all planned: we were using the Norman church near Willow Barn, which we would walk to along a winding path mown the night before (by him) through the wildflower meadow, then back for the reception in a Rajasthani tent on the lawn.

We'd also have a maypole, he insisted, with people dancing round it, for some crackpot reason of his, probably something heinous to do with fertility.

He'd practically chosen my dress for me, he was so excited about it. All his weddings had been big productions of various kinds and he just loved the whole package. So did everyone, it seemed, except me.

All my girlfriends were fixated on getting married. Intelligent women secretly longed to be Disney princesses for a day, in meringue dresses and the whole number. Even the ones silly enough to be having affairs with already-married men.

It was an obsession I really could not understand. Couldn't they see that marriage offered no security to a woman whatsoever? That was why I wanted to build my own sense of security, one that only I controlled.

And I didn't want children either, so that was no reason to seek out a more permanent male fixture. I had enough children in my life already through Ham and much as I loved them, especially Daisy, I'd also had plenty of opportunity to observe just how much they restricted and controlled women's lives.

Even successful, independent women like Nicola, the mother of Marcus and Freddie, could be felled by a couple of little toddlers. She'd had a virtual nervous breakdown from the strain. She'd got over it and gone on to have two little girls, Beatrice and Hattie, with her second husband, but I knew it was not for me.

I had tried to explain all this to Ham over the years, but he just couldn't understand it and kept telling me I would grow out of it as soon as I met the right man.

I didn't want to have an argument with him that afternoon, though. Time alone together like that was too rare and precious for us, but I could see he was looking at me with a particularly Hammy expression, as I called it.

I put my head in my hands and waited for the bomb to drop. And it did. It was a beauty.

'You know, Stella,' he said, finally. 'It's really all right with me if you're gay, you know. Just tell me. I wouldn't be at all surprised if my behaviour had put you off men entirely. I'm a shocking example of the male species for any daughter and if you've decided that you feel more comfortable romantically with other women – and you did lose your mother at a critical age, as well, of course – that's fine with me. But do tell me.'

I just looked at him, completely astonished, and then I burst out laughing.

'Ham!' I cried. 'You don't really think I'm a lesbian, do you?'

He looked sheepish.

'Well, it's just you're a very beautiful girl and you never seem to have a chap . . . And I've got some very attractive young lezzos working in the practice these days, it seems to be the way of the world, so I thought I'd better ask you, in case you were suffering, wondering how to tell your dear old dad you were secretly dwelling in *The Well of Loneliness.*'

'Oh, Ham,' I said, squeezing his hand. 'You really are so sweet, but I'm not gay, really I'm not. I do have chaps, as you call them, but nobody special enough to bore you with.'

Jay's face flashed into my mind. Could I imagine introducing him to Ham? Actually, I could. It was the first time I had ever thought that about anybody, but I pushed the thought right out again. If I told Ham about him, even in a casual way, he'd be off ordering the maypole.

'Just accept it, Ham,' I said. 'You won't ever be walking me up to the altar, it's not my thing. But you'll have Venezia to do – she's already planning her wedding, although the scenario changes depending which celebrity has just got married – and then you'll have Tabitha and Daisy to give away, so it's not like you're going to be missing out.'

He looked maudlin for a moment.

'Hope I'm around long enough to see little Daisy-day, in her wedding gown,' he said sadly. 'I won't be here forever, you know, Stella, and I just want to see you settled with a decent bloke before I go.'

I squeezed his hand. For a monstrous tyrant he could be so unbelievably soppy.

'But, Daddy dearest,' I said, determined to tease him out of his tristesse, 'haven't you always told me there's no such thing?'

It became very clear from the moment that Chloe arrived with Daisy and the teenagers, that Venezia's friend Chanel was arguably even more vain and self-centred than she was. Between the two of them, they were doing a very good job of torturing Venezia's older half-brother, Archie.

He was so clearly in love with Chanel, it hurt. Slumped like a piece of lank liquorice in his oversized hoodie, his baggy jeans hanging down below his skinny butt, his cheeks a bas relief of pimples, his mouth crammed with miniature Forth Bridges designed to control his wayward teeth; he was a festering mound of hormones.

It reminded me so much of my own unrequited passion for Alex, acted out in the same setting, it was quite painful to watch.

He'd try to impress her with witty ripostes to her vapid remarks, only to have her turn to Venezia and giggle, before one or other of them would turn back and say, 'Whatever . . .' in indescribably dismissive tones. Then they'd strut off to apply more mascara and lipgloss, all exposed flat midriffs, high breasts and endless legs.

I loved Archie. He was far too good for Chanel. I was

well aware that my big-sister credentials had little appeal compared to her golden-brown abdomen, but nevertheless he seemed quite pleased to see me.

'Hey, Archie boy,' I said, sparring with him a bit and trying, in vain, to be allowed to plant a kiss on him.

'Yeah, hi, Stella,' he grunted, not looking at me. 'Howya doing?'

'I'm fine, Archie.' I leaned my face right into his, to force him to make eye contact with me. 'But how are you?'

He finally looked at me. He had dark red kohl pencil inside his lower eyelids. It did nothing for his pimples.

'Shit, actually, since you ask.'

'Want to come and see if the tree house is still there?'

The clip-clop of Venezia and Chanel coming back down the metal staircase in their high heels distracted him.

'Chanel will still be here at dinner, Arch,' I said. 'Try playing hard to get for a while. Make her miss you.'

He looked at me for a moment, sucking on his braces, then nodded.

'OK,' he said. 'Tree house in five.'

It was one of our little Willow Barn rituals, that none of us kids ever walked to any of Ham's follies together. There were so many different ways to get anywhere in the garden, the lark of it was making sure you got to the agreed place without bumping into whoever you were supposed to be meeting there. It was just something we did.

I set off via a sliding glass door in the entirely glazed front of the house, while Archie headed off towards the kitchen.

I stood on the lawn, now fully green as spring had properly taken hold, breathing in the clear country evening air, watching the hawks wheeling over the hillsides of that ancient-looking landscape and pondering which way to approach the tree house.

It was beyond the old hay barn, spanning a stream on the far side of the orchard. I reckoned Archie would be taking the route via the kitchen garden and decided I would go down the drive, climb over the stile into the paddock, cross that and then enter the tree house from the other side of the stream.

With a bit of jogging, I arrived almost simultaneously with Archie.

'Nice work,' he said, as we smacked palms. 'Did you go drive–stile–paddock?'

I nodded. 'Yeah. A predictable classic, but I like it. How about you? Kitchen door–courtyard–herb garden–vegetable garden–orchard–hay barn–tree house?'

'Nah, much better than that. Kitchen door–courtyard–guest wing . . .'

I made an appropriate 'ooh' noise, to mark the originality of his route.

'. . . guest-wing sitting-room French window–pool house–orchard–hay barn–tree house.'

I nodded appreciatively. 'Good work,' I said. 'Quite tangential.'

We grinned at each other, in joint satisfaction at a family tradition perfectly upheld. Then we just sat in silence for a while, soaking in the tree house's familiar atmosphere.

Ham had built it himself, over a week one summer, in one of his fits of excess creativity between big architectural projects, and it was rough-hewn, to put it mildly. It was splinter hell, if you weren't careful.

'Ow,' said Archie, alternately inspecting and sucking one

of his thumbs. There was flaking black varnish on the nail.

'So why's everything shit?' I asked.

He shrugged.

'Mum?' I pressed him. He just pulled a face. 'School?' I continued. He crossed his eyes. 'Stepdad?' He pretended to hang himself. 'Venezia?' He gagged. 'Chanel?' He hung his tongue out and panted.

'She might not be good enough for you . . .' I suggested.

'I'd like the chance to find out,' said Archie and for the first time, his face split into the grin I had loved so much when he had arrived in my life as a cheeky little boy.

As conversations went with Archie these days, this was a good one. A victim of his own hormones, he'd turned from such a perky little chap, so enthusiastic about his Power Rangers and model cars, into a block of uncommunicative lard, with attitude.

It had happened almost overnight on his sixteenth birthday, as far as I could tell, and I reckoned all I could do was be there for him until he emerged from the other end of whatever tunnel he was in.

'Fucking Gerald's a total wanker,' he spat out, suddenly.

'Yeah?' I said. 'Any particular kind of wankerness?'

'Well, he won't let me have a drum kit, even though I'm already in a band, and I'm the drummer – duh? – and he won't let me go and see Cradle of Filth and he's confiscated my Marilyn Manson posters and he's just a total fuckwit. He won't let me have *Grand Theft Auto: Vice City*, either. He's not even my dad and he thinks he can, like, totally control me. And Mum's useless. She just does anything he wants, as long as he buys her stuff.'

He paused for a bit and picked some black varnish off his

little fingernail. The one that was really long and ugly.

'I can hear them having sex,' he said, quietly. 'They do it all the time and it is so gross. I can hear what they're saying, it's disgusting. Venezia just puts her iPod on and turns up the volume, but he's confiscated mine as well as everything else, just because I wouldn't take it off at dinner one night.'

I felt really sorry for him. The sex thing was gross. Really gross. Suddenly he looked up grinning.

'The other night they were doing it and I just got up and put on Dismember's new CD really loud.' He was nodding his head enthusiastically and laughing his awkward, choking, mirthless laugh. 'That stopped them. He's confiscated that now as well, the tosser.'

He was quiet for a moment and then he looked up at me. There were tears in his eyes. He punched the wall.

'Ow, ow, ow,' he said, nursing his fist under his arm.

'Oh, Arch,' I said, touching his arm. I knew that was as much physical contact as he would allow.

'It's shit,' he said.

'Yes, Archie, it is. It's total shit.'

By the time we got back to the house, dinner was on the table – and Alex had arrived with Toby and Tabitha. My stomach turned over when I saw him. He still had that effect on me, although I didn't know whether it was a genuine involuntary reaction to the man standing up to greet me, some kind of throwback sense memory to my thirteen-year-old self, or simple embarrassment.

I just had time to register that he was still rather good-looking, in a superannuated public schoolboy kind of way, and to say a rather gabbled, 'Hi, Alex,' when I was rugby tackled by my twelve-year-old half-brother, Toby, and in a more ladylike fashion by his twin sister, Tabitha, who wanted to show me her newly French-manicured nails.

Although they were the same age, Toby still seemed a boy, affectionate and innocent, while Tabitha was still sweet, but moving into the awkward years, made more so by the presence of Venezia, who would now extend her unpleasant, snubbing behaviour to her, as well as to Archie. Another half-sibling to torture was her idea of good sport.

'Hey, you two,' I said, hugging them back. 'Great to see you.'

But before I could say any more, Ham was loudly clapping his hands.

'Come on, you lot. You can do that later,' he was saying. 'It's dinner time.'

And like the children we all still were, in his eyes, we sat down obediently at the round table.

Ham always had round dining tables, with various tops to cater for different numbers. It was all part of his orchestrated manipulation of space and relationships; he didn't like the idea of a hierarchy at a family table, although it was quite clear to all of us that wherever he sat was the head. He just wanted the rest of us to feel equal, as his subordinates.

Apart from a few opening snarky remarks between Archie and Venezia, and some snickering between her and Chanel with regard to Tabitha, dinner looked set to be pleasant enough.

Chloe's food was superb as always – it was steak Diane, she was writing a book called *Kitsch Cuisine* – Ham was in very good spirits, surrounded by the fruits of his loins, as he called us, under his own award-winning roof, and good wine was flowing.

I just felt so hopelessly self-conscious around Alex.

I always seemed to be looking at him by mistake when he looked over at me, and whenever he addressed a remark to me, I had just filled my mouth with food. It was like my body was still programmed to react to him the same way it had when I was thirteen.

It was so unfair, it was really beginning to annoy me. I didn't even fancy him any more. OK, so he was quite good-looking, my friends were always telling me that, although I thought his features had coarsened a little, and in all honesty, I found him pretty boring.

He was a solicitor, working for some big bank in the City, and he'd developed that falsely jovial and extremely patron-izing way of interacting that those City boys have, especially with women.

He got my back up early on in the proceedings by asking me lame questions about the paper.

'So, Stella,' he said, with forced Rotarian warmth. 'You're still working for the rag, I see. All the girls in the office love your articles.'

'Yes,' I said, barely able to hide my irritation. I hated it when people didn't show due respect for the *Journal*. 'I am still working for the bestselling, most respected broadsheet paper in the country, thank you. Are you still slaving for Mammon?'

He laughed in a rather empty, corporate good-guy kind of way and I was relieved when he didn't address any more remarks to me.

Instead, he was having long conversations with Ham

about cars and rugby, just about the only two dull subjects my father was interested in – and he was really interested in them. So with them tied up with man talk, the teenagers acting out their own little Pinter play, and Chloe constantly up and down to the kitchen, I spent most of the dinner talking to Toby.

'Stella,' he said, earnestly, after he had finished separating all the food on his plate into careful sections so that none of it touched. 'Do you like McFly?'

'I'm not really sure, darling,' I replied. 'I know Venezia used to like them, but now she very much doesn't like them and Archie hates them with a passion, but I haven't really got a stand on them. How about you?'

'I think they're pretty lame actually,' said Toby. 'I like Gorillaz, but Tabitha loves McFly. It's weird. She's got pictures of them all over her bedroom walls. She's even got them on the ceiling.'

'Hey, Chanel,' said Venezia, overhearing. 'Tabitha likes McFly. Ooh, Tabitha, do you love Dougie? Do you dream of him? Are you going to marry him?'

Then she and Chanel went into a fit of unpleasant snickering, singing what even I recognized as a McFly song, in stupid voices. Tabitha looked outraged and upset in equal measure. She clearly didn't know whether to defend Dougie and her other McFly heart-throbs, or to pretend she didn't like them, so she could fit in with the older girls. She was trying not to cry.

I looked at Alex, who had a pained expression on his face. He caught my glance and for the first time, I felt a connection with him. I raised my eyebrows, and he nodded in acknowledgement. Tabitha was his little sister too.

'Hey, Tabs,' he said softly. 'Have you told Venezia about your modelling yet?'

Tabitha's exquisitely pretty little face lit up and Venezia's darkened with suspicion. She wanted to be a model even more than she wanted to star in *The OC*, or be a Pussycat Doll.

'What modelling?' she said, her cunning eyes darting between Alex and Tabitha, in case it was a set-up.

'I'm going to be in the Boden catalogue,' said Tabitha proudly.

'Are you, darling?' said Ham, suddenly taking notice. 'That's marvellous. You'll be a beautiful model. You've got the best head in the family.'

I saw an expression of pure jealousy cross Venezia's face. Chanel looked pretty pissed off too.

'Boden?' said Venezia, in her most contemptuous tones. 'I wouldn't wear Boden if they were the last clothes on earth. They are the most lame clothes in the whole world. I'd rather wear cling film than wear Boden. They so suck. They're just for stupid children or old women.'

Tabitha looked a bit crestfallen, but even she knew Venezia was just jealous.

'Only total lame-arses wear Boden,' Venezia was still going on. 'Boden makes me want to puke.'

'Shut up, Venezia,' said Ham suddenly. 'You really are being very unpleasant. In fact, I've got a good idea, why don't you and Chanel leave the table now. I really don't want to see you until the morning.'

'Good,' said Venezia. 'We were going anyway. Come on, Chanel.'

And she stomped off towards the metal staircase that led

up to the kids' bedrooms, her shiny blonde hair swinging, Chanel following behind.

Chloe broke the silence at the table, by standing up to fetch the pudding and getting the younger ones to come and choose what flavour of ice cream they wanted to have with theirs. Alex came over and took Toby's place next to me.

'Is she always so unpleasant?' he asked me.

'Venezia?' I said. 'She's a monster. A foul creature. And having a crony with her just makes her worse.'

'Well, she'll have to reckon with me, if she has another go at Tabitha,' he said.

I smiled at his fraternal loyalty. It was quite endearing, but I knew it was useless. Teenage mind games were way beyond the control of even the most well-meaning grown-ups. They ran their own course impervious to outside interference, which usually only made matters worse.

Indeed, mentioning the modelling the way he had would only have wrecked all hope of Tabitha being included by Venezia and Chanel for the rest of the weekend, which they would now devote to revenge. I knew all that from the battlegrounds of our own shared adolescence and I was surprised he had forgotten.

He was looking thoughtful.

'Is she like her mother?' he asked.

I laughed bitterly.

'Oh, boy,' I said. 'She's delightful compared to her mother. Her mother is an utter monster. Why do you think Archie's here? He's not even Ham's son – well, I know you're not either, but anyway – Kristy's gone off to Paris for the week-end and she's just dumped Archie here for convenience.'

'Poor you,' said Alex, quietly.

I just looked at him. I wasn't sure what he meant.

'Poor you having her as a stepmother,' he continued.

I was really surprised.

'Well,' I said. 'It was a rude shock after your lovely mum, but I survived. How is Rose by the way?'

'She's great,' said Alex. 'It suits her being single. She's still got the two young ones to look after and with her garden and the house and the dogs, that's enough for her. She doesn't need a husband to worry about as well.'

He smiled, wryly, at me.

'We've got a lot in common really, haven't we, Stella?' he said, looking me right in the eye. 'With the state of our families it's hardly surprising we're both still single.'

I was lost for words at his presumption. How dare he comment on my marital status? And imply I gave a flying fuck about his? I was instantly furious, but before I could pursue it with him, Chloe arrived back at the table with a baked Alaska and the moment was gone.

5

I just couldn't get to sleep that night. Mainly because I wasn't really happy being shoved over in the guest wing, which had to be entered across a courtyard at ground level, even though it was built right on to the side of the main house.

Keeping it separate was all part of Ham's intention to contrive the feeling of a tight family unit in the main house; he didn't want the guest wing to become just another space for us to spill over into.

He also believed guests were happier if they had their own zone to retreat into, and it had its own separate kitchen, sitting room and a terrace, where visitors could sit outside, without being in view of the main house.

He held mini architecture conferences at Willow Barn from time to time, as well as having a constant stream of eminent international colleagues and clients to stay, so it was all part of his professional world.

One architecture student – presumably with aspirations to work only on domestic projects for the very rich – had done her whole dissertation on Ham's theories of guest accommodation.

I remembered how he had laughed when a copy of it had arrived in the post from Los Angeles one morning. 'Beyond the Cabana – the Power and Politics of Guest Spaces in the Work of Henry Montecourt' it had been called.

But famous though Ham's opinions on guest wings were, I was so used to being in one of the row of six cell-like children's rooms which ran along one wide corridor on a mezzanine floor in the main house – all identical and completely separate from the master bedroom suite, which was in a small turret one floor up – I did feel a little cast out of Eden.

Although one architectural critic had likened Ham's 'kiddie corridor' to a battery henhouse for children, it had achieved its purpose of throwing us all together every night on an equal footing. He'd made the corridor extra wide so it could act as an informal meeting area, but with no seating, to keep things moving and 'loose', as he called it. Nothing was accidental at Willow Barn.

And now, while I was in the much more lavish and adult accommodation of the guest wing, I just didn't feel so comfortable there. I was also painfully aware of Alex sleeping in the next room.

It reminded me of one particularly hormonal summer when I had contrived to have the room next to his in the kiddie corridor. None of us had our own dedicated room there, we had a different one every time we came to stay, another aspect of Ham's overall scheme – and I had been determined to get the one next to Alex that school holidays.

Then I'd lain awake night after night, knowing he was lying in his bed, right next to me, just on the other side of the wall. I had spent hours with my ear pressed to a wine glass, trying to hear him breathe through the frustrating bricks and mortar.

I couldn't, of course, but I'd convinced myself I could

and that he was sighing in his sleep because he was dreaming about me. I really had been potty about him.

What was it, I wondered now, that had made me so in love with him then? OK, so he had been dashing-looking, sporty and fit, but was that really enough to inspire such devotion?

It probably had more to do with his apparently abundant self-confidence, I decided. To a rather lonely and bewildered girl, already on her third mother, he had seemed so sure of where he stood in the world, something I had been very confused about – and still was.

After an hour or so lying there in the guest wing, with all those memories flooding back, and trying unsuccessfully to go to sleep, I became gripped by a mad idea.

I got up and opened my bedroom door as quietly as I could, then tiptoed through the sitting room to the kitchen. I was going to get a wine glass to see if I could hear him breathing through the wall.

I knew it was crazy, but after all the teenage angst at the dinner table and being thrown back together with Alex, I felt so in touch with the thirteen-year-old me, I just had to do it out of solidarity with her.

I got the glass out and then decided that as I was up anyway, I might as well make some hot chocolate to try and help myself get off to sleep. I'd just bent down to get the milk out of the fridge – I was wearing a very short Agent Provocateur baby-doll nightie – when I heard a noise behind me.

I stood up very quickly and turned round to see Alex standing there, his hands over his face, in mock horror.

'Oh, I'm so sorry, Stella,' he said. 'I heard a noise and I just came to see what it was.'

He was wearing pyjama bottoms and nothing else, and I couldn't help noticing he still had a really good body, although he had grown some hair on the once perfectly smooth chest and stomach that used to render me so speechless with admiration round the swimming pool.

He slowly brought his hands down from his face and I could see he was laughing. I started laughing too. Nervous tension, really.

'Are you having a midnight feast?' he asked, looking determinedly at my face. My nightie was pretty much see-through, as well as ridiculously short. I couldn't imagine what had possessed me to bring it for a family weekend, it was just the first one that I grabbed out of the drawer. I folded my arms and crossed my legs, which wasn't easy standing up.

'Um, yeah, I can't sleep,' I said. 'I'm making some hot chocolate. Would you like some?'

'I would, actually,' he said. 'I can't sleep either. It's a bit weird being back here . . .'

'. . . and sleeping in the guest wing?'

He nodded. 'Yeah, that's really weird.'

I smiled at him. I put the milk down on the kitchen worktop and reached up to get the hot chocolate out of the cupboard, when I suddenly realized what I was doing and folded my arms again quickly. Alex put his hands back over his face.

'I'll go and see if I can find us some bathrobes,' he said.

He came back a few minutes later – averting his gaze over one shoulder – and threw me a huge sweatshirt.

'I couldn't find any dressing gowns, but I found these.'

I put it on quickly – it came practically to my knees – and looked down to read the slogan on the front. 'The Architecture of Emotion – Willow Barn Revisited' it said.

I burst out laughing. I knew the sweatshirts were left over from a big domestic architecture forum Ham had held here a couple of years before, but they could have been specially printed for my reunion with Alex.

'Your father isn't kidding, is he?' he said, smiling down at his own sweatshirt. 'I remember now, how I used to feel like his puppet down here sometimes, the way he could manipulate us all so brilliantly, just by moving us round in this house and garden.'

He did a little puppet dance with his hands, then we looked at each other, as the significance of his words hit us simultaneously. I was doing a mental tally of the number of children who were staying that night and I was sure he was too.

Unless Chanel and Venezia were staying in separate rooms – which was very unlikely, seeing as staying up all night talking was the main point of having a friend to stay at their age – there were enough bedrooms in the kiddie corridor for at least one of us to have stayed there.

Yet Chloe had been very firm, when I'd called her that morning to say I would be getting down there early, that I was to make myself comfortable in the guest wing.

'How's that cocoa going then?' said Alex suddenly, returning to his hearty City-boy persona and deftly changing the subject.

I was glad he had. I was suddenly feeling very uncomfortable with the situation and I could see exactly what Ham was up to. There were eight bedrooms in the guest wing but only two of them had been ready, with beds made up, when I'd arrived. He'd put Alex and me right next to each other

– in adult rooms – completely deliberately, the old goat.

'Yeah, I'm on to it,' I said briskly, bustling with the saucepan and milk, very happy to have the subject changed, but then I couldn't help myself.

'Get the mugs out would you – Pinocchio?' I said.

Alex looked at me and then we both cracked up. We laughed until we had tears running down our cheeks.

And with that tension cleared, and a mug of cocoa inside me, I didn't have any problem going to sleep at all.

The next morning I was very glad Alex and I had formed a pact the night before, because when we went through to the main house for breakfast – it was always at nine sharp at Willow Barn on Saturdays, no excuses – it was like the hounds of hell had just been loosed.

At every place around the dining table was a sanitary towel, liberally decorated with what appeared to be tomato sauce. And suspended from two ceiling beams across the main living space was a banner made from several sheets of A3 paper, emblazoned in red felt tip with the words: 'Tabitha's got her period.'

Archie was sitting bolt upright on a sofa with a wool beanie pulled right down over his face. Toby was closely inspecting a sanitary towel and trying to get someone to tell him what it was. Daisy was wailing in Chloe's arms – just picking up the tension. And Ham was holding Venezia and Chanel by the scruffs of their necks – well, by their T-shirts anyway – and shouting at them.

'You foul creatures,' he was saying. 'You vicious little vixens. You are both going to pay for this.'

The only person missing was Tabitha.

Alex and I stood in the doorway and took it all in.

'What the fuck is going on?' I said to Chloe.

'Oh, Stella,' she said, with tears in her eyes. 'Venezia really has gone too far this time. She found the sanitary towels in Tabitha's bag – she's only recently started the curse, poor lamb – and she did this.'

Alex had gone pale with fury.

'That little bitch,' he said, looking at Venezia, then he turned to Chloe. 'Where's my sister?'

'She's in our room,' said Chloe, softly, touching his arm to restrain him. 'But I think maybe Stella should go to her, Alex.'

He frowned for a moment and then nodded in understanding that this was women's business.

'But you could make yourself very useful taking Chanel to the station, if you wouldn't mind, Alex,' continued Chloe. 'Ham has rung her mother and she's going home on the next train.'

'Good bloody riddance,' I said. 'I'm going up to Tabs.'

I could hear her before I could see her; the sobs of utter misery were audible at the bottom of the spiral staircase leading up to Ham's turret and when I walked into the room, I could see a little hump shivering under the covers.

'Go away!' said Tabitha's voice, before I could say anything.

'It's all right, Tabs,' I said. 'It's only me, Stella.'

I sat on the bed and hugged her through the covers. She said nothing, but eventually her sobs lessened and her wretched little head emerged.

'Oh, Tabs,' I said. 'Poor you. That was so horrible of them. I'm really sorry they did that to you.'

'Now everyone will know I've got my period,' she said, which brought on more wailing tears.

'I know,' I said. 'It's awful. I still hate having them, but everyone will forget. Nobody really cares about it except you. Honestly.'

'But I don't like Daddy knowing,' she said, and started to sob again.

'I know,' I said. 'I was furious with Rose — your mum — when I first got my period, because she told Dad. I took to my bed, just like you have. But he's got lots of daughters, Tabs — and he's had lots of wives — he's used to it. It's only natural, anyway.'

She looked a little bit comforted and then her face crumpled again.

'Are Venezia and Chanel still down there?' she said.

'Chanel is going home straightaway,' I said. 'And Venezia is in serious trouble for this, Tabitha. I don't think she'll be coming down here again for a while. I've never seen Ham so cross.'

She looked comforted.

'Can I stay in bed?' she said.

'Of course you can,' I said. 'And do you know what would be really nice? You could have a lovely bath in Chloe's bathroom and then get back into bed. That will make you feel better.'

'Stella,' she said, wiping her nose on the sheet and looking desperate again. 'She's taken all my sanitary towels. I haven't got any more. What am I going to do?'

'Don't worry, I'll get you some more. In fact, I'll get you all the different types there are and you can see which you like best.'

She smiled faintly.

'What do you use, Stella?' she asked shyly.

'I'll bring what I use to show you and we can talk about it all.'

I could still remember how much it had meant to me having Claudia – Alex's sister, who was four years older than me – to talk to about all that, when I was Tabitha's age. Having loads of stepbrothers and sisters of various ages did have its benefits.

I put the telly on to a comfortingly babyish programme, gave her a hug and then ran down to catch Alex before they left for the station.

Sanity seemed to have resumed downstairs. The sanitary towels and banner were gone. Venezia was nowhere to be seen and Archie, Toby and Daisy were sitting having breakfast with Ham. Chloe was darting between the kitchen and the table, as usual.

Alex was just walking out of the front door, herding Chanel in front of him.

'Alex,' I called. 'Wait, I'm coming with you.'

I ran to catch up with them and took a certain pleasure in directing Chanel to sit in the back seat, after she arrogantly opened the front door of the car. She started to protest.

'Get in the back seat and shut up,' said Alex. She did.

'How's Tabs?' he asked me.

'As you would imagine,' I answered. 'Very upset.'

He shook his head. 'Unbelievable.'

'It is, but she'll be all right,' I said and patted him gently on his knee.

He glanced over at me and smiled faintly.

'Where's Venezia?' I asked him.

His smile broadened.

'Ham has locked her in her bedroom. He says he needs some time to consider her punishment.' He started laughing. 'But he's already smashed her mobile phone to pieces in front of her – with a hammer.'

We put Chanel on the train to London without saying another word to her and Alex went to buy the papers, while I went to Boots and bought every kind of sanitary protection they had – including some enormous maternity pads, which I hoped would make Tabitha laugh.

I was just paying for it all when my phone rang. It was Ham.

'Are you still in Lewes?' he said.

'Yes, why?'

'Excellent. You can help me construct Venezia's punishment. I would like you to go and buy the most unfashionable and unflattering outfit you can find for a fourteen-year-old girl with a very good figure. Preferably from a charity shop and a bit smelly. Can you do that?'

'I most certainly can,' I said.

Alex laughed out loud when I told him what Ham had asked me to do and we had a hilarious time picking over all the charity shops on Cliffe High Street to find the most hideous things we could.

It felt so natural to be with him, fooling around, trying on old hats and arguing the case for the particularly foul garments we each found. Although we hadn't seen each other for ages, we seemed to slip into a totally relaxed state of casual companionship, the way you do with old friends. I also realized what a deep reserve of shared history we had, of old family jokes and memories.

'Hey, look,' he said at one point. 'Here's a dress with one of those awful one-shoulder set-ups. Remember Claudia had one like that for my twenty-first? She looked so hideous.'

'And this looks rather like what you wore ...' I said, holding up a particularly vile red polyester bow tie and cummerbund set.

We had a really good laugh and once we felt we had sourced Venezia's nightmare outfit, Alex suggested we went down to Bill's for a coffee break.

The Saturday morning rush was in full flow and while we waited for a table to become free, we checked out the fruit and vegetable display, selecting some exotic Italian salad greens to take back to Chloe.

After we'd paid for them, I nipped off to the loo, and when I came back after a long wait in a queue, I couldn't immediately spot Alex in the throng. The girl who had served us at the veggie counter saw me looking lost and smiled at me.

'Your husband's sitting at a table outside,' she said, smiling kindly, and turned back to her customer.

For a moment I just stood there stunned, as it dawned on me that was exactly how we must look together. Similar ages, clearly from the same kind of social tribe, and so comfortable and relaxed in each other's company, of course anyone would assume we were a happy couple.

I made my way to the outside tables and found Alex sitting with two coffees already in front of him, clearly looking out for me.

His handsome face broke into such a warm smile when

he saw me, I felt like some kind of impostor. I wanted to go back and tell the girl on the till that we weren't married, he was just my stepbrother. My ex-stepbrother actually, who I didn't really know and hardly ever saw any more. And who I found a bit dull, quite frankly.

I felt painfully self-conscious, as I squeezed into my seat, to be sitting there with him, surrounded by our bags of shopping, the Saturday papers on the spare chair next to us.

We were such a living cliché, in our smart-casual clothes and our designer sunglasses, we could have been in an advert for a building society.

The next frame would have shown us smilingly opening the door of our dream home, then cutting to five years hence where we'd be settled in with a toddler in tow and a babe in arms.

But even through my discomfort, I couldn't help thinking how I was momentarily living exactly the future the thirteen-year-old me had planned. If I had been shown back then a glimpse of my future self, sitting there with Alex like that, I would have been sure all my dreams had come true. How misleading visual impressions can be, I thought.

Alex was clearly blissfully unaware of it, though.

'I ordered you a cappuccino,' he said, smiling his most winning creasy-eyed smile, and pushing it closer to me. 'I hope that's OK. Would you like the *Journal* mag to look at?'

I nodded distractedly, even though I hated cappuccino. I was strictly an espresso girl. Or tea. And no, I didn't want the magazine, I wanted the news pages – the foreign news pages, with the really gory stories and the long words and the difficult concepts and the unpronounceable names.

But I wasn't going to make a thing of it. I just wanted us to drink our coffee and leave, before he also realized how embarrassing it was for us to be sitting there playing Mr and Mrs Young Professional Couple, when we were really just fucked-up human fallout from a particularly dysfunctional family.

That family was looking even more bonkers than normal when we eventually got back to Willow Barn. Ham had a big bonfire going in the orchard and Venezia was scream- ing out of her bedroom window, as he tossed her clothes, shoes, accessories and make-up on to it.

'You can't do that,' Venezia was screaming. 'My mother bought me those clothes. I'm going to call the police.'

'What on, darling?' Ham shouted back, clearly enjoying himself enormously. 'I don't think your mobile's working very well just at the moment. Shall I send them a smoke signal for you?'

'You bastard! I'm going to make Mum SUE YOU!' Venezia was screaming. And as Ham waved her favourite Diesel jeans in the air, before tossing them on to the pyre, she burst into hysterical tears and slammed the window.

'I don't think she'll forget this in a hurry, do you?' he said to me and Alex. 'Did you get the outfit? Let's see.'

I pulled it out of the carrier bags. There was a really nasty pair of black platform-soled school shoes; some white towelling sports socks; a foul pair of red polyester elastic- waist trousers; a jade and purple anorak; and the pièce de résistance – which Alex had found in a record shop – a McFly T-shirt. Size: XXX Large.

Ham clapped his hands with delight.

'Perfect,' he said. 'Until her cow of a mother collects her from my house tomorrow night, this will be all she wears.'

Leaving Ham and Alex to stoke the flames, I went up to see Tabitha and we had great fun with all the 'sanpro', which I explained to her was the generic name for all those kinds of products. She found that very amusing, declaring that she was going to call Venezia 'sanpro' from now on, and the huge maternity pads induced a very healthy state of hilarity in her, just as I had hoped they would.

Chloe and Daisy came up to join in.

'Don't laugh,' said Chloe, squealing when she saw the maternity pads. 'I had to wear those after Daisy was born. It was like having a futon down my pants.'

But while we fell about laughing, Daisy thought they were lovely and was very happy putting her dolly to bed on one of them.

After that bit of girly bonding, Tabitha felt ready to come downstairs for lunch and a relative sense of normality returned to the weekend.

When we'd finished eating the chicken à la king, with a rice salad featuring garish cubes of red and yellow peppers – Chloe was still testing recipes for her book – Ham disappeared off somewhere, so I told Chloe that I would look after Daisy while she had a well-earned rest.

Daisy was delighted.

'Ooh, Stella,' she said, swinging on my hands. 'Can we make biscuits? Can we make little cakes? Can I put the pretty bits on? Can I do licking?'

So we did. Even though Chloe was always baking with

Daisy, she never tired of it, and although I was no cook, Daisy had an excellent children's cookery book with recipes even I could master.

As soon as they heard us getting the mixer and the cake tins out, the others all came to join in. Even Archie liked baking and when Alex heard the commotion in the kitchen, he put down the paper – he was reading the motoring pages, I noticed – and came over.

Soon we had the radio blaring and we were singing and dancing around like idiots, while weighing the ingredients, sieving flour and greasing tins. It was the best fun – and we knew we could make as much noise as we wanted and we wouldn't disturb Chloe, up in her turret bedroom.

We were just getting the first batch of fairy cakes out of the oven when a very droopy figure appeared – wearing a foul anorak. It was Venezia, looking properly shamefaced. We all stopped what we were doing and stared at her. She was holding a piece of white paper.

'I'm sorry, Tabitha,' she said, in the smallest voice I had ever heard out of that arrogant mouth. 'Will you please accept my apology? I was really out of line and I'm sorry. I was jealous about your modelling, that's why I did it. I'm sorry.'

It was a pretty good apology, I thought, and doing it in front of all of us earned extra points too. She handed over the piece of paper. Tabitha took it, read it and nodded.

'OK,' she said. 'But do you really promise you won't be horrid to me any more?'

'I promise,' said Venezia and finally raised her eyes to take in what we were doing. 'Can I decorate some cakes?' she said immediately, and I had to smile. Underneath it all, the bitch-queen teen was still a little girl.

'Yes,' I said. 'Of course you can, but only if you take that anorak off.'

She did and the full horror of the McFly T-shirt was revealed. Everyone roared with laughter and the drama was over.

A little later, while Venezia was helping me wash up – she really was on her best behaviour – I asked her how she had got out of her room.

'Dad let me out,' she said. 'He said I could come out as long as I apologized to Tabitha – and I've got to wear these horrendous clothes for the rest of the weekend. But it's better than being stuck in there, I suppose, and at least they were only my second-favourite pair of Diesel jeans.'

I had to admire her spirit.

By dinner time, everything was very much back to normal, including Venezia's appearance. She had customized the McFly T-shirt, by cutting off the bottom three quarters to reveal her abdomen, as per normal. Then she'd hacked off the sleeves and cut the faces out from the band photo, to create a peekaboo effect just above her breasts.

With the polyester pants chopped off into crop pants and rolled right down to her hips, she had managed to make it look just as provocative as her usual outfits and almost stylish.

She'd even jazzed up the terrible shoes, cutting out the toes to reveal fluorescent pink, yellow and green painted toenails and decorating the remaining uppers with sparkly little gems from the craft cupboard in the kiddie corridor.

Ham barked with laughter when he saw her and ruffled her artfully styled hair.

'You're a little bitch, Venezia,' he said, fondly. 'But you're *my* little bitch.'

Then, inspired by what she'd done with her terrible outfit he suddenly decided we must all wear customized clothes for dinner that night – a very Ham thing to do. He loved spontaneous happenings and sent us all off to the art supplies cupboard to find inspiration.

'No dinner for anyone wearing uncustomized clothes,' he said. 'Apart from Chloe. She's absolved because she's cooking.'

Alex looked a bit wary. He had never felt comfortable with this kind of thing when he'd lived with Ham, and I felt a bit sorry for him.

'Come on,' I said, giving him a sisterly nudge. 'I've got an idea for us two.'

I nipped upstairs to get some glue and glitter and then we went back to the guest wing.

'Do we have to do this, Stella?' asked Alex, with a pained expression.

'Oh, come on, Alex, you know what Ham's like. He wants everyone to have fun – whether they like it, or not.'

'Not,' he said. 'I work in the City, Stella. I'm not the spontaneous fun type like you are. I slave for Mammon, remember?'

'Shut up and get that sweatshirt you found last night,' I said.

I took the scissors from the guest-wing kitchen drawer and slashed the necks off both sweatshirts. Then I turned them both over, laid them flat on the table and picked up the glue.

'OK,' I said to Alex. 'What shall we write?'

He looked puzzled.

'We need a slogan,' I said. 'To write on the back. Something funny – and cool, of course – to make a statement about our identity. Now let me think . . . something about the guest wing. Let's make a point to Ham.'

Alex smiled.

'Guest-Wing Gurus?' he suggested.

'That's good,' I said, rather patronizingly. 'That's the kind of thing I meant, but it doesn't quite express our feelings of rejection, isolation and manipulation, does it? Hmmmm, how about Reluctant Guest-Wing Guests? No . . . I know! It's a Guest-Wing Thing? No . . .'

'West Wing?' said Alex.

We both laughed.

'It's good,' I said. 'But not good enough. Guest, best, zest, pest, messed . . . Best Western . . . CZ Guest . . . One flew Over the Cuckoo's Guest . . .'

Alex bit his lip and narrowed his eyes, while he thought. It suited him and I had to snap myself out of it when I realized I was gazing at him gormlessly. It was just that thing he did with his front teeth nibbling his lower lip. I remembered it so well from school-holiday games of Scrabble and Trivial Pursuit.

'How about, "Out of the Nest Wing"?' he said suddenly.

'That's perfect,' I said, more than a little surprised. And using the glue and the glitter, I wrote it in curly 1950s script on the back of the sweatshirts.

Then I styled us both up. I wore my sweatshirt like a 1980s minidress, hanging off one shoulder, with a pair of high heels I had thrown into my weekend bag on a last-minute whim, and I did my hair and eye make-up to match – big and heavy, respectively.

94

After some protest, I got Alex to agree to wear his sweat-shirt upside down as a skirt – with my nightie as a top, and a tie around his neck. He looked completely mad, but kind of cute too. I spiked his hair up with my gel and made him sit in a chair while I put black eyeliner on him.

As I was bending over him, very close to his face, apply-ing it to his upper lash line, he gently placed a hand on my hip and, almost imperceptibly, squeezed it.

It was such a tiny gesture, but so quietly intimate I just froze. Then he opened the eye I wasn't working on and looked straight at me. No twinkle, or creasy-eyed smile, just a completely direct look. My stomach turned over.

It would have been the easiest thing in the world to have moved my face just a few centimetres closer and kissed him. Then with one movement I could have been sitting astride him, kissing him, consuming him, all those things I had imagined doing so many times in years gone by.

But I froze. There was too much import in that moment. Too many years of history and too many implications. If we hadn't had sex there and then, it was inevitable that after one kiss, we would have seethed with lust through dinner and done it later. After all, we were in adjacent bedrooms.

And even apart from all the baggage, the next person I wanted to have sex with wasn't Alex, it was Jay. For just one moment there, it was very tempting, but it wasn't right. No way.

So I finished his eyeliner as quickly as I could and pulled away, turning round before he could see how flustered I was by his unexpected touch.

Dinner was hilarious. Archie had rescued the charred remains of Venezia's jeans from the embers and was wearing them as a ghastly hat, with the ashes from the bonfire smeared all over his face.

Tabitha and Venezia – now buddies in the way that only girls who have recently fallen out very seriously can be – had swapped clothes, so that Tabitha was now wearing the McFly T-shirt and loving it, even without the faces. While her Hello Kitty T-shirt – now cropped into little more than a bikini top – looked positively illegal stretched across Venezia's voluptuous body.

Ham had done himself proud, of course, fashioning a kind of grass skirt out of branches he had hacked off shrubs in the garden, topped with a very loud Hawaiian shirt – a present from a grateful student – and his old straw gardening hat, with more greenery pinned round the brim. He had some bright green poster paint smeared across his nose and cheeks.

'I am the Green Man,' he was booming. 'The Spirit of Spring unleashed.'

He roared with laughter when he saw the guest-wing statement on our sweatshirts, the final confirmation I needed that the whole thing was a monstrous set-up.

Which was why, after we had finished dinner, quite late and quite drunkenly, with my eyes meeting Alex's rather more often than felt completely normal all the way through it, I did something very cowardly.

After he had sloped off to the guest wing, yawning ostentatiously, but sneaking a covert glance at me to see if I was following, I went up and slept in the empty kid's room.

6

Sunday breakfast was at eleven a.m., but I was up long before that and ducked back to the guest wing to get changed out of my crazy outfit. I felt strangely furtive as I ran down the stairs, although it was nobody's business except mine where I chose to sleep. Or why.

By the time I emerged from my guest-wing bedroom, showered and dressed, Alex was sitting in the kitchen with a cup of coffee. Sitting on the same chair where I'd done his eyeliner the night before. My stomach fluttered slightly at the memory.

I had no idea if he knew whether I'd slept there or not. If he did know I hadn't been there, it could only be because he had come into my bedroom to find me, so I could hardly ask him.

'Sleep well?' he said in his best let's-pretend-nothing's-going-on, gung-ho style.

I nodded, wondering whether he had inherited that technique from his mother, or learned it at school, but clearly it was his default setting. If anything gets at all weird, just act jolly until it passes. It was a very English way of coping, I thought.

'Want some coffee?' he continued, in equally cheery tones.

I shook my head.

'I think I'll go over to the main house and get some tea,'

I said. 'Ham has a great selection over there.'

I was getting as vapid as him, I thought. I was nearly at the door, when he spoke again.

'Stella,' he said suddenly. 'When are you going back up to town?'

'After lunch sometime.'

'Well, as you don't have your car here and the trains are so terrible on Sundays, do you want a lift up with me? The twins are going back with Chloe and it would be really nice to have some company on the drive.'

He'd given me so many reasons why it was a good idea – and well-rehearsed reasons, judging by the way he had just gabbled them out – that, caught on the hop like that, I couldn't think of any excuse to decline, although the idea of spending two hours in a small space with Alex did make me feel rather uncomfortable.

'Yeah, great, thanks,' I said, trying to sound more enthusiastic than I felt. 'That would be great.'

'Great,' said Alex. 'We'll go after lunch then.'

'Great,' I said again and then I legged it over to the main house.

I avoided Alex for the rest of the morning, sticking my head into the papers – which I did have to read for work and had been planning to do on the train – and keeping it there.

Ham had looked so pleased when he'd heard we were going back to town together, I set about ignoring him too. I didn't want him getting all maypole-y on me.

We were halfway through lunch – baked gammon with pineapple, another recipe from Chloe's future book – when my mobile rang. I had it in my pocket, as I had to be on duty on Sundays in case something came up and the news desk needed me urgently to write a story for Monday morning's paper.

I answered it at the table – I was the only one Ham permitted to have a mobile anywhere near it – to find it wasn't the news desk. It was Jay.

I nearly choked on my Russian salad, I was so surprised.

'Hi, beautiful,' he said. 'I hope I'm not interrupting anything.'

'No,' I squeaked. 'I'm just having lunch, hold on.'

Judging by the way everyone round the table was looking at me, it was quite clear from my face that it wasn't the news desk.

'Excuse me,' I said to Ham, who hated people leaving the table during meals only marginally less than people who talked on mobiles during them. 'I'll take this outside.'

'Hang on,' I said to Jay and practically galloped across the sitting room, through the French windows and into the garden. I kept walking, across the lawn, until I reached the summerhouse.

'Hi,' I said, breathlessly, as I sat down. I was so surprised to hear his voice on that phone. 'How are you?'

'I'm fine,' said Jay. 'Are you sure this is an OK time?'

'Yeah, it's great, I just had to come outside for some privacy.'

'Where are you?' he asked in such an intimate tone it made my stomach turn over. And much more violently than it had with Alex just a short time before.

'I'm at my father's place in the country. I've been here for the weekend.'

'Willow Barn?' said Jay.

'Yes,' I said, amazed. 'Have you heard of it?'

'I told you, I'm seriously into architecture and it is quite a famous house, as you probably know. Is it as great as it sounds?'

I looked back up at it; the whole wall of glass in front of the two-storey space that was the living area, with the mezzanine floor off to the right, which housed the kiddie corridor and the little turret beyond that, which was Ham's lair.

'Yes, it is,' I said. 'It's totally great.'

'When are you coming back to town?' asked Jay. 'I would really love to see you.'

'This afternoon sometime.' I paused for a moment. This was no time for game playing. 'And I'd like to see you too.'

We breathed down the phone at each other for a bit, the sense of possibility hanging so palpably between us.

'I've got an idea,' said Jay suddenly. 'I'll come down and pick you up. How long does it take to get there from Chelsea?'

I was so surprised, I forgot to protest.

'About two hours,' I said. 'But I'd have to ring you back with exact directions. It's really hard to find. Maybe it's better if I just meet you in town,' I added, as the implications of him turning up down there started to hit me.

'What's the post code?' said Jay.

I was still in such a state of shock I told him.

'OK,' he said. 'I'll be there soon. Don't go anywhere.'

And he hung up.

'Who was that?' asked Ham, with his usual bluntness, when I walked back in to finish my lunch. They were all on their pudding – kiwi fruit pavlova.

'Just a friend,' I said, much too quickly. I could see he was looking at me beadily. So was Alex. Oh, God.

'Actually,' I continued, thinking the only way to do it was to get it over with quickly. 'He rang to say he's coming down this afternoon to fetch me, so I won't need that lift back now, Alex, but thanks so much for offering.'

Ham was looking very beady now.

'I hope you gave him decent directions,' he said. 'Or the poor bugger will never find it.'

He laughed heartily.

Just over ninety minutes later, while I was still trying to read the papers, but not taking anything in, there was the unmistakable crunch of tyres on the gravel outside the front door.

'He got here quickly,' said Ham, with his usual tact. 'Must be keen.'

I glanced at Alex. I'd rather hoped he would have been gone before Jay arrived, but too bad.

I got up slowly to go to the door, trying to be a bit cool. Mistake – Ham beat me to it, moving with uncharacteristic speed.

'Bloody hell,' he said, looking out of the window. 'Nice bloody motor. Look at this, Alex.'

And he threw open the double front doors to reveal Jay, climbing out of a vehicle that looked more like an alien space probe than a car. With his deep tan, his pale blue shirt, his jeans and his sunglasses, he looked like something out of a 1970s Martini advertisement. Sort of perfect.

Ham was out to meet him before I could even make it to the door. And Archie and Toby overtook me on the way. Alex was a little slower, but even Chloe and Tabitha were coming out for a look. Daisy and I brought up the rear together. I picked her up. I needed an ally. I was suddenly feeling extraordinarily shy. I mean, I hardly knew the guy and here he was mingling with practically my whole family. The first boy I had ever brought home.

I arrived outside just in time to see Ham pumping his hand.

'Great to meet you,' he was saying. 'Henry Montecourt. Stella's dad. This is my wife, Chloe, my stepsons, Archie and Alex, various other children. This is Stella's friend, Jay, everyone. I must say, this is a hell of a car. It's an Enzo, isn't it? I've been dying to have a proper look at one of those. May I?'

Before I could even say hello to Jay, Ham was levering his huge bulk into the passenger seat and it looked like they were going off for a spin.

I could hardly see them through the tinted windows, but the driver's side suddenly opened and Jay's head popped out.

'Hi, Stella,' he said, grinning at me. 'Back in a minute.'

They were, but then Archie and Toby had to have turns as well. Then Ham took it for a slow drive down past the paddock and back, all on his own, and then he and Alex and Jay had a look under the bonnet.

It was such a display of male bonding, they should have been wearing penis gourds.

By the time they came into the house, I was almost losing interest. Almost. And the girls were doing a good job of keeping it up.

'He's rather gorgeous, Stells,' said Chloe. 'You've kept very quiet about him.'

'I've only just met him,' I said.

'Well, he must be very smitten then, to come down here to collect you like this,' she said. And for once, her sweet, uncomplicated nature really irritated me.

'Now *he* is seriously hot,' Venezia was saying, coming back downstairs. The little trollop had gone up specially to put lipgloss on, I realized, snitched from Tabitha.

'*He* is seriously hot,' echoed Daisy, in her piping tones, just as Jay walked into the house with Ham and the other boys. Ham had his arm round his shoulder. They were laughing in that hearty brothers-in-testosterone way about nothing in particular.

'Would you like some tea, Jay?' said Chloe immediately, to distract attention from Daisy, who was now singing 'He's hot, he's hot, he's seriously hot' as a jolly little tune, and I loved her all over again.

'That would be lovely, thank you, Chloe,' said Jay and it was Chloe's turn to beam at him. He was like a human charm offensive.

'Wow,' he said, looking around and taking in the space. 'So this is Willow Barn, it's just as amazing as I've heard.'

'Jay's interested in architecture, Ham,' I said. I couldn't help myself.

'Would you like a tour?' said Ham and off they went.

Ham's official tour of the house always started in front of the closed front door – the first stage of the 'emotional journey' and all that claptrap – and as they disappeared back out of it, I went over to the kitchen to help Chloe with the tea. I was getting the cups out of the dishwasher as Alex walked past us and out of the back door to the guest wing.

Shortly after, he was back, holding his weekend bag.

'I'm going to split, Chloe,' he said, not looking at me. 'I need to get back to town. Please thank Ham for having me, it's been great. Bye, Stella.'

He kissed us both quickly on the cheek and left.

I felt a bit bad about it for a moment, he was clearly feeling a bit usurped, but then Ham and Jay came back and I kind of forgot about him.

'It's amazing, Stella,' Jay was saying. 'I really love that turret room. It feels so intimate after all the space down here. A real haven. And now Henry says you are going to show me round the garden.'

I glanced at Ham who was looking beady again. Boy, I thought, he could change horses quickly, but I wasn't complaining. As far as I was concerned, he was now backing the right one. Gee up, neddy.

We left the house through the French windows, as I had done to take Jay's call, and as we turned round to look back at the building from the far edge of the lawn, he caught hold of my hand and squeezed it. I squeezed back and immediately dropped it. I strongly suspected Ham was watching us through the telescope in his turret room.

'It's great to see you, Stella,' said Jay, looking at me with those intense blue eyes, his head tilted to one side. 'I like your family a lot.'

'Not as much as they like you. My dad is the world's biggest petrolhead and you could not have made a better move than arriving in that mad car. What is it anyway?'

'It's a Ferrari Enzo,' he said casually.

'Aren't Ferraris always red?'

'They are mostly. But this one's black. I don't like red cars.' He smiled at me. 'Now show me the garden. Preferably some bits that are well out of sight of the house.'

I led him through the rose garden and down the steps into the bamboo thickets, over the stream via the Chinese bridge into the wilder wooded area, and finally to Ham's shell grotto.

'Wow,' said Jay when we got inside. 'This is really wild.'

It was. Ham had found a small natural cave in the side of the hill when he was excavating the garden and had seen fit to have it entirely covered in shells, in mosaic designs featuring erotic scenes in the classical style. We'd found it hilarious as children. Now it was having more of the intended effect on Jay.

He pulled me into his arms.

'You left me in a terrible state last week,' he said, kissing me gently between his words. 'How could you do that to me?'

I smiled at him, as I breathed in his wonderful smell again, but I couldn't relax into his embrace. And this time I wasn't playing games. It had all been just a little too weird having him pop up fully formed in the family part of my life, which I normally kept so firmly separated from my love life. So I was still digesting all that, plus I felt extremely inhibited by the close – and all too knowing – proximity of my father.

Luckily, the shell grotto was not the most comfortable place for intimate encounters, so I was able to prise Jay out of it fairly easily. Then, after finishing the rest of the garden tour at high speed, we went in for tea, during which Ham managed not to embarrass me too much, although Venezia filled the gap, pouting and posing like a bunny girl, despite death-ray glares from Chloe.

Then it finally seemed like time to start getting back to town.

I nipped over to the guest wing to grab my things and saw that Alex had left my nightie on the bed for me. There was a note by it.

'*It looked better on you. A.*'

That was it. There was no kiss, and I was surprised how much I minded.

The entire family came out to see us off, which was slightly mortifying, and then as I was about to get into the car, Ham came over and whispered in my ear, with surprising discretion.

'You made me wait long enough before you brought someone home, you little minx, but it was worth it. You've got yourself a serious Alpha Male there, Stella. And I like him too.' He put his hands on my cheeks and turned my head, looking right into my eyes. 'Don't blow it.'

I knew exactly what he meant. Follow Daddy's rules, if you want to hook him, that's what he was saying. Make him wait.

I smiled at him and kissed him on the cheek. The old goat.

Jay and I talked all the way back to London. We were never lost for something to say and I felt really comfortable with him, except for the occasional moment when his hand strayed a little too far up my leg and I could hardly breathe, let alone form a sentence.

But fortunately for our conversation – and Ham's rules –

Jay's driving style required both hands on the wheel most of the time. I love fast cars, but even I was gripping the seat as he zoomed along the M23 like it was a German Autobahn.

'I knew Michael Schumacher had one brother . . .' I was saying, as he overtook a red Porsche, at warp-factor speed.

'Red-car asshole,' he was saying, smiling triumphantly in the rear-view mirror. 'What did you say? Schumacher? I'd like to take him on. Do you like Formula One?'

'It's OK,' I said. 'I don't find it very riveting television – although Ham adores it – but it can be quite fun in the corporate tents.'

He turned and smiled at me warmly, all blue eyes, white teeth and suntan.

'Where did you get your tan?' I asked him.

'Mustique, mainly. And a bit of skiing. Do you ski?'

'No,' I said, firmly. I'd been once, to St Moritz for a John Frieda shampoo launch and I was useless. Apart from posing around in the furry boots, I had loathed it.

Jay looked surprised, like I'd said I couldn't swim, or maybe read.

'Really?'

'We never went as kids,' I said. 'It's not Ham's scene. He'd rather go and look at museums than go downhill at high speed.'

Jay nodded, as if it all now made sense.

'Your dad is so great,' he was saying. 'He's awesome, but tell me about the rest of your family. Who were all those kids?'

So I explained about the six wives and the six children who were my half-brothers and sisters, plus the various ex-stepsiblings and semi-steps.

'Whooah,' said Jay. 'That is seriously complicated. Do you all get along?'

'Mostly,' I said and then I told him about Venezia's little outrage of the weekend.

'That is seriously nasty,' said Jay. 'Why is she so bad?'

'I think it's a combination of nature and nurture. Her mother, Kristy, is a total witch – the only real gold-digger Ham has ever been sucked in by . . .'

Jay's head turned suddenly to look at me.

'Hmmm,' I added. 'That was an unfortunate turn of phrase in the context, wasn't it? Although I'm sure it was entirely her skill in the "love arts" which lured Ham into her clutches. She was his mistress on and off for years, before they got married.

'Venezia was conceived and born while he was still married to Rose – the twins' mum – two years before they came along. So that must be a bit weird for Venezia. She was Ham's secret daughter for quite a long time. The rest of us may be a mixed-up bunch, but at least we were legitimate. Then on top of that, she's really bright – she definitely got that from Ham – and the combination is pretty lethal.'

Jay was shaking his head.

'Phewee. You'll have to draw me a diagram to understand all this. I thought my family was messy, but you guys really take the prize.'

'Why is your family messy?' I asked innocently.

His head shot round and then just as quickly back.

'Oh, the usual stuff, divorce shit, half-siblings – but only one in my case.'

I could sense him shutting down as he spoke, but I wanted to know. He knew about my mad family, in all our gory detail, I felt I had a right to ask about his.

'Where did you grow up?' I pushed him.

'Oh, mainly in New York, although we had a place in Rhode Island too. Partly over here. My grandmother was English . . . Hey, don't you want to know how I got your number?'

As subject changers went, it was a good one. I'd been puzzling about that, but had decided not to ask him.

'Yes. How did you get my number?'

'Well, no thanks to you, little Miss Mystery. I rang the *Journal* repeatedly and they'd never heard of you. Do you really work there? I was seriously starting to wonder. They kept saying we don't have a Stella Montecourt, we have a Stella something else, but not a Stella Montecourt. I was getting really pissed off in the end. I knew your name was Montecourt, because of your dad, so what was that all about?'

'Oh, no, I forgot to tell you,' I said, my hand flying up to my mouth, and it was the truth. I had forgotten. 'I don't use that name at work. My byline is Stella Fain. The full family name is Montecourt-Fain, but it's so pompous we don't use it much, and I don't want people to immediately connect me with my dad by just using Montecourt, because it's so identifiable, so I just use the Fain part.'

'Well, it was one way to get rid of some lame guy you didn't want to see again,' he said, turning to smile at me. 'Did you get my flowers?'

I thought quickly.

'What flowers?'

'OK, I guess you didn't get them then, because I put the wrong name on them too. Shame, they were nice flowers.

Roses. I chose them myself. I put my cell number on the card – I was nearly put off when you didn't call me. But only nearly.'

I quickly reviewed the flowers situation. Jeanette must have recognized Montecourt on the card. Funny she hadn't mentioned it.

'So do you want to know how I got your number, or not?' he said.

'Yes. And I also want to know how you found Willow Barn without directions.'

'Oh, that was easy. I had the post code. I just tapped it in here . . .' He gestured at the satellite navigation thing on the dashboard. 'And Miss Bossy Boots delivered me to your door.'

He pressed a button and an incredibly officious woman's voice said: 'After five hundred metres, take the next exit.'

'Did she tell you my mobile number too?' I asked him, cheekily.

'No. That wasn't so easy. I tried to get it from Jericho's PA, but she pretended she'd never heard of you, so I swallowed my pride and called Amy. Which was really humiliating, thank you, Stella.'

He pretended to punch me on the arm.

Excellent, I thought. Result.

'So,' said Jay. 'Now I've finally found you, what are we going to do? Dinner? Where do you like to go? What do you feel like?'

'I feel like going somewhere I've never been before.'

Jay grinned wickedly. 'How about my apartment?'

Then, just as I was wondering how to play things from

there, my phone rang. This time it really was the news desk. Brilliant.

'Stella?' said the gruff voice of Eric, the deputy news editor. 'Something's coming over the wires from Australia about a designer from there getting the big gig at Gucci. Is that a story for you?'

'It certainly is,' I said, trying not to sound as thrilled as I really was to have a valid excuse to torture Jay a little more. 'I've been tracking that rumour for a couple of weeks, it's a huge story. I'll come straight in.'

I snapped my phone shut and looked at my watch.

'I'm really sorry, Jay,' I said. 'But that was the news desk. I've got a big story breaking and they want it for tomorrow's paper. I do work there, really, and I'll have to go in to the office right away.'

I didn't have to at all. I could have done the story perfectly easily from home and emailed it in, but I wasn't going to tell him that.

He looked quite crestfallen.

'I'm really sorry,' I added. 'After you've driven all this way and everything . . .'

'I'll take you to your office,' he said, recovering quickly. 'Where is it?'

'So far east it's practically in the North Sea. Are you sure you want to? You can just drop me anywhere in town and I'll get a cab.'

'I like driving,' he said. 'And I like being with you. I want to spend a little longer in your company.'

He gave me a look I would come to know well in the months ahead. It was the real Jay, at his most open and appealing. He may have been like a clam about his family, but in any other context, he could be amazingly, touchingly honest about his feelings, and it was probably the thing I liked most about him.

'If you're only offering me crumbs,' he said, 'that's what I'll take. I like you enough to accept crumbs.' Then he grinned, wickedly. 'But you'll have to give me a down payment on the full cake.'

And he pulled over into the next lay-by and kissed me until my head was spinning.

By the time we drew up in front of the docklands skyscraper which housed the *Journal*'s offices, I really was getting worried about meeting my deadline, which made getting out of the car a lot easier.

I had just opened the door and swung my legs out, when Jay put his hand gently on my arm.

'Not so fast, cub reporter,' he said. 'You're not leaving this automobile until I have your home, work and cell-phone numbers. And your email address and preferably your IRS number. I'm not going through that again.'

'I never answer the work phone,' I said. 'So don't bother with that, but here are the rest.'

I scribbled my home and mobile numbers on the back of my business card and handed it to him. But I didn't ask for his.

'Hey, Stella Fain,' he called out to me as I walked up the steps towards the building. 'I'll be looking for your story in tomorrow's paper. OK?'

When I made it up to the thirty-first floor, where my desk was, I could hear a phone ringing, which was quite unusual late on a Sunday afternoon. When I got nearer to my work station, I realized it was my phone.

For once I broke my rule and answered it, because I thought it might be someone ringing me with an important lead about the Gucci story.

'Stella Fain,' I said in my most professional voice.

'Just checking,' said Jay, laughing, and put the phone down.

I sat at my desk and smiled. I liked his style. I liked it a lot.

7

I liked it even more the next day, when another – bigger – bouquet of Moyses Stevens roses arrived on my desk, five minutes after I had sat down at it, and this time delivered without Jeanette's help.

I was just reading the card for about the twenty-fifth time – '*Nice story this morning. Dinner tonight? J xxx*', I was up to three kisses, excellent – when I became aware of a commotion going on over on the other side of the office.

'Is this your name?' a voice was asking in raised tones. An unmistakable voice, with a strong Scottish accent, punctuated by the sound of a fist hitting a newspaper. 'Is this your bloody name? Did you write this? Did you put this filth in my paper?'

It was Doughnut and he wasn't happy.

I had to look. I might have been the fluff correspondent, but I was still a newspaper reporter – and needing to know what is going on, when it is absolutely none of our business, is a trait that unites us all. I raised myself gingerly from my seat and peeped over the partition.

'Uh-oh,' said Peter, the writer who had the desk nearest me. 'Someone is seriously in the soup. Can you see who it is, Stella dear? Your eyes are younger than mine and so much more acute.'

'Oh, sod off, Peter,' I said. 'You just don't want to get caught rubbernecking. I can't see from here actually. I'll make a tactical trip to the loo and report back.'

I strolled casually over to that side of the office, just in time to see Doughnut, alarmingly red in the face, shredding a copy of the *Journal* in front of someone's head. The object of his fury had his back to me, so I couldn't see who it was, but it was male and youngish.

'If you want to write excrement like that,' Doughnut was saying, 'I suggest you go and work on *The Daily Tits*, because you don't belong on my paper.'

I dodged into the loo as he stomped past me, his ginger eyebrows meeting above his nose in a chevron of fury. I was followed in by Rita, one of the features subs and a fabulous gossip.

'Hooeee,' she was saying. 'That was a scorcher. Poor bugger.'

'What was the problem?' I asked, continuing our conversation over the partition between the cubicles.

'Did you read that story in features today about Essex girls who are into customizing cars?' said Rita. 'That guy Ned wrote it and he used the word "tits" in it – and not in a quote. Somehow it got through subs, and Doughnut read it this morning and nearly had a fit over his croissant.'

'Ouch,' I said. 'Is he new? This Ned?'

He had to be. Anyone who had worked on the paper for any time at all, knew that while his own language was richly peppered with obscenities and profanities, Doughnut was obsessive about keeping up what he called 'Empire standards' in the paper. He was a stickler for grammar and correct usage, and manically against the use of 'vulgarities'. 'Tits' was a major vulgarity misdemeanour.

He didn't have a problem with maverick creative flair

– Doughnut was a great champion of originality and had nurtured some of the brightest writing talents in British journalism – but he felt that being amusing without resorting to base language was part of the challenge.

'He's been here a couple of weeks, but I don't reckon he'll be asked to stay after his trial period now, do you?' said Rita, who loved office dramas more than anything. 'He'll be just another notch on Doughnut's sacking sword.'

I nipped back to my desk to tell Peter the news.

'Poor fellow,' he said. 'And a shame, because I think he's got promise, that young man. I liked that piece, it was an insight into a subculture I didn't know about, although I did baulk at the word in question myself when I read it this morning.

'Although, of course,' he continued, leaning back in his chair and fixing me with a gimlet stare over his bifocals and down his bony nose, 'the person Duncan should really be telling off is not the young writer, but our dear features editor, is it not? Did she not read the piece in question? Is it not her job to do so, when it is to appear in the section which she allegedly edits? It is, indeed. But no, she did not read it and she has allowed someone else entirely to take the blame – and that is business as usual round here these days, is it not, my dear girl?'

I smiled indulgently at Peter. He went on like a pompous vicar, but I loved him dearly. It was a privilege to sit next to him. He'd worked for the paper for over four decades, from when it was still on Fleet Street and the type was set each day by hand in hot metal, on printing presses housed in the basement below the editorial offices – another age, really.

He had a block of old metal type spelling out his byline –

all back to front, of course – on his desk, next to his manual typewriter.

He still did all his writing on that old thing – with multiple carbon copies – and then had one of the editorial assistants type it into the computer for him. It was against all the rules and the clattering of that old Olivetti had driven me nuts at first, until it became part of the general hum of my working day, but everyone made allowances for Peter.

He was a legend on the paper. He'd actually been editor of it at one point, and news editor and letters editor and obituaries editor and features editor, as well as doing practically every kind of reporting; he could still do shorthand at 150 words a minute. And after all that, he had earned his current privileged position quietly turning out just one perfectly written opinion column a week and the odd feature, as it took his fancy.

Some of the younger journalists thought he was a has-been old windbag and couldn't stand him, but I adored him. He'd taken a liking to me, for some reason, when I'd first arrived in the features department as a trainee, and I strongly suspected I had him to thank for being offered a full-time job on the paper.

Only two of us, in my group of eight graduate trainees, had been asked to stay on and when I ended up sitting in the desk next to him, I don't think that was a coincidence either.

In fact, I knew Peter had a lot more influence with Doughnut than most people realized. But even more importantly than that, there was so much you could learn from him, if you only listened – because you don't survive in newspapers for forty years without being pretty smart.

'Shall we take that unfortunate chastised young man out to lunch, Stella?' he said suddenly. 'Cheer him up. You go over and ask him. A friendly face is what he needs to see right now – and one as pretty as yours will be particularly welcome, I should think.'

I didn't particularly want to – I had my celebrity brands piece to finish and when I didn't have an unavoidable work lunch to go to, I preferred to stay in the office – but I had learned it was worthwhile going along with Peter's ideas. There was usually something interesting at the bottom of them.

Whatever this was about, Ned Morrissey seemed delighted when I appeared at his desk and asked him out for lunch. I didn't couch it in general terms, there wasn't any point, I just came out with it.

'Hi, Ned,' I said to him. 'I'm Stella Fain. I write all the luxury fluff in features. We all heard the hard time Doughnut gave you just now, and Peter Wallington – you know, the op ed columnist? – and I wondered if you'd like to come out for lunch with us today. Shiraz and sympathy and all that . . .'

'Hi, Stella,' said Ned, in a broad Australian accent I hadn't been expecting. 'I know who you are. That was a very nice news story you had in the paper last week about Jericho. She sounds like a silly cow. I'd love to have lunch with you and Peter Wallington. The man's a legend. Shall I come over to your desk at one?'

I nodded and went back to my desk, rather amazed. He was so relaxed. I'd been expecting a human jelly, in pieces after what had happened to him, but he didn't seem remotely fazed, either by Doughnut's tongue-lashing, or by my sudden invitation.

Now I could see why Peter was interested in him.

Jay called me just before lunch.

'Thanks for the beautiful flowers,' I said right away. 'They're gorgeous.'

'I'm glad you like them. I got them from my mom's favourite London florist. I thought it was more your style than one of those trendy places with green flowers like sputniks.'

'Your mother has excellent taste,' I told him.

'So, do you like Italian food?'

'I love it,' I said carefully. 'But I can't have dinner tonight, Jay. I'm busy.'

I wasn't. I had no plans that night beyond painting my toenails pink. I was just playing games with his head.

He said nothing and I was suddenly worried I had pushed it too far, but I couldn't go back now.

'Well, I can't do tomorrow,' he said, flatly.

Immediately I wanted to ask him why not? Who was he seeing? Where was he going? Shit.

'Can you do Wednesday night?' he asked eventually, although I definitely detected a note of irritation in his voice.

'Yes,' I said enthusiastically. 'I'd love to. Where shall I see you?'

'I'll pick you up. What's your address?'

I couldn't give him my address. Nobody came to my place, not even my girlfriends. He'd already invaded my territory hugely coming down to Willow Barn like that, and he certainly wasn't getting inside my secret little nest so easily. I gave him the address of Ham's house.

'It's my father's London place,' I explained. 'That's where I'll be.'

'Great,' said Jay. 'And Stella – don't cancel me, OK?'

I giggled a little, I couldn't help myself.

'I won't,' I promised.

I strongly suspected he was on to me.

Lunch with Ned and Peter was extremely, well, interesting. That was the only word for it. It was hard to imagine a more disparate trio really, yet we were united by whatever quirk it was in our personalities that made us newspaper people.

'So, Ned,' said Peter, as we settled into his table at Gino's, the Italian trattoria that had opened expressly to service the staff of the *Journal*, when the paper had moved to docklands from Fleet Street twenty years before. Peter ate lunch there every day – having the same wine and the same food at the same table.

'Tell me why you used the word "tits" in your piece,' Peter continued, nodding at the waiter to fill our glasses with his usual Amarone. 'I thought it was a bold, and rather unnecessary, inclusion when I read it – in what was a very good piece of reporting. I could tell you had entirely won the trust of those young women you interviewed. How did you do that, by the way?'

'I wore a tight shirt,' said Ned, without blinking.

Peter and I both roared with laughter. Ned cracked a small smile, but I knew he wasn't joking. I glanced at his chest. He was a pretty beefy guy. I hadn't noticed at first.

'Oh, that's marvellous,' said Peter. 'But, go on, tell me why you felt it was appropriate to use the word "tits", when it wasn't a quote and really wasn't germane to the build of the story.'

'Do you really want to know?' said Ned.

'I do,' said Peter.

'I wanted to see what Duncan McDonagh would do.'

Peter was lost for words, which was a first in my experience.

'I've heard so much about his famous scary temper,' continued Ned. 'And I just wanted to see how bad it was, in case I ever want to do something really naughty. I didn't think "tits" would get through the subs, but I tried it anyway and it did.'

Peter was looking at him so sharply now, his bony old nose looked like an eagle's beak.

'How interesting,' he said eventually. 'And where did you work before you came to the *Journal*?'

'At *The Age*, in Melbourne.'

'Are you political?' asked Peter bluntly.

'Is this a job interview?' said Ned. 'I thought we were just having lunch.' His face cracked into a smile that made deep lines appear on either side of his mouth. He wasn't handsome exactly, but he had an interesting face.

Peter softened his expression again, but the steely look didn't go out of his eyes. He didn't ask Ned any more of his very direct questions, but by the end of the lunch, they both knew a lot more about each other.

'Where did you do your training, Peter?' Ned asked him.

'At the *Journal*, of course,' said Peter. 'Like young Stella here, but an awfully long time ago.'

'How long have you been at the paper, Stella?' he asked me. He had green eyes, I noticed. Very green eyes. As he looked at me steadily, I could see why those Dagenham girls had let him into their hot rods. He was charismatic, that was the only word for it.

'Gosh, it's over five years already,' I said. 'I came as a graduate trainee, as Peter said, and I'm still here.'

'Didn't you ever want to go and work anywhere else?'

I hated that question, it made me feel like a loser, but Peter answered it for me.

'Why leave when you're already established on the world's greatest newspaper?' he said, like the true *Journal* man he was. For him there was no other paper. The others were only good for lining hamsters' cages, as he often said.

'To get broader experience,' said Ned, looking him straight in the eye. He was fearless. He was rattling Peter and he knew it.

'An admirable intention,' said Peter, in his most patronizing tone. 'But if you resigned from the *Journal* you could never expect to come back. Certainly not while Duncan is still editor. He prizes loyalty as much as he does hard work and flair. You'd be stuck on a lesser masthead, reading the *Journal* every morning and feeling forever slightly on the outer. I've seen too many smart people do that. They get very bitter.'

I could see Ned taking note.

'Thanks, Peter,' he said. 'That's really good advice. I appreciate that. But there must have been a lot of attempts to poach you over the past forty years.'

Peter smiled. He was being flattered and he didn't mind.

'Yes. The BBC – radio, of course – was the only offer which tempted me, but I declined. I'm a newspaper man to the bone – and I rather suspect you are too.'

They smiled at each other. It was a meeting of minds.

Dinner with Jay was perfect. He'd picked me up at Ham's place, just a few elegant minutes after the allotted time and paid me what seemed like a sincere compliment about my appearance.

He'd stayed for a few minutes, being very nice to Chloe and Daisy – Ham wasn't there, to my great relief, he'd gone to Stockholm to give a lecture – and then he'd whisked me off in that silly car to the River Café. Which just happens to be my favourite restaurant.

Then we pretty much sat there and beamed at each other across the table. I could hardly eat, which was a shame, considering how great their food is, and I could hardly drink which was also a shame, because Jay had ordered some pretty serious wine. Really, I just wanted to sit and gaze at him.

'Hello,' he said, suddenly, when we'd been holding eye contact for ages, like a couple of love-struck teens. Then he reached out and took my hand, blinking at me slowly like a contented cat.

'Hello,' I said back, softly, not caring how soppy I sounded.

'There's something between us, isn't there, Stella?' he said, quietly.

I nodded.

'I don't normally sit and stare at people I'm having dinner with, do you?' he continued.

I shook my head.

'Just checking,' he said. 'And here's another thing I want to check – you're not going to run off to work on me tonight are you?'

I shook my head again and he smiled at me, so sweetly, I almost couldn't bear it. I always found it disarming when I saw that side of Jay. There was something about the combination of that gentle sweetness with his smoothie James Bond good looks that just did me in.

'You know, Stella,' he said, after a moment. 'This is amazing food and all, but I find I'm not real hungry right now. Shall we split?'

I nodded my head. I didn't care about playing the game any more. It was time to go with my feelings.

So I did. I went with Jay, in his ridiculous Thunderbirds car, back to Chelsea, to a huge flat on Sloane Avenue. Where we made love all night.

And it was like that, it was making love and all that corny old stuff, it wasn't just hot sex. Which is what it would have been, I thought, if we'd gone for it that first night – or morning – in the South of France, but in the days since then, something had grown between us and expressing it together, at last, was a beautiful thing. Not to mention supersonically orgasmic.

Eventually, Jay went off to sleep, but I couldn't. I lay awake for what seemed like hours, just looking at him and thinking. I must have dozed off eventually, though, because I was woken by light coming through a small chink in the heavy brocade curtains of his bedroom. He was still out, like an exhausted puppy sprawled across the huge mattress of his four-poster bed.

I had been surprised by that bed, when I saw it, as I was

about everything in Jay's place. I'd expected him to live in some kind of groovy loft, all mid-century furniture and modern art, the flat equivalent of his car, but this place was more like something out of Harry Potter, with wood panelling and Persian rugs, huge stone fireplaces and the four-poster. There were even paintings of horses and dogs on the walls.

He'd smiled, when I'd expressed my surprise, the night before.

'Well, I didn't decorate this apartment myself,' he said. 'My grandmother did, but I like it like this and anyway, it doesn't matter, because very few people see it. I don't bring people here.'

He pinched my cheek.

'I'm honoured,' I said, thinking how alike we were in that regard.

'No, I'm the one who's honoured,' he said and he pulled me into his arms. 'And now I'm going to be honoured all over again.'

When the chink in the curtains was clearly full daylight, I leaned over and woke Jay up with a kiss. He was smiling before he had even opened his eyes.

'Hello, beautiful girl,' he said, rolling over and kissing me tenderly on the forehead. 'It's good to see you. Do you like daylight at this time of day, or are you the vampire type?'

'Daylight,' I said, firmly. I had no blind on the skylight in my bedroom at home, and I liked being woken up by the sun.

He reached for a remote control by the bed and the heavy brocade curtains – or drapes, as he called them – slid open automatically.

'That's better,' he said. 'Now I can see what I've got for breakfast . . .'

And he made love to me again. Twice.

I got to work a little late that day – nearly two hours late – but at least I got there. Jay had been amazed when I'd told him I was getting up to go home to change and then to work.

'But I want to spend the day with you,' he said. 'Don't go.'

'I'd love to stay,' I said, getting out of bed. 'But it's Thursday. It's a workday. I have to go.'

'Can't you call in sick?'

I looked down at him lying there, all toffee-brown skin and white teeth and gorgeous. It was tempting, but I had stuff I needed to get on with at the office.

I had to put the last bit of polish on the celebrity brands story for my pages in the next day's features section and I had a phone interview set up with the CEO of Gucci that afternoon about the new designer. Big stuff, in my world. But it wasn't just that I had to go to work – I wanted to go.

I shook my head. 'You can't do that on a newspaper,' I said. 'My work won't wait.'

I sat down on the bed again and put my arms around him.

'I've had a wonderful time, Jay. It's been great. I'd love to see you again soon.'

It was a lot more than I should have said if I was playing Ham's teasing game properly, but it was how I felt. I was over the game.

'You will,' said Jay. 'You totally will.'

But I didn't. I had a text while I was at work that day – a

text! – saying how great it had been and how he couldn't wait to see me again and he'd call me soon. But he didn't.

And I was so cross with him for sending me an impersonal text, rather than calling, I deleted it, so I didn't even have his number. At that stage I still thought he would definitely ring me any minute, or I might have held on to it – but he didn't.

After a few days, I just felt completely stupid. I couldn't believe what had happened. I had been certain there was something special between me and Jay, and I didn't know if I'd lost him by letting the game go and sleeping with him, or by playing the stupid game too long, when he clearly knew what I was up to.

Or maybe he hadn't felt anything for me at all and it had all been just talk and another kind of game for him. Whichever it was, our little fling was clearly over and I was surprised how miserable I felt about it.

On top of that I was really dreading Ham asking me about him. I knew he would be ridiculously overexcited about the first boyfriend I had ever brought home, so I was deliberately avoiding him.

I worked long hours at the paper, declining all invitations to events after work – there was nothing big happening, so I could – and spent every evening at home, doing what I liked to do best when I was alone.

Curling up on my big brass bed in my silliest baby-doll nightie, and watching CNN and BBC World into the small hours.

8

It was well over a week since I'd last heard from Jay and I was still in the office at well past eight p.m. – wallowing in my self-imposed work purdah – when Ned Morrissey appeared by my desk.

I was always pleased to see Ned. We'd had coffee a couple of times since the lunch with Peter and I found him a really interesting character.

He hadn't yet been fully absorbed into *Journal* culture and his fresh eye on it all fascinated me. I'd been there way too long to see anything clearly any more.

'You're working late again, Stella,' he said, sitting on the edge of Peter's desk. 'You've worked late every night this week.'

'Well, if you know that,' I said, 'then you must have been working late every night too.'

He picked up Peter's piece of old metal type and weighed it in his hand, before putting it down again.

'You're not wrong,' he said. 'But I've still got something to prove here. I'm killing myself just to keep my job since the tits incident, but you're fully established. Why are you doing it?'

'I'm never complacent,' I said.

He narrowed those green eyes.

'You snooze, you lose, in this game,' I continued. 'Just like the cliché says. There are a lot of people who would love to have my job, Ned, so I never assume it's mine by right. I'm still always striving to be the best.'

'You *are* the best at what you do, by all accounts.'

'For what it's worth,' I said, somewhat bitterly.

'What do you mean?'

'Luxury . . .' I shrugged. 'Really? Who gives a shit?'

He just looked steadily at me. I carried on talking.

'The whole luxury industry basically comes down to a fairly small bunch of grotesquely spoilt women and status-obsessed men with penis-size issues,' I was babbling on. 'Or men and women who aspire to live as they do. The values at the base of it all are repugnant, yet it's presented as life on some kind of a higher plane. Like you're a better person because you can afford to waste money on pointless shit. It's all bollocks.'

There was something about Ned that made you a little indiscreet like that. Probably because he knew when to say nothing. Peter always said that was one of the characteristics of the best interviewers and it clearly came naturally to Ned. I was still going on.

'I never wanted to write about bloody diamonds. I just ended up doing this by accident, and it is worth it to have a job here, but it's not why I wanted to be a journalist.'

I smiled at him sheepishly. 'I wanted to be Woodward and Bernstein.'

Ned barked with laughter.

'I still do,' he said. 'I still want to be them. That's why I'm here. Do you think I'll end up writing about handbags too?'

'No,' I said, laughing with him. 'But I'd watch yourself if you ever get asked to do anything for the motoring section.'

'You're not kidding,' said Ned, still smiling, then those canny eyes narrowed again. 'But if you don't love the luxury world, Stella, you're keeping some pretty swanky company.'

'What do you mean?' I asked him.

He handed me a copy of *Hot Stuff!* magazine, a celebrity gossip trash weekly. It fell open at a page of paparazzi photographs and my eyes nearly popped out when I saw what was on them: pictures of me and Jay, arriving at Wonderland, and on the dance floor, in a tight clinch, mixed in with other shots of Jay with Jericho.

'What the fuck?' I said, but Ned had gone.

'See you later, Stella,' he was saying as he disappeared round the corner. 'Don't work too hard.'

I took a few deep breaths and looked down at the pictures again. I felt quite sick, just seeing them, it was such a shock. Jay was just as gorgeous as I remembered him, which was distressing in itself, but it got a whole lot weirder when I read the copy that went with the photos.

'JAY'S CHOICE: POSH or SCARY?' said the headline, in screaming red and pink type and then 'SCARY?' was repeated over Jericho's picture and 'POSH?' over mine.

The copy that went with it was even more bewildering.

> Poor little rich boy Jay Fisher found himself in a messy love triangle with two hot babes fighting for his attention at the French Riviera's hottest nightclub Wonderland recently.
>
> The billion-heir playboy who stands to inherit the Fisher family fortune – reputed to be around a cool $10 billion – was seen arriving at the lavish

club with It girl peer's daughter the Hon. Stella Montecourt, eldest child of leading architect Lord Montecourt of Cliffe.

But while those two seemed pretty close on the dance floor, who should show up to claim Jay but megastar songstress Jericho – who had been seen getting cosy with the deliciously single billionaire in Aspen just a couple of weeks before.

Adding to the spice of it all, the famously hot-tempered Jericho stormed out of her press conference in a fury the next day – right after being asked a question by the Hon. Stella, who has a play job on the *Daily Journal* newspaper.

But it doesn't look like either of these girls is going to be the one to bag this particular Mr Big. He was last seen in Buenos Aires, at the 25th birthday party of beautiful Argentinian heiress Patrizia Fernandez.

Tough luck, girls. This Jay has flown away.

I didn't know which bit of the story to be most amazed about. I had certainly never been described as an It girl before and I was furious to have my career dismissed as a 'play job', but of course the part that really left me speechless was the revelation of who Jay really was.

I checked the date on the front of the magazine – it wasn't due to come out until the next day – and then I turned back to the story and just kept going over it, almost unable to believe what I was reading.

But at the same time, it was all falling into place in my head. Everything that had been a bit weird about my time with Jay now made perfect sense. Including his absence.

An investment manager! That was what he'd said he did. He wasn't kidding. His loose change was probably more than most people's life savings – then I remembered the wad of notes he always carried. He always paid cash, I'd noticed that. I'd thought it was odd, but it must have been something to do with being so loaded. Who knew? That kind of money was another universe. And no wonder he'd gone all weird whenever I'd mentioned his family.

Then another thing struck me – it wasn't surprising he knew all about my father. Ham had won the competition to design the Fisher Institute in Boston, a new museum commissioned to house some of the priceless works of art that the Fisher family – Jay's family – had donated to the American nation, complete with the landmark building to house the collection.

It was Dad's most prestigious project by far, and he'd won it by designing a public building specifically to have the feeling of a family home, to reflect the dynastic nature of the Fisher Trust.

What was even odder was that Ham hadn't made that connection himself, but then when I looked back at the day Jay came to Willow Barn, I didn't think I'd ever mentioned Jay's full name, so why would he? Ham didn't read the gossip mags any more than I did, so he probably wouldn't have known what Jay looked like either.

I felt so stupid, I just wanted to go and hide myself away. I slunk out of the office and went home, but I'd only been back at my place for a few minutes when the phone rang. So few people had that number I answered immediately. It was Ham.

'I saw your light on,' he said, in a rather strained voice. 'Can you come over?'

It was such an unusual request, I said I'd be right there.

Ham was sitting at the kitchen table, with a large glass of whisky, looking at a magazine – it was *Hot Stuff!*.

'Have you seen this?' he said, holding it up by a corner, like it was a rather smelly dead fish.

I nodded, sitting down. 'About an hour ago,' I said.

'Why didn't you tell me he was Jay *Fisher*?' said Ham. He sounded really hurt.

'I didn't know, Ham,' I said. 'Well, I knew that was his name, but I didn't make the connection with the Fisher banking family, I just thought he was a guy called Jay Fisher. I didn't know he was a multibillionaire called Jay Fisher.'

Ham looked incredulous.

'Hadn't you heard of him?' he said.

'I think I had,' I said, slowly. 'But I just didn't make the connection. He told me he was an investment manager and I thought he was just another overpaid New York/London banker-wanker boy. I meet a lot of them, doing what I do, and normally I'm not that keen, but I really liked Jay, from the moment I laid eyes on him and the penny just didn't drop. And he certainly didn't spell it out to me. Anyway, what's the big deal?'

He was rubbing his jaw and frowning. I nodded at his glass.

'Can I have one of those, please?' I asked in a small voice.

'Of course you can, number one duckling,' said Ham, clearly relenting a little about whatever had upset him, and he got up and poured me a large shot of single malt.

'I'm really sorry, Ham,' I said, when he sat down again. 'But I wasn't being sneaky not telling you, I'm just incredibly stupid.'

'You certainly are not, but I would have thought that with what you write about, you would be a little more au fait with all those silly jet-set socialite types.'

I pulled a face.

'That's the part of it I can't stand,' I said.

'But you love going out to fancy restaurants and staying in five-star hotels, don't you?'

'Yes,' I admitted. 'But on my own terms. I like visiting that world as a kind of lifestyle tourist, but I certainly don't aspire to dwell in it all the time. The people who do are mostly utter twats.'

'Well, that's a relief,' said Ham, smiling broadly, but then a frown settled on his brows again. 'And that leads to my other concern with regard to your friend, Mr Fisher.'

'I don't think he is my friend any more,' I said, my voice wobbling slightly as I fought tears.

Ham's bear-like hand reached out across the table and covered mine.

'Has he dumped you?' he asked, gently.

I nodded. My eyes were now fully teared up. One slid down my cheek.

'He hasn't called me for over a week,' I whispered.

'Had you slept with him?' said Ham, very quietly.

I screwed my eyes up and nodded. Then I burst into tears.

Ham came round the table and enveloped me in his huge arms, while I sobbed uncontrollably on to his shoulder until

I had let all the pent-up sadness and anger pour out and was just hiccupping a bit.

He dried my eyes on his shirtsleeve and then pulled a chair over, so he could sit with one arm round me.

'My poor little poppet,' he said. 'God! Men are frightful. Just don't say I didn't warn you.'

'That's what makes it so awful,' I said. 'I knew what to do and I messed it all up.'

I looked up into Ham's big craggy, kind face.

'No,' he said. 'He did.'

I felt all teary again, just talking about Jay.

'I really liked him, Ham,' I said eventually, in a tiny voice. 'I had no idea he was stupidly rich, I just really liked him. Not just because he's good-looking, and I didn't even like the flashy car and all that nonsense. It's just that he has such a gentle side to him and he's so kind and funny and interesting and he always knows what to do – the way you do. I felt safe with Jay. He's lovely.'

I had another little bout of sobbing, with Ham saying, 'There there,' and patting my head, until I finally recovered enough to ask him what he had been about to say before I'd broken down.

'Ham, you said that you had another concern about Jay. What was it?'

'Ah,' said Ham, looking uneasy. 'That. Well, surely you must remember I have a connection with that family.'

I nodded. 'The museum in Boston. I did finally figure out that was how Jay knew all about you.'

'Yes,' said Ham, sighing deeply. 'I did the Fisher Institute and it was the most painful project I have ever worked on.'

I blinked at him. 'Why?'

'His family are an utter nightmare,' said Ham. 'I cannot tell you the crap I had to put up with from them over that building. I wouldn't care if it burned down tomorrow, they made it such an unpleasant experience.'

'Not Jay?' I said, horrified.

'No,' said Ham. 'He had nothing to do with it. I'd never seen him until he turned up at Willow Barn, although he did look vaguely familiar, now I come to think of it. It's the rest of them. The generation above him. His father! Don't start me. He's as cold as a sphinx. His mother wasn't involved with the institute – they're divorced – but his father is married again to a woman so avaricious she makes Kristy look like Mother Teresa. And then there are the truly terrible uncles. The Fishers are a huge clan of sociopathic fuckwits. They're messed up in a way that only the inherited megarich can be. Those people scare me.'

I just gawped at him.

'But Jay's not like that,' I said, after a moment.

'Well, he seemed very nice, I must say, but I can't imagine where that comes from, because the rest of them are completely appalling. Greedy, paranoid, ungenerous, petty . . . it just goes on.'

He leaned forwards.

'Do you know what his Uncle Edward did? He's the obsessive–compulsive pederast, by the way, as opposed to Michael, the masochistic dipsomaniac drug addict. Anyway, he went through every single receipt in my personal expenses claim from the project and refused to reimburse any mineral water that was on restaurant bills. He said I should have had good American tap water. True story. It amounted to about fifty pounds – in a project that was costing over two hundred million dollars.'

I shook my head in disbelief.

'But if they're that mean,' I said, 'how come they were giving away such an amazingly valuable art collection to the American people? Why didn't they just keep it all? Uncle Edward could have had the Renoirs in his loo.'

Ham rolled his eyes.

'Tax break,' he said. 'No, the Fishers really are as vile and mean-minded as only several generations of inherited wealth can make people, and the thought of you being involved with a family like that is simply horrendous to me. They are poison.'

I put my face in my hands and groaned. I didn't know what to be more upset about. That Jay had dumped me, right after I had slept with him? That I had been stupid enough not to realize who he was? Or that the only man I had ever had proper adult romantic feelings for, had turned out to be from a tribe of money-obsessed psychomonsters?

Then I was distracted by another thought.

'But how on earth did you come to see *Hot Stuff!* magazine, Ham. It's certainly not your normal kind of a read. Or Chloe's, I'm happy to say, and it's not even out until tomorrow.'

His eyes creased up into a wry smile.

'Kristy told me about it. It's her favourite magazine – she's a subscriber, so she gets it a day early. This is her copy. She dropped by with it earlier and to say she's very keen for Venezia to see Jay again. And she's looking forward to meeting him herself as well.'

We looked at each other for a moment and then burst out laughing.

'Oh,' he added. 'And then Venezia called a bit later to say – and I quote – "There is *so*, no way Stella's an It girl . . ."'

That just set me off again, until I was nearly crying with laughter. It was a welcome release, but it wasn't quite the end of it. We chatted about other things for a while and then I told Ham I was going home to bed.

I started to stand up, when he put his hand on my arm.

'There's one more thing, Stella,' he said, looking serious.

I sat down again.

'You're a very sensible girl,' he continued. 'Which is pretty amazing considering what silly flighty parents you had, but I need you to promise me something about all this.'

I looked back at him. It wasn't his usual style, but these weren't usual circumstances.

'What is it?' I asked him.

'Promise me you won't see Jay Fisher any more. From what you've told me it's already over, but if he does get back in touch with you, promise me you will have nothing more to do with him.'

I stared at him, in surprise.

'He won't make you happy, Stella,' Ham said, earnestly. 'None of that family are capable of being happy and I don't want to see them ruin your life along with all of theirs. They're noxious. Deadly. So I want you to promise me that. Will you?'

It was strong stuff and I was really taken aback, but Ham had never asked me to promise anything before and although I felt a bit uncomfortable, I agreed.

I mean, I wasn't going to see Jay Fisher again anyway, was I?

*

My head was still spinning with it all when I fell into bed that night.

It was just too much to compute and after an hour or so of lying there, going over every moment I had spent with Jay and analysing all the little things he had said and done which could have tipped me off to his true identity, I started to feel like my brain was coming out of my ears.

In the end I decided there was only one way to cope with it. I'd just throw myself back into my work more than ever and I wouldn't give Jay Fisher another thought.

That proved rather hard when I got into the office the next day. The article from *Hot Stuff!* had been blown up to A3 size on the colour photocopier and was plastered all over the noticeboard above my desk.

Just to make it even worse, the photo of me and Jay in an intimate clinch had been enlarged separately, so I could see every detail of his beautiful face and how happy I had looked gazing into it.

'Hello, Posh Spice,' called out Rita, as I walked past the subs' desks on my way to make a cup of tea in the staff kitchen.

'Oooh, it's our very own It girl,' said another. 'Give us a loan, Mrs Fisher.'

'You'd better watch out,' said a third. 'I think I saw Jericho lurking near your desk, with a stiletto shoe in her hand . . .'

They all shrieked with laughter. I smiled weakly and stepped into the kitchen, only to see that the article had been pinned up on the noticeboard in there too. Rita followed me in.

'How exciting, Stella,' she said, her eyes gleaming with the thrill of it. 'What's it like dating a billionaire? He's really cute, I must say. Has he bought you any good presents?'

I just looked at her. I wanted to tell her to fuck off, but I couldn't blame her. As office gossip went, it was pretty hot stuff. I tried to smile ruefully. I probably looked like I had wind, but I knew I had to make an effort. Being a good sport was all part of being a success on a newspaper. If you showed the teasing bothered you, you'd be torn to pieces.

'Oh, only a new Mercedes,' I joked.

'Has he really?' said Rita, clearly ready to believe anything in her keenness to get hold of some juicy details to share around.

'No, you noggin,' I said, playfully punching her arm. 'And I'm not dating him. I just met him at the Jericho launch and a whole gang of us went out that night and I just danced with him and somehow they got those stupid pictures. God knows how, I didn't even see a flash go off. It's a classic trash mag beat-up. They must have been desperate for a story.'

Rita's face hardened a little.

'So how come you had a romantic dinner with him at the River Café as well?'

I just looked at her. That hadn't been in the piece in *Hot Stuff!* How did she know about that? But I couldn't ask – I couldn't let my guard down.

'Wouldn't you?' I said and winked. Then I got out of the kitchen. It was getting a little too hot in there.

When I got back to my desk Tim was waiting there for me, keenly examining the article on the noticeboard. I reached past him, tore it down, screwed it up and threw it in the bin.

'Morning, Timothy,' I said, with an edge in my voice.

'Morning, It girl,' he replied.

I slumped into my chair.

'Not you as well, Tim,' I said. 'I've already had a roasting from the bloody subs. You're supposed to be my friend, remember?'

'I *am* your friend,' he said, retrieving the article from the bin and smoothing it out so he could carry on reading it. 'That's why I'm here. So what's all this about? Are you really dating Jay Fisher? I don't know about the *Family Fortunes* side of things, but if he's as cute as he looks in these pictures, I wouldn't blame you.'

'No, I'm not dating him,' I said firmly. 'I met him at that Jericho launch and we did go out dancing, but I'm not dating him.'

'So how come Rita tells me you've been seen at the River Café with him, since these pictures were taken, and that you left there without finishing your meal and went back to his place and didn't leave until after ten the next morning, when you came out wearing the same clothes you had on the night before?'

'How the fuck does she know all that?'

I didn't have to pretend with Tim. He really was a friend.

'Her boyfriend's a paparazzo. He was probably trailing you all night. Or one of his pals was.'

I just sat there and let it all sink in. I knew they did that. I may have worked on a broadsheet newspaper that would never have lowered itself to such base forms of journalism, but I knew that freelance paparazzi did stuff like that all the time. It was hardly an industry secret.

'Bloody hell,' I said. 'Do you think they stake him out all the time?'

'Anyone who has been seen up close and personal with

Jericho is immediately a marked man, obviously. But they'd probably keep a bit of an eye on him anyway, wouldn't they, considering how rich and handsome and single he is. Didn't that occur to you?'

I shook my head.

'I didn't really know who he was,' I said quietly.

Tim looked at me for a moment, in disbelief, and then threw his head back and roared.

'Oh, my little hard-news wannabe, you are hilarious. You write about luxury and you didn't recognize Jay Fisher? He's a luxury brand in human form and you really didn't know who he was?'

I shook my head.

'You don't read *Hot Stuff!*, do you? Or *Hello!*, or any of them. Do you, Stella?'

'Sometimes in the hairdresser's . . .'

'Who is the president of Afghanistan?' he said suddenly.

'Hamid Karzai,' I said.

'Uzbekistan?'

'Islam Karimov . . .'

'What was Pope Benedict's name before he was pope?'

'Cardinal Joseph Ratzinger . . .'

'Paris Hilton's last fiancé?'

I shrugged.

'Oh, Stella,' he said. 'You are hilarious.' Then his face went serious again. 'Don't worry about this rubbish, it will all blow over when Jericho's linked to someone else, and dating a billionaire will be marvellous for your reputation in the world you work in. You'll be seen as an insider – and a possible customer – not just a hack. Tamara Mellon is probably planning to invite you round for drinks as we speak.'

'I'm not dating him,' I said quietly.

'A quick fuck and a fuck you?' said Tim, referring to his own preferred style of relationship.

'Yeah,' I said emphatically. 'I was just fooling around. He is bloody cute, like you said.'

Tim looked at me thoughtfully.

'Well, just keep your eyes open for men on motorbikes with cameras, OK? They'll probably watch you for a while now, in case you are the future Mrs Fisher – and Jericho's love rival is a fairly prominent role in its own right.'

He put his hands on my shoulders and looked right into my eyes.

'And do try and be a little less naïve, Stella. You were playing in a very high-stakes game for a moment there. It can be dangerous in that world. And read the bloody trash mags every week, not just *New Internationalist*. Right, lecture over. I also came over to say goodbye. I'm going back to Iraq this afternoon. What's the name of the president there, by the way?'

'Jalal Talabani,' I shot back.

He roared with laughter again, kissed me on the cheek and left.

The office teasing carried on for a day or two and then it calmed down. That was the great thing about newspapers; every day really is a fresh start and nobody who worked at the *Journal* had much to speak of in the way of an attention span.

But out of those confines, I didn't feel so secure, because Tim had been right – the paparazzi were trailing me. Only a couple of them, but they were there. They were waiting outside the office when I left at night, on their motorbikes. They tracked me back to Notting Hill and then sat outside my place, presumably waiting for me to leave to meet Jay, or for him to turn up there.

I continued to decline invitations, and whenever I was forced to be on the street I made sure I was dressed down, with my hair pulled back in a ponytail and shades on. It was my attempt to stay inconspicuous, and after a couple of days of me going into my house and not coming out again, they appeared to give up on me.

One night, exactly a week after the story had come out in *Hot Stuff!* I was sitting at my desk working late when Ned loped over.

It was the first time I'd seen him since he'd tipped me off about it. I'd been over to his desk a couple of times to try and find him – I'd wanted to thank him – but he'd never been there.

'Hi, Ned,' I said. 'I've been looking for you.'

'I know,' he said. 'Rita told me.'

'Oh, you can rely on Rita,' I said. 'She's more reliable than a front-page lead in the *Journal* if you want to get a story circulated.'

'I'd figured that,' said Ned. 'What did you want to say to me, anyway?'

'Thank you,' I said. 'Thank you for showing me that horrendous thing in *Hot Stuff!* It was so humiliating and if I hadn't known about it before I came into work that day, I would have been mortified – well, even more mortified. But tell me, how come you had an early copy? Are you a subscriber?'

'My girlfriend works there,' he said. 'She always bikes it

over to me as soon as it comes in from the printer, in case I can get a story out of it.'

I nodded. 'Well, thanks to both of you.'

'Are you OK?' he said. 'It must have been pretty weird to find yourself suddenly the subject of journalism – especially that kind of crap.'

'It was horrendous,' I said. 'But I'm OK now. It's all rubbish anyway, I'm not dating him. I never was.'

I didn't care if Rita had told him all the gory details about the River Café and all that; I wasn't dating him and that was that.

'Shame,' said Ned. 'Most girls would dream of being with a guy like that.'

I just looked down. I suddenly felt a bit teary. I didn't want Ned to see.

He stood there for a while, saying nothing, in that way he had.

'So,' he said after a moment. 'If you're not dating a billionaire, how would you like to come out with some ordinary people? You've been working late every night again. People are talking about it – and not just Rita. So why don't you give work a rest for a while and come out? A crowd of us are going to the Amused Moose to see a few acts, so why don't you come with us, have a laugh, get out of yourself?'

I knew the Amused Moose was a comedy club somewhere in Soho, but I'd never been there. But it so wasn't my scene, it suddenly seemed a really attractive prospect.

'When?' I said.

'Now,' said Ned, smiling sweetly.

I thought for a moment. Why not? Why shouldn't I just go out after work with my colleagues, like any normal person?

I was even appropriately dressed for it. Normally I had to get a bit togged up for work, because I was always off to The Wolseley for lunch, The Berkeley for tea, and cocktails at Claridge's, but in my present low-key persona, I was wearing cord jeans. Perfect for a comedy club. No one but me would know they were Sevens and cost nearly £200. I'd fit right in.

'You know what?' I said. 'I would really love to.'

And I turned my computer off with a flourish.

9

When Ned had said 'a crowd of us' were going to the Amused Moose, I'd thought he meant a crowd from the office, but it turned out to be a group of his non-work friends.

It was rather strange to be out with a load of complete strangers, but actually quite wonderful. I felt completely free of expectations and after all the ribbing I'd had to put up with at work – plus a lifetime of being Ham's daughter – that was a very pleasant relief.

They were nice enough people, as far as I could tell, but comedy clubs don't give you much of a chance to make small talk, so I didn't really get to know any of them. And I didn't have to tell them anything about me. Excellent.

Whoever they were, none of them looked like *Hot Stuff!* readers and they didn't seem to recognize me. They were so different from the people I normally mixed with, whether through the luxury world, my family, or friends from university, it was almost like going on holiday in another country. Everyone drank beer, in pints, smoked roll-ups, and wore cheap clothes. The women and the men.

And the really funny thing was that, in my jeans, with my hair simply pulled back – I usually had it blow-dried at John Frieda, but I hadn't bothered that week – I fitted right in. I wasn't even carrying a major statement handbag, for once. I'd put my wallet and keys in my pocket and left my Bottega

Veneta tote in my locker at the office. It was almost like being in disguise.

The other thing that made me feel protected was that whenever there was a break in the show the person I ended up talking to was Ned. He sat next to me the entire evening and was very solicitous, in his easy way, so I didn't feel left out, or exposed.

As the evening went on, he seemed to sit closer to me, I noticed, and after a while he casually put his arm along the back of my chair.

I was a little surprised by his attentions, especially as I had expected his girlfriend to be there. Considering her connections with *Hot Stuff!* magazine, I was rather glad she wasn't, but I had been interested to see what she would be like. Ned was so enigmatic, it was quite hard to picture what his type would be. In the end I just came out and asked him about it.

'Where's your girlfriend, Ned?' I said. 'I was looking forward to meeting her.'

'Oh, she's out with her mates,' he said, moving his arm off my chair. 'We don't live together or anything, we're not like a really couple-y couple, we lead our own lives.'

I nodded. I could relate to that. That was how I liked to conduct my relationships too.

'So you don't have a boyfriend yourself?' he said. 'Apart from the odd date with a billionaire?'

I shook my head.

'I find that very surprising. You're the kind I'd expect to see with one of those City types, in a Porsche and all that.'

Jay's car popped into my head, whizzing past all the Porsches on the M23. I just smiled weakly at him.

'Mind you,' he said. 'That wouldn't fit in with the Woodward and Bernstein side of your personality, would it? Guess I'm just buying into your superficial luxury persona here – perhaps you'd be more likely to be carrying on with a bit of rough instead, eh?'

He smiled, to show he was teasing and I hoped my eyes hadn't popped open in surprise. I wondered what he'd think if he knew what I got up to with Jack. But maybe he wouldn't be as shocked as I might think. I found Ned very unsettling sometimes.

'Well, I'm quite surprised that you've got a girlfriend who works on a gossip mag,' I countered. 'If you want to talk stereotypes, I'd see you more with a social worker, or maybe a human rights lawyer you'd been going out with since you were at university.'

Ned laughed.

'My last girlfriend was a lap dancer,' he said, and before I had a chance to pursue it, the next act came on.

My night out in a different world had almost been like going on safari. The novelty gave me a real boost and Ned's cheeky comments, about being able to picture me with a bit of rough, put the idea of Jack into my head.

A little rendezvous with him was just what I needed to get me fully over Jay, I decided in the cab home from the Amused Moose. I was surprised I hadn't thought of it sooner, really, so the next day I called him up.

'Wotcha, Posh,' he said, which stalled me for a moment, until I remembered that was what he had always called me – he wasn't referring to the piece in *Hot Stuff!*

'Busy?' I asked him.

'I'm busy now,' he said. 'I'm a hundred and twenty feet above the ground fixing the pointing on this here steeple, it's in a right old mess. But I'm not busy later. Got anything in mind?'

'You,' I said. 'Six thirty?'

'It's a done deal, darling.'

'Don't fall off, Jack,' I said.

'Don't worry, sweetheart, I'm an expert with tall erections, as you know.'

I hung up, with a big smile on my face.

Just talking to Jack put me in a good mood. Even apart from his talent and enthusiasm for sex, which were considerable, the whole notion of him turned me on. I liked his rough hands and his cheeky humour – and I loved the secrecy of our arrangement. It made me feel like some kind of wicked eighteenth-century courtesan.

Looking forward to meeting him was a big part of the thrill, and I left work early to go home and pick up some of my sauciest underwear for his delectation. He loved all that corny old stuff in a really unapologetic way. Jack just loved totty, full stop.

But from the moment he walked in that evening it wasn't right. Nothing was different on the surface. I had arrived first, showered and changed, had a vodka from the mini-bar, draped a scarf over the bedside lamp, slipped into my lingerie and arranged myself seductively on the bed.

Jack arrived in his work clothes, nice and dirty, and after admiring me for a while, from various angles, he took some of them off, while quietly telling me, in the filthiest terms, what he was planning to do very shortly.

I looked at him bare-chested, in his dusty jeans – which

he was just pulling down over his hips – and I could see how sexy he was, the gay fantasy of the hunky construction worker, complete with the steel toecapped boots, but I just wasn't feeling it.

I'd been in a state of heightened excitement all day, thinking about him, but now he was here, I felt nothing. Just a bit stupid really, in my stockings and balcony bra.

Jack got on to the bed and slowly worked his way up my body, with his usual finesse – very surprising, if you judged only by his appearance – and I went through the motions, thinking the rush would kick in at any moment, but then suddenly he stopped.

'It's not happening for you, is it, Posh?' he said, sitting up.

I shook my head. 'How can you tell?'

'I just can,' he said, shrugging.

I should have known. Jack had some kind of sexual sixth sense when it came to my body, of course he would have known.

He slapped me gently on the buttock and smiled at me, a bit sadly.

'Go home, Posh Totty,' he said. 'What are you doing here with me anyway? A beautiful girl like you. It's been great, Posh. I've been a very lucky man, but it's time for you to go and find yourself a nice bloke. You're too good for this, darling. So do yourself a favour, OK?

'I'll miss ya,' he said warmly, as he got off the bed and zipped his jeans back up. 'It's been great.'

He pulled on the rest of his clothes and then he leaned down to kiss me on the cheek. He stayed there for a moment looking into my eyes with a surprisingly caring look.

'And another thing,' he said. 'Don't go shagging no more men on trains, all right? You were lucky with me, Posh, I'm a nice bloke, but there's lots more out there who ain't. I'd hate anything bad to happen to you. Promise?'

I nodded. And after one last slow look at me, he left.

My disastrous assignation with Jack left me feeling so hollow, it was all I could do to get up the next day. Although he had been so nice about it – and I knew deep down inside that he was right – I still felt cheap, rejected and stupid. Between him and Jay, I found I was left with a very low opinion of myself.

In fact, I felt like a complete slut.

I decided I wasn't going to have sex with anyone for a very long time, because it seemed like whether you did it as part of a loving relationship – which is what I'd foolishly thought I'd had with Jay – or simply for the physical release, you still seemed to end up feeling used afterwards.

Ham was right. All men were bastards and I was much better off without any of them. Except him, of course.

I spent the whole weekend cocooning in my little house, with my mobile switched off. I'd picked up some food at Fresh & Wild on my way home from work on Friday and I didn't leave once, or speak to anyone, until Sunday afternoon when my phone rang.

It was Chloe.

'We know you're in there, Stella,' she said, laughing. 'Come out with your hands up.'

Then she turned a bit more serious.

'I need your help, Stella,' she said. 'Henry feels really bad about your friend, Jay. He thinks he's made the whole thing much worse for you by telling you about the family and how ghastly they are. So will you come up and have dinner with us all tonight and cheer him up? Please? It's been like living with a depressed Fozzie Bear for nearly two weeks now and I can't stand it. And I'd like to see you as well, of course,' she added.

I loved Chloe, and while I still really didn't feel like seeing anybody, I couldn't refuse her.

When I walked into the house, though, I wished I'd paid more attention to her exact phrasing. The place was empty, but when I saw the dining table had been laid for eleven people, I remembered that Chloe had specifically said the words: 'Have dinner with us *all* . . .'

She wasn't kidding about the all part. There were place cards round the table and I could see that all of Ham's kids were coming, plus his two favourite ex-stepsons, Archie and Alex. It was very unusual for so many of us to be together like that, because it was usually too complicated to arrange, not to mention utter mayhem.

'What's going on, Chloe?' I said, feeling uncomfortable, when she emerged from the pantry. I didn't like having that kind of thing sprung on me. 'This is like some kind of spooky surprise party.'

'Oh, don't worry,' said Chloe. 'It's not *This Is Your Life*, Henry's just having one of his sentimental moments. You know what he's like. He just needed to see all his babies.'

'But Alex and Archie aren't his babies,' I said crossly.

'No, but Alex is bringing the twins – they've been staying at his place this weekend, because Rose is in France at a gardening conference – and Henry just plain loves Archie. I think he wishes he could trade him in for Venezia, really.'

'I'd second that,' I said. 'But where are they all?'

She glanced automatically at her flow chart.

'Ham's gone to Kristy's to pick up those two, Nicola's dropping off the boys any minute, Daisy is upstairs having a late nap and Alex is bringing Tobes and Tabs. But I wanted to see you alone, Stella. I've got something I want to tell you myself.'

'I knew it,' I said. 'I knew something was going on. Spit it out.'

Chloe wiped her hands on her apron and leaned against the steel counter. I knew what she was going to say, before she even got it out, and couldn't stop myself grinning.

'I'm having another baby,' she said.

I rushed round the bench to give her a hug.

'I wanted to tell you first,' she said, wiping her eyes. 'We're going to tell the others tonight, but I wanted to tell you myself. You're such a good friend to me, Stella.'

I was amazed. I felt like I was the one who was always being looked after by her.

'Really?' I said.

She nodded.

'It's not always that great dealing with the ex-wives club, you know, and you just accepted me so warmly from day one. You never made me feel like an interloper.'

'Well, that was no problem,' I said. 'You're the nicest wife he's ever had and I want you to stick around. When's the baby due?'

She smiled broadly.

'Christmas Day.'

I roared, it was just the sort of thing Ham would adore.

*

Dinner was great fun. Ham had told all of my various siblings the good news in little batches and everyone was very happy about it. Daisy was ecstatic.

'I'm going to have a baby! I'm going to have a baby!' she was telling anyone who would listen, thrilled that she was no longer going to be the youngest. I pulled her on to my knee and gave her a big cuddle.

'I'm a big girl now, Stella,' she said very seriously, nodding her head that way she did.

'You're a very big girl,' I said, mentally preparing myself to spend a lot of time with her when the new baby eventually came along, and she wouldn't be feeling quite so thrilled about it. I'd seen a lot of that over the years with my father's growing family.

There was a fair amount of sibling rivalry going on round the table that night, although things were more equable than they might have been because, to my great delight, Venezia hadn't joined us after all. She'd reacted very badly to the news of the baby and had refused to come. Suited me.

'What's her problem now?' I asked Archie, who was sitting next to me, in a placement which had been drawn up by Ham, as usual.

He was surprisingly keen on table plans – it was all part of his interest in the emotional manipulation of space and proximity. He'd even had dinner parties where he had deliberately done the most ill-advised plan he could come up with, to see how much it really did affect the dynamic. Monstrously, by all accounts.

But I was delighted to be next to Archie. Despite all his adolescent angst, there was something so strangely sensible about him.

'What?' he was asking me incredulously. 'You're asking me why Vomezia' – it was his new name for her – 'doesn't want another half-sibling?'

'Yes, that's what I'm asking. I'm delighted, aren't you?'

'Stoked, and it won't even be related to me.' He laughed his painful Beavis and Butt-head snigger. 'But Chloe's totally great and any kid of hers will be way cool. I love Daisy, so yeah, great, but Vomezia isn't happy because it's just one more little chip away from her inheritance.'

'Are you serious?' I said.

'Yeah,' said Archie, nodding so vigorously I was almost blinded by the spikes of his new vertical hairstyle. 'I bet she's got her calculator out, right now, working out how much her share has just decreased by.'

'I'm speechless,' I said. 'Doesn't she know about Ham's opinions on inherited wealth? He's not leaving any of us anything – he's always telling us that – doesn't she get it?'

'Have you ever met my mother?' said Archie, and I had to laugh.

A more disturbing feature of Ham's table plan was that he had put Alex on my other side. Not exactly subtle, I thought, but I was quite glad to get the first post-Jay meeting with him out of the way really. It had to happen sooner or later and I just wanted to get our relationship – such as it was – back on to its old bland footing.

But, for once, Alex seemed reluctant to let that happen.

'So,' he said, looking at me intently, the moment I turned to him, so I couldn't just look away again. 'Are you still seeing Jay Fisher?'

I pulled a face.

'You saw *Hot Stuff!* magazine then?' I said.

He looked completely blank.

'What's that?' he said, as though I had changed the subject.

'You didn't see that thing in a magazine about me and Jay?'

'No,' he said, looking very surprised. 'I didn't realize it was that serious. Are you "dating" him, as Americans say?'

'No, I'm not,' I said, quickly. 'I met him at a press thing and I think he just wanted to see the house really, so that's why he came down that time. He's a huge fan of Ham's work. You know, with the museum and everything.'

Alex was looking at me steadily. I was babbling, I didn't care.

'But if you didn't see that thing in *Hot Stuff!*,' I continued. 'How did you know who he was? I didn't think I'd introduced him by his full name.'

Alex looked incredulous.

'You didn't need to introduce him. I knew who he was the minute I saw him.'

'Oh,' I said, hoping to end the conversation right there. I certainly wasn't going to tell Alex that I hadn't had a clue all along.

'The bank I work for handles quite a lot of investments for the family,' Alex was saying, with a funny look in his eye. 'I've met his father quite a few times – he's the main trustee. I had to go over to New York to see him just a couple of months ago in fact.'

'Ham says he's a nightmare,' I said. No point in pretending.

Alex just smiled at me gently, in an I'm-saying-nothing-which-says-a-lot kind of way. He was amazingly discreet, I thought. No wonder he was doing so well in his job.

'So,' I said brightly, deciding to take a leaf out of his book. A book which could be entitled *Hiding Your True Feelings The Good Old Empire Way*. 'What have you been up to? Going anywhere nice this summer?'

Alex laughed heartily; he knew exactly what I was doing, but like the true Brit he was, he played along and we had a very pleasant conversation comparing the attractions of Corsica, Tuscany and Sardinia for our prospective holidays.

Before we were forced to find another bland subject to discuss, Ham tapped his wine glass with a spoon.

'OK, tribe,' he said, standing up. 'I want to talk to you all. Now, this is a very special occasion as you know, celebrating the wonderful news that our darling Chloe is to have another child in December, a Christmas baby for us all. So I wish to make a toast to my beautiful wife,' he said, gazing at her and raising his glass. 'I give you – Chloe.'

We all drank to her, followed by toasts to 'the baby' and 'Henry', and then Ham said he wanted to propose the most important toast of all, which was to: 'Family.'

We all did what we were supposed to do and I thought that would be the end of it, but Ham was clearly loving it and had no intention of leaving it there.

'Now,' he was saying. 'I want to use this marvellous moment, when I have all my ducklings gathered together – apart from Venezia, of course, the silly girl. It happens all too rarely, so I am going to grab the opportunity to embarrass you all horribly.'

My heart was beginning to sink. I loved my family, I adored Ham, but I really couldn't stand this touchy-feely stuff. The years he had spent studying in California still had a lot to answer for, in my opinion.

But there was no getting out of it now, I could see. He had that gleam in his eye. I was beginning to sink down in my seat, praying for it to be over quickly, when I felt something gently prod my ribcage. It was Alex, nudging me. I turned to look at him and he very discreetly crossed his eyes. I felt giggles rise in my chest.

Ham was oblivious and had embarked on his mission, which was to tell each child, one by one, why he loved us.

'Daisy, you are my most recently hatched egg,' he was saying. 'But not for long. You are about to grow up into a big sister, my adorable little chick, but you know how your daddy cherishes you, the product of my love for your beautiful mother, Chloe . . .'

Oh no, I thought, this was going to get really cheesy. The full Paxton & Whitfield. Alex nudged me again, harder.

It went on in the same vein, with Ham getting more and more like a talking Hallmark card. It really was amazing how someone so brilliant and sophisticated could be quite so syrupy.

Archie clearly felt the same way as me and Alex, and it was my turn to nudge Alex, as I noticed my favourite toxic teen was sliding very slowly down his chair, like a piece of spaghetti, until he was actually on the floor under the table.

Alex and I started to shake with barely controllable laughter, as Archie then very slowly started to inch his way across the floor, away from the table, moving on his elbows like a commando.

Ham – by then in full flow about Freddie, so he was clearly

working up through his children by age – was completely oblivious.

Trying to hide the tears of laughter that were threatening to pour down my cheeks, I made the mistake of turning my head to the side and caught Alex's eye. That was it. With a great combined guffaw, we simultaneously leapt up from the table and literally fell through the open glass door into the garden.

'Oh, for GOD's sake,' I heard Ham saying, as we made our exit. But it was too late, we couldn't go back.

The relief of being able to let the tension out was so great that we were both rolling around on the lawn, kicking our legs in the air.

'Oh, my God,' Alex was saying. 'The full cheese counter, with extra relish. Gag.'

'Ham and cheese on rye, or what?' I agreed.

We finally recovered ourselves a little and sat up on the lawn, but as soon as we looked at each other, we were off again.

'Oh, my little duckling,' Alex was saying. 'Your tiny egg so recently cracked into the great omelette pan of life . . .'

I was laughing so much, my stomach was starting to hurt. Then I looked back through the wall of glass – a feature of all Ham's houses – and saw that Archie was now halfway down the hall, away from the kitchen, still moving like a centipede, on his stomach.

That set us off all over again, until I was just lying there panting. That was when I noticed how wet the grass was. I turned my head to look at Alex, who was rubbing his face with his hands and groaning. He turned suddenly and looked at me.

'My arse is getting soaked out here,' he said.

'So's mine,' I said, jumping up and looking behind me to see a big wet patch on my skirt.

'Oh no,' I said, looking back into the house. 'He's still only on Marcus. It's going to take ages.'

I made a split-second decision.

'We can't go back in there,' I said. 'Do you want to come and have a drink at my place until it's all over?'

'That would be great,' said Alex, looking pleased and rather surprised.

I almost regretted my invitation as soon as I had made it, but Alex was family really, and I did occasionally have Chloe in for coffee and Daisy was a regular visitor, so it wasn't like a real intrusion. But apart from Ham, he was the only man who had ever been in my place.

Alex looked very big in my tiny little sitting room and he smiled sweetly as he took it all in.

'Well, Stella,' he said. 'I had no idea you were such a girly girl at heart.'

I looked at it afresh through his eyes. The sofa he was sitting on was covered in sugar-pink velvet, with a pompom trim. I was mixing drinks at my mirrored console table, by the dim glow of the twenty strings of fairy lights I had festooned around the various gold mirrors and floral paintings on the walls.

I giggled a little as I handed him his vodka and tonic, and sat down in one of my French bergère chairs, which were upholstered in leopard-print fabric.

'It's my secret den,' I said. 'I don't have to make concessions to anyone else's tastes or needs in here.'

I stood up again suddenly.

'My bum really is wet,' I said. 'I think I need to change. Do you want to borrow something?'

He felt the back of his jeans and nodded.

'Yes, but not a frilly negligee, please.'

I smiled to myself as I opened my wardrobe. Frilly negligees were something I had plenty of and when I was home alone, I flitted around my little house got up like Eva Gabor in *Green Acres*.

I was momentarily tempted to put one of them on – perhaps the sheer pink organza with the marabou trim and matching mules? – just to make him laugh, but stopped myself.

Just at that moment I was feeling on a really good even keel with Alex for the first time since that weird weekend at Willow Barn. Being united in hilarity about Ham's hideous sentimentality – something we had both hated when we were young – had got us back on to a comfortable footing again and I was suddenly aware how easy it would be to unbalance it.

I peeled off my wet skirt and put on a nice neutral pair of jeans, and then found a sarong for him to wear.

I took it down to him and then went through to the kitchen to get some ice, returning a heartbeat too soon, just as he was about to wind the sarong around his hips.

He had his back to me and I was treated to a view of just about the finest pair of bare male buttocks I had ever seen. Alex still rowed, I remembered. It showed.

I nearly dropped the small silver bowl I was carrying, but just managed to hold on to it and dodge back into the kitchen, before he realized I had seen him.

I had to take a few deep breaths to recover before I could

go back in, but not only because of the physical jolt of coming face to face with such a magnificent display of man flesh. The thing that had made me nearly drop the bowl, was that it could have been Jay's rear quarters I'd been looking at.

The two of them didn't look anything alike from the front. Their faces were completely different – with Jay more movie-star handsome, it had to be said – although Alex was still a good-looking guy, in a particular pink-cheeked English way.

Jay's hair was darker, but physically, I realized, they were startlingly similar. The same height, the same build, the same broad shoulders – and the same fabulous bottom. The only difference was that Jay had really sexy tan lines on his – his buttocks were stark white against his tan, where his trunks had been.

I almost wished I could ask Alex to take his sarong off and turn round, so I could see if he also had those wonderful lines running down from his abs to his groin, like Jay had. I thought he probably did.

I made a bit of noise, clunking around in the freezer as though I was doing something useful, until I felt fully composed again. I was sure it was the similarity to Jay which had unsettled me so much, but I couldn't escape facing the truth that anything vaguely sexual in connection with Alex made me feel deeply uneasy.

He was only my stepbrother – and my ex-stepbrother, at that – but he was definitely part of my family, not my love life. I wasn't going to make the same embarrassing mistake my adolescent self had made and mix them up again.

I needn't have worried. Blissfully unaware of the ringside

view I'd just had of his butt – and of the extensive collection of saucy seduction wear I had upstairs – when I finally went back into the sitting room, Alex was still happily operating in what I thought of as our 'fond cousin' mode, which enabled me to slip back into it too.

'Hey, Stella,' he said. 'Do you remember the time Henry made us play that loathsome game where we all had to write the things we loved about our siblings on pieces of paper and then he read them all out and we had to guess who had written what about whom?'

I groaned.

'Oh yeah,' I said, remembering all too well. 'And if someone guessed yours right you had to hug the person you had written about? It was terrible.'

What I remembered was that I'd written something horrifically embarrassing about Alex and I was now immeasurably grateful to Ham for not reading it out – although at the time I had been furious with him, because I had been gagging for an excuse to hug my stepbrother.

Happily oblivious to that, Alex was now laughing about something else and shaking his head.

'I wrote that I admired Rowan because he was a very skilled butcher,' he said, chuckling away. 'Ham read it out and was really pleased – he thought it was something to do with Boy Scout barbecues, or something, and had no idea butchery was our slang for wanking. You know – beating the meat?'

I shook my head at him.

'You boys,' I said.

As Ham was always telling me, the sexed-up savage was never far below the surface with men, however civilized they appeared to be on the surface. Alex was clearly no exception.

By the time we re-emerged back in Ham's kitchen about an hour later – after carefully checking from the garden that his one-man love-in was definitely over – it seemed he had already forgiven me and Alex for our sudden exit.

'Sorry we missed it, Ham,' I said, pecking him on the cheek. 'We just weren't in a Californian sort of mood.'

'That's all right, you cheeky little buggers, I loved you up anyway – both of you – in absentia.'

And as he beamed at us and invited us into the library for a cognac, while the younger children watched a DVD in the living area, I reckoned his irritation at our rudeness was probably cancelled out by his delight in seeing us bonding.

Whatever Ham was up to with us – and nothing to do with human relationships was accidental if he had anything to do with it – was clearly going to plan. I was happy to let him have his little fantasy.

10

The next week, satisfied that the paparazzi were no longer on my tail, I felt able to start accepting invitations again. It was about time. I needed to get out there working my contacts and sniffing out the big stories before the competition did.

But while I was still shuffling through the folder of invites on my desk, I got another one I certainly wasn't expecting when Doughnut's secretary, Sheila, sent me an email asking me to call her.

'Mr McDonagh is having lunch in the boardroom today,' she said. 'And he would like you to join him.'

I was thrilled. Lunch in the boardroom was a big deal at the *Journal* – I'd only been twice in my five years on the paper. It was such a splendid room. They had moved the original one over from the old Fleet Street building, panel by panel, so that a corner of this soaring office block was forever the 1920s. It was an art deco gem on a par with the Savoy, with the original furniture, sculptures and paintings, and I loved going up there.

I was just about to hang up on Sheila, when I remembered to ask her what this lunch was in aid of.

'I'm not sure,' she said. 'But I think it's something to do with features.'

I presumed that meant the ghastly Jeanette Foster would be there, which slightly dampened my enthusiasm. Jeanette

166

was the editor of the daily 'Journal Plus' features section, where my weekly pages appeared, and she clearly thought she was my 'boss', although that was an honour I reserved mentally for Doughnut and no other.

After all, I worked for the news pages almost as much as I did for features – and for the Saturday 'News Review' section and the colour magazine. I even wrote the odd book review, if a biography of Christian Dior came out, or something like that. Once, I had even reviewed a car.

But Jeanette – or the Lovely Jeanette, as Peter Wallington sarcastically called her – relished her little power trips and would frequently pull stunts like making me rewrite a perfectly good feature, just because she liked to make me suffer.

Over the year or so she had been features editor, I'd got her measure, though. I'd just rewrite the first two paragraphs and she'd think I'd done the whole thing again, because she'd never actually read it to the end in the first place.

'That's so much better, Stella,' she'd say in her smug voice, loudly, so the whole office could hear. 'I think it's a much better read now you've re-nosed it as I suggested.'

'I'll re-nose her, if she carries on picking on you,' Peter had muttered as she'd minced off in her ultra-flat shoes.

Peter hated her. He could be really bitchy when he didn't like someone, and it amused me intensely.

'I don't mind the fact that she is so brazenly talentless,' he had said to me on more than one occasion. 'Or even that she is lazy and ordinary and has never had an original thought in her tiny little suburban life, although she is always fast to claim those of others as her own. I don't even particularly mind that the only reason she has her job here is because her husband is a great friend of our managing editor, Mr Ryan. No, what I really can't tolerate about the Lovely Jeanette is the way she looks. I don't like her teeth.'

I had roared with laughter. She did have funny teeth. They were strangely long and narrow.

I loathed the way she looked too, but for different reasons. She wasn't unattractive really, she just offended my personal sense of aesthetics. She had brutally straight, cropped hair – without the beautiful bone structure to justify it – dyed a hard mahogany red, and she favoured 'art jewellery' of a particularly clunky kind, which she thought very sophisticated. She always referred to it as 'pieces'.

'Oh, what a marvellous necklace,' Peter would say, completely disingenuously, when she'd turn up sporting the latest bit of anodized scrap metal some charlatan had flogged her.

'Oh, thank you, Peter,' she'd say, through her frightening ventriloquist's dummy teeth. 'I do think it's rather a special piece. I got it at the weekend from a favourite little gallery of mine in Brussels.'

She was always dropping Brussels into the conversation – to the point where the subs called her Sprouts. Her husband was a Liberal Democrat MEP and she loved swanning over there on taxpayers' money.

Brussels was another reason Peter hated her so much. He was so anti the European Union, he refused even to go to France on holiday any more, which caused great distress to his wife, Renee, as they had a beautiful house in the Luberon.

If I wanted to wind Peter up I would put a five-euro note on his desk while he was in the loo. He'd hop from foot to foot like Rumpelstiltskin when he came back and saw it – usually tearing it to shreds in his rage.

We did have some funny times in that office.

I was just spraying myself with my favourite Frédéric Malle fragrance, Musc Ravageur, before heading up to the thirty-fifth floor for the lunch, when Jeanette walked past towards the lift.

She was wearing a particularly nasty pair of oversized earrings and her mouth was smeared with a brutal slash of her signature dark red lipstick. She was definitely going to Doughnut's lunch. I recognized her warpaint mode.

'There goes liver lips,' muttered Peter, then he glanced over at me. 'Are you ready for the lunch too, my fragrant one?'

I'd had no idea he was going too and must have looked surprised, which clearly delighted him as he stood up, slipped on his suit jacket and put out his arm for me to take.

'The thirty-fifth floor, madame?'

He never missed a bloody trick that one. But I was even more surprised when I walked into the boardroom and saw Ned already installed there.

He was standing chatting to the managing editor, Martin Ryan, and a man and woman I didn't recognize, which meant they probably worked on the advertising side of things. They all turned round when we came in and I caught Ned's eye. He raised an expressive eyebrow at me.

I went over to him.

'Bet you're surprised to see me,' he said, smiling cheekily.

'I sure am,' I said. 'But I'm pretty amazed to be here myself. It's only my third time up here. Have you any idea what it's all about? Those two are from advertising, aren't they? Doughnut doesn't normally have much to do with them.'

'I've been doing some investigative reporting while we waited for you,' said Ned, his eyes twinkling. 'I think they're starting some kind of new section and from what I can gather, it might be good for you and me.'

Before he could tell me anything else, Doughnut arrived with Jeanette, which was odd because I'd seen her on her way up before Peter and I had even left our desks. She'd probably lurked near the lift so she could accidentally-on-purpose emerge and get into it with him, I realized.

And you had to hand it to her – it was a constant campaign of those kinds of sneaky manoeuvres that had got her where she was on the paper. From the self-satisfied look on her face as she swept in through the double doors with him, you'd have thought Doughnut had invited her to enter on his arm.

But things didn't go quite so well for Jeanette for the rest of the lunch. She was clearly rattled when she saw that I had been seated on one side of Doughnut, with the woman from advertising on his other. Jeanette was between Ned and Martin.

'Right,' said our esteemed editor-in-chief, the moment we had all sat down. He never was one for small talk. 'I bet you're all wondering why you're here. Well, it's simple – money. But first of all, let me introduce you to Tony and Gillian. Tony is our advertising sales chief and Gillian is new to his team. She's come over to us from Condé Nast, so that we can steal as much of their advertising as possible. That's right, isn't it, Tony?'

Tony nodded, smiling.

'Now, Tony and Gillian, I would like to introduce you to the people who are going to help you do that. Martin, my managing editor, you already know. Peter Wallington, I hardly need to tell you, is the senior journalist on the paper and the best newspaperman in the business. He was my mentor when I joined the *Journal* as a young reporter, many years ago.'

Well, I hadn't known that. That explained a lot.

'Stella Fain there,' he gestured at me, 'is one of my best writers – a star on the paper and certainly the leading authority in British journalism on the luxury world. Ned Morrissey is new to the paper, a very bright talent, with a fresh voice and a particularly sharp eye for the youth market.'

For a moment it seemed he wasn't going to introduce Jeanette. She'd already looked pained by his glowing description of me, and now she looked as though she were being strangled.

'Oh,' he said, as an afterthought. 'And that's Jeanette Foster, features editor.'

There was a pause while the boardroom butler served the starter and then Doughnut resumed.

'Right. Tony and I have been talking and we have come to the conclusion that there is a large segment of the advertising market which the *Journal* is missing out on. Now you in editorial will know that I am not particularly interested in advertising, except in so far as it funds my journalists, in which case I am very interested in it.

'And as the board are once more trying to make me cut costs – and have even made such preposterous suggestions as closing our Jerusalem bureau – it is in my interests to help boost the advertising revenue. With this in mind Tony, Gillian and I have been discussing how we can work together to do that. Now over to you two.'

Tony and Gillian then went into long explanations of how the paper was failing to maximize the potential advertiser appeal of its well-heeled readers because it didn't have an editorial 'platform' suitable for ads from companies such as Chanel, Hermès and Louis Vuitton.

'The only part of the newspaper family that is getting that spend at the moment is the Saturday magazine,' said Gillian. 'Which obviously has a separate budget structure from the main paper . . .'

'Meaning it won't fund my Jerusalem office,' interjected Doughnut, before indicating that she might continue.

'But we don't see why we wouldn't be able to persuade the prestige brands to increase their overall spend with us and the more niche brands to start advertising here,' she said, 'channelling the new revenue directly to the paper, by providing a new editorial platform in the broadsheet week – which will also enhance the reader experience.'

The jargon was doing my head in – and Ned crossed his eyes at me when I looked over at him – but I thought I had grasped the main gist of it. They were going to start some kind of new features section in the paper, expressly to attract advertising from the kind of companies I wrote about. Sounded OK.

Jeanette had clearly got this message too and I could see her eyes flicking backwards and forwards between Gillian – who was still talking – and Doughnut, as she tried to suss out what was in it for her. But I had an urgent question of my own.

'That sounds great,' I said, when Gillian had finished her spiel. 'Obviously I am delighted to hear there will be more space for coverage of the luxury market in the paper. But what concerns me is that if this new section is being set up expressly to attract advertising from the brands I write about, where does that leave me with regard to my editorial independence? In short – if they do something rubbish, can I still say so?'

I asked, because I was sincerely concerned about the answer. I knew the girls on *Pratler* couldn't say anything even vaguely negative, or even cheeky, about any of the magazine's advertising clients and I seriously did not wish to be in that position myself. Then I really wouldn't be able to stomach being the fluff correspondent.

I was a bit worried it wouldn't be a popular topic to bring up, with advertising executives in the room, but seeing the beam that lit up Doughnut's face and the fond smile on Peter's, I knew I was OK.

'That's absolutely right, Stella,' said Doughnut. 'You have hit the nail on the head. We will carry on telling the truth, however uncomfortable, in the great *Journal* tradition – even as we take their advertising money. And that is exactly what will give the section its credibility and make it the one that they simply must all have an advertising presence in.'

'That's fantastic,' I said.

'And that's why we want you to edit it,' said Doughnut, smiling broadly at me.

Jeanette dropped her fork. That was not what she'd been expecting.

'Yes,' continued Doughnut, oblivious to her discomfort. 'We are going to drop the features section on Fridays and turn it over to you and Ned. Obviously, the crossword, telly et cetera will still be in the back of it, but the rest of it will be called "The Good Life".

'We want to get it up and running in a month, so I'm taking you two off features from now on and, as editor, you'll have your own office, Stella, and Ned will work alongside you, concentrating on the male side of the subject matter. Peter will work with you to develop the section, and I would like to see a dummy for it by the end of next week, OK?'

And with that, the lunch was over – and it would be hard to say which of us left it more surprised, me, or Jeanette.

I was thrilled with my promotion, but the only thing that made me a bit sad about it, was the thought of packing up my desk to move into my own office. I wouldn't be sitting next to Peter any more.

'I'll miss you,' I said, as we got back to our little corner after the lunch. 'I'll even miss your thundering typewriter. I've got used to being deafened while I try to write.'

'We're going to be working together very closely on this section,' he said. 'You'll probably get sick of me. Anyway, are you pleased with your new role?'

'I'm totally thrilled,' I said.

'Did you see the look on Jeanette's face?' he added, wearing his most wicked expression. He looked like a mischievous old pixie.

I just giggled. Peter started to chuckle too.

'Mind you,' he said, leaning close to me and speaking quietly. 'That's nothing compared to when she finds out you're moving into her office.'

He threw his head back and roared with laughter.

'No!' I said. 'I don't want to, it'll have bad feng shui. And she might leave some earrings behind.'

'No, don't worry, I'm just kidding. It would probably smell of feet as well. But I do think we'll have to make sure you get a bigger one than hers, with a better view. Actually, Stella, I think we should go out tonight and celebrate this new era, don't you? Let's see if Ned can come too.'

So I flicked through my invitation file and found a clutch of cocktail parties for us to hit and the three of us, that unlikely triumvirate, went out on the town in a major way.

It was a truly great night. I decided that if Ned and I were going to work together he might as well have total immersion in the luxury world and we started out at a very intimate cocktail party for elite press and best customers, in the Anya Hindmarch boutique in Pont Street, looking at the new range of summer bags, which had just gone in store.

Peter fitted in absolutely anywhere, but Ned looked rather uncomfortable surrounded by glossy young women in skimpy tops and very high heels, all sporting handbags which had cost three times as much as his work suit. After we'd been there ten minutes, he was still standing in a corner, holding his glass of champagne like it was a pint of lager.

'Look, Ned,' I said, walking over to him and holding my glass up in front of his face. 'You hold it by the stem.'

He looked puzzled.

'Champagne flutes,' I continued. 'You hold them by the stem, so the champagne doesn't get warm, which makes it go flat.'

I saw him glance around the room and take in the fact that everyone – including Peter – was holding their glass by its stem. He adjusted his and then, looking me right in the eye, he downed it in one go.

'Is that right, Stella?' he said, wiping his mouth on the back of his hand. 'Any more of this piss on the go, do you think?'

I grinned at him. I knew we were going to have a really good time working together.

The next event was in the Cartier boutique on Bond Street, hosted by my friend Becca, the in-house PR, who always threw a great party. I knew she wouldn't mind me turning up with a couple of extra guests and she whooped with delight when she saw us.

'Stella, my darling,' she said in her throaty theatrical voice. 'Two spare men, how clever you are. We never have enough men at these things.'

She stopped a passing waiter, so we could get some drinks and Ned picked up a flute of champagne by its stem and raised it to me. He was a quick study, I thought.

Leaving the boys to get to know Becca better – she was someone Ned would need in his new role as cool fluff correspondent, as we had already dubbed him – I did a quick once-around-the-room, collecting compliments on my recent articles, and one or two catty comments about Jay Fisher.

I was ready for them, though, and dismissed it all with a gale of laughter about what a hoot it was for a hack like me to be the victim of a trash mag beat-up.

The person I was really looking for, though, was Amy Ticehurst. It was weeks since the Jericho trip and I hadn't heard a word from her. Of course, I hadn't been out much, which was how I normally kept in touch with Amy – it was that kind of a spontaneous friendship, we never arranged to meet, we just did, on the party circuit.

But I had thought she might ring, or send me a sympathetic email, after the piece came out in *Hot Stuff!* I'd even tried her mobile once, but the message bank had been full.

It was also very surprising for her to miss a Cartier party – she knew they always gave great door gifts. In the end I baled up Becca and asked her if she knew where Amy was.

'Amy? She's on safari. Kenya. She's been gone for ages, but she's due back any day now. It was all very last minute, I think. A really good freebie came up and she added on, you know how she does . . . Going to do a big piece for the mag.'

That made sense. Amy loved Africa. She'd gone on her first safari as a press trip ten years before and she'd been on a permanent mission to get back there, as often as possible – preferably for nothing – ever since.

'I had a freebie in Aaaaafrica . . .' was one of our ongoing jokes.

As we left Cartier, Ned was amazed to be given a pair of gold cufflinks as a going-home present. I told him to get used to it.

'Your life will now be a shower of gifts,' I said. 'You'll never need to buy anyone a birthday present ever again. You can just pass on some useless bit of tat that has been given to you.'

'Excellent,' said Ned.

'If you choose to accept them,' said Peter, who had politely declined his.

Our next stop was a quick whirl through a private view in a Cork Street gallery, which was dull, and then there was only one place to go. It was time to introduce Ned to The Groucho Club.

Peter was a founder member. He'd been on the original membership committee when it opened in 1985, and he had very kindly sponsored my application when I was a young reporter at the *Journal*.

'I've heard a lot about this place,' said Ned, as we signed him in. 'Is it as great as they all say?'

'No,' said Peter. 'It's not at all what it was, but it's still the best there is.'

I agreed with him. I went to all the private clubs from Soho House to Annabel's in the course of my work and play, but The Groucho was still the one I felt most at home in. It seemed to have the same kind of non-judgemental, mad mix of people as a newspaper office. If you belonged, you belonged and that was it.

We had a great time. Peter got straight into the champagne, which I knew he would happily put through on expenses, and between him and me, we knew so many people in there it became quite a party.

We eventually rolled out at one in the morning, having ordered cabs to three different destinations. Notting Hill for me; Regents Park for Peter; and Whitechapel for Ned.

We really were a rum crew.

The next morning I was back at my desk consuming a bacon sandwich in an attempt to soak up a horrendous hangover, when my mobile rang. It was Amy.

'Darling,' she said, in a concerned tone. 'Whatever have you done to Jay Fisher?'

'What?' I squeaked.

'He's an absolute mess. I saw him in Mombasa last week and he was asking me all about you, what kind of girl you are and all that. He was really agitated. Did you do something terrible to him?'

'No, I did not,' I said, astonished and confused in equal measure. 'Where are you, Amy? Are you still on safari, or are you back in London?'

'I'm in town, darling, got back last night. I would have rung you about this sooner, but my phone didn't work properly out there. Are you all right?'

I decided just to be honest.

'No,' I said. 'Actually, I'm really confused about, er, the person you were talking about . . .' I was suddenly aware of ears flapping all around me – even having my own office was no guarantee of privacy in that place. For all I knew Rita had planted a listening device in my phone.

'Look, Amy,' I said. 'Could we have lunch? I can't really talk about this in the office.'

'Love to, sweetie. It's always nice to go out to lunch the first day back at work, isn't it? Get back in the swing of things gently. I'll see you in The Wolseley at one? OK?'

I got there first and ordered a Bloody Mary, to try and make myself feel less nauseous, although I wasn't sure whether the sick feeling in my stomach was the hangover, or the anticipation of talking about Jay with someone who had recently seen him.

Amy arrived with a magnificent tan, her arms jangling with Masai bracelets up to her elbows, with a huge necklace and a beaded rawhide shawl finishing the effect.

'Hello, Mrs Blixen,' I said.

'Oh, if only . . .' she said, taking a deep drink from the glass of champagne which had been delivered without her even having to ask for it. 'I had such a marvellous time. But what about you? What on earth has been going on?'

So I told her – the whole unexpurgated story, including the not insignificant detail that I hadn't twigged who Jay was until after he appeared to have dumped me. Amy laughed so much at that, her champagne came down her nose.

'Oh, you little twit,' she said. 'How could you be so stupid? Don't you read *Pratler*?'

'I mainly look at the pictures,' I admitted.

'I did wonder, when you asked him what he did for a living,' said Amy, still snorting with laughter. 'But I thought you would have worked it out by the time we were cruising around in a stretch limo being fawned over at every private club on the Riviera. My God, Stella, even that drag queen door-bitch at Wonderland knew who he was. Didn't that seem a little odd?'

I shrugged.

'Yes, but I thought she must have known him from New York,' I said feebly.

'And you didn't figure out Spotter's role?'

I looked blank.

'Bodyguard, you moron.'

Now it was my turn to choke.

'I mean, they're mates, too, and everything,' said Amy. 'But Spotter's ex-SAS and Jay takes him along whenever he thinks he needs a little extra protection. He doesn't need him in London, but the Riviera is a famous hunting ground for kidnappers, as you know.'

I just stared at her. I didn't know any such thing. It was

a completely alien notion to me. Then I remembered our long ride back to the hotel on a stolen moped.

'*Roman Holiday*,' I said out loud.

Amy looked at me strangely.

'What?'

'Oh, nothing,' I said, but I was realizing just what a carefree interlude that must have been for someone who felt he needed the protection of an ex-SAS giant, just to go to a nightclub. The only difference was that Jay was in the pampered princess role, and I was the dumb journalist.

Then I remembered what Amy had said about Jay being agitated over me. That was the bit I really wanted to know about.

'You said Jay was upset with me, when you saw him – and come to think of it, what was he doing in Mombasa anyway? He was in Buenos Aires the last time I heard of him.'

'I don't know,' said Amy, shrugging. 'He was probably seeing friends, or going to a party, something like that.'

I sat and took that in. He'd been at the Cap Mimosa, just for the hell of it, then a brief spell in London, before heading off to Buenos Aires for a party, and then on to Mombasa, possibly just for drinks. That was how he lived. Crazy. No wonder he didn't understand me rushing off to work all the time.

But I still wanted to know what he was so upset with me about.

'Go on,' I said. 'I need to know exactly what he said about me . . .'

'Well, I think he rather likes you actually, but he was very upset about something that had come out in a magazine. Presumably that thing in *Hot Stuff!* you just told me about. Yes?'

I shrugged.

'Hmmm,' she said, looking thoughtful. 'Now, you say reading that was when you discovered who Jay really was, yes?'

I nodded.

'Well, that's interesting, darling, because Jay is under the impression that you sold them the story . . .'

'What?' I was so incredulous, I nearly fell off my seat. 'How could he possibly think that? I'd never do something like that – and how could I, when I didn't even know who he was?'

'Quite, and I believe you, darling, I know you would never do something like that – plus I fully believe you are dim enough really not to have known who he was. And that's a good point actually, do you think Jay realized you had no idea who he was, if you see what I mean?'

I thought for a moment.

'Definitely. I'm sure he knew I hadn't twigged who he was . . . And I've wondered ever since if that's why he appeared to like me, because it must have been such a novelty.'

'That's what he kept saying, that he'd thought you were "untainted" and then it seemed you'd done this terrible thing, but he still couldn't believe that you'd been stringing him along the whole time.

'"She seemed so real," that's what he kept saying, and that was what he was trying to find out from me – whether you were as nice as he had thought you were. I said you were, of course, but he was still very shaken by the magazine thing.'

'But who told him that I'd sold them the story?' I asked, suddenly. 'I don't get that either, and it didn't even come out until after he'd already dumped me.'

'Someone from the magazine got hold of him in advance to try and get a quote. Lord knows how they get the numbers, but they do. That's why people like Jay are always changing their mobiles – the number you would have is out of date, by the way. Anyway, he "no commented", of course, but then he asked them how they'd got the story and they said it was direct from you.'

'So someone from *Hot Stuff!* told him I had sold them the story?' I asked her, wanting to be sure I had it straight.

Amy nodded.

It was so weird, my head was spinning, but even in shock I realized there was one consolation I could cling to: I had a direct conduit to *Hot Stuff!* through Ned, so with his help I might be able to find out exactly what – and who – was behind all this nonsense.

My first impulse when I got back to the *Journal* after lunch was to run to Ned and get him to find out immediately from his girlfriend who had really sold the story to *Hot Stuff!*, but I stopped myself.

I knew I needed to keep a cool head and to figure out my tactics carefully, and while I liked Ned enormously, I still didn't know him well enough to fill him in on the whole thing. So I decided to bide my time, before I pursued it any further.

I'd moved into my new office the day before – it was bigger than Jeanette's, as Peter had promised, with great views west along the Thames – and I emailed Ned to come in so we could do some brainstorming for the section.

It was really fun. We were going through a huge pile of international magazines which had just come in. We'd tear out anything we felt had the right feel for the section, then when we both had a large pile we'd compare notes and pin the best ones up on the blank wall opposite my desk. It was starting to look very enticing, that wall.

We'd been in there for about an hour, reading, ripping and pinning, and the phone on my desk had rung a few times. As usual, I didn't answer it, but then it began to ring more and more often until another call would come in, right after the last one ended.

Then it got even stranger. It would ring three times, stop,

then ring twice and stop, then once and stop, and then the whole cycle would start over with the same rhythm.

'I think you better get that,' said Ned, after it had happened three times. 'Someone really wants to speak to you.'

The next time it rang, I picked it up.

'Stella Fain,' I said in my most professional voice.

'It's Jay,' said the person on the end of the phone.

I glanced at Ned, who was already standing up.

'I'll see you later,' he mouthed, reading the situation with his usual instinct.

'Hello,' I almost whispered, as I kicked the door shut with my foot.

'You really don't pick up that phone, do you?' said Jay.

'Er, no,' I said. 'Why didn't you call my mobile?'

'I deleted the number,' he said, sighing. 'I was so angry with you, Stella, and I was wrong. Luckily, the switchboard number is in the phone book like you told me.'

'You were misinformed, Jay,' I said, getting back to the point. 'And I can't believe you thought I'd do something like that.'

'I'm sorry, Stella. I'm really really sorry. It's just I have been done over so many times by people, it can be hard to trust anyone. I should at least have called you and asked you straight up if it was true, but I was just so sad and disappointed, I wasn't thinking straight.'

'I couldn't have done it anyway, Jay, even if I'd wanted to. I had no idea who you were until I read that stupid article.'

He laughed, gently.

'I know, baby,' he said. 'I know that . . . and if only it could have stayed that way. I was working up to explaining it all to you, I knew I had to, but I was enjoying being a blank page so much, I just never got round to it. And then you had to find out like that. What a dumb mess.'

'I was followed by the paparazzi, Jay,' I said, feeling completely at ease with him again, as I always had. 'It was awful. They were sitting outside my house, waiting for me.'

'Sorry again, but welcome to my world. I live with that shit twenty-four/seven, Stella, and if you would like to see me again – and I really hope you will – you'll have to live with it too.'

I just sat and took that in for a moment – both parts of the statement. I didn't feel quite ready to answer.

'Did Amy call you?' I asked him, instead.

'Yes, she left a message saying she'd just seen you and that I was completely wrong and that you were exactly the sweet, untainted English rose I had thought you were. Those were her words, but I agree with them, of course.'

Now it was his turn to pause.

'Do you want to see me again, Stella?' he asked finally, very quietly.

My promise to Ham flashed through my head. I had expressly promised him I would never see Jay Fisher again. It was the only thing he had ever asked me to promise him – and he had never broken any of the promises he had made to me, from earliest childhood.

It was something he had always stressed. 'I may be a faithless hound to all the other women in my life, but if I make a promise to you, Stella, I will always keep it,' he'd say.

And he had. If he'd promised he'd be home in time to read me a story, he had been. If he'd promised to take me to see Father Christmas in Lapland, he had.

'Yes, Jay,' I said, almost immediately. It was done, the promise to Ham was broken, I couldn't help myself. 'Of course I want to see you.'

The moment I heard his voice I'd known I wanted to see him again. As soon as possible. Despite all the complications I now understood would be involved, from the attentions of the paparazzi, to his tendency to flit off to parties in Argentina, and, of course, my father's deep disapproval, I still wanted to see him. Desperately, actually.

Jay had touched something in me which no one else had ever got near. I still didn't quite know how and why, but I wanted more of it.

'Where are you?' I asked him, suddenly realizing I had no idea. He might still be in Mombasa for all I knew.

'New York,' he said, casually. 'But I'll come back to London as soon as I possibly can. Now, can you give me all your numbers and your email again?'

And just a few minutes after he rang off, I had an email from him – with all his numbers on it. I must have been still beaming about it all a few minutes later, when Ned came back into the office.

'Good news, then,' he said, smiling wryly, as he walked in.

'Oh yes,' I said, realizing that I had to maintain complete discretion about Jay from this moment onwards. 'It was an old friend I haven't heard from for ages. Great to speak to her. She's, er, having a baby.'

My new double life, as Jay Fisher's girlfriend, had begun.

When I got home that night, I got straight on the phone to Amy. I was already too paranoid to call her from the office about it.

'Thank you,' I said to her. 'Thank you for clearing my name. You are a true pal.'

'Did Jay call you then, darling?'

'Yes, he did. Thanks to you.'

'Oh, I am glad. So are you going to carry on seeing him?' she asked, switching to her most confidential gossip tones. I could just imagine the twinkle in her canny eyes.

'I don't think so,' I lied shamelessly, slipping so easily into my new duplicitous role. 'Too complicated, but I'm so glad that at least he knows I'm not a tabloid tart. I think we can be friends.'

'Oh, what a shame you're not going to go out with him,' said Amy. 'I hardly need to tell you now what a coup that would be, but it's up to you, darling. I'm just happy I could help sort things out a bit. Do me one favour, though – next time he changes his mobile, would you let me have the new number?'

I promised I would, gaining another little insight into how Amy's world worked.

A few hours later I was lying in my bath, up to my neck in bubbles, with music blaring out when my phone rang. It was Jay.

'Hello, beautiful,' he said. 'I just had to call you again, I hope you don't mind.'

'I don't mind at all,' I said. 'Hang on a minute, though, I'll turn the music down.'

I stepped out of the bath and padded over to the stereo in my bedroom, still holding the phone, leaving large patches of bubbles on the floorboards.

'Hey,' said Jay, when I got back into the bath and put the

phone up to my ear again. 'That was Joni Mitchell you were playing. *Blue*, right?'

'Yes,' I said. 'Do you like her?'

'Are you kidding? I love her music, especially that album. My mum used to play it all the time when I was a kid. She actually used to live near her one time, in LA, before I was born.'

I sat up in the bath.

'So did my dad,' I said. 'Topanga Canyon?'

'Yeah,' said Jay.

'Gosh, how weird is that? My dad loves her music too, he got me into it. He plays it all the time.'

'Oh dear,' said Jay. 'This is no good at all, too much spooky synchronicity, nought degrees of separation and all that. I'm going to have to come over there real soon.'

We talked until my bathwater went cold and I had to keep topping it up. I still didn't quite understand what it was about him yet, but we just had so much to say to each other. Not only soppy lovey-dovey stuff – although there was some of that going on too – but interesting things.

Jay had his own angle on everything, but not in a monologue-y way. He never lectured, but he made me think. He stretched me and made me feel brighter than I felt with anyone else.

The physical side of things with him had been sublime, but that was much easier to find than this kind of 'brain fuck' that we had going on. That was his name for it and described it perfectly. I was as turned on by his brain, as I was by his body.

After he rang off, I was in such a swoon I sank down into the water beneath my bubbles.

*

189

Jay rang and emailed me every day from then on, usually more than once, but he still hadn't been able to get back over to London. He was a bit vague about the reasons, something to do with family commitments, as far as I could gather, but while I was longing to see him, I had plenty going on at work to keep my mind off him.

Doughnut had extended our deadline for getting the dummy of the new section together, which was a relief, because there was a lot more to it than I had realized.

Peter was a great help, but it was still daunting creating an entirely new framework for a section that had never existed before – and the ghastly Jeanette was doing her best to undermine me at every turn.

With my new status as a section editor, I now attended the weekly Monday meeting of all the section editors on the paper, so we could all discuss what we were planning to run over the next week, to make sure there weren't any overlaps.

Although my section wasn't happening yet, Peter had said it was important for me to start going to the Monday meetings to get to know the other section editors and how they worked. Very quickly, though, the meetings became a major forum for Jeanette trying to make me look – and feel – I wasn't up to the job.

It was quite subtle the way she did it, just the odd little reference to how experienced everyone else there was at editing, and using technical terms about production that I didn't understand. Then she'd ask me some direct question about how I was planning to do something on 'The Good Life', which I couldn't possibly answer and I'd feel all tongue-tied and stupid.

I started to dread those meetings – especially as they were chaired by the managing editor, Martin Ryan, who I had never liked, and who had, I was quite sure, an equally low opinion of me.

He was great friends with Jeanette for one thing – he'd been at university with her husband and they were still very tight. But apart from that there was something really cold about Martin that made me wary. He didn't say much, but you could see him taking everything in, like a big lizard. It was much more scary to me than Doughnut's hot temper.

'He's a useful grunt,' was the best Peter had ever said about him. 'That's the only reason Duncan has him around the place, I'm certain of it. He does the actual sackings, for example. Duncan may have a terrible temper, but he's a decent man at heart, and he doesn't really enjoy sacking people, whatever anyone thinks. But Martin does. He relishes the power trip.'

I also discovered Jeanette was mounting a campaign against me with key writers on the paper. I got my first inkling of that when I took the fashion editor, Natalie, out to lunch one day, to talk about how she could contribute to the new section.

Natalie and I didn't have the easiest of relationships. She'd only been on the paper a few months and when she'd arrived, from a rather recherché fashion magazine, she'd been extremely arrogant for someone with no newspaper experience.

She really seemed to think she was doing us all a favour by being there and that filing copy by deadlines and checking facts and spellings were beneath her as a creative being.

As a result, the subs really hated her, which was never a good position for anyone on a paper.

I had tried to be friendly when she'd first started, but she seemed to have a problem accepting that it was totally within my remit to write about Louis Vuitton, Chanel, Gucci, and all the other luxury brands she felt were her exclusive territory, just because they happened to make clothes.

She had been particularly furious the time I had been invited to Milan instead of her, to do an exclusive interview with Miuccia Prada.

Making matters worse between us, the person who had come to her aid, when it seemed she might sink under the consistent lack of cooperation from some very pissed-off subs, was Jeanette.

Natalie was a seriously groovy girl and I felt at heart she didn't really relate to creepy Jeanette and her sack-like 'art' clothing and feature jewellery, any more than I did, but she clearly owed her one.

She certainly made it immediately apparent that she wasn't at all interested in cooperating with me on the new section.

'I really don't know what your section has to do with me, Stella,' she'd huffed, when I'd asked her to have lunch with me. 'You're the one who has always been at pains to remind me that fashion and luxury are quite separate.'

I took a deep breath.

'Can we at least talk about it?' I persevered.

She reluctantly agreed to meet me in the café on the ground floor of the building, but then kept me waiting for over ten minutes after the agreed time.

While I was sitting there waiting, Jeanette came through the door and was clearly making for a table where two of the most highly respected feature writers on the paper were already sitting, when she saw me.

A succession of expressions crossed her smug face. Irritation, concern and cunning, one after the other. Then she snapped her fingers as though she had just remembered something, turned on her heel and walked out again.

I glanced over to the feature writers, who were looking at Jeanette's receding back with extremely puzzled expressions. Shortly afterwards one of them answered his mobile phone and then they both got up and left.

Was I being paranoid, I wondered, or was that very strange? And was it really all a result of Jeanette spotting me? It seemed far-fetched, but I just couldn't see any other reason for what I had just witnessed.

Before I had any more time to ponder on it, Natalie arrived, not even apologizing for her lateness, and sat down opposite me with her arms folded. I decided just to be honest.

'Listen, Natalie,' I said. 'I know you don't like me because you think I write about stuff which is your brief and you probably don't want to cooperate with me on the new section, in case you accidentally make me look good, but I just want to ask you to think about it a bit more carefully before you reject it.'

She had the grace to look surprised, at least. She started to protest that she'd never said she didn't like me, but I just waved her away.

'That's all irrelevant, Natalie. I honestly don't care if you like me or not. This is work, not fun time, so just let me finish,' I said. 'This new section I am editing is Doughnut's baby. It's all his idea and he has a lot invested in it professionally. It's really going out on a limb for him, to do something in his paper which is expressly designed to bring in advertising revenue and he really wants it to work.

'If it does work – and I'm going to make sure it does, with or without your help – everyone involved with it will get a large boost in Doughnut's estimation. So just have a think about that, before you tell me you're not interested, OK?'

She looked quite puzzled.

'Got any questions?' I asked, in a milder tone.

'Was it really Doughnut's idea?' she said.

'Yes,' I said. 'He wants the revenue to finance the Jerusalem bureau, and he came up with this idea in cahoots with the advertising bods. They've even got in some hotshot from Condé Nast to help woo the luxury clients. Why do you ask?'

'Well,' she said, looking distinctly shifty. 'I had lunch with Jeanette the other day and she told me that the section was your idea – to expand your empire, as she put it – and that you had got Doughnut to agree to it, by flirting with him outrageously, and because he knows your dad.'

I just sat and stared at her, I was so amazed. She looked a bit more uncomfortable for a moment, and then continued.

'And she also said that it wouldn't last more than a few months and it would be the laughing stock of London and anyone who was involved with it would look really lame.'

I sat there stunned for another couple of seconds and then I burst out laughing.

'Are you serious?' I said. 'That is hilarious. My God, she's even more desperate than I thought she was. Doughnut does know my dad, but they're not big buddies; they both know a lot of people and they go to the same parties. Jeanette's just pissed off about this, because they've taken her Friday section away from her and her little empire has shrunk by one fifth.'

Natalie's eyebrows were nearly at her hairline.

'Would she really make all that stuff up?' she said.

'Well, that's up to you to decide,' I said. 'You can only believe one of us, but if you want to check my version of the story, you could ask Ned, or Peter Wallington – or Doughnut actually. I didn't ask for a section to edit, they gave it to me, out of the blue. It's about luxury, which is what I write about, so it was a no-brainer to get me to do it really, wasn't it? Of course I'm excited, but it's a hell of a lot of work, and I'm a bit freaked out by it, if you really want to know.'

Natalie looked quite shattered.

'I'm sorry, Stella,' she said, eventually. 'I've been really unfair to you, but Jeanette has just always made me feel like you were someone to be seriously wary of and I've had such a hard time since I came to this paper, I just didn't want to risk getting close to you in case you stitched me up – as Jeanette said you would at every opportunity.'

'Well, I'm flattered she thinks I'm so deadly,' I said. 'But really, Natalie, I'm just a newspaper reporter trying to do my job, I've never hankered after anyone else's, not yours and not Jeanette's. I'm too busy doing my own as well as I can.'

'Well,' said Natalie, looking quite punch-drunk. 'I'm on board with "The Good Life", if you still want me.'

I smiled and put my hand out to shake hers. I reckoned from then on we would get on just fine.

*

Once I was back in my office and had a bit more time to reflect on what Natalie had told me about Jeanette, I stopped finding it quite so funny. It was treacherous – slanderous – what she'd done. And that wasn't the end of it. I'd been right about what I'd seen in the café.

Later that afternoon, Tim called me on my mobile, from his side of the office where he was re-installed, back from Iraq.

'Cabbage crates over the briny,' he said. 'Red eagles fly tonight.'

It was his way of saying: meet me at the fire escape as soon as possible. I knew the score.

'Ten four, rubber duck,' I said and went straight out to meet him.

By the time I got there he was already inside the 'conference room' as we called the fire stairs. That stairwell was the only place in the *Journal*'s open-plan office where you could have a private conversation.

Even the few offices with doors were hopeless, because they all had glass walls looking straight on to the news floor. Some people ascribed Rita's amazing powers of gossip gathering to lip-reading through those glass partitions.

'Hello, sweetie,' said Tim, who was sitting on a concrete step, with an unlit cigarette between his lips. 'I have some intelligence for you. Not nice. Jeanette is fully trying to stitch you up. Greg Turnbull has just told me she took him and Roger Fullman out for coffee and told them you'd only got this new section because of your father's friendship with Doughnut – plus his immature penchant for slender brunettes with good legs.'

I laughed, bitterly. Greg and Roger were the writers I'd seen in the café earlier when Jeanette had done her strange about-turn.

'Well, funnily enough, I did have an inkling about this,' I said. 'Go on, tell me the rest.'

'She also said that writers of their reputation would be mad to write for the section because you were only doing it so that you could arse-lick all the luxury brands who take you on all those glamorous overseas trips and send you all the free gifts and bouquets.'

I groaned. I was no longer finding Jeanette's machinations amusing. It was all getting to be a huge drag.

'Surely, they don't believe Doughnut would let that happen on his paper?'

'Well, I'm just telling you what Greg said. Of course, I told Greg I believed that you were entirely ethically scrupulous, but I think maybe you need to talk to him and Roger yourself.'

'Thanks, Tim,' I said and told him about my own meeting with Natalie.

Tim made appropriately disgusted noises, then we sat in silence for a moment. He pretended to take a draw on his unlit ciggie and extravagantly blew out the imaginary smoke. Then he looked at me sideways. It was an expression I knew well.

'How do you like working with Ned?' he asked innocently.

'Great,' I said. 'He's a great guy.'

'So I hear,' said Tim, archly. 'I wouldn't mind being bent over a computer console with him myself. You've been shut up in that office together very cosily, I must say, and Rita tells me you've been going out to loads of events with him too. So, are you shagging him then?'

'Tim!' I said outraged. 'We work together. You know I'm not into that office-affair bollocks and he's not my type anyway.'

'Maybe he should be . . .' said Tim, and he got up to start the descent down the thirty-one flights of stairs to the ground floor, which was the only way out of our conference room once you'd closed the one-way fire door.

I left Tim happily puffing outside the building and went back up to my desk – via the lift – feeling quite sick about what was going on. It just amazed me that someone who seemed to do as little work as Jeanette, could find so much energy to put into trying to destroy someone else's career. If only she channelled that vigour into her actual job, she wouldn't have lost the Friday section in the first place.

One thing happened to cheer me up that afternoon, though – another beautiful bouquet arrived from Moyses Stevens. A huge spray of glorious garden roses and a card which said '*For my untainted English rose. J. xxxxx*'.

Five kisses. Excellent.

I was a bit surprised, though, the next day, when another bunch arrived. So I rang the florist to tell them they must have made a mistake, because I'd received a bouquet from them the day before from the same person. The girl on the phone said she'd check the order book. She came back on the line after a few minutes.

'That was from Mr Fisher, right?' she asked me and I confirmed it.

'No, that is correct,' she continued. 'He ordered pink

roses yesterday and mixed roses today. There should have been a different message today too, did you get that?'

I told her I had. I could remember it quite clearly.

'*Soon . . .*' it had said. '*J. xxxxxxxxxxx*'.

The next day, I got another bouquet. White roses, mixed with white lilac, and another lovely card. And the next day another. Mixed lilac. My office was so full of flowers, I had run out of places to put them and the smell was overpowering – and my colleagues were starting to make comments.

'It's like the Chelsea Flower Show in there,' said Peter, as he passed my office on the Friday morning.

Rita, as usual, was more to the point.

'Bloody hell, Stella,' she said, leaning forwards to sniff the lilac and clearly trying to see if there were any cards lying around she could sneak a crafty look at. 'Who's sending you all these amazing flowers? Have you got another billionaire boyfriend?'

I thought quickly.

'Oh no, Rita,' I said. 'It's just the new section. All the luxury brands have heard about it, and they're all trying to crawl up my arse.'

'Oooh,' she said. 'Well, when you get a free set of Vuitton luggage, chuck a little one my way will you?'

It got me off the hook regarding Jay, but that little lie quickly caused other problems. Tim sent me an email.

'Nice flowers, Stella,' it said. 'I've just heard Jeanette tell Greg they're all from luxury PRs – just the start of the freebies you will be creaming off via the section. Thought you should know.'

When that day's delivery arrived – a glorious purple

wisteria in full bloom, in a large terracotta pot – I knew I had to do something.

I took all the bouquets to the editorial assistant and asked her to have them sent to the nearest hospital. I got Tim's friend in the delivery bay to send the wisteria to Ham's address.

That night when Jay called, I knew I would have to bring it up with him. Every other night that week I'd thanked him for the beautiful flowers and it was going to be hard to ask him not to send any more without seeming really churlish. Luckily, he brought it up first.

'Did you get your tree?' was the first thing he asked me.

'Yes, thank you, it's so beautiful.'

'Do you know why I sent that? Because when I first saw you, you were sitting beneath a cloud of that purple in the pool bar at the Cap Mimosa. A flower among the flowers.'

'That is so gorgeous,' I said. 'I did wonder if you were making a reference to that. I've brought it home, so I can keep it in my courtyard. I'm going to grow it up my garden wall.'

'Oh, that's nice,' said Jay, sounding surprised.

'I hope you don't mind,' I said, seizing my chance. 'But I had to give some of the other bouquets away this afternoon. I couldn't bring them all home and I couldn't bear to think of them just dying in the office over the weekend when someone could be enjoying them. You're not hurt, are you? I could hardly get into my office for flowers by this morning.'

Jay didn't say anything for a moment.

'You still had them all?' he said eventually, sounding puzzled.

Now I was puzzled. 'Well, yes. What did you think I'd do with them?'

'Doesn't your maid throw them out each night?'

It was one of those moments when I realized just how great the chasm was between our experiences of life. He came from a world where women expected new flowers every day. I came from one where they were still a huge treat – and I got a lot more flowers than most people.

'Well, I don't really have a maid at work,' I said, gently. 'The cleaners don't touch flowers, or anything unless it's already clearly in a bin, that's the rule, and there was no way I could chuck a beautiful bouquet of perfect roses into the garbage.'

Jay laughed. 'You are so cute,' he said. 'So what flowers would you like next week?'

'Oh, Jay,' I said. 'You really don't have to do that. They're beautiful, but I know you're thinking of me without them. Just one bunch every now and again would be gorgeous.'

'Would you prefer I sent them to your home?'

'No, there'd be no one there to take them in – I don't have a maid at home either, Jay.'

That was clearly such an out-there statement he didn't even comment on it – and anyway, he had better things to tell me. He was calling from the First Class lounge at JFK. He'd be back in London the next morning.

I 2

Of course, I was absolutely thrilled that Jay and I were finally going to be reunited, but I could have done with a bit more warning.

For one thing, I seriously needed to get my legs waxed, but more importantly, it meant I had to get out of going down to Willow Barn that weekend. And it wasn't just any old weekend.

It was Freddie's seventh birthday the following week and children's birthdays were a big deal in our family. Ham always threw a party on the nearest weekend – he insisted the child in question spent the actual birthday with their mother, because 'she'd done all the hard work', as he put it – but he liked to mark the occasion with special cakes, mad games, fancy dress and a firework display, at the very least.

I'd been looking forward to it for weeks – seven was a particularly good age for birthdays, old enough to be really excited at the prospect of presents and parties and a cake, and not yet 'over' it.

I'd bought him a tepee, which I'd had sent straight down to the Barn. The plan was that Ham and I would erect it the night before and then on the morning of the big day, Chloe and I were going to surprise him with a suitably Western breakfast, which we would eat cross-legged round a campfire, powwow style. I'd bought Ham a feather head-dress to wear. Big Chief Hambone, I was going to call him.

And now I didn't even want to go. I wanted to spend the whole weekend with Jay.

I spent a couple of hours wrestling with my conscience about it, telling myself that Freddie would be so overexcited he really wouldn't care if I was there or not, and at least he would have the fun present that I had already organized, so I wasn't letting him down completely. The people who would really be disappointed were me and – I had to admit it to myself – Ham.

He so loved us all being down there together and it was very important to him to be reassured that the whole crazy patchwork of children he had created, really did love each other.

'I need to know the love goes from side to side and not just up and down,' he'd told me once, trying to explain it. 'I want to know you'll still be knitted together as a family, after I've gone.'

So there was all that, plus feeling bad about Chloe, as I knew my absence would mean she would get absolutely no help with any of the cooking or clearing up. But on top of all that, the overriding superguilt was that I was not only dropping out of a family birthday – I was doing it to be with the one man on earth Ham didn't want me to see.

So I was lying to him and breaking the only serious promise he had ever asked me to make. Not pretty.

But even as I struggled with my guilt, I already knew deep down inside that I wasn't going to Freddie's birthday party. The feelings I had for Jay were just too special. I had simply never felt that way about anyone before and one of the things that made me certain it was different with him, was that I wanted to have him to my place – to stay.

When I knew I had made up my mind, I rang Willow Barn and told Chloe that something had blown up at the paper, with regard to my new section, and that I would have to work right through the weekend.

It was lucky for me that she answered. Ham had popped round to see the neighbours, to warn them about the firework display, so I didn't have to hear the disappointment in his voice, but I already felt bad enough, hearing it in Chloe's.

'Oh, no, that's such a shame, Stella,' she said. 'I've been so looking forward to the wigwam breakfast, but don't worry, we'll still do it. Archie's here, so he can help Ham put the tepee up and make the campfire and all that, and I'll do the sausages and beans, just as we planned. I'm going to make some cornbread as well,' she added excitedly.

I felt like a total shit. And later that night, as I attempted to wax my own legs, very badly, with some strips I had bought from a 24-hour pharmacy on Queensway, I marvelled at how quickly I had become an accomplished liar. I deserved every painful rip.

Jay rang me as soon as his plane landed at Heathrow on Saturday morning. It was just after six a.m., but I didn't mind. I'd sent him a text the night before asking him to phone.

'Good morning, baby,' he said. 'I'm here. Ol' red eyes is back.'

'Welcome back, Jay,' I said, a severe case of butterflies taking hold of my stomach.

'So, where do you want to meet me?'

'Well,' I said, deciding to launch in, but feeling incredibly nervous. 'I wondered if you'd like to come and stay at my place this weekend . . .'

I felt so strange asking him. It was so alien to me as a concept even to ask someone over for coffee, let alone to stay. Of course, there was no way he could have any idea what a big deal it was to me, but if he'd said no, he'd really rather meet me at a nice anonymous luxury hotel, I would have been gutted. I knew what hotels meant – just close enough and no closer. And I wanted Jay as close to me as was possible.

'At your place?' he said, sounding surprised. 'That would be totally great. I was going to suggest mine, but I'd love to see where you live.' He paused for a moment. 'Where *do* you live?'

I laughed and gave him the address and he said he'd get a cab straight over. Then, as I put down the phone, I did a little dance.

I threw open all the windows, changed the sheets, lit a few scented candles and then wandered around wondering what my place would look like through Jay's eyes.

I loved my little house, but it was seriously – ridiculously – girly-girly and I really didn't know what he would make of it. But as he was about to find out that I shared my decorating tastes with Miss Piggy and Lady Penelope, I thought I might as well go for it.

So after a quick shower and applying one of those 'no-make-up make-ups' that are a girl's best secret and walking through a squirt of scent, as advised by the late Estée Lauder, I put on my favourite pale pink marabou-trimmed negligee, over a very cheeky Agent Provocateur half-cup bra, with stockings and suspenders, my highest-heeled fluffy mules on my feet. I was going for the full Vargas Girl look. I hoped he'd get it. I knew not all men did.

I had just finished pouring myself into the stockings when he knocked on the door.

I was so simultaneously nervous and excited, that in that frozen moment I almost felt like not answering it. I'd read Dorothy Parker, I was all too aware of the way reunions can so often be better in the anticipation than the reality. Maybe I'd built Jay up into something he wasn't. Perhaps there was something wrong with him – he seemed so keen on me, maybe it was all too good to be true.

As these thoughts were crowding into my mind, my hands were opening the door. And there he was. Tanned, smiling, gorgeous, still the Jay I remembered. I swallowed hard.

'Hey, baby,' he said, looking at me with his head on one side. Then he put his hands out and took mine in his, squeezing them gently, then bringing them up to his lips.

I just stood there, frozen.

'Can I come in?' he asked, after a few seconds had passed.

'Oh, God, yes, come in,' I said, completely flustered. Then as he crossed the threshold I couldn't restrain myself. Before I knew what I was doing, I had flung myself at him and was clinging on to him like he was a life raft. So embarrassing, but I couldn't help it.

'Don't go,' was all I could say, speaking into his shoulder. 'Don't go.'

'Hey, sweetheart,' he said. 'Don't worry, I'm not going. I'm here. Hang on there a minute, let me get my stuff inside.'

Still holding on to me with one arm, he reached through

the door with his other and pulled in three bags, which I couldn't help noticing were those giant-sized Hermès Birkin holdalls, in perfectly worn-in tan leather. He threw them on the floor, kicked the door shut and then took me in his arms.

He held me really close and then pulling away slightly, he looked into my face. I wasn't quite crying, but I was very close.

'Well, that was a welcome,' he said, smiling so sweetly and lifting my chin up with his fingers, so he could see me better. 'Are you OK?'

I nodded quickly, hoping my no-make-up make-up wasn't now smudged all over my cheeks.

'I'm so sorry,' I said. 'It's just it's been a bit intense. The whole thing. I'm really embarrassed. But I'm just so glad to see you again.'

When I looked up, Jay was checking out my sitting room. As he took in the oversized chandelier, the zebra-skin rug, the shocking-pink walls, the sugar-pink velvet sofa, the pompoms, the leopard-skin Louis chairs, the mirrored table, the gold-framed mirrors, the floral paintings and the abundance of fairy lights, a huge grin spread across his face.

'What a great little place,' he said, shaking his head slowly. 'It's so cute and quirky. Who's your decorator?'

The chasm again, I thought.

'I did it myself, Jay,' I said. 'I don't use decorators. Well, only the kind who use paint rollers and white spirit.'

He pulled me into his arms again and rubbed his nose against mine.

'Well, you're a very clever girl, then. Now, tell me, is the bedroom in the same style?'

I giggled and led him up there by the hand.

'Wow,' he said, when he saw my huge brass bed with the skylight over it, starched white linen pillows piled up, and the early-morning sunshine pouring in. 'That's what I call a bed.'

Then he picked me up and threw me on to it.

'I love what you're wearing,' he said, as he stood over me, unbuttoning his crisp white button-down shirt, not taking his eyes from mine, which were flicking shamelessly from his face to his beautiful brown stomach as he revealed it, button by button. It was like a reverse action replay of the first night I had met him.

'You look like a Vargas Girl lying there,' he said. 'My boyhood fantasy come to life. So don't take it off. Leave that to me . . .'

We spent the whole morning in bed, with occasional inter-missions for me to make Jay coffee, to keep him awake – it was still the middle of the night in New York and his post-coital naps were in danger of turning into eight hours of deep sleep. I was under strict instructions to wake him if he slept for longer than fifteen minutes.

'You know, Stella,' he said eventually – after I'd just woken him up for the third time. 'Bed is not the greatest place to beat jet lag. Let's go take a walk. I love Hyde Park in May. All the chestnuts will be flowering.'

'So do I,' I said, delighted he cared about those kinds of things too. 'But the paparazzi won't see us, will they?' I dreaded the return of those dark riders back into my world.

'No,' said Jay. 'They don't know I'm here yet. There were

some creeps at the airport, but they were after Liz Hurley, not me, so I snuck past, while they were hassling her. They didn't see me. As long as we stay away from the obvious places, we'll be fine. Just dress down, tie your hair back – and I presume you have some large, dark glasses . . .'

I felt like a naughty schoolgirl sneaking out into Notting Hill with Jay, wearing a baseball cap and the largest shades I owned, a pair of old Ray-Ban Aviators I had pinched from Ham years before.

Jay joked that they weren't nearly big enough, or dark enough, for proper paparazzi avoidance, but he took my hand anyway, and we walked quickly through the streets where we were most likely to see people either of us knew.

Once we hit Bayswater Road, I relaxed a little, and by the time we were in the park, I felt quite elated. We just strolled along like normal people, holding hands, fooling about, chatting and laughing. It was glorious.

By the time we were heading out of the park again it was mid-afternoon.

'I've just realized something,' said Jay, rubbing his stomach, in what I had come to recognize was a rather endearing habit of his. 'I'm absolutely starving. Can we eat something?'

'I'm starving too,' I said. 'What do you feel like?'

'It's not so much what, as where?' said Jay. 'Anywhere we'd want to eat out is much too visible.' He thought for a moment. 'Can we eat at your place?'

'Sure,' I said, my heart sinking. 'But I have to warn you, Jay, I can't cook. I'm really useless at it. I'm very spoilt, because I eat lunch out a lot for work, so most nights I don't want anything and when I do want to eat at home, I just go up to my dad's – his wife writes cookery books and her food is amazing.'

'Don't worry, I'll make it,' said Jay.

I turned to look at him in amazement. I'd thought that America's Little Lord Fauntleroy would expect to be cooked for and waited on.

'You cook?' I asked him.

'Sure. I love to cook. And by the way, I remember how good Chloe's cake was that time I came to Willow Barn, I can't wait to try some more of her food.'

Oh dear, I thought. There was no way Jay was going to be eating at Ham's table anytime soon and I was going to have to find a way to explain that to him. Later, I thought, I'd do it later.

'So,' he said, smiling happily. 'Do you like Thai? Spicy noodles? A bit of chicken thrown in? Lots of ginger and coriander. A nice hot wok. Mmmmm, I can smell it already.'

I nodded enthusiastically.

'OK, well let's go buy some food.'

My first thought was Fresh and Wild because that was pretty much where I did all my food shopping – such as it was – but then I thought better of it. It was just the kind of place we'd be recognized, so I steered him to one of the ethnic supermarkets on Queensway for the noodles and exotic bits, then to M&S for the chicken breasts.

'You've got chilli sauce, right?' said Jay, as we walked back to the house, laden with shopping bags. He'd vetoed my suggestion of hailing a cab, saying that the drivers often recognized him.

'They're one of the great sources of info for the paparazzi

assholes. They drop you at a hotel, call the creeps, tell them where you are, and get slipped a few quid. Them and the bellhops are among the worst. They do it for such a paltry amount of money and totally ruin someone's life. I'd pay them more not to do it.'

'Gosh,' I said. 'I had no idea. But, er, no, actually on the chilli sauce front, I haven't got much in the way of ingredients at my place actually. Or utensils. Or a cooker, really.'

He stopped and looked at me, putting his shopping bags down. He put his hands on my shoulders and leaned into my face.

'Do you have a microwave, Stella?' he asked.

I nodded.

'And a well-used toaster and cereal bowl?'

I nodded again. He roared with laughter and hugged me.

'Oh well, I'm sure I can rustle something up with a bread knife and a frying pan.'

I wasn't at all sure – I didn't have a frying pan, but I was hatching a plan.

When we got back to the house, I showed Jay the waste-land that was my kitchen. A fridge, mainly full of face creams, scent and nail varnishes, with one bottle of vodka and a few ready meals in the freezer, then a microwave, a toaster and a kettle. That was it. And I only had one plate and one bowl. Lots of mugs, though.

'Well, that is seriously minimalist,' said Jay, smiling and shaking his head. 'You really don't cook, do you?'

'No, but as I said, Chloe seriously does, so why don't we go and use her kitchen?'

'Great,' said Jay. 'That would be really cool, but are you sure she won't mind?'

'Well, they're not there – they're down at Willow Barn – and I know she wouldn't mind anyway. They're always telling me to use the house when they're away. It's better for security, apart from anything.'

'Is it far?' said Jay, picking up the carrier bags again. 'I'm ready to faint with hunger.'

I smiled. 'Not far at all. Follow me.'

Jay laughed when I opened the gate in my little courtyard – where the wisteria was still blooming beautifully in its pot – and he could see up Ham's lawn to the kitchen, clearly visible through the glass wall at the back of the house.

'This is where I picked you up that night – this is your dad's place. You live out back, that is so funny.'

Jay was thrilled when he saw Chloe's kitchen, with its professional stove, huge, abundantly stocked fridge and larder, and every culinary utensil you could dream of hanging from a handy overhead rack.

'Rock and roll,' he said, throwing a piece of ginger up into the air and catching it behind his back. 'She's even got a ginger grater.' He kissed it theatrically and got to work.

My job, he said, was to mix some drinks, get some music going and find him something he could put in his mouth immediately. 'And I don't mean your left breast, delicious though that is,' he added.

Without even asking him what he wanted, I made him a beauty of a negroni. I might have been a total waste of space in the kitchen, but I seriously knew how to mix drinks. I'd learned it from Ham's second wife, Margot, who was a world-class alcoholic, but with a lot of style.

Her gift to me as a child, was to work our way through a 1950s book of cocktail recipes. While other little girls might have played teddy bears' tea parties, I mixed drinks like a Savoy barman.

I mixed them and decorated them – using all the right glasses and trimmings, which she had lined up ready in a fabulous old cocktail cabinet – and she drank them. We both had a fine old time.

I was still really fond of Margot. She was in pretty poor shape these days – you can't drink with the kind of commitment she had to hard liquor and hold on to your health – but I still loved her company.

She'd been in my life for only three years – from four to seven – but that's an impressionable age and she had definitely made a big impact on me. My taste for marabou-trimmed peignoirs definitely came from her. She had lounged around in hers all day drinking the cocktails I made her, with Dean Martin crooning on the hi-fi.

It was Ham finding out about our daily cocktail sessions, which went on while he was working, that finally led to the end of their marriage, which had never been well advised. And I think, in that way kids have, I somehow thought it was my fault. She'd never married again, but had spent the years since drinking herself to death on Ham's alimony.

So out of a mix of affection and responsibility, I still visited her when I could, in the residential care home where she now lived. She rambled a lot these days, in between bouts of rib-wracking coughing – she smoked as much as she drank and with similar elegance, always with a cigarette holder – but she would still come out with nuggets of kooky brilliance.

'The thing about your darling faaaaaather,' she used to say, in her wonderful 1950s RADA voice – she was older than Ham and had been a Rank starlet in her youth, 'the old rat, is that he's too much cock and not enough cocktail.'

Then she'd take a big drag on her ciggie and smile at me like the Mona Lisa, the smoke billowing out of her nose, completely forgetting what she'd just said.

It was sad to see her like that, her hair still always perfectly done, her nails always painted, always in high heels, but her brain shot to bits. But one thing I had learned from Margot, apart from how to mix a mean martini, was to have healthy respect for booze and cigarettes. I knew what they could do to a girl.

Jay was suitably impressed by his drink – and my choice of music. I'd put Van Morrison on, because another thing we'd discovered we had in common, over our twice-daily phone calls, was that we both really preferred music from the seventies to anything that had come out more recently. We even agreed on the exceptions – which were mainly tracks that were just great to dance to – but for music to chill to, we liked the old stuff.

I sat at the kitchen counter on a high stool, sipping my drink, nibbling on the Twiglets and olives I had found in the cupboard and watched him cook. He clearly loved it and he never so much as asked me to chop an onion, which was fine by me.

We'd been singing along to Van the Man and were just getting into a discussion about seventies films – and what seemed to make them more interesting than contemporary ones – when my mobile rang. I had to answer it. It might have been the office.

I turned the music off with the remote control and told Jay I would take the call in the next room. I was glad I had — it was Ham.

'Are you still in that bloody office?' he said.

'Hello Big Chief Hambone,' I said, feeling almost sick with guilt. Not only had I broken my promise to him, I was doing it in his house. I was no better than men who cheated on their wives in the marital bed. 'No actually, I'm not at the office — I'm at your house. I just got here.'

I didn't say where from. The less actual lies I told Ham, the better.

'Well, you should be down in this bloody house. I'm so sad you're not going to be here tomorrow.' Then he switched to his most conspiratorial tones. 'You should see the cake — Chloe's done Freddie a Harry Potter cake, but with a photo of him for the face. It's marvellous. I've got a massive firework display set up — do try and come down tomorrow if you can, darling, it won't be the same without you.'

'I'd love to, Dad,' I said and I meant it. If only he didn't have such a problem with Jay we'd both be down there already, I thought. That was the maddening thing. Jay would have loved it, I knew him well enough already to know that.

He could have helped Chloe with the cooking, he could have put the tepee up, and I could just imagine him leading a tribe of whooping Indian braves through the garden. He would so fit in.

But of all the men I had ever met — and the only one I had ever brought home — he was the one Ham didn't want me to see. I still couldn't believe my luck, or lack of it.

I would have to take it up with him again sometime soon, I told myself, but this was not the moment. I was up to my neck in dishonesty in a hole I had dug for myself, and for the time being I was stuck there.

'Well, my senior duckling,' Ham was saying. 'I've got a good mind to give Duncan a call and tell him to release you tomorrow, but I know you wouldn't like that. But if they do see fit to set you free, just get straight down here, OK? Anytime. And help yourself to anything in that house. I like to think of you up there.'

I rang off, praying he wouldn't ring Doughnut – and feeling like a total piece of poop.

'Food's up,' said Jay, looking completely relaxed and happy, when I walked back into the kitchen. 'Do you want to eat at the table, or in front of the TV? Either's fine by me. Your dad has a fine selection of Scorsese movies on DVD, I've just been looking through them.'

I'd been feeling really miserable after that phone call, but I had to laugh. Here I was, for the first time in my life, doing the full domestic thing with a man. It was everything I despised in my friends' relationships – and I was loving it.

'The table,' I said. There were limits. I wasn't ready for the full DVD and dinner-on-the-sofa experience yet. Just playing house with Jay was enough of a breakthrough for one day.

I opened a bottle of wine and we sat down at Ham's round table to eat Jay's delicious food.

'You really can cook,' I told him, after the first mouthful.

He smiled. 'My mom taught me. She's a great cook. We spend the whole day cooking when I go see her. We pick the veggies from her garden, make bread, the whole works. She has her own vineyard too. It's a blast. I'll take you to meet her one day.'

'Where does she live?'

'New Mexico. Just outside Santa Fe.'

'I love it there,' I said. 'I went there once to interview Tom Ford, on his ranch.'

Jay's face lit up.

'Oh, you know Tom, that's great – he's a good friend of Mom's. They live real near each other out there. He's a great guy, I really like Tom.'

'So do I,' I said. 'He's one of my heroes.'

'Well, if he's around when we're there, we'll have him to dinner. You can mix him a drink.'

He beamed at me, while I sat and pondered that latest reminder of the chasm between us.

'This is another great domestic space of your dad's,' he said, after a while. 'I can see how he has the energy flowing through it again. Will you show me round after dinner?'

I nodded. Just another little betrayal of my father couldn't hurt. I was stacking them up thick and fast. Maybe I should have jungle sex with Jay in Ham's bed, I thought. That would top it all off nicely.

'I'd love to see your dad again,' Jay was continuing. 'I'm such a fan of his ideas and he's a great guy too. I really enjoyed meeting him that time at Willow Barn. He's a blast.'

It was time to tell him, I thought. OK, so it meant possibly destroying the first – and blissful – domestic evening I had ever spent with a man I was also having sex with, but I couldn't lie simultaneously to both the men I loved.

And as I thought it, I realized it was true. That was why

it was all so different. That was why I wanted him to stay at my place. That was why I was happy shopping for food and cooking dinner and being soppy about song lyrics with him.

I was madly in love with Jay. Scary.

13

'There's something I have to tell you,' I began, fiddling nervously with my wine glass.

'I'm listening,' he said, smiling happily.

'It's about my dad . . .'

He put his head on one side, looking all boyish and interested. It was agony, but I had to get it out.

'It's about my dad and you . . .'

He frowned a little.

'Well, you know he's a life peer and all that?' I blundered on.

He nodded.

'Well, the thing is, he's a *Labour* peer . . . he's sort of a socialist and, well, you see, he has a big hang-up about inherited wealth.'

Jay put his knife and fork down with a clatter.

'Here we go . . .' he said, his face instantly tightening up. It was such a contrast from the gentle way he normally looked at me. I hated to see that hard look on his beautiful face.

'So your dad hates me because I have too much money. Ay yay yay.' He shook his head bitterly. 'Most of the world is trying to crawl up my ass to get their hands on it, and the other few – mostly the nice ones – hate me because I have it. Great.'

'It's not the amount, Jay. Ham – Dad – has a lot of very wealthy friends, it's not money itself he has a problem with.

It's just that you didn't make it yourself. He doesn't think that's good for people.'

'Well, that's hardly my fault,' he said, his voice getting even more tense. He looked like he was on the verge of blowing up. 'I didn't ask to be born a Fisher, just like a kid in Africa doesn't ask to be born starving. I just was.'

'I know that, Jay,' I said. 'In all honesty, I don't think my dad is entirely rational about it, but he just doesn't want me to be with someone who comes from a huge pile of inherited money. He doesn't think it makes people happy.'

'Doesn't he?' said Jay, with a sarcasm I had never heard from him before. 'But aren't you going to be one of those people yourself one day? He can't be short of a few bob himself. He is one of the best-known architects in the world.'

'Actually,' I said, sounding more defensive than I wanted to, 'Ham has hardly got a penny. He's been married five times before this one, remember, and everything he makes from the practice goes in child and ex-wife support. He has six kids who are still under eighteen – three of them are still under ten, for heaven's sake – and now Chloe's pregnant again. That's a lot of school fees still to pay, then university . . . It doesn't leave much. Plus, he does a lot of lecturing and consultancy work in developing countries for nothing.'

'Well, if he's such a socialist,' said Jay, 'why does he send his kids to private schools?'

I didn't have an answer for that. It's just the way things were.

'Anyway,' he continued. 'He might not be particularly liquid, but you're all going to inherit plenty when he goes from the property alone. This place is prime London real estate and Willow Barn would be worth a fortune even if it wasn't so famous. But with its architectural significance, it's almost priceless.'

'Ham doesn't own Willow Barn,' I told him blankly, slightly offended by his casual assessment of our family assets. 'He was given the money to build it by a group of his patrons. They set up a trust to pay for the house, in the interests of furthering architectural theory and trying out Ham's ideas for real. He gets to use it freely in his lifetime, but as soon as he dies, it goes back to the trust and it will become a study centre for students of domestic architecture.'

'Oh, really?' said Jay, in that maddening off-hand American way.

'And this place will go straight to Chloe,' I continued. 'And she's only a few years older than me. So I'm not going to inherit anything. I've never expected it and I've never hankered after it and that's why my career means so much to me. I've already got my little house, Ham gave me that, I'm very lucky, but apart from that, I'm on my own.'

Jay was leaning back in his chair, looking thoughtful. It was his turn to look at me across the chasm, I thought.

'So, how do you feel about it?' he asked me, eventually, in a more even tone. 'How do you feel about my money, my filthy inherited wealth? Does it revolt you too?'

'I don't really understand it,' I answered, completely honestly. 'I really can't conceive of how much money you might have and what that really means. Over a thousand pounds it's all the same to me really. I write about handbags costing twenty grand, which I know is more than a lot of people earn a year, but there are waiting lists in London for those bags. Over a certain amount, money just turns into blah blah in my head. Zero zero zero blah blah blah.'

Jay smiled again, and squeezed my hand.

'Oh, you are so cute,' he said, shaking his head. 'Because I know you mean that.'

'Of course I mean it,' I said urgently. 'I'm not joking. So tell me, Jay, how much money do you have? It said "billions" in that magazine. Ten billion was it? What does that actually mean? What does that look like? How much is a billion dollars in terms of someone's life?'

Jay's face clouded over again. He had an expression on it I hadn't seen since the South of France, when Laura Birchwood had said his name. In retrospect I understand that I had just asked him the ultimate no-no question – how much money do you have? But back then, I still didn't properly understand all that and, even if I had, I still would have said it.

This time he recovered quickly.

'You know what, Stella?' he said, looking at me tenderly again. 'I really don't know how much money I have – and I don't really care. Yes, it's a lot. The family trusts are huge and I am the main heir, by another accident of birth, or rather death. My older brother died in an accident nearly twelve years ago.'

He sighed and looked sad for a moment. I squeezed his hand.

'I'm sorry,' I said. Now he had mentioned it, a tragic death in the Fisher family rang a bell somewhere in my head, but this didn't seem the moment to ask him about it.

'Anyway,' he said, gathering himself. 'I don't know how they come up with figures like "ten billion". I think they make it up, because it's hard to assess. A lot of it's in property – Fishercorp owns quite a bit of midtown Manhattan. Then there is a whole load of investments and other stuff, even apart from the banking, so when people talk about "billions", it's not money in sacks, it's the aggregate value of all the things that we own, which we will never sell. It's almost like virtual money.

'As far as how it affects me, I guess I'm rich enough not to have to think about money on a day-to-day level – except that I am not allowed *not* to think about it, because everywhere I go people treat me as some kind of a freak because they know about it.'

He paused.

'Do you know I have people – total strangers – come up to me and touch me for luck. And not in India, or Mexico – in New York City. Do you know how weird that is?'

I shook my head. 'That *is* weird. That's horrible, actually.'

'And do you know who else never allows me to stop thinking about the fucking money?'

I shook my head.

'My goddam family. It's all they ever think about.'

His eyes narrowed suddenly.

'Did your father mention my family? You know, when he was warning you off all Fishers?'

I didn't want to answer that. I just looked down at my plate.

'Did he mention my dear Uncle Edward, by any chance?'

My head snapped up to look at him, before I could stop it. Jay was nodding. He raised his wine glass to me and took a big swig.

'That'll be it. Your dad had to work with Uncle Ed on the museum project.'

He leaned towards me, across the table.

'My Uncle Edward is a nightmare. He and the equally appalling Michael Fisher. They're radioactive, they're so awful. My dad isn't much better, but a little less crazy, because he was born before them, so he's the big swinging dick of their generation. I suffer because I'm next in line for that role – they suffer because they're not.'

I didn't say anything, but Jay was spelling out exactly the reasons Ham felt inherited wealth screwed people up. It was too ironic to be funny.

'That whole museum project was mainly set up by my dad to keep Edward occupied,' Jay continued. 'And to make him feel important. It was also a desperate attempt to stop Michael drinking himself to death, by having to turn up at the odd board meeting. So I can quite see why knowing them would make your dad wary of me.'

He paused again. I smiled weakly. I wasn't going to betray Ham any further by repeating what he'd said about Edward and Michael Fisher. That was potentially damaging to his career and I wouldn't do that to him, not even for Jay.

'But your dad's met me,' said Jay urgently. 'Surely he could see I'm not like them.'

'He did say how much he liked you, Jay, but he's got it into his head that however nice you seem on the surface, the context of your inherited wealth would not be good for me – and . . .' Now I had to get the really hard part out. 'And he's made me promise not to see you again.'

'Was that before or after today?' Jay asked quietly.

I laughed bitterly.

'Before,' I said. 'It was when that stupid article came out. That one little article made so much trouble for us, didn't it?'

'You got it . . . The power of the press, something you should know all about in your job.'

That stung, but I let it pass. Jay leaned back in his chair, looking at me with a sombre expression.

'So,' he said. 'Are you planning to carry on breaking your promise to him?'

'If you still want me to, after hearing all that.' I glanced away for a moment and then back at him. 'I don't normally break promises so easily, Jay,' I said, quietly.

'I believe you,' he said. 'And much as I respect your father, I would like you to continue betraying his trust, to see me – as long as you really think I'm worth it.'

That handsome face, with its playboy tan, looked quite vulnerable for a moment. So I got up, sat myself on his knee and held him really tight.

The rest of the weekend was charmed. It was a huge relief to have got the Ham business off my chest to Jay, so I could just surrender myself to enjoying his company and this novel game of playing house.

I have to confess, I was so wrapped up in him and the little bubble we had created that I completely forgot to ring Freddie to say Happy Birthday until it was nearly noon on the Sunday. And I'd switched all my phones off.

'There you are!' said Ham, who picked up the phone after one ring. 'I've been calling your home phone and mobile all morning and of course you never pick up that work phone, do you? I was so worried I was ready to drive back to town, if you hadn't called by lunch.'

'Oh, don't be so silly,' I said. 'I'm just so wrapped up in what I'm doing here, I forgot to put my phone on this morning. Anyway, how's the birthday going? How did the tepee go down with Freddie?'

I was getting so good at these not-the-whole-truth lies, I amazed myself. It was a strange kind of comfort not to be telling actual brazen porkies about being in the office, although I knew inside that such semantic details would be immaterial to Ham if he knew what I was really wrapped up in.

I had a brief word with the birthday boy, who was in a state of extreme excitement, and then I was free to go back to the only thing I really cared about at the moment. The beautiful man who had just been rubbing my neck and was now tenderly kissing it . . .

After a leisurely brunch cooked by Jay in Chloe's kitchen, we decided to go out for another walk in Hyde Park. We should have been warned when the first people I saw on opening Ham's front door were my friend Becca – the Cartier PR – and her sister, Toria, who lived just round the corner in Chepstow Villas.

They were good friends of mine; we were all single girls and we often met up at the weekend for breakfast and a long walk, which is what I presumed they were on their way back from.

It would have been a disaster, I realized, if they'd seen us. They both would have recognized Jay immediately. It was Becca's job to know who he was and Toria was a banker who'd spent a few years working on Wall Street – she probably knew his dad.

And Jay and I had agreed the night before that the only way it was going to work was for us to maintain absolute secrecy. If we didn't want my father or the paparazzi to know what we were up to, we basically couldn't tell a soul. As Doughnut liked to say: 'The only way to keep a secret is not to tell anyone.'

Luckily, I managed to jump back inside the door before Becca saw me and after that fright, we decided it was safer to leave from my house, where we could emerge discreetly at the end of the mews.

By the time we got into the park, I had forgotten the near miss and was just revelling in Jay's company on the beautiful spring afternoon. We lay down in the rough grass for a while, my head on his stomach, not even talking much, just happy and easy together.

As usual on a sunny Sunday, there were lots of families in the park, and I was rudely shaken from my reverie when a football hit me on the head, closely followed by the grinning toddler who had kicked it.

His parents rushed over to apologize, and I told them not to worry. He was a very cute little boy and I was reminded for a brief poignant flash of how sweet Marcus and Freddie and Toby had been at the same age. I tweaked his cheek and he giggled wildly.

'Do you want to have kids, Stella?' Jay asked me, after they'd gone.

'No,' I replied firmly. 'No way. No kids, no husband, no people mover, I don't want any of that.'

Jay was so surprised he sat up.

'Are you serious?'

I nodded. I was.

'You don't secretly hanker for the full happy-ever-after, orange-blossom scenario, like every other woman on earth?'

'I like orange blossom the way it's meant to be,' I said. 'Still on the tree. Preferably still in the ground, somewhere nice in the Mediterranean, with a cold glass of wine not far away.'

Jay smiled at me.

'You are a very singular girl,' he said.

'That's how I like to be,' I said. 'And that's how I want to remain – singular.'

'Sorry, I didn't mean to make a lame joke, I meant it the other way – unusual.'

'I know you did, but it fits me both ways. Most people don't believe me, but it's true.'

I paused for a moment. This was very personal stuff for me. I'd copped a lot of flak about it over the years, because no one believed me, and it had rather put me off talking about it. I normally just sidestepped those kinds of questions, but Jay's own family set-up was clearly so weird, I didn't mind telling him some of the dirty truths about mine.

'Do you want to know why I feel this way?' I said, eventually.

'I sure do.' He grinned at me, wickedly. 'I wish more women did, it would make life so much simpler. God, I hate that thing when you just know they're designing the towel monogram on the first date.'

I smiled to myself. All of my girlfriends were like that. A man just had to look at Becca and she was planning the Conran Shop wedding list. I'd seen just how quickly it put them off her too.

'Well,' I started. 'The reason I want to stay singular, is that since I was a little girl, I have watched women come and go through my father's life like they were rented on short leases. And I've seen what can happen to women who have been traded in, once they get past a certain age.'

I was thinking about Margot, of course, but there were others. Ham had worked his way through quite a few mistresses and girlfriends, as well as the actual wives. I'd seen some sad cases over the years. As far as I could tell, he wasn't joking when he said men were bastards.

'So,' I continued. 'I'd rather just be on my own right through than get used to playing happy houses and then suddenly be thrown out to survive by myself.

'I mean, I don't want to be alone all the time,' I added, I didn't want to put him off completely. 'I'm not a hermit, I want to have boyfriends, lovers, companions, whatever you want to call it, I just don't want it to be tied down and formal. I like things to stay fluid.'

'But what about kids,' said Jay, his eyes narrowing. 'You really don't have that urge? Isn't that inescapable biology for women?'

'Not for me,' I said, shaking my head. 'I'm surrounded by children, so I don't need to have any of my own, to get that kiddie hit. And, as I told you, there's another baby on the way in the family this year and before he or she is even grown up, my other siblings will start to produce the next generation of children, so I'm never going to go short of baby energy.'

Jay was looking a little sceptical.

'I mean it,' I said. 'I love my big-sister role – it's got all the advantages grandparents talk about. You have all the love and fun of kids, the cute drawings, the cuddles and the school nativity plays, but then you get to give them back. And you don't have to do the maths homework, either.'

He smiled at me, but I could still see a dubious look in his eyes.

'And, the other thing is,' I continued, 'as I've already told you – I'm really into my career. I love my job, I love newspapers and I don't want to give that up for kids.'

'Well, surely you don't have to, these days,' said Jay.

'No, of course you don't, lots of my female colleagues have kids, but I've studied the working mother thing close up with my stepmother Nicola – she's the previous wife, the mother of the two youngest boys – and it's not pretty. She nearly went bonkers trying to do all that juggling when they were small.

'Of course, she did have all the stepchildren to cope with as well, plus the large child who is my father – but for a while there I don't think she was a good publisher, or a good mother. So I think you have to make a choice: work or breed. I'm going to work.'

'Phew,' said Jay. 'That's pretty tough.' He got a cheeky look in his eye. 'But at least I don't have to worry about the towel monograms with you then . . .'

'I've already got monogrammed towels, Jay,' I said. '*My* initials – and I'm not changing them.'

'You're a one-off,' he said, starting to tickle me.

'Yeah, and I'm staying that way,' I said, pretending to fight him off and loving it.

After that we went for a long walk, right over to the Serpentine and back, and stopped to take a break on a bench near the statue of Peter Pan. As we sat there, Jay took his sunglasses off, so that he could get some sun in his eyes – the best cure for jet lag.

Suddenly, with no warning, he snatched away his arm, which had been round my shoulders, jumped up from the bench and started walking away. I was so surprised I jumped up too, but then an instinct told me to sit down again. I watched Jay out of the corner of my eye, as he strode off. After a few minutes, my phone rang. It was him.

'It's me,' he whispered. 'I just saw someone I know and I think they spotted me. Stay where you are for now. I'll call again in a minute. And keep your sunglasses on.'

I sat there for what seemed like ages, feeling rather lost. I kept checking my phone, but there was no sign of a missed call, or a text. Time continued to pass and I was just starting to wonder if I should head for home, when Jay appeared again, breathless.

'Oh boy,' he said. 'They did spot me and it was very hard to get out of chatting to them. I am so sorry. I just couldn't get away – they are really good friends of my best friends, if you see what I mean, so I couldn't just brush them off.'

'Did they see us?' I asked.

'I don't think so. Kelly asked me who I was sitting with and I just said, no one . . .'

He glanced away for a moment.

'I hated denying you like that, but it is the only way for now, isn't it?'

'Well, between my dad and the paparazzi, I think so.'

He shook his head. 'Sometimes, I think your dad might be right about me. Not worth the trouble.'

He sighed deeply, then he put his arm round me and gave me a squeeze.

'Come on, beautiful, let's go home.'

It was after four by the time we got back to my place and I was starting to get a bit nervous. Ham and Chloe and the rest of them would be back sometime that evening, but I didn't know exactly when, and it was making me edgy. I knew Ham wasn't going to burst into my house or anything, but it felt just too sneaky to hide Jay away in there, so close.

In the end I called them, ostensibly to see how the party had gone, and found out that they had decided not to come back until Monday morning, which was very handy for me.

Just the same, we didn't go up to the big house to make dinner that night, but sat in bed eating a chicken tikka I'd unearthed in the bottom of my freezer.

'There you go,' I said. 'Microwaved food's not so bad is it?'

'Not if you have a nice side salad to go with it,' said Jay, disappearing under the covers.

We spent the rest of the evening just lying there, flicking between channels and chatting. It was gorgeous. And amazingly, Jay liked to watch the same kind of things as me – mainly BBC World and the History Channel, although I did notice he lingered a little over the sports channels too.

'I've had an idea,' said Jay, after we'd watched a documentary about Mozambique. 'We should go away somewhere. Then we could have some time together without worrying about being seen. We can go somewhere nice and obscure where we can hang out without having to act like amateur spies.'

He turned to look at me. I smiled back at him, it was a lovely idea.

'Where shall we go?' I asked.

'Oh, I have a number of secret locations I like to go to, when I want to be left alone,' said Jay. 'I'll take you to one of those, it will be a surprise. Now, where did I put the phone? I'm going to book it.'

'When do you want to go?' I asked.

'Tomorrow?' said Jay, completely serious.

In that moment, the chasm really yawned between us.

I pulled a face, because I didn't know what to say.

'I have to go to work tomorrow,' I squeezed out eventually.

'Really?' said Jay, frowning. 'Do you have to?'

'Yes!' I said laughing. 'I told you yesterday, I've just had this big promotion, and I've got to get a whole new section together, plus I'm fighting a guerrilla war on my left flank. I can't go anywhere. I've never been so busy at work.'

Jay looked crestfallen, like a disappointed child.

'Can't you – what do you call it? – chuck a sickie?'

'No – I've just explained. I'm in the thick of it at the moment – and I love it anyway. I wouldn't chuck a sickie, even if I could.'

He slumped back against the pillows.

'Well, that's a pain in the ass. What am I going to do here while you're at work? I told those people I saw today I'm going back to New York tomorrow to get them off my back, so now I'll have to hide out in the apartment all day tomorrow, until you get let out of the factory, then we can stay in and have home delivery. Wowee, what a wild life the rich and pampered lead. I wonder what's on *Ricki Lake* tomorrow?'

We both laughed, but it wasn't a very scintillating scenario, put like that.

'Haven't you ever had a girlfriend with a job before?' I asked him.

'Sure I have,' he said. 'But not one they wouldn't pull a sickie on, to go away with me.'

He punched me playfully on the shoulder and I stuck my tongue out at him. I was on the verge of suggesting maybe he should get a job himself, so he would have something useful to do all day, but as he pulled me into his arms, I thought better of it.

The next morning, Jay was very sweet and understanding about sneaking off early. We agreed to speak during the day and to meet later at his place. Then I forced myself to go up and see Ham. I had to get it over with.

They'd just got back when I walked in and Chloe was like a human whirlwind, trying to get the boys ready for school, negotiating on the phone with Kristy about who was going to take responsibility for Archie, while Daisy clung to her legs.

I scooped the little girl up and Chloe beamed her thanks at me.

'Hello, crazy Daisy,' I said, kissing her on the nose. 'Did you enjoy the party?'

'I had cake,' she said, nodding. 'Two lots. It was nice. I like cake.'

'So do I,' I said in the same serious voice and nodding back.

'Shall I ask Mummy if you can have some?' she asked, her blue eyes wide. It was a big deal, cake.

'Oh, yes, please,' I said.

Freddie raced in and ran over to thank me for the tepee. 'It was brilliant,' he said.

'We had breakfast in it,' said Marcus.

'Daddy wore an Indian chief's hat,' added Freddie. 'It was really funny. Why weren't you there?'

Two innocent little faces looked up at me, squinting a little. So they had missed me.

'I had to work,' I said lamely. They looked suitably blank.

'You missed the best firework display ever,' said Freddie.

'And we had sausages for breakfast *and* tea,' said Marcus.

'I had about twenty-five,' said Freddie.

'I had forty-five . . .' said Marcus and they ran off in a babble of upwardly spiralling sausage claims.

Ham was up in his dressing room – he thought it was important to keep clothes, and particularly shoes, out of the bedroom – packing. He was heading off to an architectural conference in Rome, later that morning.

'Ah *ciao, bella. Che bella ragazza*,' he boomed, when he saw me. He couldn't really speak Italian, but he always said he felt Italian and got very excited when he was going there.

'Five days of marvellous food,' he was saying. 'I can't wait.' He paused, choosing between two of his favourite brightly coloured shirts. Ham wasn't one of those architects who wear grey shirts done up to the neck with no tie. In this instance, the gaudier of the two won. It was daffodil yellow. 'I'll miss all my ducklings, though.'

He looked up at me. 'Keep an eye on Chloe for me, would you, darling? I don't like leaving her this long when she's pregnant, but I committed to this event last year. I'm making the big speech.'

He cocked his panama hat at me, then rolled it up and chucked it into his bag. Then mashing down the lid – he still travelled with an ancient Globetrotter suitcase and thought bags on wheels were for wimps – he snapped it shut and left the room singing '*La Donna è Mobile*' very badly.

I was very grateful, at that moment, for Ham's tendency always to look forwards, rather than back.

14

Heavenly though my domestic bliss with Jay had been over the weekend, I was quite relieved to get back into the more familiar territory of the *Journal*.

I found the hum of newspaper offices immensely reassuring. The gentle tapping of keys, the constantly moving pools of chatter and murmuring voices, with the odd shouted phone call, bursts of hysterical laughter and occasional screaming matches, added up to an aural landscape that really felt like home to me.

I didn't get in until after ten that morning, which didn't give me much time to get ready for a meeting with Peter at ten thirty. He wanted to see how things were developing with the section.

I showed him what we'd pulled together so far and he made a lot of helpful suggestions, and then I decided it was time to tell him what had been going on with Jeanette.

He listened carefully to what I had to say, nodding sagely, with the tips of his fingers forming a little steeple over his mouth.

'So what should I do?' I asked him, when I'd finished the sorry tale.

'Nothing,' he said, in a particularly Yoda-ish voice. 'Just stay aware of what she is up to and defuse it gently when you can – exactly what you have been doing already in fact – and I'll do the same.'

He narrowed his wily old eyes and nodded slowly.

'It's very important that she thinks she's winning, you see, because that will be her downfall. The thing is, with people like her, who try to scheme and scam their way to the top, is that it gets them to a certain point, probably more quickly than simple hard work and talent would have done, but then it generally blows up in their face.

'It's a type who seem to be particularly attracted to news-papers for some reason – or maybe there are just loads of them everywhere. Anyway, you watch. The Lovely Jeanette is going to go up like a bag of penny rockets.'

He smiled at me with all the serenity of a Buddhist monk.

'I love fireworks, don't you?'

I always adored Peter's pronouncements, but it was hard to stick to his advice that afternoon, when I would have liked to have gone round to Jeanette's office with a chainsaw.

It all started when two carrier bags – one Prada, one Louis Vuitton – arrived in the loading dock, with my name on them. For some reason – and I strongly suspect it wasn't an accident – the post boy delivered them to her office and not to mine.

She produced them in the section editors' meeting.

'Oh, Stella,' she said, when it was just about over, but before anyone had actually left the room. 'These arrived for you.'

She held them up like Exhibit A, so that everyone in the room could see exactly what they were.

There were a few snarky 'Oooh' noises and one 'Pra-di-dah, darling . . .' from the editor of the food section.

'You must be very far ahead with your section, Stella,'

continued Jeanette, 'if you're already calling things in for shoots – and you're nowhere near launching yet.' She left a just long-enough pause. 'Or maybe these are just some more of your lovely gifts?'

I didn't know what they were. I hadn't called anything in from Prada or Louis Vuitton, so it was possible they could have been presents – or they could have been press releases in carrier bags, which luxury brands did sometimes, to make sure you looked at them.

But whatever they were, it seemed very unlikely to get two on the same day – and as I really didn't know, I couldn't defend myself.

She handed them to me – one at a time, for added effect – with a plastic smile of Julie Andrews brilliance and then turned away again immediately, leaving me alone holding the 'evidence' in a room full of highly cynical and competitive section editors.

'Go on, then,' said the food editor. 'Open them. I want to see what they are.'

Every head in the room swivelled back to look at me.

'I wasn't expecting anything,' I said, too flustered to think. 'I'll open them later. I need to get on.'

Then I fled from the room.

When I got back to my office and did open those carrier bags, I wasn't sure whether to be deeply relieved or furious that I hadn't opened them in front of my colleagues.

In the Prada bag there was a pair of their latest cult sunglasses; the huge black TV-screen shades every fashion editor in London was gagging for. The Louis Vuitton one contained a fabulous logo baseball cap. And they were both presents – from Jay.

Although I wasn't sure how I was going to ask him not to send me any more designer presents to the office, I rang immediately to thank him.

'Well, if you're going to sneak around with me,' he said, 'I thought you should do it in style. And talking of sneaking around, I've had an idea for something fun we can do later. I really don't feel like staying in another night, do you?'

He wouldn't tell me any more – it was becoming clear to me that Jay loved springing surprises on people – and we just agreed that I would go round to his place as soon as I could get away from work.

I found Jay at home in his workout gear. He had a running machine set up in front of the TV and Led Zeppelin blaring out of the sound system.

'I'm a celebrity, get me out of here!' he shouted, as he opened the door to me. 'I'm going nuts stuck inside.'

'Have you been in all day?' I asked.

'Yep. Too many people I know live round here. If I stepped outside too freely, it would be all over. I did manage to put some gasoline in the car this afternoon – in Kilburn; they know me at all the gas stations round here too – but that was it for today's fun.'

'So what's your plan for tonight, then?'

'We're going to go over to see my pals, George and Zaria. They are great people, you're going to love them and I really want them to meet you.'

I must have looked as surprised as I felt, because he put his arms round me and continued.

'I know we agreed to tell no one, but I really can trust them one hundred per cent not to tell anyone about us,

240

OK? George is my oldest and closest friend and he has, er, similar issues to me. He gets it. Our secret will be safe with them. Fort Knox safe. Trust me.'

I pulled away from him.

'Jay,' I said. 'You are seriously whiffy. You must have been pounding that running machine.'

He sniffed his armpit and grinned.

'You're right. I need to take a shower badly.' He grabbed my hand. 'And you can come in with me . . .'

With my new sunglasses and baseball cap in place, Jay told me to leave first and wait for him on the corner and he would pick me up in the car shortly.

I did as I was told and looked out for the black Ferrari. I felt really stupid standing there in my cap and dark glasses, and when a vintage-looking car in a light brown metallic colour pulled up, I thought I was being kerb crawled. Then the passenger window went down and I saw Jay grinning at me.

'Want a ride, pretty lady?' he said.

'I was looking for the Ferrari,' I said, climbing in.

'Oh, I took that back,' he said. 'It wasn't really my thing. Too obvious. I only had it for a test drive. I prefer old cars.'

'What's this one?' I asked him.

'It's an Aston. You know, Aston Martin? It's a DB6 Mark 2. It's my favourite car. Do you like it?'

I nodded, it was ringing a bell with me.

'Isn't this what James Bond drove?' I said. I only knew that because Ham was obsessed with these cars. He had a Dinky toy of one of them in his office.

'Close, Moneypenny. Although that was actually the

DB5. But watch out anyway. You're in the ejector seat.'

George and Zaria, whoever they were, lived in Kensington Palace Gardens. It's a private road right on the edge of the park – so private, in fact, that you have to get a security guard to let you through the barrier.

It was clear they were expecting us, though, because the barrier shot up as soon as Jay gave his name. They waved 'Mr Pêcheur' right through.

Although I had lived within walking distance of it all my life, I'd never actually been along that road before. It was too forbidding even to stroll down, but I knew about it. Everyone in London knew about it. Especially since one of the houses had gone on the market for £85 million, a few years before.

I had thought it was pretty much all embassies, but Jay drove up to the Bayswater Road end, where there was a sleek, modern seventies apartment block overlooking the park.

'OK,' he said, as we pulled up. 'Like I said, George is my best friend since school days. We kind of grew up together. He married Zaria a couple of years ago. She's an old friend of mine as well – I introduced them actually. No kids yet. They're both great people. Just be yourself and they will love you too.'

He squeezed my hand reassuringly. I didn't quite understand why he seemed to be briefing me about his friends, but I liked it anytime Jay used the word 'love' in relation to me, especially with 'too' nearby.

'Great,' I said, squeezing his hand back.

It wasn't until he pushed the buzzer that I understood why he had prepped me that way. The label next to the button Jay had just pressed read: G and Z Xydis. Now that was a surname even I recognized.

They were one of the great Greek shipping families. There was Onassis, Niarchos and Xydis. And I knew who Zaria was too. She was one of the famous Taylor sisters.

There were four of them, from a majorly moneyed American family – shopping malls or something, and relatively recent, but that didn't matter in America – they were all preposterously beautiful and they had all married spectacularly well. I'd seen the Xydis wedding in *Hello!* at the hairdresser's. I remembered marvelling at her monogram.

It didn't make any rational sense, but now I knew who they were, I couldn't help feeling a little nervous. For the first time I began to understand the odd way people reacted to Jay, when they knew who he was at first meeting and, at that moment, I was very glad he was still holding my hand tightly.

'The Xydis residence,' said a strongly accented woman's voice over the intercom.

'It's Jay Fisher,' said Jay.

'Please come up, Mr Fisher,' said the voice. I knew it wasn't Zaria.

When the lift doors opened, we were met by a tiny little woman in a full-on maid's uniform. The white apron and everything.

'Hi, Flo,' said Jay.

'Good evening, Mr Fisher,' she said. 'Mr and Mrs Xydis are expecting you.'

She turned to me.

'May I take your coat, miss?' she asked.

I handed her my jacket, wondering if she'd notice the Warehouse label.

'Please go through,' said Flo. 'Mr and Mrs Xydis are in the drawing room.'

Jay clearly knew his way around and headed off to the right, still holding my hand. I wished he would slow down a bit, so I could take in the decor. It was seriously fabulous – a perfectly balanced mix of mid-century classics, and more recent signature pieces – set against a sleek background of polished and textured surfaces, topped off with a quirky combination of modern art and tribal artefacts.

It was beautiful, but one of Ham's expressions did run through my mind: decorator salad. It was clear Zaria hadn't chosen the rugs herself.

We had just reached a large set of double doors, when they flew open to reveal a deeply suntanned man with very black hair. He was even browner than Jay, with even whiter teeth.

'Jay, my main man,' he said, in an accent as mixed-up as Jay's, although his definitely had a twang of something exotic there. Greek, presumably. They embraced heartily.

'I'm so glad you were in town,' said Jay. 'It's great to see you and . . .' He turned to me. 'I really want you to meet Stella. Stella, this is Georgiou Xydis; George, this is Stella Montecourt-Fain.'

'Stella, great to meet you,' said George, or Georgiou – I wasn't sure any more – shaking my hand and giving me a kiss on both cheeks. 'Jay has told me all about you. He was a bit blue about you for a while back there . . .'

He smiled at me. I liked him immediately, whatever his name was. He had a naturally friendly face. He was nothing like as good-looking as Jay, in fact he was a bit on the short and chubby side, but he was so warm, you just felt comfortable with him right away.

Jay punched him playfully on the bicep.

'Hey, Georgie boy, that's enough of that – don't give away all my secrets now. Where's Zaria?'

'Oh, she's here somewhere ... Zee Zee? Honey?' he called out.

He led us into the next room and then into the one after that, and the one after that – it was clear the apartment covered the entire top floor of the building – but still there was no sign of 'Zee Zee'.

'Now where is that wife of mine ...?' George was saying, as we passed through a couple more reception rooms. 'She was right here a minute ago. Ah, there she is.'

And there she certainly was, standing outside on a vast terrace, her golden skin perfectly lit by the last of the evening sun, the gentle breeze just disturbing the strands of her long blonde hair, the curves of her slim silhouette outlined against the sheet of water that was falling down the wall behind her.

Now, I'm no Teletubby, but I took one look at Zaria Xydis and felt as dumpy as a Shetland pony – and about as well dressed. She was wearing a slip of a frock, which I happened to know was by Alberta Ferretti, and suddenly my white Earl jeans, wittily paired with a flimsy top from New Look, didn't feel nearly as chic as they had when I left home.

My girlfriends were always complimenting me on my knack for finding great bits and pieces in chain stores and mixing them with designer gear, but looking at Zaria, I felt as cheap as my top. I was so glad I had a great pair of Prada heels on. New season, too.

'Jay, darling,' she said, coming towards us, a beatific smile on her face. 'We're so excited you're here. We haven't caught up for so long, it's crazy.'

There was a big hug and lots of smacking kisses, until Jay extracted himself and put his arm out to bring me into the aura of golden glow that seemed to surround Zaria.

'Zee, this is Stella – you know, the girl I was telling you about?'

'Hi, Stella,' said Zaria, putting out her hand to shake mine and while Jay looked happily on, she smiled sweetly at me. 'Great to meet you.'

But as George distracted Jay, to come into another room to see some photograph he'd just bought, Zaria's friendly smile went out like a light and she looked me full in the face, eye to eye for a few distinct beats. It was a very significant look and it clearly said: And who the hell are you?

I felt distinctly uncomfortable.

'Come and sit down,' Zaria – or Zee – said eventually. 'Flo will bring us some drinks. Champagne?'

I nodded. 'That would be lovely.'

But when the drinks arrived Flo handed Zee a long glass of mineral water, with a twist of lime.

I also noticed that when she took the canapés around, she never offered them to Zee, which made it even harder for me to say no, even though I didn't particularly feel like a slab of foie gras the size of a paperback book at that particular moment.

'So, where did you meet Jay?' she asked me, without any warmth, after Flo had gone to take flutes of champagne through to the 'boys', as Zaria called them.

'At the Cap Mimosa,' I said. 'We were both there for the

Jericho jewellery launch and a mutual friend introduced us.'

'Oh, that's right,' said Zaria, in unashamedly icy tones. 'You're a *journalist*, aren't you?'

'Yes,' I said as brightly as I could, although the way she had said it, the name of my profession might more normally be used for the words 'crack dealer'.

'Who do you hack for?' she asked.

'I'm a senior writer on the *Daily Journal*,' I said, just managing to keep the edge out of my voice. 'I write about luxury brands – the designers, the artisans, the hot trends and the history, right through to the business side of things.'

She remained stony-faced. Clearly my description of my job – which was subtitled: Look, bitch, I don't do gossip bullshit, so back off – hadn't done anything to impress her.

'Do you know the paper?' I asked eventually, out of desperation.

'Oh, I don't know,' she said, shrugging. 'George gets all the papers, they're all the same to me. I only read the *Times* really. The *New York Times* . . .'

There was another long pause. What was I supposed to say? So, what do you do, Zaria? Apart from having your nails painted and paying someone to redecorate the odd island? They'd been given an island, I remembered, as a wedding present, from one of their fathers. I couldn't recall which one.

Really, there was nothing for me to say to her. If there was sometimes a chasm between me and Jay, there was a black hole between me and Zaria. And she clearly wasn't planning on building any bridges across it.

I was just starting to feel seriously can-I-go-home-now-please uncomfortable, when Zaria crossed her legs. It was the first time I'd noticed her shoes. They were exactly the same as mine.

'Nice shoes, Zaria,' I said brightly, raising my own foot in the air and waving it around so she couldn't miss it. They were even the same colour. What the hell, I thought, I had nothing to lose with her. This might be the only thing we ever had in common.

Zaria looked at my foot and an expression of horror came over her face.

'Oh!' was the best she could come out with, she was so clearly taken off guard. Then her features tightened up again. 'Did Jay buy those for you?'

I laughed.

'No, he did not. I bought them for myself. In Milan. I love these shoes, aren't they great?'

That was it. I wasn't going to take any more of that ice-maiden shit from her, I didn't care if she was Jay's best friend, she was being a bitch to me and I wasn't going to play her game.

'Look at this, guys,' I said, when he and George came back into the room. 'Zaria and I have the same shoes on, isn't that hilarious?'

'That is so funny,' said Jay, looking delighted. 'I knew you two would get along.'

Zaria, who had clearly missed her vocation in Hollywood, was suddenly all delighted beams.

'Isn't it so cute, George?' she said. 'You'll have to take our picture, with our shoe cousins on, eh, Stella?'

'I can't wait,' I said gaily. 'Shame we can't breed 'em, eh?'

Flo came round with some even fattier hors d'oeuvres, once more bypassing Ms Lemon Rind and heading straight for me. I declined, without a pang of embarrassment and asked her loudly if I could have a glass of mineral water – with a lime twist.

'Don't you like Cristal, Stella?' said George, sounding sincerely concerned, and clearly willing to crack open the Krug, or the Dom, or whatever would make me happy.

'Oh no, I love it,' I said. 'It's just I'm a little thirsty and I don't want to swig it down like lemonade. I want to savour it.'

Zaria was looking at me with narrowed eyes. She knew I was giving her the finger. I didn't care. I smiled brightly at her and waggled my foot. I really didn't give a shit any more. It was one of the great advantages of not being fixated on marrying the man you were sleeping with, I thought. You didn't care if his best friends hated you.

Flo came in again and spoke to Zaria.

'The dinner is ready, madame,' she said. 'Would you like me to serve it?'

'Oh no, that's fine, Flo,' said Zaria. 'You go home now. We'll see you tomorrow. And thank you so much.'

Well, I thought, at least she was nice to the help.

Things were much easier over dinner, mainly because the two boys were there all the time and, unlike his poisonous wife, there clearly wasn't a malicious or snobby bone in George's chubby body. He really was a lovely chap – and I thought it reflected very well on Jay that they'd been friends for so long.

'So, tell me again,' he was saying, 'why is it you two are hiding out like a couple of bank robbers?'

I glanced at Jay. I didn't know how much he would have

told George. Did he know it was partly because my father had made it all into a ridiculous Montague and Capulet situation?

Jay looked back at me and raised an eyebrow. I got the message. Leave it to me, he was saying.

'Well,' he said. 'It was the usual gutter-press shit. Stella and I met in the South of France, when we were both at that Jericho jewellery thing and we went out dancing – we went to that club Wonderland. Have you two been there yet? It's nuts.

'Anyway, somehow the paparazzi creeps found out we were there and because I'd been seen having a drink – and believe me, nothing more than that, I value my balls – with Jericho in Aspen just a whiles before, they sold the pictures to an English rag and then, because of who Stella's dad is, they blew it up into a big story and after it came out, poor Stella got seriously hassled by the paps back at home.

'And, of course, her dad wasn't too happy about that, which is understandable, so we have to play it cool for a while.'

Nice work, I thought, making it sound like I was the one the paparazzi were after, and I was gratified to see Zaria's head flip round towards me just at the moment Jay mentioned my dad. That was logged, I thought. Good.

'So you don't want to risk being seen together again in case you get more paparazzi hassle?' said George. 'We went through all that, didn't we, Zee baby, when we first started dating?'

She nodded.

'But now we're just boring old married farts, they leave us alone,' he continued, laughing heartily. 'Which is a great relief. Did they stake out your home and everything?' he asked me.

'Yes,' I said. 'It's really scary when you're not used to it. Of course, I'm a journalist myself ...' I glanced at Zaria. 'But the paper I work for doesn't do that kind of thing. It was quite a shock.'

'Oh, that's right,' said George, getting enthusiastic. 'You work for the *Journal*, Jay told me. Now that is a seriously great newspaper ...'

He was clearly about to ask me more about the paper, when Zaria cut in.

'Why don't you just go to New York for a while?' she said, like it was the most obvious thing. 'You won't get hassled there.'

She glanced at me, with narrowed eyes the 'boys' couldn't see – a nobody like you won't get hassled there, was what she meant, of course.

'You tell her, Stella,' said Jay, smiling at me mischievously. 'You tell Zaria why we can't go away, like I want to.'

I stuck my tongue out at him.

'I work,' I said loudly, to the whole table. 'I have a job. A job I love and that I'm very committed to. I've just been promoted and I can't take any time off right now.'

'Well, good for you,' said George. 'That's great.' He looked a bit pensive for a moment. 'You're really lucky, you know, having a job you love, something you really want to do.'

'I know,' I said, deliberately misinterpreting him. 'I tell myself that every day – I could be stacking shelves in a supermarket, or working on a chicken-plucking line, and instead I work on one of the world's great newspapers. I feel very privileged.'

Take that, Lamebrain, I thought, but she was already on to something else.

'So who is your father?' she asked me directly.

'Oh, yes,' said George, beaming again. 'Jay told me about him. Stella's dad is the guy who did the museum for the Fishers, you know, Zee . . .'

'The Fisher Institute in Boston?' said Zaria, her eyebrows almost meeting her immaculately highlighted hairline. 'Wasn't that Lord Montecourt . . . ?'

'Yes,' I said, smiling cheerfully at her. 'That's Daddy.'

'Stella's dad is *so* amazing,' said Jay. 'You should see their country place, it is a seriously radical take on the family home . . .'

And he went into a long and loving description of Willow Barn, and then the London house, while Zaria appeared to thaw before me, like a time-release film of a glacier melting.

By the end of the meal, she was practically sitting on my lap.

'We would love to meet with your father,' she was gushing. Her habit of talking in the royal 'we' was seriously starting to irritate me. 'And we would love to see Willow Barn. We have a property on Long Island where we are going to build our beach house and your father is one of the architects we are thinking of commissioning for the project.'

Take a ticket, join the queue, I thought, Ham's time was booked up for years. And the likelihood of me ever introducing him to Jay's best friends looked very slim indeed.

'So how did you like them?' Jay asked, beaming happily at me, in the car on the way back to his place. He had clearly had a great time.

'George is lovely,' I said.

Jay's head snapped round to look at me.

'Was Zee a bitch to you?' he said.

'Somewhat,' I said. 'Until she found out I had a famous father. With a title . . .'

'Oh, shit,' said Jay. 'I'm sorry about that. I really hoped she wouldn't do that to you. The thing is, Stells, Zee is a little overprotective of me. She's seen me in the clutches of too many miners . . .'

'Minors?' I said, horrified.

'Diggers? Miners for precious metal . . .'

'Oh, I see,' I said. 'Zaria thought I was a gold-digger, mining for the Fisher billions. How hilarious.'

'Yeah, well, coming from money herself, she knows just how many users there are out there. Plus, she and I used to date, back in the day – don't worry, way back – and I guess she feels she has some kind of extra proprietary role with regard to my romantic life. And then, I'm George's best friend and so she's just a little possessive. I did ask George to tell her to behave towards you, but I'm afraid he's blind to his wife's little personality defects.'

'He seems like a really lovely guy,' I said, sincerely, and glad to shift the focus off beastly Zaria.

'You know what? He really is. And he hasn't had the easiest time, with his mom dying when he was so young . . .'

As he spoke, that sad story came back to me – his mother had killed herself, when he was a young boy. It was one of those classic jet-set tragedies and there had been a huge piece about it in *Vanity Fair* not long ago. It was twenty-five years since it happened, or something.

It was a perfect story for that magazine – the beautiful

French showgirl from a humble background who had married the Greek billionaire and then couldn't cope. Well, he clearly hadn't inherited his mother's height, I thought, but he must have got his charm from her, because his father was a famous tyrant.

Jay was still talking. I tuned back in.

'So, after his mom died, he spent most of his school holidays with me at my mom's place – he doesn't really get along with his dad, something we have in common – so we're pretty close. He's like another brother to me really. Anyway, I'm real glad you two hit it off and I'm sure you and Zaria will get along fine. She just needs to get to know you better. Give her another chance, would you? For me?'

He squeezed my hand. I lifted it up to my mouth and kissed it tenderly. But I couldn't help thinking, as we drove on, that Zaria was exactly the kind of product of inherited wealth my father had warned me about. And although I liked him enormously, so was poor motherless George.

Despite the difficulties of our self-imposed purdah, Jay and I continued to spend every night together. Most evenings, I'd have some kind of event to go to for work, so I'd speed in and out of that and then get over to Sloane Avenue, as fast as I could, for yet another night in.

Apart from George and Zaria, he still wasn't in town as far as his friends were concerned, and I was seriously paranoid about word getting back to Ham via the paparazzi if we were seen, so we sneaked about, getting food sent up from local restaurants. And he always paid for it with cash.

Now I understood why he always carried wads of

banknotes and never paid for anything with credit cards, if he could avoid it – a black Amex card emblazoned with the name J Fisher was the equivalent of a neon sign over his head.

For someone who had always dreaded the cosy sofa supper, I sure was having a lot of them.

During the day, I would go to work and he would hang out with George, mainly playing tennis at obscure suburban courts where no one would know who they were.

When the weekend came around George insisted we borrowed a really pretty cottage on the Xydis family estate in Berkshire. It was gorgeous.

Total isolation – just the two of us – country walks, cooking, napping and just hanging out. We even risked a trip round the local Spring Flower and Produce Show together, which really took me to a new level of cosy coupledom. And no one recognized Jay among the displays of giant gladioli.

And then, at last, after ten days of our oddly proscribed bliss, the moment I had been dreading arrived. We were lying in the bath together on the Monday night – one at each end, having races with wind-up bath toys – when he brought it up.

'I'm sorry, Stella, but I can't stay over here much longer,' he said, abruptly.

'Is the solitary confinement getting to you?' I asked him.

'Yep,' he said. 'It *is* a huge pain – although it's worth it for you . . .' He made a small turtle walk up my thigh. 'But even apart from that, I have to go back to the States.'

He sighed deeply and put his head right back, leaning it against the edge of the bath, running his hands through his wet hair. Something about his exposed throat made my heart turn over with lust and admiration and tenderness, that brand-new mixture of feelings I had whenever I looked at Jay.

'It's the anniversary of my brother's death next week,' he continued, lifting his head and looking back at me again, causing another minor earthquake in my abdomen. 'And it's always a really hard time for my mom, so I usually go and stay with her for a while and we go on hikes and cook and do all the stuff we do and I help her through it.'

I smiled sadly at him.

'You're a good son,' I said.

Jay laughed, bitterly. 'Oh, boy. I don't hear that very often. From her, yes, but from the rest of them – I'm just a useless piece of shit.'

He crashed the turtle down into the water so hard it made a huge splash. Then he shuddered, quite violently, as if trying to shake the association off.

'I'm sorry, babe, but just thinking about my dad makes me angry.'

'What's his problem?' I asked gently, wary of going over the line.

'Oh, I'm the problem – not serious, not interested in the trusts, not properly respectful of what the name Fisher stands for. "A playboy not a player", that's his latest one. God, sometimes I understand why my uncle Michael drinks. Do you know what having dinner with my dad is like?'

I shook my head.

'You can be in the most beautiful restaurant in the world – beautiful decor, beautiful people, beautiful food – and it is like having a twenty-ton weight on your head. He just crushes any energy out of you with the sheer pressure of his disapproval. No one is good enough for him – me least of all.'

I didn't know what to say. Jay was pretty perfect as far as I was concerned.

'Why do you think he is so down on you?'

Jay shrugged.

'He always has been. My older brother was the golden boy – I mean, I loved my brother, but he did have a lot more in common with Dad than me. I don't know if it was because he always knew he was the heir from the day he was born, whereas I knew I could just cruise it – or thought I could – but really, I think it was just genetics.

'Bob was more like my dad and I'm more like my mom, and I don't know why they ever got married, so Dad and I are just plain incompatible like they were.'

He picked up a small plastic whale, threw it high up into the air and caught it.

'I wish I could divorce him too.'

The next day, Jay left London for New Mexico and I minded even more than I had expected to. Spending every night at his place had been a bit distracting when I was so busy at work – especially as he used to ring me there all the time and send me filthy emails – but now he was leaving, I felt quite desperate. And it seemed he did too.

Calling from the departure lounge at Heathrow on Tuesday afternoon, he had almost begged me to come out to New York to be with him, as soon as he got back from seeing his mother in Santa Fe, and I had to tell him I just couldn't.

But I promised I would take a holiday the moment it was

possible and he promised to come back to London as soon as he possibly could. Neither of which seemed nearly soon enough.

When we hung up I realized I was crying.

15

While I missed Jay enormously once he was gone, there was another part of me that was quite glad to get back to my funny old singular life – and to spend some time with my family. It was very unusual for me to see so little of them.

It had been a happy accident that Ham had been away for five of the days while I had been with Jay, but once he was back, I knew I would have to make myself a bit more visible at his place, or arouse suspicions. And apart from that – I really wanted to see him and the rest of them.

So the day Jay left, I rang Chloe and asked if it was all right for me to come up for supper that night. She seemed surprised I'd even asked, and said they would love to see me.

The sincere enthusiasm in her voice triggered multiple twinges of guilt that I hadn't been looking after her, as Ham had specifically asked me to while he was away, so I just added that to the big pile of guilt that was already in my head and got back to work.

That evening I made sure I got up to Ham's place before seven thirty, so I could put Daisy to bed. It was one less thing for Chloe to do – but it was also one of the great pleasures of my life, and I'd missed it.

Daisy was gratifyingly excited to see me.

'Stella, Stella,' she said, holding her little arms up to me to be picked up, in a gesture I adored and dreaded her growing out of. 'Will you put me to bed? Will you tell me a story? Will you tell me the one about you and Alex and the tree house and the whispery leaves?'

Daisy had loads of books, but the stories she really loved were the ones I told her about her older half- and step-siblings and the high jinks we had got up to when we were kids at Willow Barn.

I gave her a bath and then once she was tucked up in her pink pyjamas in her boat-shaped bed, I squeezed in next to her, so close our faces were practically touching, and told her the story she'd asked for.

'Once upon a time, a very long time ago, before you were even born,' I began – it was the ritualistic start to all her bedtime stories. She snuggled up to me contentedly and put her little arm around my shoulder. 'There was a little girl called Stella . . .'

'That was you, wasn't it?' said Daisy, nodding. 'You were a little girl then and Alex was a little boy.'

I nodded back and then went on to tell her the story, which was a fictionalized account of a true event.

It was the end of our first summer holidays together. Alex had been fourteen and I was eight – and already start-ing to develop my crush on him, although I left that aspect of it out when I was telling it to Daisy – and one night he declared he was going to sleep in the tree house, which Ham had just built.

Alex's younger brother, Rowan – who was ten – had insisted on joining him, but came back to the house after about half an hour, because he had 'heard something rustling'.

Despite such dangers, in the middle of the moonless night, I went out on my own to join Alex. But with carrying my duvet and a teddy, I dropped my torch, and got completely, terrifyingly disorientated in the dark orchard, until he heard my desperate cries and came out to find me.

It wasn't funny at the time – I had been absolutely petrified – but it had passed into family legend. The gallant Alex had taken me to the tree house, where I had insisted I still wanted to sleep, and had given me the last of the cocoa from his Thermos. And his last Jaffa Cake.

About half an hour later, by which time I was in a state of teeth-chattering terror at all the whispers and rustles of the country night, he had accompanied me back to the house.

I had thought him the biggest hero – although, of course, the adult me understood I had actually given Alex the excuse he needed to come back and sleep inside too – a humorous point I made much of, when I told the story to Daisy.

By the time I finished telling it to her that night, she was fast asleep and I carefully edged my way out of the bed, so as not to wake her, then bent down to kiss her precious blonde head, before I went back downstairs.

Telling that story brought back a lot of happy memories about those early days at Willow Barn. Embarrassment and shame about my debilitating pash on Alex generally made me remember the painful times more than the good ones, but when I looked back more rationally, mostly it had been very happy there, and he had been a kind and gracious stepbrother.

I really ought to make more of an effort to stay in touch with him, I thought to myself, as I went back down the stairs. Those shared memories were very precious and we'd had a really good laugh the last time we'd seen each other, at Ham's cheese fondue, as Alex had dubbed that cringe-making family dinner. Plus, I thought, I might be able to set him up with one of my legion of unhappily single gal pals.

But most of all because being proper friends with one of my ex-steps – especially one who was a bridge to two of my younger half-siblings – was one thing I could do to make Ham happy. At a time when I was doing so much that would make him very unhappy, if only he knew about it.

My beloved dad was home when I got back downstairs and I was treated to a full Hamburger, with relish and large fries, as I called his over-the-top bear hugs.

He was still full of his trip to Italy and had brought me back a beautiful Fornasetti teacup and saucer, as a present.

'There you are *cara mia*,' he said. 'I bought Chloe a splen-did *mezzaluna*, but I thought this was more suitable for your idea of cooking.'

Dinner was great. Apart from the sleeping Daisy, Venezia and Archie were the only kids in residence – the four younger ones were with their respective mothers – and the terrible teens were both unusually civilized, probably because Ham allowed them both to have a little wine and they felt they were being treated as adults.

I was surprised to see Archie there in the middle of the week and while Ham and I were out in the garden admir-ing the borders together, I took the opportunity to ask him about it.

He glanced back towards the kitchen and spoke amaz-ingly discreetly for him.

'He's living with us full-time at the moment,' he said, rais-ing and dropping his eyebrows in a significant way.

'Had it just got too awful with Kristy and Gerald?'

'Yes,' said Ham. 'He turned up here on his bike late one night last week – in tears, poor little sod – and I've told him he can stay as long as he likes. Venezia seems to deal with that terrible man better, but then she's a tough little cookie, isn't she? Just like her mother.'

'Doesn't Kristy mind Archie being here?' I asked him.

Ham snorted.

'Are you kidding? She's delighted. One less child to look after.'

'Knowing her, she'll probably expect you to start paying his school fees too.'

He grinned at me sheepishly.

'I already am,' he said.

Archie was clearly delighted to be living with Ham and appeared to be making a huge effort not to fight with Venezia, however much she goaded him. He also kept springing up from the table to help Chloe, without ever having to be asked. Apart from my own efforts, it was the only proper help I'd ever seen her get.

Being released from the stress of living with his latest and loathed stepfather had also allowed Archie's true personality to shine through again and he was highly amusing over dinner. As he entertained us with impersonations of his poor beleaguered physics teacher and foul classmates, which made Ham roar with laughter, I was relieved to have the attention diverted away from me.

Ham did ask me some dutifully interested questions about how things were progressing at work, but I didn't feel I was under the searchlight of one of his major interrogations. Plus, he wanted to go on at length about his trip to Italy and was still prone to bursting into Verdi without warning.

Mainly, though, the conversation was about the family in general, as they brought me up to date with the latest goings-on among the junior members, particularly Toby, who had been looking after a friend's pet rat one weekend, when they had stayed up in town, and had promptly lost it in the garden.

'Poor Tobes,' Chloe was saying. 'He had this terribly worried look on his face, but he wouldn't tell me what the matter was. Then after a couple of hours with him on his hands and knees in the garden, but still not saying what had happened, Alex suddenly turned up. Toby had rung him secretly to come over to help him find it – Scabbers, its name was. They didn't, but they sourced a very good doppelgänger at a pet shop.'

'How is Alex?' I asked her.

'He just rang, actually,' said Chloe. 'While you were putting Daisy to bed. He's coming down to Willow Barn this weekend, with Rose. Henry wants some advice on planting.'

Alex's mother, Rose, was an accomplished landscape architect and plantswoman. It was how she and Ham had met and they still worked together sometimes on schemes for his domestic projects around the world. It had been an amazingly amicable divorce, that one – especially considering the circumstances with Kristy and Venezia. I had always suspected that Rose, with twins to cope with, was secretly relieved to get Ham off her hands.

'Yes, I want to rethink the lower garden entirely,' said Ham, getting a particular gleam in his eye, which meant *grands projets* were afoot. 'I went to see the Villa Orsini garden again while I was in Italy and it's given me some ideas . . .'

'Isn't that the one with all the huge terrifying giants?' I asked him.

He nodded, smiling wickedly.

'Yes, it's the one that gave me the idea for the grotto originally. Rose is going to advise me. You should come down, senior duckling.'

He looked at me a bit beadily, but nothing too obvious.

'I'd love to,' I said, in all honesty. 'It would be lovely to see Rose. I haven't seen her for ages.'

I was just going to make damn sure I wasn't sleeping in the guest wing this time.

Although I was relieved not to have to lie to my father on a daily basis, as the days passed I found I was missing Jay more and more. And what I hadn't been prepared for was that I would miss him even when I was home alone.

Suddenly my secret little nest, which had always been my sanctuary away from the world, didn't offer the instant comfort it had always delivered before.

Every time I walked into my bedroom I could see Jay lying in my bed, his brown chest magnificent above the white sheets, his arms behind his head, the sun pouring down on to him through the skylight. I could see him in my kitchen, making coffee, with just a towel around his waist; and his marvellous rear view through the steam in my bathroom, as he stood in my bath under the shower.

Every time I put music on I would remember him going through my CDs – and my bookshelves – and shouting out with delight every time he came across one of his own favourites, which happened frequently in both cases.

It was almost like having a ghost in the place and it

confirmed why I had never allowed a lover in there before. I'd allowed him to breach my fortress and it would never be the same haven again.

So, feeling like that at home and still rather on guard at my dad's place, in case something slipped out, the office began to feel like my only refuge, which was ironic, considering how the pressure was building in there.

With Jeanette's smear campaign still in full flow – my various spies were keeping me informed – I had until the end of that week to prepare the final presentation of the new section, to show to Doughnut and the advertising executives. The boardroom was booked for Friday morning.

In the days leading up to it Ned and I started early and worked late every night, in between the increasing number of events we had to attend. It was a busy time in the luxury world, with a final flurry of boutique and product launches to be fitted in before the start of the summer social season, and before August, when that whole world came to a dead halt – or at least transplanted itself to Sardinia, the Amalfi Coast, Croatia, or wherever was the hot destination that year.

It was much more fun going to things with Ned in tow, but eventually I accepted that we would have to split the party load, and with some trepidation I sent him off on his own to a black-tie dinner at Asprey, wearing his normal terrible work suit, a creased old shirt – and his favourite pair of pink Converse All Stars.

As it turned out he actually made quite a splash at that dinner. The PR was Tara Ryman, and she rang me the next morning to tell me about it.

'Jade was very taken with that new chap you have working with you. The Aussie guy,' she said. 'She especially asked for him to be moved next to her after the main course . . . Is he single, by the way?'

And so, it turned out, after all my years in the luxury world, I had something to learn from Ned – which was that even in that rarefied little enclave, with all its complicated little codes and signifiers, you could actually get ahead by breaking the rules, if you had enough confidence. And Ned had plenty of that.

'So how did you like Jade Jagger?' I asked him the next morning, after he had arrived in my office with the two large coffees which were his customary order from the staff canteen.

He looked mystified.

'The woman you had pudding with last night?' I prompted. 'Tiny, beautiful, long hair, designs the jewellery . . . ?'

'Is that who she was?' he said, a grin splitting his face.

'Don't tell me you didn't know . . .' I replied, incredulous.

'Didn't have a clue,' he laughed merrily. 'I called her Jane all night.'

He didn't seem to be joking and it made me feel slightly better about not having a clue who Jay was when I'd met him.

'She's a nice girl, anyway,' Ned was saying, as I smiled to myself. 'Sexy little thing. I got her number, actually . . .'

He grinned at me, shamelessly. I thought he was probably kidding about that bit, but I wasn't sure – Ned was incorrigible when it came to women, but I didn't mind. I found it amusing. I suppose he reminded me of my father in that regard.

The more I got to know Ned generally, the more I liked him and increasingly, I found I was looking on him as a friend, not just a colleague. We'd had a lot of fun putting the dummy together, and the pressure-cooker atmosphere that had been building up towards giving the presentation that Friday, had made us get quite close very quickly.

I had let him in on what was going on with Jeanette and he'd proved to be as good an office detective as Peter. While Peter always knew what was going on 'upstairs' in Doughnut's inner chambers, and the executive levels above that, Ned's efforts were concentrated with the clerical staff.

As far as I could tell, every PA and editorial assistant in the place – from the old-stagers who were hanging on for retirement benefits, to the recently recruited school-leavers – was in love with him.

He had a way of sitting on the edge of their desks, and using their names a lot, in that accent of his, while making lingering eye contact, which reduced them all to quivering jellies. Even the special needs post boy adored him.

The result was that we could get anything done ridiculously quickly, from colour photocopying and binding, to bike deliveries and mass mailouts. He also had the newspaper's cuttings and photographic library at his beck and call for research purposes. He just had to saunter in there and lean on the counter and half a dozen pink-cheeked librarians – of both sexes – would come running.

The other benefit of Ned's close relationships with this section of the paper's genome was the insights he got into what Jeanette was up to. A lot of the reporters and editors on the paper seemed to forget that the clerical staff existed and would conduct the most indiscreet conversations fully within their earshot. All of which came back to Ned, with the gentlest of coaxing in his Russell Crowe tones.

The other person who was in love with Ned, was – more surprisingly – Natalie, the fashion editor. He denied it, but it was obvious to me. I was pretty sure she was living with someone – one of those moody art photographers, by all accounts – but there was no missing it, Ms Cool Hoxton Trousers was all tongue-tied and flustered in his presence. She'd also started wearing very flimsy clothes to the office and leaning over his desk a lot.

I had plenty of opportunities to observe this mating behaviour close up, as she was making a big contribution to the new section, in ideas, contacts and sheer legwork – something I felt I largely had Ned's charisma to thank for.

And there were other benefits for me springing directly from her crush on him, as I found out that morning after the Asprey dinner.

'Natalie was at that dinner last night, as well,' Ned told me, slurping down a coffee in one hit.

'Did she crack on to you?' I asked.

'Oh, give it up, Stella,' said Ned. 'She's got a boyfriend, she's just lonely on the paper and I'm the only person who's nice to her.'

'Not as nice as she'd like you to be . . .' I persisted. I couldn't resist it. I loved teasing Ned, because it was usually me who copped it from him.

'Anyway,' he said, tapping me on the knee with a rolled-up copy of French *Vogue*. 'I had a very interesting conversation with her last night. Something you might like to hear about.'

'Really?' I said, sceptically, whacking him back, much harder, with the new edition of *W*.

'Yes,' said Ned, stretching his arms above his head, so his shirt tightened across his chest. 'It actually ties up with another line of enquiry I have been pursuing on your behalf for some time now.'

'Good heavens, Mr Woodward,' I said. 'I don't know where you find the energy for it all.'

'Keeps me interested between the jewellery dinners, Mrs Bernstein,' he said. 'Anyway, shut up and listen.'

He got up and quietly closed the door. When he sat down again he rolled his chair closer to me.

'Remember that nasty paparazzi article about you that appeared in *Hot Stuff!* magazine a while back?' he said, in soft, confidential tones.

I nodded, suddenly keenly interested. I remembered it all too well. It had nearly ruined my life, although Ned had no idea about the full, ongoing extent of it.

'Well, I know who put it there,' he said.

He smiled at me grimly and I just stared back at him. I had pretty much given up on the idea of ever finding that out. Ned had split up with the girl who worked on that magazine not long after the night we went to the comedy club, and with that contact gone I had lost hope.

'I thought you broke up with that girl . . .' I started.

'I did,' he said. 'But not before I'd found out a bit of key information.'

'Why didn't you tell me?'

'I wanted to see if anything else came out first, to make it all hang together, before you overreacted and blew my cover – and last night it did.'

Although my heart was beating so fast I felt a bit sick, I couldn't help smiling. He so loved the chase.

'So?' I said, impatiently. 'Tell me! Who the fuck was it?'

'Jeanette,' he said bluntly.

'Jeanette?' I said, incredulous. 'How the hell did she know?'

'There was a woman on that Jericho trip called Laura Birchwood, right? Writes for the *Post*?'

I nodded. I should have known she was involved.

'Well, she's Natalie's best friend – they went to college together . . .'

I took that in for a moment. I'd known they knew each other, but I hadn't realized they were besties.

'Anyway,' Ned was saying. 'She told Natalie that she'd seen you with Jay Fisher the morning after, as it were, when he was supposedly there with Jericho – and the state you were in you'd clearly shagged him . . .'

He got a cheeky look on his face. 'I'd like to have seen that actually.'

'I did not shag him, Ned . . .' I said, impatiently. Not then anyway.

'Well, that's what Laura told Natalie and the thing is – and Natalie feels really bad about this now – she told Jeanette.'

I slammed my hand down on to my desk.

'I'm going to kill her,' I spat out. 'She can forget working on this section. God!'

'Hang on a minute, Stella,' said Ned quietly. 'Just cool it and listen first. Natalie feels really bad.'

'I hope she bloody does . . .' I started, but as Ned gently put his hand on my arm to restrain me, I took a deep breath and tried to calm down, before I lost it completely and told him the entire reason I was so upset about it all.

'Just listen, first,' he said. 'She didn't know then how vile Jeanette is and she just told her as a bit of office gossip – Jeanette was the only person she had on her side at the paper back then, remember, and gossip is currency here, as you know – and then thought no more of it.'

I pondered for a moment.

'I still don't see how that proves Jeanette gave them the story,' I said. 'I mean, it makes sense it would be her, she clearly hates my guts, but how do we know for sure? It could have been any of them. It could have been Laura – or Natalie for that matter.'

'We don't know for sure,' admitted Ned. 'But I'm convinced it was her. Of the three of them who knew – Laura, Natalie and Jeanette – she's the only one nasty enough to do it, and the only one with a real motive.'

'Laura Birchwood doesn't like me much either,' I said.

'But do you really think she'd do that?'

I thought. I didn't like Laura, she just wasn't my kind of girl, and she may well have wanted my job, but I didn't think she was that much of a monster.

'No,' I said eventually.

'And Natalie wouldn't do something like that, now, would she?' continued Ned.

I would happily have barbecued Natalie at that moment, but I had to agree. She wasn't a monster either. Jeanette was.

'There you are,' said Ned. 'That's why I'm convinced it was Jeanette and I'll tell you something else; whoever did it is quite an operator. Shelley – that was the girl I used to go out with from *Hot Stuff!* – told me at the time that the "contact" had put them in touch with someone on the staff at the hotel who confirmed they had seen you arrive back at the hotel that morning in compromising circumstances with Jay Fisher.

'So, whoever it was who rang *Hot Stuff!*,' he continued, 'had the story – and a contact that the mag could check out for confirmation – already in place before they made the call, which is pretty professional stuff.'

'But how did they get the pics?' I asked, still not quite understanding how it had all come together.

'That's the easy bit for a mag like *Hot Stuff!*, isn't it? Once they'd had the tip-off from Jeanette – presuming it was her – that Jay Fisher had been seen dancing on the Riviera with the glamorous daughter of a life peer, while he was supposed to be having a fling with Jericho, they just got on to the paparazzi who had been following the whole Jericho party down there to see if they had any pics from the night. And they did.'

I leaned back in my chair with my hands behind my head and sighed deeply. It was exhausting just thinking about it.

'How come the paps were at that club?' I wondered. 'It was nowhere near the hotel we were all staying at.'

'The club would have tipped them off that Jericho was going to be there that night – or her management would have, for that matter. You know how she loves publicity. And luckily for the whole sleazy lot of them it turned out that while they were waiting for her to arrive, they took those pictures of you and Jay Fisher on the dance floor – just in case. And it paid off for them.'

'So if Jeanette – or whoever – hadn't tipped *Hot Stuff!* off, those pictures of me and Jay Fisher would probably just have been chucked out?'

'Probably,' agreed Ned, shrugging. 'I mean, with a guy like that – a "billion-heir" as they call him – anyone he dances with is going to come under some scrutiny, aren't they? It's just that they probably wouldn't have found out who you were, if they hadn't been tipped off by our friend here.'

'I would just have been the "mystery girl" . . .' I said, then something else occurred to me. 'So did Shelley say what name the "contact" used when she rang the magazine?'

'Oh, yes,' said Ned. 'I'm glad you asked me that – that's a good one. She pretended to be you.'

I sank back into my chair and just let it all swirl around in my head. Well, that all fitted perfectly with what I already knew. The reporter at *Hot Stuff!* had told Jay it was me who had sold them the story, and now it turned out it wasn't just a line, to fob him off. That was what they had believed.

And why wouldn't they? There were always people prepared to do things like that to promote themselves and for anyone wanting to boost their personal profile, some intimate pictures with Jay Fisher would be excellent exposure. Especially when he had been recently linked with someone as hugely famous as Jericho. Fame by association and all that.

'But how come they didn't call me here to check?' I wondered.

Ned shrugged. 'She probably gave them a mobile number that she pretended was yours. You know, bought a cheap pay-as-you-go phone, which she used just for that, put a message on it pretending to be you. People do it all the time.'

He leaned towards me.

'And anyway *Hot Stuff!* didn't care who the story was from.

They had the pics, they had the confirmation from the hotel snitch, and they knew it was you in the pictures, just from looking at your byline shot from this paper, so it was more than solid as far as they were concerned – and juicy too.

'A nightmare superstar who's famously unlucky in love, a billionaire bachelor playboy and a bit of London posh totty. A jet-set love triangle on the French Riviera – it's a great story.'

I put my head in my hands, trying to take it all in. It was almost too much to process, but one question kept rising up out of the great swirl of competing thoughts. I looked back at Ned.

'There's one thing I don't understand in all of this,' I said to him. 'That all happened way before this new section even came along – so what I want to know is: Why does Jeanette Foster hate me so much?'

Ned looked uncharacteristically serious.

'That's what I'm going to find out next,' he said.

16

That night when I had my regular bedtime conversation with Jay, I told him all about it.

'OK,' he said, when I'd related the whole story, as figured out by me and Ned. 'Let me get this straight – you're telling me it was one of your colleagues at the paper who called the magazine and tipped them off about us? And she'd been given the information by another colleague, who'd been told by one of the other journalists who was at the Jericho thing? Have I got that straight?'

'Yep,' I said. 'That's it.'

'OK,' said Jay. 'So is this normal when you work on a newspaper? I mean, I know what the press do to people like me – but you're telling me they do it to each other as well?'

He had me there.

'Well,' I started. 'I think this was quite an unusual case, but yeah, it can be pretty bitchy. People get very ambitious – and jealous – and they do try to stitch each other up. It's very competitive.'

Jay said nothing, he didn't need to. He'd made his point – this was the marvellous job I loved so much, the job that was keeping us from being together at that very moment.

I sighed. I could see how it looked to him, but his resentment of my work was just about the only thing that irritated me about Jay. I mean, I was pleased that he wanted to be with me so much that my job pissed him off because it was keeping us apart, but I somehow felt he should show it a little more respect. Especially as he had never worked a day in his life, as far as I could tell.

But apart from that, things were as sweet as ever and even though our only contact for the time being was phone calls, texts and emails, it wasn't showing any signs of wearing thin between us.

I just hoped it would last until he could come back to London again – because I couldn't see myself taking time off to go to New York anytime soon.

He'd told me he was going straight on to LA from his mother's place, to catch up with some old friends, and I couldn't help imagining the kind of women he would meet there – and how pleased they would be to see him.

Although I tried not to fret about it – telling myself that Jay was a free man, just as I was a free woman – I was aware that the longer we were apart, the greater was the likelihood of him meeting someone else. Who perhaps wasn't quite so irritatingly committed to her day job.

For the time being, though, with him five and a half thousand miles away, my job was still my main focus and despite all Jeanette's efforts to undermine me, the presentation that Friday morning was a triumph.

Ned's revelation about the source of the *Hot Stuff!* story had left me momentarily battle weary, but that soon turned to cold fury – the perfect state of mind to show I would not be beaten by Jeanette and her mean tricks. I'd win out through talent, application and hard work. And I think I was also a little driven by the need to prove something to Jay.

Ned and I did the presentation as a kind of double act, acting out the part of *Journal* readers, with me as the seasoned and sophisticated luxury shopper and him as the less-experienced but cashed-up younger consumer, both explaining how the various parts of the section we had created appealed to us and served our needs.

From the first slinky lounge beats of the opening sound-track – Ned's idea, he'd got a DJ friend to put it together – and the way I had styled the boardroom with ranks of designer carrier bags, our presentation had been smart, funny and clever, and it had worked brilliantly.

Between doing my bit of the yackety-yak and keeping on top of the technology – we had the mocked-up dummies of our proposed pages projected on to screens from two laptops, with light pointers and all that malarkey – I hadn't really been able to take in their reaction while we were doing it. I was concentrating too hard.

But when we'd finished, I looked up to see Peter beaming at me like a proud uncle. That was all the confirmation I needed that it had gone well, but it didn't hurt to see that Doughnut and the advertising execs looked equally happy – and that Jeanette looked like she had just been forced to eat a plate of cat food. Result.

I looked back at Ned and it was clear he had just clocked her too. He grinned and winked at me.

'Bravo,' Doughnut was saying, leading a little spattering of applause, which I could see it was nearly killing Jeanette to join in with. 'That was superb. I'm feeling quite excited about this section now – I think it's going to add some real energy to the paper at the end of the week.

'So, well done, you two, excellent work. Now, take yourselves off for a good lunch on expenses somewhere and don't come back this afternoon. You can start commissioning all this on Monday.'

Ned and I were so excited that we did a little victory dance around my office when we got back down there, whooping and hollering with glee.

He grabbed me for a spontaneous burst of polka and on one of the giddy turns, I thought I saw a face staring malevolently in at us through the glass wall of my office. It was Jeanette, I realized, but by the time I had broken free from Ned and turned around, it was gone. I shuddered involuntarily and before I could say anything to Ned, Peter appeared in the doorway, clapping.

'Bravo, bravo,' he was saying. 'That was marvellous, quite brilliant. Donald is thrilled, as you may have gathered. And I think you can rest assured that your future here is secure, Ned.'

Ned punched the air in triumph, as Peter walked over to me and put his hands on my shoulders.

'Oh, did you see the expression on her face?' he almost sang into my ear. 'Pure bile – such bliss.'

Then he disappeared off to Gino's for his customary lunch.

'So,' said Ned, turning himself round and round on my chair, like an excited little boy. 'Where shall we have lunch then? Can you get us into The Ivy? The Wolseley?'

'Probably,' I said, laughing. 'You've developed a taste for the high life pretty quickly, matey, I must say, but I've got another idea – are you doing anything this weekend?'

'Getting pissed and sleeping it off probably. Getting laid if I'm lucky.'

'Have you got a girlfriend at the moment then?' I asked tentatively. I didn't want to make the offer I was about to, if he did.

'No,' he said, one of his cheeky smiles spreading across his chops. 'But I've got a reputation to keep up.'

I balled up a press release and threw it at his head.

'Well, I was just wondering if you would like to skip the lunch today and come straight down to my dad's place with me for the weekend. There's going to be loads of us down there, it'll be a bit crazy, I warn you, it always is, but good fun. You could nip home for your kit now and I'll meet you at Victoria in a couple of hours.'

Ned looked really surprised – but pleased.

'I'd love to do that, Stella,' he said. 'It won't matter that I'm an uncouth colonial?'

'Don't be ridiculous,' I told him. 'My dad might be a lord by name, but he's a total savage by inclination and he's going to love you. You two have a lot in common . . .'

It only occurred to me as I said it, but it was true. They'd either love each other on sight, or it would be a clash of the testosterone titans. Ned was very much an Alpha Male, in his own particular way.

After he left to get his things, and I gathered up my own bits and pieces to leave the office, I hoped I wouldn't regret the invitation.

It had been a completely spontaneous impulse to ask him down – I'd almost been surprised to hear the words come out of my mouth as I'd said them – but I knew Ham and Chloe wouldn't mind, they were always urging me to bring friends there.

In fact, Ham would be delighted – once he had got over

his initial disappointment that Ned wasn't a future son-in-law – to see that I had a friend of any kind.

He was always telling me I could have the whole place for the weekend anytime I wanted to 'with a crowd of mates'. His face got so sweetly excited whenever he suggested it, because he loved the idea of me having a wild time down there with great gangs of 'young people', using the house to its full capacity, but I just didn't have a crowd of friends in that way.

I had workmates, like Tim, Peter and Ned, who I rarely saw outside the office; I had the people I knew from the luxury circuit, like Amy and Becca; there were a few bods I kept in touch with from school and university; the odd person I had met on holidays over the years; my human handbags; and various ex-boyfriends I was on good terms with, but I saw them all as separate friends, not as a cohesive crowd.

I just didn't particularly like introducing friends from different compartments in my life to each other. It made me feel uncomfortable and exposed, as though I would some-how be revealed if they could get together and compare notes on me, so I always saw them separately. It's just the way I was.

Even introducing friends to my family was unusual for me, so this weekend with Ned would be quite a new experience. It had been a spur-of-the-moment idea, inspired by the triumph of our collaboration, but as I walked to the Tube, it did occur to me that having him there that particular weekend would also help to make sure there wouldn't be any more overly intimate moments with Alex this time.

That last one had been so weird, I really didn't want to

risk it again – and it seemed my subconscious had taken care of that for me.

It turned out to be one of the legendary weekends at Willow Barn. The weather was great – a mini heatwave – the garden was blooming in its June splendour, the strawberries were ripe, and with all his biological children, plus a couple of ex-stepkids, an ex-wife and his new best friend (Ned, they did bond) in residence, Ham was at his most ebullient.

It really was a 'house party'. Not in the snobby stately-home sense, but because there was such a festive atmosphere spread over the entire place that the house seemed very much a part of the event – just as it was designed to be.

All the windows and doors were permanently open and people were constantly coming and going, in ever-changing combinations. Hordes of kids would come racing in through one door and then disappear out of another, and whichever part of the house or gardens you went into you would come across little knots of people happily engaged in various activities. It was – to use a Henry Montecourt buzzword – completely 'fluid'.

With all the children in situ – including Archie – I did end up in the guest wing again, but it was fine. Ned and Rose were sleeping there too, as well as me and Alex, and we ended up being quite a tight little unit of our own. Plus it helped that I had a bedroom on the ground floor next to Rose, with the two boys in rooms on the upper floor.

Apart from anything else, it was great to see Rose again. After Chloe, she was my favourite stepmother and she'd been in my life at such a formative stage – from eight to seventeen – that she'd been a huge formative influence on me. She was certainly the reason I couldn't cook. She never cooked herself, she had very little interest in food and just couldn't be bothered with it.

What I loved about Rose was that, despite such talent gaps, especially of one so crucial when raising a large family, she was completely unflappable. She was very creative – a brilliant garden designer and a good watercolourist too – but there was none of the neurosis that often goes with that temperament.

She wasn't a very good housekeeper at all, completely chaotic actually, but it never mattered somehow. She had just always made sure she had a reliable and devoted team of domestic help to look after things for her.

She was always finding a 'marvellous little chap in Lewes' who would cook all the food for a Willow Barn weekend in advance and deliver it, ready to be heated up, and 'such a sweet girl from the village' who would clean and organize the house, making sure all the ironing was done and the beds immaculately made.

Really, the ability to find such people and make them slavishly loyal to her, was as much a talent as being able to do it yourself, I had decided.

Ned and I were having a quiet drink on the terrace of the guest wing on the Friday evening when she and Alex arrived.

'Where's that darling girl?' I heard Rose saying as she came in – she was always already talking to the people in a room before she entered – and I sprang up to meet her.

It was a couple of years since I'd last seen her and she hadn't changed at all. Still as skinny as a teenager, with the same kind of sporty spring to her limbs, and her hair – which now had a lot of grey mixed in with the natural blonde – in the same boyish Christopher Robin cut.

'Let me look at you,' she said, holding me at arm's length. 'Marvellous. I always knew you were a beauty, even though I was your stepmother during those terrible awkward years girls have. She was quite the ugly duckling, weren't you, sweetheart?'

She roared with laughter and introduced herself to Ned.

'Oh, brilliant,' she said, eyeing his packet of Camels on the table. 'Another smoker. We can be untouchables together.'

By the time Alex emerged on to the terrace we were having a great time, with Rose and Ned wreathed in smoke, a bottle of white wine well on the go.

'Alex,' I said, standing up to kiss him. 'Great to see you. This is my colleague, Ned Morrissey. We work at the *Journal* together. We had a bit of a triumph today and so Ned's come down here to celebrate with me.'

They shook hands and I continued to babble slightly.

'Ned, this is my ex-stepbrother, Alex. He works in the City. Rose is his mum and she used to be married to my dad.'

I knew I was talking too much, and like a five-year-old, but I couldn't help it. The first few swigs of wine had gone straight to my head, the way they do when you're a bit excited and haven't eaten anything, and it was really impor-tant to me that Ned and Alex both understood exactly where they both fitted into the picture.

I thought I'd done a pretty good job – and I had tried to

prime Ned with the complications of my family tree on the way down on the train – but I could still sense they were eyeing each other up a bit, that way men do, trying to see who is the dominant wolf in the pack.

But by the time we'd got over to the main house for dinner, the 'boys' as Rose was calling them, seemed to have bonded and were having an involved conversation about the various codes of football, including something called 'Aussie rules' – yet more sport Alex was keen on, and the first I had ever heard Ned express an interest in.

I thought his only sporting activity was chatting up the more attractive media students who came into the paper to do work experience, and his scores in that regard were pretty high, as far as I could tell.

When we got over to the house Ham was frowning down at the huge round dining table – it had its biggest top on – and puzzling over his seating plan.

'Aha, the out-of-the-nest wing,' he said when he saw us, quoting the slogan Alex and I had put on our sweatshirts, the last time we had been here together.

I felt immediately uncomfortable, and the unexpected reference to that night made my eyes flick over to Alex before I could stop them – just as he looked at me. Our eyes locked for a millisecond that told me he was still as self-conscious about the events of that evening as I was. I looked away immediately.

'Now, you lot,' Ham was booming. 'I need your help with this plan. Can you count heads for me, Alex, to check numbers? You're the best with figures. You see, I think we've got thirteen tonight. Chloe suggested putting Daisy to bed early to make it twelve, but I don't think that's fair, she deserves her place at the table, so I suppose it will have to be a teddy, which I've always thought was horribly twee . . .'

I was about to go looking for a large Pooh Bear who lived in the kiddie corridor, when I noticed Rose and Alex were looking at each other and giggling. Rose was nodding excitedly at him.

'Actually, Henry,' said Alex, 'I think we might be able to solve that problem for you. I'll just nip out to the car.'

Ham looked bewildered, but shrugged and carried on shuffling the index cards he had with our names written on them.

After a couple of minutes Alex returned – with a small, plump fawn-coloured pug on an emerald-green lead.

'Monkey can take the fourteenth place,' said Alex. 'He has very good table manners.'

Rose shrieked with laughter. Monkey was her most treasured dog and she'd brought him with her, even though canines had been strictly forbidden at Willow Barn, ever since she and Ham had split up. He'd told me once that it was having several dogs in bed with them every night which had caused that marriage to fall apart.

'Oh, I know I wasn't supposed to bring him, Henry,' Rose was saying. 'But I couldn't leave him behind. He's so devoted to me. The others don't mind, they're all staying with Mrs Plimmer, who does my house, and they all adore her. But Monkey is so devoted to me, he just would have pined terribly.'

Ham looked cross for a moment, but Monkey looked up at him and put his wrinkled little head on one side in such an appealing manner, Ham couldn't resist him.

'Oh, all right, Rose,' he said. 'We can't leave the poor little bugger in the car all weekend. Here – write his name on this card.'

The twins, who had come down to the house with Chloe, were thrilled to see their favourite dog and Daisy was simply beside herself. She wanted a dog more than anything, but Ham was intransigent on the subject.

'They're dirty,' he always said. 'And smelly and needy and farty and they shit all over the garden. I've done dogs and I'm not having another one.'

'We'll see about that,' said Rose to me, out of the side of her mouth.

With Monkey in situ between Rose and Daisy, and sporting a black tie which Tabitha had put on him, it was a very funny dinner from the outset.

By the time we'd finished the first course, both Monkey and Daisy were asleep at the table, and Rose and I took them off to bed – we just didn't tell Ham it was the same bed.

Children gradually peeled off – to sleep, or just to do their own thing – until it was just the six adults who were left. While Chloe made coffee, Ham switched the table top to a smaller one, to make it more intimate, and with just him, Chloe, Rose, Alex, Ned and me, it was a surprisingly successful combination.

There was certainly no awkwardness between Rose and Chloe, who had established a very good relationship from the outset with regard to the movements of the twins between the two households – greatly aided by Alex, who helped as much as he could with the ferrying.

The two women were having great fun ganging up against

Ham and teasing him, which he clearly adored; Ned and Alex were getting along famously in a blokey kind of way; and Rose and Ned kept popping out of the glass doors for what she called intercourse ciggies. It was generally a very successful evening.

It was nearly midnight and we were getting into the eau de vie – always the sign of a really good dinner – when my phone started ringing. In all the excitement I had completely forgotten it was in my pocket, but I knew who it was the moment it started: it was Jay calling 'to put me to bed'.

From the first trill of the ringtone, every face around that table was looking at me.

'It's a bit bloody late for phone calls,' protested Ham. 'Even from that office of yours that makes you work weekends and God knows what.'

Oh no, I thought, as I saw Ned look at me oddly. He knew I didn't work weekends – and I knew that a casual remark like that, which might have gone over most people's heads, would be instantly logged in the Woodward and Bernstein hard drive of his brain.

I pretended to look at the number – like I didn't know what it would be – then I turned the phone off with a flourish, cutting it out in mid-ring.

'Sorry about that,' I said, way too brightly. 'It was a New York number. They're still at work over there and they must have forgotten the time difference. Probably some airhead from Ralph Lauren. They've always got loads of ditzy rich kids doing play work there.'

I could have swallowed my tongue as I said it. Why did I have to overegg my explanation? Now I noticed Alex was looking at me keenly and I was sure he was remembering the last time my phone had rung at that table – and was wondering when the black Ferrari would arrive at the front door.

From that moment on, sitting at the table was torture for me. I was so terrified of opening my mouth in case I made another gaffe, that after about ten minutes I hurriedly made my excuses, saying it had been a big day with our presentation that morning and I had to crash.

I went straight to my room and rang Jay. I shouldn't have done it. I should have just texted him an explanation but I was pressing return call before I'd even thought about it, because the thing was, with the white wine before dinner, all the red during it and the hard stuff at the end, I was just too pissed to think sensibly.

'Hi, honey,' said Jay in his most affectionate tones, when he answered. 'I called you to say g'night and I got cut off.'

'Omigod,' I blurted. 'It was such a nightmare, I was at dinner at my dad's house – I'm down at the Barn, remember, I told you? And I realized it was you and I could see everyone was looking at me and I knew Alex was thinking about you and then I said this really stupid thing and I could see Ned looking at me too and I was just, oh my God . . .'

There was a short silence before he responded.

'So, there's quite a gang of you down there then,' he said. If there was a slight coolness in his voice at that point, I didn't pick it up.

'Oh yes,' I was off again. 'It's been so much fun – until your call. Oh what a nightmare that was. Anyway, Ham really loves Ned, which is great, and Rose is here – she's Alex's mum – and I really love her and it's really good to see

Alex too, because my dad really wants me to be friends with him and I do love him really, and all the kids are here and really it's the house being used exactly as Ham had always envisioned it. It's a perfect Willow Barn weekend, really.'

'Well, I hope you all have a lovely time,' said Jay, and now, even through my boozy funk, I could hear the chill in his voice. 'And now I'm going surfing. Goodbye, Stella.'

And he hung up.

I was so surprised I didn't think I could have heard him right. Had he really hung up on me, or had I missed something? And as my fuddled brain tried to make sense of it, I fell into an ugly open-mouth sleep.

I normally loved the early birdsong from the woods at Willow Barn, but the next morning I could quite happily have nuked the lot of them. Not only did their insistent tweeting make my very tender head throb unbearably, they had woken me up into the realization that I had said some inconceivably stupid things to Jay the night before.

I sat bolt upright in bed, as the conversation replayed itself in jagged snatches in my brain. Then I groaned and threw myself face down on to the pillow and hammered my feet against the mattress.

Jay didn't even really know who Ned was and I had been happily babbling on about how lovely it was that Ham liked him – oh – and how great the evening had been until Jay had rung. I groaned some more.

'A perfect Willow Barn weekend,' I could now remember saying. A perfect weekend at the place Jay would love to visit again and never could, because my dad hated him – unlike Ned and Alex, who he loved, and so did I.

How could I have been so tactless? I groaned a bit more, but it just made me feel more sick.

I was never going to drink again, that was clear, but my more pressing concern was how I was going to make it up to Jay – especially as he was on LA time. It was hours until I could ring him.

By the time we were having breakfast at the main house, I was almost glad of my hangover, as a cover for my tender emotional state. The combination of remorse and anxiety, with the tyranny of the time difference, and the need to keep it all under wraps, was making me feel quite hysterical.

I was so jumpy at the breakfast table I knocked over the milk jug and then literally fell off my chair, trying to avoid the resulting deluge. It was so embarrassing. I was just relieved Alex wasn't there to see me – he'd gone off to a specialist shrub nursery with Ham and Rose – but Ned, Archie, Venezia et al. clearly found it hilarious and Daisy was bouncing up and down in her chair with delight.

'Stella had an all fall down,' she was squealing, before hopping off her own chair. 'All fall *down*!'

'I think I must still be drunk,' I said, hauling myself up from under the table.

'Cool,' said Archie, followed by a burst of his staccato Butt-head laughter, which was like a painful assault on my ears.

I put my head in my hands and sighed.

'I have to go back to bed,' I said. It was all too much, being surrounded by so many people when I was in that condition. But when I got back to the guest wing and was all alone, I felt even worse.

Particularly awful phrases from the conversation – 'It's been so much fun – until your call . . .'; 'Ham really loves Ned, which is great . . .'; 'It's a perfect Willow Barn weekend, really . . .' – went round and round in my head, until I felt like some kind of crazy Hitchcock heroine, going bonkers.

On top of that I couldn't stop myself looking at my watch constantly, to see whether I could call him yet, even though I knew he wouldn't be up until it was late afternoon in East Sussex.

I made myself a strong cup of tea in the guest-wing kitchen and went to sit outside on the terrace, hoping the fresh air might clear my head. Then I had a brainwave and rushed back up to my room to get my phone – to see if maybe he had sent me a reassuring text while I was asleep. He hadn't.

I was sitting there staring down at the phone wondering whether I trusted myself to send him one, when Ned walked out on to the terrace.

'How's your head?' he asked me.

'Shocking,' I said. 'I shouldn't drink white wine. It really doesn't agree with me.'

He laughed.

'I shouldn't drink the equivalent of the English Channel in alcohol,' he said. 'It doesn't agree with me. I'm going to have a swim. Your dad's back and he just told me the pool's open. Maybe you should have one too, it might sort you out.'

'What a brilliant idea,' I said.

I went back into the main house to see if I could borrow a swimsuit from Chloe, and as I was walking back through the sitting room carrying two ridiculously small pieces of shocking-pink Lycra, dating from her pre-Daisy life, I bumped into Alex. He saw the bikini and his face lit up.

'Is the pool open?' he said.

'So Ned tells me,' I said. 'You coming in?'

'You bet,' said Alex.

I went straight to the pool house to change and as I came out into the bright morning sunshine there was a big splash as someone dived into the pool.

I was standing on the edge at the shallow end, weedily dipping my big toe in to see if the water was bearable, when a large seal burst out of the water at my feet. It was Ned. His normally messy black hair was slicked back by the water, and his eyelashes were stuck together in thick clumps against his green eyes. He grinned at me and stood straight up in the water. I nearly fell into the pool.

He had the body of a god.

I couldn't help staring. Seriously broad shoulders, a perfectly smooth muscular chest, a taut flat stomach with a tantalizing line of hair down it – and those hip lines, just like Jay's, but deeper.

There was something about those lines that did me in. Gazing at Ned, I remembered the first time I'd seen Jay in the pool at the Cap Mimosa, but while that gave me a pang of guilt, something still fluttered inside me where it really shouldn't have.

I couldn't believe I'd been sitting inches from this body for weeks at work, putting together the new section, and I hadn't realized. I mean, I knew he was well built, but this was something else again. Did all the other women in the office have X-ray vision? Because they had clearly seen something I hadn't, beneath that shambolic suit he always wore.

Just as I caught myself, and tried to look away, I realized that he was brazenly checking me out too. He wasn't even pretending not to. His eyes were on their way back up for another look, when he suddenly shifted his gaze to my eyes – and unfurled his slowest, most wicked smile.

'Nice bikini, Stella,' he said, and took off back down the pool at high speed.

17

On top of my already feeble state, a sudden surge of highly inappropriate sexual attraction was almost too much to deal with. I lowered myself quickly into the pool via the steps and got my head under the water. I needed to cool down.

What was it about that place? Every time I went down there I had some kind of close encounter of the seriously weird kind. Maybe Ham was pumping some kind of hormonal love potion into the water supply, as an experiment. I wouldn't have put it past him.

I swam up and down a few times until I felt a bit calmer, and then got out and lay down on a sunlounger. For once in England, it was properly hot and I planned to spend the day as inert as a lizard.

Ned was still pounding up and down the pool like an Olympic swimmer – he even did proper racing turns at the deep end, I noticed – and I was glad that he was leaving me alone.

I was even more relieved when Alex appeared with a number of children in tow, although I couldn't help noticing he looked pretty dandy himself in a pair of Speedo trunks he'd found in the pool house. Daisy was wearing her first real swimming costume – it had an adorable little frill round the bum – and was very proud of her Barbie rubber ring.

Toby and the younger boys jumped straight into the water and immediately had Ned teaching them how to do tumble turns, while Alex bounced Daisy around in the shallow end.

'Look at me, Stella,' she was shouting. 'I'm swimming! Come in, Stella, come in! Come in and swim with me!'

I couldn't resist her and got up to join them in the pool. But as I walked over to the shallow end, I suddenly felt extremely self-conscious in Chloe's tiny bikini.

She had been really skinny when she'd first got together with Ham, with much smaller breasts than me. Now I was all too aware that mine were spilling out of the flimsy halter-neck top – and that both Ned and Alex were steadily watching my progress along the side of the pool.

'Was that right, Ned?' shouted Toby, emerging from his latest spluttering attempt at a racing turn, but Ned wasn't paying attention. He had his arms extended along the edge of the deep end of the pool, and was shamelessly watching me.

It was too much, I pulled a face and stuck my tongue out at him, and with one movement he turned and pulled himself up out of the water, so I had a quick rear view – nice – and then he was standing on the edge, his hands on his hips. Homo magnificent. He shook his head, so the water flew off his hair like a dog coming out of the sea and then he raked it back with his hands.

Our eyes locked for a moment and a knowing smile flickered across his lips, before he turned his attention back to the kids.

'Right, you lot,' he was saying to the boys. 'Now I'm going to show you how to do a proper racing start. Watch . . .'

And with another splash, he was back in the pool.

Alex clearly hadn't missed a beat of it.

'Great bod, eh?' he said, nodding his head towards Ned, who was now speeding back down the pool again away from us, but then just happening to stand up himself, revealing his rower's chest and shoulders.

I splashed water at him.

'You're not exactly Mr Blobby yourself, Alex,' I said and turned away from him. 'Right, Miss Daisy, I want to see those frog legs kicking.'

While all that was going on, Chloe had arrived at the pool and was rubbing suncream into her swelling belly, before she got in the water and took over Daisy's swimming lessons. I got out and lay back down on my sunlounger, and was soon joined by Alex on one side and Ned on the other.

This gave me ample opportunity to notice that Ned wasn't wearing proper swimming trunks, but just had on a pair of black underpants – those ones like little biker shorts, but made of ribbed cotton jersey – and wet as they were, I could see a very clear outline of what was inside them. I swallowed, hard.

So that was what I saw if I turned my eyes left. If I looked right, I had a grandstand view of Alex's beautiful rear. He was lying on his front, reading the business section of the paper. One side of his trunks was slightly caught up, just revealing the crease at the bottom of his buttock.

It was like being in a Gucci ad. I decided I'd better close my eyes.

But surrounded by male pulchritude, even as I was, the minute I closed my eyes, my thoughts returned to Jay. I wondered how he'd feel if he could see me lying there like that, because I knew exactly how I'd feel if I saw him in the reverse situation: gutted. And considering where he was

– LA, the world capital of the body beautiful and the rapacious bimbo – he probably was.

For all I knew he was lying in bed at that very minute with a couple of ravishing starlets or surfer chicks – he'd said he was going surfing as he'd ended the call, I suddenly remembered – one on either side. I felt simultaneously ill and homicidal at the thought of it.

It was a completely new feeling for me. I'd never really been bothered by those kinds of thoughts before – jealousy, I supposed it was – because I'd always kept my sexual relationships as low-key as possible.

The thing with Jack had been the extreme version of it, but even with the more conventional 'boyfriends' I'd had over the years, I'd always been at pains to keep it light and easy – and slightly distant. So no cosy double dates with friends, no meeting the family – mine, or his – and no demands and expectations. Just fun and good times, when the moment was right.

As soon as a bloke had shown any sign of assuming that I wouldn't accept a dinner invitation from someone else if I felt like it, or that he would automatically be seeing me on a Friday night, it was over. Not interested.

So it was strange to feel these uncomfortable new emotions for the first time. I felt I had to grow them, like a tadpole growing legs – and so far all they were doing was making me unbearably restless.

In the end I couldn't stand it any more and I got up and went back to the guest wing. I had decided I couldn't just leave it like that between us, I had to leave a message for Jay to get when he woke up.

I didn't even plan what I was going to say as I dialled his

number, I was just going to see what came out, and I was completely taken aback when he answered his phone.

'Jay,' I whispered. 'It's Stella. I'm really sorry – it must be the middle of the night there – did I wake you up? I was just going to leave you a message.'

'Hey, baby,' he said, a bit croaky, but the usual warmth was back in his voice. 'I couldn't sleep. I'm so glad you rang. You're the reason I couldn't sleep . . . I was really mean to you before.'

'Oh, no,' I protested. 'I was awful. I was really drunk and I didn't realize and I just babbled on and said so many stupid things. I'm really sorry . . .'

My voice caught a little.

'Hey, stop that,' said Jay. 'It's fine, really. I was stupid. I was jealous, Stella. I was jealous of Alex and Ned – whoever he is – being there with you at your dad's place and me being stuck here like some unwanted exile and I just lashed out.'

'I'd so much rather you were here than any of them,' I said, and I meant it.

'Who is this Ned, anyway?' said Jay, pretending to be stern.

'Oh, he's just a guy I work with,' I said.

A guy I work with who incidentally had a body like Ian Thorpe, but never mind that.

'We did the presentation together yesterday morning,' I continued. 'You know, about the new section? And it went really brilliantly, so I invited him down here to celebrate, that's all.'

'That's great, sweetheart,' he said. 'I'm really pleased for you. I'm proud of you.'

I could tell he was making an effort to be enthusiastic about my job. I was touched.

'How are things with you, Jay?' I asked him, gently.

'They're OK,' he said, sounding a bit low.

'You don't sound OK,' I said.

He sighed deeply.

'Well, I'm being virtually stalked by a woman I met at a dinner here. I'm going to have to change my mobile; she got hold of the number and she just won't stop ringing me. Then she "just happened" to turn up where I was having dinner tonight. It is so boring when this happens, Stella, and I have done nothing to encourage her, believe me. But women like her are just convinced that if they try hard enough you are going to suddenly fall in love with them and marry them. It's unbelievable.

'And then on top of that, I've got some kind of shit coming up with my dad – I've got to go back to New York tomorrow and see him. He's sending his plane for me, so I really can't get out of it. Big Daddy hollers, I gotta go,' he said, in a mock Southern accent.

'Poor you,' I said.

It sounded pathetic, but I didn't know what else to say, considering I had no idea of what kind of 'shit' went on between him and his father – and how nauseous I was instantly feeling at the thought of all the women who must have been chasing him over there.

'Yeah, well, maybe when I'm through with that,' he said. 'I can get over to London to see you again.'

And then after a few more minutes of rambling sweet nothings, we rang off.

*

On the Saturday evening we all – including Monkey – had dinner together again, and it was a bit more formal, as Saturday nights down there traditionally were, so none of the kids, except Daisy, were allowed to leave the table until Ham formally released them after pudding.

For once there didn't seem to be any psychodramas going on – apart from Venezia doing some full-beam flirting with Ned, whom she had clocked that afternoon at the pool, prompting an immediate reversal of her 'swimming is for kids' policy.

She had disappeared back to the house and returned very quickly in a tiny bikini with a Brazilian thong bottom. God knows where she'd got it from, although it looked like something her mother would take on her annual January trip to Barbados. Venezia was always plundering her mother's wardrobe for inappropriately sophisticated clothes.

Ham had exploded at first sight and told her to go back inside immediately and change into something 'decent', before issuing his most terrible threat as far as she was concerned.

'If you don't learn to behave with a little more decorum, Venezia Montecourt-Fain,' he said, 'you will leave me no choice but to despatch you to a convent in Scotland for the rest of your education. A closed order. And I'll make sure you wear regulation school-issue flannel knickers at all times.'

'I think she's more suited for St Trinian's, don't you?' said Ned quietly to me, watching her pert fourteen-year-old bottom bouncing back to the house.

She was still at it over dinner. She'd even committed the huge crime of changing Ham's seating plan, so she would be next to Ned, but he laughed it all off with great tact.

I was so distracted by Venezia's embarrassing behaviour and by laughing at Archie's barbed comments about it, that I hadn't noticed anything was wrong with Tabitha.

I helped Chloe clear the table after the main course and when I came back carrying one of the three huge trifles that were for pudding – she was still researching *Kitsch Cuisine* – I noticed her place was empty.

I assumed she'd gone to the loo, but when we had all finished our trifle – and had seconds and thirds – and she still hadn't reappeared, I began to wonder if she was all right. Kids were strictly not allowed to leave those dinners until Ham said they could, and Tabitha was usually an obedient girl – and very keen on her puddings.

I turned to Alex, who was sitting on my left.

'Do you know where Tabs has gone?' I asked him, quietly.

He looked surprised, he clearly hadn't noticed.

'The loo?' he suggested.

I shook my head.

'She's been gone since before pudding,' I said.

'That's not like Tabs,' he said, but not looking particularly concerned. 'She's probably snuck off to watch a DVD, or to send some text messages. She's surgically attached to that phone, these days.'

It occurred to me that Alex had probably forgotten just how strictly Ham liked to enforce the house rules down at Willow Barn, so he wouldn't appreciate the full significance of her absence.

I didn't say any more – I didn't want to attract Ham's attention to it – but got up quietly and went to ask Toby if he knew where she was. He didn't, but Archie, who was sitting next to him, overheard me.

He raised his eyebrows at me and I leaned towards him.

'Tabitha's not happy,' said Archie, with his customary bluntness. 'She left the table. Crying. No one noticed.'

'Any idea where she went?' I asked him.

He just shook his head.

'Girl stuff, probably,' he said dismissively, and helped himself to another huge bowl of trifle.

I checked the telly room, the kids' corridor, all the bathrooms, Ham's turret and even the guest wing. There was no sign of her. On my way back into the house I bumped into Alex in the kitchen courtyard.

'Any sign of Tabitha in there yet?' I asked him, nodding my head at the main house.

'No,' said Alex, looking surprised. 'Isn't she in the telly room?'

'No, I've looked everywhere and I can't find her. I think she must be in the garden somewhere. I'm going to look for her.'

'Right,' said Alex, finally looking concerned. 'I'll look too. I'll do this side and you take the front, OK?'

I nodded.

I snuck back into the guest-house kitchen to pick up a torch and went down the side of the front lawn, so that no one sitting inside the house would see me – I didn't want to have to explain.

It was getting close to the longest day and the evening light had lingered until after nine, but now it was fully dark. I checked the summer house and all the way down to the shell grotto, which was decidedly spooky at night. Confident I was far enough away from the house not to be heard down there, I called her name into the bushes and trees, but there was no response.

I came back up through the bamboo walk, the slender trunks clicking eerily as they were knocked against each other by the light summer breeze. I shivered a little. It reminded me of the night Alex and I had slept in the tree house – and immediately, I realized that was where Tabitha would be.

I walked quickly back towards the house, skirting to the left behind the monkey puzzle tree, and then jogged up through the orchard to the tree house.

I could hear her crying before I got there and I climbed up the rope ladder as quickly as I could.

Just as I put my head through the door, and saw Tabitha lying on her side in the fetal position, wracked with sobs, another head appeared through the opposite door – Alex.

'Hey, Tabs,' he was saying.

We climbed in simultaneously and she was so surprised she sat up and stopped crying. Then once she'd taken it in, she fell back down on her arms again, weeping.

Alex stroked her head and made soothing noises. I lay down on the floor so my head was right next to hers.

'Tabs, sweetheart,' I said. 'Whatever is wrong? Tell me – tell us. We love you, tell us what's wrong, please.'

She sobbed a bit more and then she spluttered a bit and wiped her nose on her sleeve.

'Mum and Dad . . .' she managed to gasp out, and then fell down sobbing again.

Alex and I exchanged glances.

'What about them?' said Alex, but I had an idea I already knew what she was talking about.

'Is it seeing them together?' I asked quietly.

She opened her eyes wide and looked at me, clearly surprised that I understood. She nodded and wiped her nose again.

'Yes,' she croaked. 'How did you know?'

I sighed. 'Well, it did occur to me that it might be a bit weird for you, seeing them together like that.'

The twins had only been two when Rose and Ham had split up (as a result of Kristy turning up on the doorstep one evening with Venezia in tow . . .). And it had struck me, as we had all sat down at the table that evening, that just as I didn't remember my mother, Tabitha and Toby wouldn't have any memory of what it was like to have their parents together as a family unit. No wonder she was in shock.

Tabitha sobbed a bit more and I looked over at Alex. He had such a sad expression on his face, I felt like he needed comforting too.

'Oh, my little sausage,' he said. 'It never occurred to me. It must be really strange for you.'

'It is,' said Tabitha, sitting up at last. 'It's been so lovely having them both together and you two here as well, sitting round the table like a normal family, and tomorrow we're all going to split up again and . . .'

She started howling again.

'Why does my family have to be so weird?' she said, between splutters. 'Why do we all live in different places? It's never the same, it's always different people and I just want to be in a normal family.'

I pulled her towards me and put my arm around her, so her head was on my shoulder.

'Don't lots of your friends at school have divorced parents as well?' I asked, gently.

'Yes,' she said. 'But no one is as weird as us. Most people's dads have two wives. They have the first one, who is their mum, and then they have the new wife, who is like Chloe, but I'm the only one with all these weird stepmothers and half-brothers and sisters and stuff . . .'

'Well,' said Alex. 'Stella and I have a lot of weird half-sisters and stepbrothers as well, you know.'

She sniffed and blinked at him, then wiped her eyes.

'I suppose so . . .' she said, smiling a little bit.

'And Stella's had five different stepmothers, haven't you?'

I agreed, thinking – and no real mother, either, but I didn't need to burden Tabitha with that. She was twelve, nearly thirteen, and viewed the world entirely from her own central place within it. I could remember feeling just like that myself, and sobbing my heart out in that very tree house.

'I used to come and cry in here, Tabitha,' I said. 'Sometimes I felt so left out, because you and Toby had two living parents, and you were properly blood related too, and so were Alex and Claudia and Rowan. Proper brothers and sisters. I'm only a stepsister to any of you and I felt like some strange add-on extra – a sort of unnecessary flange on the side of the family.'

Tabitha looked at me with wide eyes, it had clearly never occurred to her, how it might have been for me having no full siblings and no mother.

'So we are weird then, aren't we?' she said. 'I'm not making it up, am I?'

'We're absolutely bonkers,' said Alex. 'The whole lot of us.'

And we all burst out laughing.

We stayed in the tree house for a long time, talking about the happy times when Ham and Rose were together, and I told Tabitha the story of the night Alex had tried to sleep in the tree house.

I glanced over at him as I was telling it, and he was smiling at me so fondly, I suddenly felt a bit awkward.

'Anyway,' I said, rushing to finish. 'So your big brother was a total hero to me that night, just as he has been to you tonight. So anytime you are finding it too weird with all your half-siblings and stepsiblings and semi-steps and God knows what, just remember you have us. All the halves and steps and stuff in our family don't matter, we are just your big brother and sister and we love you.'

'Absolutely,' said Alex.

She hugged us both and we walked back to the house together. 'Ah, there you are,' boomed Ham, over his shoulder, when we walked in from the kitchen. 'I wondered where you lot were.'

Tabitha ran up the stairs to the kids' rooms and Alex and I walked over to where Ham was installed on a long leather sofa, one arm round Rose, the other round Chloe. Monkey was on his lap.

Ned was sitting opposite, on the other sofa, looking at me and Alex thoughtfully.

'What have you two been up to then?' asked Ham, his face a mask of delight – clearly loving the thought that Alex and I were getting closer.

'We were in the tree house talking about old times,' I said, smiling back.

Ham looked like his head was going to split he was grin-ning so broadly.

'Marvellous, marvellous,' he said. 'That's exactly what I built it for. As a place to create memories – and later rekindle them.'

Ned used this as an opening to start discussing Ham's theories of architecture with him and how else he had applied them to the house. He might as well have opened the flood gates at Niagara, and fascinating though it all was, I really wasn't in the mood to hear about 'fluidity' and the 'percussion of emotion' all over again.

I yawned ostentatiously a few times, and went back to the guest wing.

I was sitting on the terrace, drinking some herbal tea and enjoying the last lingering warmth of the evening and the scent of the roses in the nearby border, when Ned came out through the French doors.

'How're you doing?' he asked me, throwing himself down into a chair opposite and putting his feet up on the one next to me. He stretched his arms into the air – effectively reminding me what lay beneath his unironed shirt, which I am ashamed to say made my heartbeat quicken a little. Then he linked his hands behind his head, looking steadily at me the whole time.

'So you were off having a cosy chat with your handsome stepbrother in the tree house, then?' he said, his eyes twinkling.

'Do you think he's handsome?' I said, acting surprised.

'Are you kidding?' he said. 'He looks like something out of *Brideshead Revisited*. So did you snog him?'

'Ned!' I said, pushing his legs off the chair.

'You did then?' he said, roaring with laughter.

'No, I did not,' I said. 'That is so embarrassing. How could you even say that?'

'Well, he must have had a go,' Ned said. 'I mean, I know Englishmen are pathetic with women, that's why I do so well over here, but crammed into a confined space with you like that, nice and cosy, a long hot day at the pool behind you, surely he tried to slip you the tongue?'

I sighed loudly.

'No, he did not,' I said, feeling really pissed off with Ned and simultaneously furious with myself for letting him get to me. In more ways than one. 'Alex is my stepbrother, so it would hardly be appropriate and anyway, we're friends, so it would be really yucky.'

'That's not the way it looks to me,' said Ned, bringing his arms down slowly and standing up. He walked towards me and bent down so his head was close to mine.

'From where I'm standing,' he said, right into my ear, in his lazy seductive voice, so close I could feel his breath against my skin, 'it looks like he's madly in love with you.'

After dropping that bomb on to my head, Ned blithely disappeared inside and as soon as I heard his bedroom door close, I went in too.

I lay in my bed in the dark thinking about the day. On the surface it had been just another perfect summer Saturday down at Willow Barn, but actually so much had gone on for me underneath the surface.

The terrible remorse about my conversation with Jay. The revelation of Ned's love-god body and the uncomfortable – well, too comfortable, actually – feelings it had sparked in me. And in Venezia. Making it up with Jay. Tabitha's tears. The closeness I had felt to Alex in the tree house. Ned's inappropriate comments about him.

A wave of irritation swept over me, as I remembered what Ned had said. It was bad enough feeling that Ham was trying to set us up, and now I almost wondered if he hadn't recruited Ned to help him with his cause. It was just the sort of manipulative game they would both enjoy.

I analysed all my interactions with Alex that day. OK, he had been a bit competitive with Ned in the pool, but that was just normal boy behaviour. And, really, any man would have felt a bit threatened by Ned's body.

He'd been a bit soppy when I'd told Tabitha the story about us sleeping in the tree house, but that was just sentimental childhood memory shit. None of it added up to unrequited love.

Looking back further, there had been The Incident, of course, but that was just boy behaviour too. All men are driven by their hormones – Ham had drilled that into me since childhood. It was a classic example of his dandelion theory.

'Put a man in a situation where he feels he has the slightest chance with a woman and he will always give it a go,' was what he had repeatedly told me. 'It's not our fault, it's just nature. It is our biological imperative to spread our seed as widely as possible. Really, we are no different from dandelions.'

So that was all it had been that embarrassing night with Alex – just nature, making him have a go. And if my body had betrayed me by reacting, that was just biology too.

And I could apply Ham's theory equally well to Ned's

flirtatious behaviour by the pool and my own hormonal reaction to that. It was perfectly normal, according to the laws of nature, for a virile man and a woman of childbearing age to experience a sexual frisson during an encounter when neither of them is really wearing any clothes.

Dandelions, the lot of us. Just fluffy, little weeds.

18

That Monday morning Jay sent me a huge bunch of flowers – lots of different kinds, but all shades of blue. They were utterly gorgeous and so was the card that came with them.

'This is the colour I am without you . . .' it said, followed by so many kisses I couldn't even count them. I wondered how he had dictated that to the girl in the florist's.

I kissed the card back and put it carefully into my wallet. He'd stopped even putting his initial on them, to be on the safe side, but I still wasn't taking any risks.

He couldn't have timed those flowers better. For one thing I was extremely relieved that we had got our relation-ship – if that was what it was, the concept was still so new to me – back on track, if not a little closer, as it would dispel any confusing feelings I might have had about Ned after the incidents of the weekend.

As relatively secure as I now felt with Jay, I knew I could put Ned – and his killer body – firmly back into his rumpled work suit and his role as my respected colleague and office mate, with any more complicated stirrings completely forgotten.

The other reason Jay's flowers were a welcome boost that morning, was something I'd just seen in the *Post*'s weekly media section, which was the most widely read one in the industry.

It was a really snide little snippet about the new section

– and the first mention of it anywhere, because it hadn't been officially announced yet. I had read it about twenty times, still hardly able to believe how horrible it was about me.

> Once again under the cosh from management to cut costs, *Journal* editor-in-chief Duncan – Big Spender – McDonagh has stooped to conquer. His idea is don't spend less – earn more, no matter the cost to the paper's integrity.
>
> So in a move that has surprised the paper's more serious journalists, he has appointed the paper's lissom 'luxury correspondent' Stella Fain to edit a weekly mini glossy magazine for the paper, with his eye on pinching some of *Vogue*'s advertising revenue.
>
> Daughter of six-times-married peer Lord Montecourt of Cliffe, the It girl journalist has recently been linked to billionaire playboy Jay Fisher and is great mates with such luxury-brand luminaries as Rebecca Rosen – the London PR for Cartier.
>
> So with the paper's apparent desperation for cash, no doubt the gushing editorial will flow as freely as the Bollie at the swanky functions and freebie five-star trips Ms Fain so regularly enjoys.
>
> Sad times, indeed, for a paper that used to be better known for its groundbreaking investigations than its PR puffs.

I was just reading it one more time, to be sure I hadn't imagined how foul it was, when Peter and Ned appeared in the door together. I took one look at their concerned faces and burst into tears.

They both moved to comfort me and even in my distress, I was relieved that Peter got there first, flourishing the starched handkerchief he always had in his pocket. I wasn't quite ready for a hug from Ned yet, not so soon after seeing what his bare chest looked like.

'Oh, you poor mite,' Peter was saying. 'That was a very nasty little piece. Actionable, actually. I just came in to tell you that I've seen Duncan and he says not to worry – we'll get the bastards.'

Ned was reading it again and shaking his head in fury.

'What a bunch of fuckers,' he was saying. 'This is so wrong.'

'But the thing is,' I said, blinking back the deluge of tears which was trying to flood out. 'I do go on free trips and I do drink bloody Bollie at launch parties and Becca is a luxury-brand PR and she is my friend, I can't deny any of that. The only thing I can say in my defence is that it really doesn't affect what I write. But that's just my word and as I do write positive things about some of the brands – the ones I really do think are great – I am compromised.'

Peter looked thoughtful, then he took the media section from Ned's hands and threw it into my bin.

'There, that's where that is going at the end of today. You've worked on papers long enough to know that things like this, while unpleasant at the time, blow over very quickly. Hamster cages and all that. It's a very upsetting experience when you're the brunt of it, but in the long term, it's just a blip, so try not to worry about it. Just carry on doing your work as brilliantly and ethically as you always have and you will be fine. Success is the sweetest revenge, I have always found.'

He patted my head, consolingly – he wasn't the most physical of people – and turned to leave my office, when something occurred to me.

'Peter,' I said. 'Before you go, one last thing – do you think Jeanette could have had a hand in this?'

'Almost certainly,' said Peter, looking rather pleased about it. 'And I'm hoping she did, because it might be just the thing finally to get her fired.'

I felt a little comforted by Peter's comments, but after he left, and Ned had gone off to the canteen to get me a comforting bun, I sat gormlessly at my desk for a moment, wondering what to do. Get back to work, I finally told myself, like Peter said, that was the only thing for it.

I clicked on to the Internet and checked out a few new luxury shopping sites I'd heard about, but I couldn't concentrate. I stared into space for a little while and then my glance rested on Jay's beautiful blue flowers and I had another idea – I logged on to Google and typed in his name.

As the screen immediately filled, I wondered why I hadn't done it sooner. There were pages and pages about him. Most of them were articles – and pictures, which made my heart turn over – in trashy magazines, but there were quite a few *New York Times* and *Wall Street Journal* stories as well, and even some Amazon links to books about the Fisher family and their fortune. I clicked on one of those.

Fishers of Fortune, it was called, with the subhead: 'How the Fisher family took control of the American banking system'.

I scrolled down and read the longer description of the book.

Leading *Washington Post* reporter, Jerry Mulhew,
analyses the rise and rise of one of America's rich-
est dynasties, from its origins as a small-town savings
and loan started by two brothers, to an international
banking empire.

The book examines the extraordinary financial brilliance of five generations of one family and also looks
into the legend of the Fisher family curse, which has
arisen from the untimely deaths of at least one son in
every generation since the bank began.

I knew Jay's older brother, Bob, had died when he was
twenty-three, but I'd had no idea about a family curse, that
was really horrible. For a moment my hand hesitated with
the cursor poised on the 'Buy It With One Click' box.

If I bought that book, I could find out all about Jay's
family in one fell swoop. It was really tempting, but instead
I closed the page and then Google. I didn't want to get
to know him in that artificial way. I would wait and put it
together through what he told me, as I would have to do
with any other man.

Ned came back with the coffee and we spent the rest of
the morning with the designer who had been assigned to us,
going through the articles we were planning to use for the
first two weeks of the new supplement.

Work was the perfect distraction, just as Peter had said it
would be, and as I went through it all I began to feel really
excited about the section again. Once it came out and people

saw how cool – and unbiased – it was, spiteful little reports like that one would be forgotten.

I also had the chance to ask Ned about his killer body. Somehow I felt talking about it openly would put an end to any further sexually-charged moments between us.

'So tell me, Ned,' I said, as we started to wrap up for lunch. 'How did you get that body of yours? I had no idea you were a man mountain beneath that terrible suit.'

He grinned at me and flexed one bicep like a cartoon muscleman.

'I used to play water polo for Australia,' he said.

'Wow,' I said. 'Very impressive. Did you have to give it up when you moved here?'

'Pretty much. I could have moved to Italy to play professionally there, but I just wanted to be a journalist, so here I am.'

'Do you still train?'

He nodded. 'Five times a week. Why do you think my hair's such a mess?'

At twelve thirty I left my office for my own preferred form of training – my Iyengar yoga class. I had just pushed the button in the lift, and the doors were closing, when someone barged in. It was Jeanette.

'Not a very positive piece in the *Post* today, Stella,' she said, with her crocodile smile. 'Rather personal, wasn't it?'

I felt like planting a smart punch on her liver-y lips, as I was pretty much convinced that she was behind it, considering her track record of planting unpleasant stories about me in the press, but I forced myself to stay cool.

'That's just newspapers, isn't it?' I said, shrugging. 'You're always going to get your share of nastiness when you're ahead, aren't you?'

I don't know how she took that, because I spent the rest of the ride looking resolutely at the lift door and was very glad when we got to the ground floor and I could speed off. She was really starting to give me the creeps.

The afternoon got off to a brighter start, when the post boy, Martin, turned up at my office door carrying a large package with a gold balloon attached to it. The balloon had the words 'Pop Me!' printed all over it.

'Can I do it?' asked Martin shyly.

I handed him my letter knife and he gleefully stabbed it, until it burst and a small key fell out on to the floor. Meanwhile, I had opened the package, to find an old-fashioned jewellery box, which I unlocked with the key.

Inside was an invitation to a fragrance launch – but not just any fragrance launch. It was from the classic French house of Huguenot for their new scent, Précieuse, and their launches were legendary, more like fabulous balls than corporate events. This one was black tie, which was always a good start.

I'd received a diary note about it a couple of weeks before, so I'd known it was coming, but there was one problem. The invitation said: 'Stella Fain and Guest'. Who could I take?

I'd asked Ned, but he'd already accepted an invitation to a major mobile phone launch the same night. Tim would have loved it, but he was back in Iraq, and I realized that with all that had been going on, I had rather lost touch with the various other men I had used before in a human hand-bag capacity.

I got on the phone to a couple of them, but to no avail.

One had acquired a proper girlfriend who, he said, would not appreciate him going out with another woman, even just as friends, while the other one was clearly pissed off not to have heard from me for so long and told me, in very icy tones, that he was busy that night – and the rest of his life.

I put the phone down on him and pulled a face at it.

If only Jay had been around, I thought. I could just imagine how heavenly he would look in a dinner jacket. But even if he had been in town – and even if Ham had not made me promise not to see him – our presence at such a public event would only have unleashed the hounds of paparazzi hell on us again.

Nothing was simple about that relationship, I thought sadly, except how much I liked being with him.

I was just wondering whether to ask Peter to come with me, when inspiration struck. I rang Alex at work and invited him. He sounded really surprised – and really pleased – and said he would be delighted to come with me. It was a relief that something seemed to have worked out neatly.

The day of the launch, I had my hair done in the morning and got changed in the office. I was wearing a taupe chiffon Alberta Ferretti dress I'd picked up in the Harvey Nichols sale, with the baroque pearl and diamond earrings Ham had given me for my eighteenth birthday and a pair of gold Manolo skyscraper heels. It was hard to see myself properly in the awful light in the office loos, but I thought I looked OK. I always felt good in gold shoes.

As I headed for the lift, I heard a loud wolf whistle. I looked in the direction it had come from and saw Ned, standing by the photocopier, grinning at me.

'Nice dress, Stella,' he said, looking me over, shamelessly, from head to toe, just as he had done that day at the pool.

Even from a distance, I could see he had that wicked look in his eyes; the one that rendered the newspaper's librarians into blushing ninnies. I wasn't going to let him do the same to me. There were strict limits to our professional relationship, as far as I was concerned.

'Nice suit, Ned,' I replied. 'Oh no, silly me – it's the same one you always wear. Anyway, have fun at your phone launch.'

'Have fun with your stepbrother,' said Ned.

Bastard, I thought. He always got the last word in.

I'd arranged to pick Alex up from his office building in the City, which was on the way back into the West End from the *Journal*. He was waiting outside when I got there and before he noticed the taxi pulling up, I had a moment to reflect on how good he looked in his dinner jacket.

I realized I hadn't seen him in one since my twenty-first birthday party and he still wore it well. Remarkably well, actually. Women pouring out of the office entrance were turning back for another glance at him.

His face broke into a broad smile when he saw me – that uncomplicated smile that used to make my stomach do cartwheels when I was a teenager. Now it gave me a simpler warm feeling; of familial affection, nothing more, whatever Ned said.

'Hey, Stella,' said Alex, getting into the cab. 'You look absolutely gorgeous.'

He kissed me warmly on both cheeks.

'You look pretty 007 fabulous yourself, Alex,' I said.

'I do enjoy getting into this rig-up, actually,' he said. 'Girls love it. I got changed far earlier than I needed to, so I could pose round the office a bit.'

He grinned at me again.

'So,' he said, 'what's this jolly all about? Something about scent, did you say?'

I explained that Huguenot was one of the classic French fragrance houses, with a long noble tradition, like Guerlain, and that they only launched a new perfume about once every five years, so it was always a big deal and the parties were extravagant production numbers.

It was apparent from the moment we arrived that this one was no exception. There was a huge marquee set up next to the Serpentine Gallery, covered in gold fabric, the entrance guarded by two muscly chaps clad Nubian-style, with loin cloths and turbans and not much else, their skin painted gold from head to toe.

Inside, the marquee had been done up like a fantasy of the *Arabian Nights*, lit by hanging lanterns, with a lot of low-slung furniture, piled with embroidered velvet cushions.

The first room was a stand-up-and-mingle area, where we were greeted at the entrance by the Huguenot luminaries. There was Jean-Pierre Huguenot-Lafalle, the CEO, who I had interviewed several times over the years; another chap I had also profiled, who was the nose of the house and created the fragrances; and Tara Ryman, who did the PR for them among her many prestigious clients.

They all welcomed me effusively, and it felt more like a party given by friends than a big corporate do – especially when I saw Becca walk in.

The nasty piece in the *Post* did flash across my mind, as I waved to her, then turned to take my first glass of Taittinger for the evening. But while I was doing exactly what I had been accused of in that spiteful piece, my conscience was clear. If I didn't like Précieuse I simply wouldn't write about it. Censure by exclusion was my trademark.

'Hi, Stella,' said Tara, warmly. 'Who's your arm candy tonight?' she whispered into my ear, while we exchanged air kisses.

'Oh, Tara,' I said, deliberately pulling back from her. 'This is my stepbrother, Alex Urquhart Muir.'

From the expression on her face as she welcomed him, I could see that Tara was just as delighted to meet him as she said she was, which was not something you could always rely on with a PR as successful as her.

Right from the start, it was clear that Alex had been a great choice as my party handbag. He fitted in perfectly with everyone I introduced him to and he totally knew how to play the corporate game – asking the nose, who was at our table for the dinner, all the right questions about the fragrance. And then, of course, he looked so good.

Many of the women I knew there, from various publications and department stores, asked me who my new boyfriend was, in clearly envious tones, and it amused me greatly to tell them that he wasn't my boyfriend – he was my stepbrother. I then casually added that he was a lawyer for a merchant bank, he was single, he owned his own house in Fulham, and I would be delighted to introduce them to him. If I could have got in his love of children and dogs I would have.

I was sure a lot of hearts were beating faster in the breasts of the single women at that party, but the one I had secretly marked out for Alex, was Becca, who was sitting at the table next to us. That was one wedding list I would have been delighted to help her plan.

After the dinner and speeches Alex and I danced a bit, but I kept finding excuses to go elsewhere whenever Becca was around so he felt he had to ask her to dance.

On about my sixteenth trip to the loo, Becca followed me in there.

'What are you doing, Stella?' she said. 'Why are you trying to fix me up with Alex – and so blatantly? It's really embarrassing.'

'Don't you like him?' I asked her. There was no point in denying it.

'Oh, don't be silly, Stella. That's irrelevant. It's not going to happen, so stop trying to engineer it. A, he's completely out of my league lookswise, in case you haven't noticed. And B, it's quite obvious he's mad about you. The two of you are the most gorgeous couple here. Everyone is saying that.'

'Oh, now you don't be silly,' I said. 'We're *so* not a couple, you know that. He's my stepbrother, I've known him since I was eight. I simply don't have those feelings about him and I'm sure he doesn't have them about me. We're just really comfortable together, because we've known each other so long. And even if he did like me in that way, it's irrelevant, because he just doesn't stir my loins,' I added, leaning into the mirror to do my lipstick and hoping she would drop the subject.

'Well, he stirs mine,' Becca went on. 'And he stirs most of the women here, so you'd better watch yourself. Eventually, he will go off with someone else and then you'll be sorry.

He's bloody gorgeous and Toria says he's doing terribly well at Weller Wright Fisher.'

I nearly gave myself whiplash my head snapped so quickly back to attention.

'What?' I said.

'Alex?' said Becca, looking at me strangely. 'He's doing very well at work.'

'Weller Wright Fisher?'

'Yes, that's where he works – oh, my God,' she said suddenly, and burst into peals of laughter. 'You were in that ghastly magazine dancing with *Jay* Fisher, that must have been so funny for Alex. Dancing with the boss's son. What a hoot – you should have put a good word in for him.'

'Yes,' I said weakly. 'We did have a good laugh about that.'

'Did you ever hear from him again? Jay, I mean,' said Becca, in more conspiratorial tones. 'He's really nice, when you get to know him, isn't he? He usually comes to the Cartier polo. What a dish. He's even better-looking than Alex actually, which is saying something. You should have got in there. Then you could have come to us for the ring.'

She roared again and I did my best to join in.

I didn't think I could have felt any more stupid about my idiocy in not realizing who Jay was when I first met him, but I did now. No wonder Alex had known who he was that day he had arrived at Willow Barn. I'd not only sprung an incredibly handsome dude in a flashy sports car on my unsuspecting stepbrother, but he was also the boss's son. No wonder he'd left so swiftly.

I felt like a total banana.

The party was still in full swing when I eventually emerged

from the loo. The DJ was great and there was a virtual queue of women waiting to dance with Alex – a situation I had spent the earlier part of the evening engineering, but all the fun had gone out of it for me.

I felt so stupid not realizing he worked for the Fishers and it made me feel really uncomfortable with him – adding a whole extra layer to the reasons why I didn't want anyone to know I was still seeing Jay.

Becca's remark that Alex was clearly 'mad about me' had pissed me off too. I wished everyone could leave me alone about that. He wasn't. We were just particularly at ease with each other.

Which was apparent almost immediately, when I slumped into a chair at our table, feeling suddenly exhausted. He came off the dance floor at the end of the track and sat down next to me.

'I'm knackered,' he said. 'Can I please have a break from dancing with single women for a while? It's exhausting being the focus of so much expectation. Excluding you, of course. I could probably find a last shred of energy if you want another spin on the dance floor. Would you?'

I smiled weakly at him.

'I'm fine thanks, Alex,' I lied. 'I'm happy just to watch the fun for a while.'

He turned and looked at me, with his head on one side.

'Have you had enough, Stells?' he said, softly. 'Want to go? It is a school night after all.'

I sighed with relief and nodded. Suddenly I wanted to go home more than anything in the world. He really could read me.

And as he effortlessly found us a taxi in Kensington Gore

and climbed into it next to me, saying he'd drop me home first and then take it on to Fulham, which was so far out of his way it was a joke, it made me understand something with renewed clarity.

There certainly wasn't a chasm of experience between me and Alex, the way there was with Jay. Quite the opposite, really. He was almost too suffocatingly close.

The next day I was very glad I had left the party relatively early. I needed all my wits about me for the day I later came to think of as Black Friday.

It started relatively normally. I got into work on time, I was checking my emails and post, the usual stuff, and about half an hour after he should have, Ned came in with a stonking hangover from his mobile phone launch, sporting several livid love bites on his neck, and carrying four lattes from his preferred coffee emporium.

We were comparing notes on our respective parties – he was smelling my bottle of Précieuse and I was checking out the full-on movie viewing feature on his new mobile – when Peter came to my office door, looking rather grim.

'Are you all right?' I said. 'Sit down, have one of Ned's many coffees.'

'Oh, I'm fine,' he said, closing the door and sitting down in the chair that Ned had just vacated for him. 'But I will have that nasty coffee, actually.'

That was when I really knew something was up. Peter loathed plastic 'baby' coffee, as he called it. He liked the plunger variety, which he had explained to me – at length, on several occasions – is actually stronger than the espresso machine variety, because it sits on the beans for much longer.

What now? I thought. A full close-up of me air kissing Jean-Pierre Huguenot-Lafalle on the cover of *Time* magazine?

'I've got some rather disappointing news for you two,' he said, taking a sip of Ned's latte and pulling a disgusted face. 'Oh God, but it's not bad enough to drink that foul coffee – take it back, please, yuk. Now listen, I've just been up with Duncan and he is postponing the launch of the section.'

'What?' cried Ned and I, in unison.

'Yes, I know, it's a frightful bore, but that's newspapers, isn't it? Hurry up and wait, that's how it goes here. Kill yourself getting something ready for a ridiculous deadline and then, no, whoops, we've changed our mind, we'll do that later . . .'

'He hasn't changed his mind completely, has he?' I asked, determined to know the full truth however awful it was. 'That stupid thing in the *Post* hasn't put him off the idea, has it?'

'No, no,' said Peter. 'He was very clear about that – he's just postponing it for several reasons. There are production issues, plus the ad people say they're not quite ready to go live, and on top of that he's got some heavy board meetings coming up that he wants out of the way before your section starts up – or any of the other new projects he's working on, for that matter.'

'Any idea how long this postponement might be?' said Ned.

'No,' said Peter, with his customary bluntness. 'But I know the board meetings are in three weeks' time, so you've got at least a month, probably a bit longer. I'd say two, in all honesty.'

'What are we supposed to do in that time?' asked Ned.

'Yes,' I added. 'Do we carry on commissioning?'

Peter looked a little uneasy.

'No, he wants you to lay off on that for the time being. Just go back to writing features, the way you were before.'

Something else occurred to me. Petty, I knew, but important in the newspaper scheme of things.

'Am I allowed to keep my office?' I asked.

Peter's face creased into a broad smile.

'That's my girl,' he said. 'You know what really matters on this paper – yes, as far as I know, you are staying in this prime piece of *Journal* real estate.'

'Actually, Peter,' I said, running the whole scenario through my head at high speed, to make sure I was quite clear about all the implications. 'I've got two more questions. Do I carry on going to the section editors' meetings – and do I have to answer to Jeanette again? I suppose I do.'

'Yes, I'm afraid you're right about that. The Lovely Jeanette is still features editor, so you will have to work to her brief again, temporarily. But that's why it's also really important that you carry on going to the section editors' meetings. You still are one – it's just on hold. OK?'

Peter left my office, followed shortly after by Ned, and I sat there for a moment, feeling a bit shell-shocked. Then I decided I might as well just get on with it.

I was going through the huge pile of press releases on my desk, when a bleep announced that I had an intraoffice email. It was from Jeanette's assistant saying that she wanted a list of features ideas from me – by three o'clock that afternoon.

She didn't lose any time, I thought, and opened the list of

feature ideas I had for my section, to see if there was anything I should pass on to her before they went out of date. I could be fair-minded and professional, even if she couldn't.

I was just about lost in my work again when the alarm on my Palm Pilot went off. I was delighted to see that it was reminding me I had a work lunch and a tea to go to that day – the perfect distractions.

I had to walk past Jeanette's office on my way to the lift and although I didn't deliberately look in – I always made a point not to – I couldn't help noticing that Martin Ryan was in there with her. Jeanette had her back to me, but I saw Martin's shark eyes watch me go by.

The lunch, in the private room upstairs at The Ivy, was the newspaper launch – they'd hit the magazines months before – for a range of vintage sunglasses.

They'd been unearthed in an old optometrist's shop in Italy, by an LA-based stylist, who presented herself as the classic la-la-land fluff bunny, but who clearly really had a steely business mind.

'Peggy Guggenheim used to buy all her eyewear from this store in Venice, Italy,' Leandra, the pretend fluff bunny, was telling us, while sporting a pair of huge black and white stripy sunglasses it was difficult to ignore. 'So I went over and found they had a whole warehouse of old stock. I bought it. So here we are, with a collection of vintage shades with an amazing provenance, but refitted to twenty-first-century eyewear standards.'

Here we are, I thought, with sunglasses at £600 a pop. But that was fine by me. I knew they'd sell out in Browns before the end of the month and I'd get a great feature out of it, which we could illustrate with a fabulous archive pic of Peggy Guggenheim wearing crazy sunglasses and a kaftan, sitting in a gondola.

It was just the kind of brainless distraction I needed, and I was feeling quite cheered up, until we got to the coffee and in a lull in the conversation, Laura Birchwood suddenly piped up.

'I hear your new luxury section has been cancelled, Stella,' she said, from the other end of the table of twelve, so everyone could hear.

'No, it hasn't,' I said. Which was the truth. And I wasn't even going to dignify her comment by explaining the situation – or asking how she'd heard that. I knew the answer to that anyway: her pal Natalie had clearly got right on the phone to her.

'So, when is it launching then?' persisted Laura.

'I really can't reveal that,' I said, as patronizingly as I could. 'It's strictly embargoed.'

I was happy with the way I'd handled it, because I hadn't expected the news to have travelled quite so fast, but I was still glad to get out of the lunch.

I had over an hour before tea at The Berkeley, so I decided that a walk through the humming centre of town to the retail bliss of the West End was what I needed. A scramble around the big Zara in Regent Street, followed by the flagship Top Shop and, if I had time, New Look and Warehouse too. Bond Street shopping was work for me, the Oxford Street chain stores were my private therapy.

I decided to make a small detour first to Coco de Mer in Covent Garden, to see if they had anything new and particularly saucy in. I'd already featured the store in my pages as a new wrinkle on the luxury market – prestige erotica – and I loved the place.

With its sensual atmosphere and all the naughty books and toys on display, just being in that shop was a turn-on, and I wished I could call Jay to meet me there and then. I bought a vintage lace blindfold as a hostage to fortune that I would see him again very soon. At £68 it was something of an investment.

It was as I stepped back to Monmouth Street that I saw them. Standing outside the Covent Garden Hotel just up the street, were Ham and a blonde woman, who from the back could have been Chloe. But when she turned to get into the taxi, I could see it clearly wasn't her, because there was no pregnant belly. Just the very slender figure of the type of woman Ham particularly liked.

I felt physically sick and told myself not to be stupid, he was probably just saying goodbye to a work associate, but then I saw him put a hand on her waist and pull her to him. There was no mistaking it. He kissed her full on the mouth and even from a distance I could tell tongues were involved. The final confirmation was when I saw his big meaty hand reach down and squeeze her buttock.

The taxi door slammed and the cab pulled away, leaving my father standing on the kerb wearing the satisfied smile of a man who has just got seriously laid.

I felt some kind of small explosion take place in my head and without a conscious thought my feet were running across the road and up to the hotel. He'd made me lie to women in the past to cover his tracks, and I'd done it for him, but there was no way I was going to let him get away with this one.

By the time I had reached him and grabbed his arm roughly, my fury had turned to ice.

'I saw you,' I said, practically spitting the words into his confused and shocked face. 'I know what you're doing. Don't do it, Ham. Not this time.'

'Darling one,' he tried to say, turning on his autopilot charm offensive. 'Whatever are you talking about, my little one?'

'Don't little one me. I know what you're up to. You just fucked that skinny blonde, don't try and deny it.'

He gaped at me. He tried to smile again, but I think he realized he was trapped.

'I've been around you and your womanizing my whole life,' I hissed at him. 'Jesus, you've even used me to cover up for you in the past, which is how I know this is one of your preferred schtupping venues, so don't bother saying anything. Just listen to me . . .'

I tapped my finger against his chest hard, as I made my points. I wanted to hurt him.

'Chloe is pregnant,' I said. 'I know you are phobic about fat chicks, but do not do this to her. I'll take her side if you do. She's the best woman you've ever had – and I include my mother in that, even though I didn't know her. So for once in your life, Dad, keep it zipped. And I don't mean your mouth.'

He just stared at me, frozen. He had tears in his eyes and I was glad.

'I'll be watching you,' I said viciously, and I turned my back on him and walked away, fast.

He called after me, but I ignored him and when I saw a cab at Seven Dials, I jumped into it.

'Hello, darling,' said the cabbie. 'Where can I take you?'

I had no idea. Suddenly Zara and Top Shop had lost all their allure and I knew I wasn't going anywhere near that tea at The Berkeley. I wasn't up to making interested remarks about a bespoke mascara service. I wasn't ready to go back to the office either and my house was way too close to Ham's territory.

I gave him the address of Margot's nursing home.

19

As we got closer to Avonlea Residential Care Home, I wondered whether a visit to Margot had been such a good idea. It was well after lunchtime and she was liable to be in a deep, alcoholic fug. She probably wouldn't even remember I'd been afterwards, but I decided to go anyway. I needed to see someone I could talk to about my dad – with no inhibitions.

I got out of the cab at an off licence nearby and bought her a large bottle of brandy, a bottle of Moët, and a carton of cigarettes. I always struggled with my conscience about doing that, but she would just buy them herself anyway and the look of delight when you turned up with those kinds of presents, was the closest to happiness I think she ever got any more.

I also bought her a pile of glossy magazines, which she still enjoyed looking at. She liked the 'gowns', she used to tell me.

'Daaaaaaarling,' she said, when I walked in, clapping her manicured hands with delight. 'What an unexpected joy. Come and tell me everything – in filthy detail.'

She was much more lucid than I had been expecting. It must have been a good day and it clearly got better for her, when she saw what I'd brought with me.

'Oooh, you marvellously clever girl,' she said in her throatiest tones. 'I did train you well. Just open that cupboard by my bed, would you, sweetheart?'

She directed me to the middle shelf and behind a frilly make-up bag, was a box of sugar cubes and a bottle of angostura bitters.

'Did you mean these?' I asked her, holding them up, her plan becoming clear to me.

She giggled girlishly and nodded. 'Champagne cocktails all round, don't you think?'

So I made us the drinks just as I had learned to, from her book of cocktail recipes – she even had a couple of champagne flutes stashed in her underwear drawer, along with some emergency gin – and between us, we quickly polished off the whole bottle of Moët.

After the third champagne cocktail, I was already so pissed I was slurring my words – and I was smoking, which was something I never did.

And in my drunken state, I told her the entire story of me and Jay, and Ham's interference, plus the problems I was having at work, all leading up to what I had seen in Monmouth Street that afternoon.

I had no idea how much of it she took in and I didn't really care. I just needed to tell someone the whole unexpurgated history and, as long as I kept mixing the drinks, Margot was all ears.

When we finished the champagne we moved on to neat cognac and after a couple of those I was beginning to feel like maybe I really had drunk enough.

I was starting to nod off a bit in my chair, when suddenly, through the pall of smoke between us, her Rank starlet tones rang out. It was as though someone had suddenly turned the radio on. To the Home Service.

'So what you are telling me, darling girl,' she said, ashing her cigarette on to the floor, with great aplomb. 'Is that for the first time in your life you are really in love with this young man – who is very handsome and frightfully rich. You are also having a tiresome time at work. Well, I really don't see what your dilemma is. You must go to him immediately. Stuff the job. Let him spoil you. Enjoy yourself. And as for your wretched father? Stuff him too. It's time a woman stood up to him – and who better than you?'

And then she fell asleep – or unconscious, there wasn't much in between with Margot – in her chair. I kissed her on her powdery cheek and left.

I rang Jay from the cab home.

'I'm drunk,' was the first thing I said to him. 'I'm really really falling-down drunk, so don't hold any of this against me, but I had to call you.'

Jay laughed.

'You do sound loaded. What's going on?'

'I've had the shittiest of shit days and I just got completely hammered with my dad's second wife. She's a total alky, but I love her.'

'What was so shit?' he said, sounding genuinely concerned.

'Oh, just all kinds of crap at work and then – then . . .' I started crying, I couldn't help myself. 'I saw my dad with another woman . . .'

Now I was wailing. The taxi driver was glancing at me in his rear-view mirror, with some concern. Probably worried I might be about to vomit all over his cab. He might be right, I thought, starting to hiccup between wails.

'Oh, you poor baby,' said Jay.

'I mean, I know my dad is a total womanizer,' I was gabbling. 'He always has been and he used to make me answer the phone and lie to women, when I was just a little girl, but I thought he might have finally grown up and he hasn't. He's just a total bastard and I love Chloe and she's pregnant. How *could* he, Jay? I mean, he drones on and on about the sanctity of "family" until it makes you want to spew, and then as soon as his pregnant wife grows a belly, he's off schtupping the first skinny blonde who hoves into view. He's such a hypocrite and a liar.'

'Oh, baby,' Jay kept saying. 'That is hard, that is real hard. I wish I was there for you.'

I wailed and hiccupped a bit more.

'Look,' he said, suddenly sounding businesslike. 'We can't go on like this. I've got a big meeting with my dad this afternoon – at the bank, nightmare – and I've got to go up to Rhode Island with him this weekend, I can't get out of it, big family powwow, but as soon as that's done, I'm coming over there. I'm going to be there for you. I'll leave Monday night, OK?'

And I just wept into the phone with relief.

I woke early on Saturday morning with a hangover from hell. Did Margot wake up feeling like that every day? No wonder she drank; the only way to get over hangovers like that would be to get loaded again.

I groped for my phone and checked to see if Jay had rung. He had, leaving a beautiful message saying he would leave his phone on all night and that I could call him whenever I wanted. There was also a short, rather strained one, from Ham, saying that they had gone down to Willow Barn and that he would try me again later. I deleted it.

Ham left several more messages over the weekend and I just zapped them all without even listening to them properly. I hadn't quite worked out how I was going to handle it with him, because if I declared war, we would have to give Chloe an explanation. Then inspiration struck. I would use the truth to cover up his lies.

I rang his mobile and left this message.

'It's Stella. Don't call me back. I'm not talking to you and I don't want to see you – possibly ever again. But don't worry, I won't tell anyone why. I'm good at keeping your secrets. I've done it all my life, after all. And you can tell Chloe I'm angry with you because of your fatwa against Jay Fisher. You're good at lying, Dad. You won't find it very hard.'

I hoped it would really hurt him.

After all that, I was more than relieved to get back into work on Monday morning, and I breezed into the section editors' meeting, feeling quite light-hearted. That was short-lived. Once everyone was settled down and ready, Martin Ryan looked up at me over his frameless glasses.

'Stella,' he said. 'This is a surprise. We didn't expect to see you here today.'

I just looked back at him, not getting his point.

'This is the section editors' meeting, Stella,' he said slowly, as though he was talking to a halfwit, his cold eyes disappearing behind the flash of the lenses. 'And as you don't have a section any more, you don't need to be here, do you? So you can go back to your desk.'

For a moment, I just looked at him, unable to believe what I was hearing and then I had no choice. I picked up my notebook and pen and left the meeting room, feeling like a schoolgirl who had been sent out of class.

By the time I got back to my desk, I was trembling with fury, but I was thinking very clearly. I got a form out of my filing cabinet and filled it in. Then I went straight up to Doughnut's office and gave it to his PA.

'This is a holiday form, Sheila,' I said. 'Starting today. I've got six weeks due to me and I'm taking it all. Will you please tell Mr McDonagh that as my section has been postponed, I might as well take some time off now, so I'll be raring to go when it starts up. And if he needs me to come back early, you just have to ring me. I'll be on my mobile.'

Sheila nodded.

'I'm sure that will be fine,' she said.

But I didn't really care whether it was or not, I was out of there. I stopped off in my office briefly to collect my stuff and to send explanatory emails to Ned, Tim and Peter, then I left.

I called Jay as soon as I was out of the building.

'Don't get on that flight tonight,' I told him. 'I'm coming over there to see you.'

'You are?' he said, sounding delighted. 'Wow, that is the best news, I can't tell you. I'm having a truly heinous time with my dad, right now, and I can think of nothing better than having you come visit.'

'So, what's your address?' I said, feeling dizzily carefree and excited.

'Don't worry about that,' he said. 'I'll meet you at the airport. And don't worry about your flight either. Just go to the BA desk at Heathrow and it will all be fixed for you. Which flight do you want to get?'

Unlike Jay, I didn't have the New York–London flight schedule off by heart, so he told me to get the next plane, which left in three hours.

'Have you got your passport with you?' he asked.

I did. I was a newspaper journalist, I always carried my passport.

'Great,' he said. 'Then just go straight to the airport from the office. We'll get you everything you need when you're here.'

I was stumped for a moment. It was such an alien concept to go somewhere without packing, but when I thought about it, if I had him to look after me, what did I really need?

For once, perhaps, I could leave my baggage behind.

From the moment I landed at JFK, my time with Jay was charmed. He was waiting at the gate when I came through from customs and I practically fell into his arms. He had a black stretch limo outside and, as we climbed in, he turned off the intercom and closed the window between us and the driver.

'Welcome to New York,' he said, smiling as he unbuttoned my shirt.

By the time we pulled up outside his building in SoHo, he'd made love to me twice. Then we went up to his apartment and did it some more.

I woke up jet-lag early the next day and leaving him sleeping, went to look at his place, which I'd hardly taken in the night before. A whole floor of a classic SoHo loft conversion, it was huge, incredibly light, and the walls were covered in books and fantastic paintings. It was exactly the kind of apartment I had expected Jay to live in.

I made myself some tea – I was pleased to see he had my favourite English Breakfast tea bags in for me, he knew what I liked – and I sat down on one of his several sofas, to take it all in.

In pride of place on a blank wall between the floor-to-ceiling bookcases was a classic Warhol portrait of a woman. I got up off the sofa and perched on the window seat so I could look at it properly. There was something familiar about her face, but I couldn't place it.

I was still gazing at it, when Jay appeared, naked, rubbing his tummy, in that sweet, boyish way he had.

'Saying hi to Mom, are you?' he said, smiling at me through blinky eyes.

'Is that your mother?' I said.

He nodded.

'She looks like you,' I said, realizing why the face had looked familiar. 'Same eyes.'

'Yeah, people say that,' said Jay, sitting down next to me and putting his arm around my waist. He kissed the top of my head. 'Hey, baby,' he said. 'It's so good you're here.'

I just sighed and rested my head against his shoulder. I felt completely relaxed with him. There was no awkwardness between us at all and sitting there with him, the various big messes I had left behind in London seemed irrelevant and unimportant.

'I suppose that's a real Warhol, right?'

'Yeah,' said Jay, casually. 'Mom was good friends with him. She was one of the first people he did in that style.'

Immediately, the Grand Canyon yawned between us again. He wasn't acting cool, it just wasn't a big deal to him.

'Oh,' I said.

From that first day – when he sent me off to Barneys in a chauffeured car, with his charge card, to buy everything I needed for my stay – there were numerous more occasions when I was reminded of that chasm, but in the end I made a conscious decision to stop letting it freak me out.

Instead, I just relaxed and let myself enjoy it. Of course, I had my own money for bits and pieces, I wasn't entirely a kept woman, but once I surrendered to it, it was actually rather nice to let him spoil me for a while. Margot had been right about that.

And as I met more of his friends – mostly other money bunnies, like George and Zaria, some hideous like her, but mostly OK in a rich-kid way – I realized that it was the differences between us, combined with all the things we shared, that made the relationship so compelling for us both.

Although we socialized a bit, most of the time it was just the two of us, doing all the things we both loved to do. Going to galleries and museums in the morning and movies in the afternoon. Browsing in bookshops. Lying on our backs in Central Park, watching the clouds go by. Whiling away afternoons just talking in all the great little bars and cafés he knew. And dancing into the small hours, sometimes in seriously cool clubs, sometimes just the two of us in his apartment.

He took me to my first baseball game and I took him to his first Iyengar yoga class and the rest of the time we made love like the pair of rampant loved-up crazies we were. It was one long magic-carpet ride.

The only irritation was Ham calling and texting me furiously for the first few days, until eventually I relented and called him back.

'Where are you?' he practically screamed down the phone at me. 'You're not in the mews and I've called your office and they've told me you've gone on holiday and I've been going out of my mind with worry. We all have.'

'I'm in New York staying with a friend,' I said. 'After what happened, I just couldn't stand to be anywhere near you and your fake family values, so I'm staying here for a few weeks.'

'Who are you staying with in New York?' he asked me, suspiciously. I just ignored him.

'Is everyone OK?' I asked him. 'How's Chloe? How's Daisy?'

'They're all fine. They all send love.'

There was a long silence and I did nothing to fill it. I wasn't going to make it easy for him. Eventually he spoke again.

'I'm sorry, Stella,' he said, and he did sound it. 'I've been really stupid and what you said that day has really made me think. I'm really sorry I have behaved so badly with women all your life. It's hardly surprising you find it hard to trust men. And you're right, Chloe is the best woman in the world and I won't do anything to jeopardize that. Please forgive me, Stella, if you can?'

I thought for a moment. He did sound sorry, but it wasn't enough. And how dare he make sweeping statements about me not trusting men? I trusted Jay implicitly. I just didn't trust *him*.

343

'No,' I said, eventually. 'I won't.'

And I hung up.

One of the most joyful things about being in New York with Jay, after our time creeping around London like fugitives, hiding from my father and the paparazzi, was the sense of freedom.

We strolled around SoHo holding hands and Jay was completely uninhibited about public displays of affection. He'd stand on a street corner snogging me, while we waited for the lights to change, if that's what he felt like doing.

I asked him about it one day, when we were sitting in our regular daytime haunt, Café Gitane, which was just round the corner from the apartment.

'Aren't you worried about the paparazzi here?' I asked him.

'Not much,' he said. 'I've seen them around a bit. I didn't tell you at the time, but one took some pictures of us coming back from that goddam yoga class of yours the other day – I still have sore hamstrings from that, by the way. But I don't think it's a problem because, with all due respect, no one knows who you are here. They'll just think you are one of my many girlfriends.'

He tickled me in the ribs as he said it.

'Am I?' I couldn't help asking, although it was a subject we never went near – exes, long-losts, other love interests, it never came up, it was one of the things I really liked about Jay. We lived in the moment.

'No,' he said, firmly. 'You're my only girlfriend and well you know it, so shut up, or I'll start thinking you're obsessing on the towel monogram.'

I stuck my tongue out at him. He so knew I wasn't.

Spending so much time together, Jay and I really opened up to each other about our respective families and I was so glad I hadn't read that book about the Fishers, as it meant I was able to react with proper sincerity to everything he told me about his brother's untimely death and his appalling relationship with his father.

The problem between them was quite simple, as far as I could tell. First and foremost, they just didn't get on and then, since the death of his brother, Jay was expected to take over running the whole empire when his father retired, and he had absolutely no interest in doing so.

The current sticking point was that his father wanted him to go and work at Fishercorp on a daily basis to get him ready for his inheritance and he just wouldn't do it.

What made Jay really furious about the whole thing, was that although neither of his uncles had children, his aunt had three sons and a daughter, all of them already working in banking, but his father wouldn't even consider any of them for the big gig.

We were lying in bed one afternoon, 'resting', as Jay liked to call it, when a call from his father's PA prompted a major outburst from him and I finally got the whole picture.

'He has this antiquated fixation that it has to pass from the oldest son to his oldest son,' he was saying, pacing around the bedroom, naked, as usual. 'Just because that is how it has always been. It's like something out of an Icelandic chronicle. Jay, son of Robert, son of Robert, son of Robert . . .

'He wouldn't even hand it on to my Uncle Ed, who has been gagging for it all his life, let alone any of my cousins.

I mean even my girl cousin, Lauren, is more interested than me. She has an MBA from Harvard and she's worked at Morgan Stanley since she left college, but no, she won't do and my banker-wanker – as you call them – boy cousins won't do either. It has to be me and I say, no. I know nothing about that world and I couldn't care less. Stalemate.'

'So why do you keep talking to him about it?' I asked, still fairly mystified. 'Can't you just tell him no, you don't want to run a bank, or whatever it is, and that's the end of it?'

'Well, I could do that – if I want to be completely disinherited,' he said, sounding irritated.

'Would that really be so bad?' I said quietly.

He looked at me like I had suddenly started speaking Swahili. I felt the great divide yawn between us again. But it was obvious to me: it was the great monolith of the family money that was making him so unhappy, but it seemed he couldn't let it go any more than his father could.

Unfortunately, I didn't leave it there.

'Would you really be completely disinherited?' I asked.

'No, of course not, he can't touch my trusts, they became mine the day I turned twenty-one, but I wouldn't get anything else. The Hippo would get it all.'

I knew that was a very sore point. The Hippo was his half-brother, Todd, by his father's second wife, Jaclyn, a razor-thin, multi-facelifted, couture-clad, major feature of the social pages, with an apparently insatiable appetite for money and prestige. And having clawed her way up to Sutton Place from humble origins in Queens, she was brutally ambitious for her son.

Jay openly loathed him and called him the Hippo,

because he was somewhat on the chunky side. He'd shown me a very cruel story *New York* magazine had done earlier that year, featuring a long-lens paparazzi shot of the two of them side by side at the family's Palm Beach house, in swimming trunks. 'The Hunk and the Hulk', it had been called.

From what Jay had told me, every pound Todd gained made Jaclyn more determined that in the long term he would triumph as the Fisher heir. And her ambition for her son was equalled only by her jealous hatred of the trim and handsome true heir. As far as I could tell, she was a major cause of the friction between Jay and his father, which she did everything possible to inflame.

'Forgetting the Hippo for a moment,' I persisted, 'aren't your trusts enough to live on?'

He started to get that small crease between his eyebrows. I should have taken it as a warning.

'You tell me,' he said, raising his arms. 'You're living on it.'

'Well, it seems like enough to me,' I said, stung, but determined to keep my cool.

'I guess it is,' said Jay, shrugging. 'But it's not as simple as that, it's not just about the money, it's the principle. You see, since my brother died, I'm the heir. It's my birthright. And like I said, if I bailed, my dear little half-brother would get it all.

'The funny thing is, though, I don't even think my father would want that. He might think I'm a useless piece of shit, but he's a very old-fashioned guy at heart, and when Bob died, I was next in line and that is how it has to be, in his book. Anyway, that's why he keeps trying to force me to become what he wants me to be, not who I am. He's determined to have me on his terms and I'm determined not to let him.'

As he spoke, Jay's face had taken on a set look I had never seen before; his jaw was quite clenched. He was incredibly stubborn, I realized – and maybe not as different from his father as he thought he was. But I could see that would not be a politic thing to say.

'And even aside from that and how much I hate the Hippo's spoilt, ignorant, bigoted butt,' he continued, 'I can't let him inherit – for the memory of my brother, I can't let that happen. Bob loathed the Hippo even more than I do. I mean, Bob was a chip off the old block. He started reading the financial pages when he was at school, and he loved going into Fishercorp – as a kid, that was a treat for him – but he was a good guy too.'

He looked at me sadly.

'I wish you could have met him, Stella, you would have loved him. He was the best of any of us. So, no, the Hippo does not inherit.'

'I think I can understand that, Jay,' I said, still not ready to give up. 'But nevertheless, how can you expect to get the whole thing, if you're not prepared to do something for it?'

The little crease was now a full-on frown. But still I didn't stop.

'I mean, you may not share his values, but it sounds like your dad works really hard to keep it all going, so why should you get it all for nothing? Surely privilege always comes with responsibilities, as well as all the good bits? Nothing's for nothing, Jay.'

I paused for a moment, before ramming my point home.

'Wouldn't Bob have told you that?'

I watched his face turn to stone before me. His eyes, which were normally so full of gentle smiles for me, were hard and cold.

'You know what, Stella,' he said, the sides of his beautiful mouth curling downwards. 'I thought you were on my side. But it turns out, you're just as uptight as the rest of them. And you know what else? You don't have a fucking clue what you're fucking talking about, so why don't you just shut the fuck up?'

And with that, he grabbed his clothes from the bedroom chair and left the room and shortly afterwards, judging by the slammed door, the apartment.

I just lay there in a state of shock. We'd never had a proper row before and this had been a really nasty one. Why hadn't I shut up? I knew even as I was saying it, that I was going way too far, but I couldn't help it, because that was what I really thought. I had to say it. I couldn't live a lie with him, it would just have festered inside me.

And, really, I didn't understand his attitude. How could he expect to inherit all that money without lifting a finger to be involved with any of the administration it entailed? It was the only thing about him that I didn't understand.

That and the way he seemed to be happy to spend his whole life merrily doing nothing. He wasn't stupid, far from it, and I couldn't compute how he could just while his life away as he did, however pleasantly.

And deep down inside there was a little part of me that couldn't respect that. I might not have shared my father's phobia about inherited wealth, but I did – I now realized – have his work ethic. Big time.

I lay there for a bit longer and when Jay didn't come back I started to wonder what to do. Was I supposed to pack and leave before he returned? I got up and dressed, just in case he'd gone out to buy me an air ticket, and then I waited around for half an hour, and when he still didn't come back, or call me, I decided to go out myself.

I didn't have a particular destination in mind, I just wandered around SoHo, looking at the shops and the galleries and the people, which normally entranced me, but none of it held any charm. Eventually I decided to head over to Café Gitane. I thought its familiarity might comfort me.

Jay was already there, sitting at our usual table with his head in his hands. I went over and sat down opposite him. He looked up, with tears in his eyes.

'Oh, honey,' he said, reaching for my hand. 'What took you so long getting here?' And his mouth curved up into its more familiar smile.

I started to speak, but he got in first.

'I'm truly sorry for swearing at you, like that,' he said. 'But I just can't deal with all that stuff, it sends me crazy. And the way you put it, you're probably right about what Bob would have said – and, if I'm honest, my mom has said something similar. So you just hit a sore spot.'

He leaned back with his hands behind his head and sighed loudly.

'It's just that when my dad gets on my back about it – and Jaclyn weighs in – I just flip in my head and it makes me even more determined not to do what he wants. I'm sorry I took that out on you. Real sorry.'

'No,' I said, reaching over to pull down his hands, so I could hold them. 'I'm sorry. I should have shut up. I know how much all that upsets you and you're right, I really don't understand it.'

'Well, go on then, let's try and talk about it.' He sighed deeply again and squeezed my hands back. 'That's what my mom always tells me I have to do – talk about it – so go on, ask me something. Anything.'

'OK,' I said, tentatively. 'If you want to have it both ways, couldn't you make a show of getting involved a bit now, just to mollify your dad and get him off your back, and then, after you inherit, hand it all over to your better-qualified cousins to look after, and just be the titular head?'

I could see he was making heroic efforts to try to stay calm.

'But I don't know where to start with any of it, Stella. I mean, I just have to open *The Wall Street Journal*, and I get a migraine. It's not just that I'm not interested, I simply have no aptitude for it. It makes me feel dumb and I'm not dumb.'

'But surely you did business at college, or something?' I asked.

That was what George and all his money-bunny pals had done. It seemed to be automatic setting for all of them, whatever they finally ended up doing – and most of his cashed-up pals had some kind of hilarious pretend job – so it seemed obvious that Jay would have done that too.

He shook his head and laughed, ruefully.

'Oh, Bob did all that, which meant I didn't have to. So do you really want to know what I did at college, Stella?

That is, until my poor brother fell off that balcony and Daddy dearest forced me to drop out . . .'

I nodded, encouragingly, and he leaned towards me.

'I did architecture, at UCLA, that's what I did. Special area of study, domestic architecture – funny, huh?'

And as I took it in, I did have to laugh. It was all such a stupid mess.

'So that time at Willow Barn wasn't the first time I'd seen your dad,' he continued. 'I went to a lecture he gave at my college. It was so great. I wrote an extended essay on your family home actually, Stella. Got an A, too. How funny is that?'

'Why didn't you tell me all that before?' I asked, incredulous.

He shrugged.

'I was embarrassed. I felt like some kind of groupie. Then, when it turned out he hated me it was too late and just seemed to make it all more complicated, so I kept quiet.'

The craziness of the situation gave me the courage to ask my other big question.

'So if you had to stop your studies, but you won't go and work at the bank, isn't there something else you could do? I mean, we've had a great time these few weeks, but don't you get bored just hanging out, Jay? Don't you want to do something with your brain?'

He looked at me, smiling sadly.

'I do,' he said. 'I just don't talk about it.'

I looked at him expectantly.

'I have a foundation,' he said. 'A charitable foundation that I set up in my brother's memory.'

'What kind of foundation?' I asked, determined to make him open up about this side of his life. 'What's it called?'

He looked a bit uncomfortable, glanced away for a moment, and then leaned towards me.

'It's called "B & Me" and it helps young drug addicts with artistic inclinations through rehab and then mentors them into careers.'

I nodded encouragingly, trying to look more impressed than I really was. Most of his rich-kid pals had toy charities like that. Zaria had set up a rest home for retired beauty-counter sales girls – her mother's one-time profession – who had fallen on hard times.

We'd gone to a gala benefit for it a couple of weeks before, which had rather sickened me. OK, so it had raised money for the home, but as far as I could tell, it was really just about having fun and dressing up for Zaria and her spoilt friends, and for getting your face in the society pages with your halo glowing.

If each of the female guests there had donated just one piece of the jewellery they were wearing, I'd thought at the time, the home would have been secure in perpetuity.

But despite my misgivings about guilt-assuaging, money-bunny charity work, I kept a positive look on my face for Jay – I was just so pleased to hear that he did something apart from enjoy himself.

'Well, you are the original secret squirrel, aren't you?' I said. 'Why didn't you tell me about it before?'

'I don't talk about it to anyone, except my mum, who's involved too; it's too personal. I keep my involvement as low-key as I can – pretty much anonymous, actually – but seeing as how you clearly think I am a total lamebrain, I've told you. That was what I was doing out in LA. Stuff to do with that, OK?'

I decided it was time for us both to lighten up.

'Anything else you want to tell me?' I said. 'Got a wife and family I should know about? A secret identity as a super-hero?' I leaned across the table to pinch him in the ribs.

He giggled like a little boy – Jay was really, adorably tick-lish.

After that, everything was fine between us again, and what had started out as a hideous row actually made us closer. But a few days later another problem reared its head – when it turned out our attitude to the paparazzi had been a little overcasual.

I was down in Café Gitane on my own one morning, while Jay was off playing tennis, and I opened 'Page Six' of the *New York Post*, to see a picture of the two of us, looking truly appalling in our yoga gear. Well, I did anyway. 'Fisher in the Shallows' was the heading.

> After Jay Fisher's dalliance with megastar Jericho, whose girl bumps are insured for almost as much as his monthly income, and his recent flirtation with succulent Argentinian beef heiress Patrizia Fernandez, it seems New York's favourite billion-heir playboy is easing off a little in the glamour stakes. He was spotted this week holding hands with this unknown grunge queen. Not exactly what you'd call chic central, are they?

By the time he got back to the apartment, he'd seen it too.

'Time to skip town, I think, honey,' he said, throwing the

paper on to the kitchen countertop. 'Did you see this?'

I nodded. 'Well, at least they didn't know who I was,' I said. 'Actually, I'm surprised they even recognized you. We look like a pair of homeless people.'

'So,' he said, hugging me from behind. 'Shall we disappear? Flee down to Mexico? Get lost in the Caribbean? Or somewhere more exotic?'

'I really don't know,' I said, feeling rather inhibited. I didn't want to sound like I was raising my hand for my ultimate dream holiday, which would probably have been a couple of weeks at an Aman Resort somewhere in the Pacific Ocean, if he had really wanted to know. 'You choose.'

'OK,' he said. 'Give me your passport and I'll fix it. It will be a surprise.'

And he disappeared off to his study, whistling. An hour or so later he emerged grinning and sent me off to Barneys again, to shop for a beach holiday, somewhere warm and, as he put it, 'not uptight'.

I didn't argue.

The next morning we were out at JFK, checking in for a flight to Venice – which Jay told me firmly was not our final destination.

'Don't get all excited about La Serenissima,' he said. 'Lovely though it is. We're just going to change planes there.'

I was so caught up in the fun and intrigue of it all that when my mobile rang, I answered it without checking the incoming number first. Mistake. It was my father and he was shouting at me.

'I know who you're staying with in New York, Stella

Montecourt,' he was shouting, 'because it's splashed all over the *Daily Mail* today. So I don't care if you're not talking to me, because I'm not talking to you either. You have completely broken your promise to me and I'm wounded. *Wounded*, do you hear me?'

And we raced to be the first to hang up. The only boring thing about mobile phones, I realized, is that you can't slam them down on people.

20

Venice looked so beautiful from above I was momentarily sad we weren't staying there – and I did have a particularly good view of it from the cockpit of the light aircraft I was sitting in. Jay put his arm around me.

'OK?' he said.

I nodded. Very OK. We'd arrived at Venice airport, collected our bags and then he'd led the way out of the terminal and along the road which was signposted 'Water Taxis to Venice', with all the other tourists.

At first I'd thought he'd been kidding all along and we were going to be staying there, after all – the Cipriani? I wondered for a thrilling moment, the Gritti Palace? – but then, just before we reached the quay, he'd pushed open the door of a nondescript building to our left.

There wasn't much in there apart from a couple of bored-looking security guards and the usual luggage X-ray machines, and it wasn't until we were putting our bags on the conveyor belt – no queues here – that I realized where we were. A well-dressed elderly couple were coming the other way, and they nodded at us as they came through.

It was a moment of recognition I had experienced several times with Jay in New York, at various elite but discreet sports clubs he had taken me to. It meant – we're rich, you're rich, we're all rich, because if you're here, you're rich. We were in the private plane terminal.

357

I'd assumed the Italian guy who had come to speak to Jay would be our pilot, but he carried our bags out to a small prop plane, opened it up, had another quick word with Jay and then handed him the keys.

'Let's go,' Jay had said, showing me how to manoeuvre myself into the cockpit passenger seat, over the wing. 'You can sit in back, if you like,' he said. 'But I'd rather have you up front with me.'

'Do you fly like you drive?' I said.

He laughed. 'I hope not.'

As far as I could tell, he didn't. After sitting around for a while to get clearance, he took off smoothly and we headed out over Venice before turning left, so we were looking straight down the Adriatic Sea.

'Do you know where we're going now?' Jay asked me.

'Croatia?' I suggested. I was good at geography.

'Not bad,' said Jay. 'Close. The next one down, actually – Montenegro. It's beautiful, you'll love it.'

It was a glorious flight down the coast and over all the islands, and then after just an hour or so, we started to descend and head inland, to somewhere called Tivat – at least, that was what it said on the roof of the terminal.

There was a man waiting to park the plane for us and we grabbed our bags off the back seat and just breezed through passport control and out towards the taxi rank. As we passed great stressed-out hordes of people waiting for their bags to arrive on the luggage carousel, I decided I could really see the point of private planes.

A driver – who clearly already knew Jay, judging by his bear-hug welcome – was there to meet us and after about twenty minutes driving at terrifying speed through a classic

Mediterranean landscape, we arrived at a small town on the coast, screeching to a halt just in time at the water's edge.

Tied up at the stone jetty was a speedboat which looked like the love child of an E-type Jag and a stealth bomber. It was so sexy, it was positively rude.

'Wow,' was all I could say. 'Is that for us?'

Jay was beaming.

'Oh, she's a beauty, Mishko,' Jay was saying to the driver, patting him heartily on the back. 'That's just the one I wanted. Thank you. I'll call you when I'm going to bring her back. OK?'

Jay swiftly concluded his business with him – I looked away when I saw he was about to hand over a massive wad of cash – and then he tossed our bags into the speedboat's cockpit, before leaping aboard, and turning to hold out his hand to me.

'So, do you like her?' he asked me.

'It's the most filthy gorgeous boat I've ever seen,' I said laughing. 'What is it?'

'This, my darling,' said Jay, patting it lovingly, 'is a Rivale. It's the latest model from Riva. You know all those fabulous teak speedboats in sixties films? The sort you'd see Brigitte Bardot riding around in? They were all Rivas and this is the twenty-first-century version. Shall we go?'

I nodded and waited while he checked everything, the way that people who really know about boats do. I just stood and admired the scene – a beautiful place, a beautiful man, a beautiful boat.

Eventually, he signalled to Mishko, who was still waiting happily on the quay, to untie us. He threw me the mooring rope and Jay throttled her up. It made more noise than the plane had and once we set off, I think it went faster too.

I sat down with a bump, taken by surprise at the acceleration. Jay was standing up, grinning into the wind, his white teeth brilliant against his skin, shades on, black hair whipping back. I'd never seen him look happier.

'Are we going anywhere in particular?' I asked, as we zoomed over the water. 'Or just going?'

'Do you mind?'

I shook my head.

'Not as long as I'm with you.'

He put his arm round my waist and pulled me to him.

'Good girl,' he said. 'And don't worry, I know these waters really well. Do me one favour, would you, though? Take my clothes off for me.'

So while he steered the boat, I undressed him. Jay was never happier than when he was naked and he was so at ease with himself in that state, he didn't look remotely silly, standing there driving a major speedboat with nothing on, so it seemed only right to join him.

'Get rid of those tan lines, eh?' he said, slapping me on my bare buttock.

We spent the rest of that day just cruising and speeding through the crystalline waters, until Jay located a deserted island that he said he'd stopped at before, and we anchored in a small bay.

We spent the rest of the day and night there. Just sunbathing, swimming, eating the lobster and salad that I had found ready prepared, in the boat's fridge, and drinking the perfectly iced white wine. The oiled-wheel nature of Jay's life was really beginning to sink in. Money was the ultimate lubricant, I now understood, it made everything run smoothly.

As I was climbing aboard after a late swim, that first afternoon, I noticed the name on the Rivale's stern. Some words in Italian, I didn't understand.

'Hey, Jay,' I called down to him, from the ladder, pointing at the name. 'You speak Italian. What does that mean?'

He swam over to me and grasped me firmly from behind. I gasped.

'It means "Extreme Bliss",' he whispered into my ear. 'And you're just about to experience some.'

The rest of the trip continued in this mode without a moment of friction between us. Whatever we were doing, Jay and I just got on – as long as we stayed off the subject of his family and my job.

We never ran out of things to talk about and were endlessly engaged by the same things, whether it was the porpoises leaping in our wake, the books we were reading, or the very particular smell sunlight leaves on skin at the end of a hot day.

After a couple of nights on the boat, our food was running out, and Jay headed further south along the Montenegrin coast, past various little towns and the odd ugly hotel development, until eventually we came in view of a particularly picturesque place, that looked like an ancient village, entirely covering a tiny little knoll of an island.

'That looks pretty,' I said.

'That's Sveti Stefan,' said Jay. 'That's where we're going.'

As we curved round to the shore side of the island, I could see it was connected to the mainland by a narrow footbridge. There was a beach club on the side where we were cruising in, and I could see the people on sunbeds sitting up to look at the boat as Jay leapt out – back in his shorts, for once – to moor us, with me slightly terrified at the wheel.

Sveti Stefan, it turned out, once a fishing village, was now a hotel – the whole place. It was a maze of little streets of houses, each of which was a guest villa. There was a restaurant, a pool, a casino, an ancient church, even a funny old hairdresser's, with bright orange seventies pod hairdryers, and a saltwater pool, set into the rock, with amazing views out to sea.

It was spectacular, but our villa, when we were shown to it, took shabby chic to new levels, in fact, it was just plain shabby. The loo was constantly running, and the taps were dripping, leaving nasty brown marks on the sink and bath. The tiles were broken, the towels were as thin as dishcloths, half the light bulbs didn't work and the nasty cheap polyester-velvet curtains were hanging off their poles. It was clean, but it was nasty.

I tried not to look dismayed, as Jay tipped the boy who had carried our bags in. He didn't seem bothered at all, marching into the room, throwing open the window and leaning out to look at the sea, crashing on to the rocks beneath.

'Do you like it?' he said, turning to me, looking so happy, I knew I would have to put up a good front. It wasn't the Cipriani, and it certainly wasn't an Aman. I did my best.

'It's, er, amazing,' I said. 'The setting is amazing . . .'

'But the rooms are foul dives?' He laughed. 'I know it's really shabby, but I love this place. I first came here when I was five years old, and I love it. Trust me, once you get used to it, it's much more relaxing here than any five-star resort.'

He came over and put his arms around me.

'It used to be a five-star resort, actually. We would arrive by yacht or helicopter, and all kinds of famous people would be here, but since the war in Yugoslavia it's been really neglected. The government runs it – really badly – but I still love it. And I hope you will too . . .'

I wasn't convinced, but I was prepared to put on a good show, for him. That night, though, even Jay's patience was stretched to its limit.

We went to bed early, after a pretty terrible dinner on the stunningly beautiful restaurant terrace, only to find that if we so much as moved a leg, the bed creaked and twanged like an orchestra tuning up. We couldn't even get comfortable, let alone do anything more active.

'What the fuck?' Jay was saying, after rolling over to put his arm around me and setting off a noise like someone throwing a grand piano off a tall building. He bounced up and down a little to test it – it was deafening.

I moved a little, to see if it was just his side. It wasn't. Just moving my hips a tiny bit sounded like someone hurling saucepans down metal stairs.

We bounced up and down together and it was so unbelievably noisy, we collapsed into hysterical laughter. It was the ultimate irony for Mr Eveready, as I had christened him – a hotel bed you couldn't move around in.

We laughed for a long time, setting each other off by seeing just how small a movement it took to make it jangle – and scratching your head could do it – until eventually Jay started to get properly pissed off.

'Actually, this is a joke,' he said. 'Forget screwing – we're not even going to get any sleep on this damn thing.'

363

He lay motionless for a moment and then sprang up – sparking a noise like Beethoven's Fifth, played backwards.

'Get up a minute,' he said, and then he pulled the mattress off the bed and threw it on to the floor. 'That should do it,' he said, putting his hand out to me. 'Madame?'

The next day, he had the hilarious bed taken away, and an extra mattress brought in to put on top of the other one, and with the loo, taps, curtains and lamps fixed immediately, with a bit of his folding banknote persuasion, we settled in very comfortably.

And he was right. It may have been rough and ready, with sunloungers which could have been used in a Sean Connery-era James Bond movie, but Sveti Stefan was a uniquely relaxing place.

We read, swam, snorkelled and sunbathed by day, sometimes taking the Rivale out for a run. We went for long walks along the coastal path in the evening, had dinner at local fish restaurants, and went early to bed, if not always to sleep. All my cares were forgotten.

I made a sneaky call to Chloe, to make sure she and Daisy were OK, but that was the full extent of my concern about the place I called home, and Chloe made no efforts to try and intervene between me and Ham. She knew there was no point. Mostly, I hardly gave him a thought – and the same went for the office.

One afternoon, when we'd been there over a week and I had relaxed into an almost inert state, I was sitting on the terrace outside our villa, idly checking my phone for text messages to delete.

I'd been away from home for over a month by then and had pretty much stopped even reading them – when I saw I had a new one which made me stop and look. It was from Peter Wallington.

Peter despised text messages even more fervently than he did milky coffee and the euro – probably because they didn't suit his grandiloquent style of communication – so if he had sent me one, something was definitely up.

'*Please telephone me as soon as possible. Peter.*' That was it. Probably the shortest sentence he had ever written.

I wouldn't have responded to anyone else – except Doughnut, of course – but I had to know what was going on. Jay was having a post-lunch nap inside the villa and so as not to wake him, I walked round to the resort's little *salon de thé*, to make the call.

Peter answered his desk phone on the second ring – something was definitely up.

'Ah, Stella, at last,' he said. 'I've been leaving messages for you, but you haven't returned them, you naughty girl. In the end I had to resort to "txt"-ing, or whatever you call it.'

'Are you all right?' I said. 'I knew it must be serious for you to send one of those . . .'

'Well, no, nothing's all right really, Stella. The thing is, you see . . .'

I was starting to feel really uneasy.

'Yes?' I said.

'Duncan's been sacked,' he said finally.

'Oh, shit!' I said.

'Quite,' said Peter.

'What happened?'

'Oh, it's all to do with these wretched budget cuts they want to make. Remember I told you he had some difficult board meetings coming up? Well, a couple of the new board members – the ones who want the big spending cuts – got together and campaigned against him and they used what they called his "poor showing" at the board meetings to oust him. It's appalling. It's all about the share price here now, not the journalism. It's sickening.'

He was right, I did feel physically sick. Then a terrible question raised its head.

'So who's the new editor?' I asked, tentatively.

'That's the really bad news, darling. It's Martin Ryan.'

I just groaned. There was no way of looking at the bright side of it, there wasn't one.

'I suppose that's the end of the section, then?' I said, already knowing the answer.

'I fear so, my dear girl,' said Peter.

'Oh, well, thanks for letting me know,' I said, my heart starting to pump with stress. 'I suppose I better come back, hadn't I?'

'I would,' said Peter. 'And quickly. They're moving your things out of that office as we speak.'

'What?' I said.

'Yes. Not into packing cases, but back to your old desk. I thought you'd want to know. Come back soon, Stella. I miss you.'

And he hung up. I just sat there, my arms hanging by my sides, feeling like I had been punched in the stomach. My head was whirling with the implications. Martin loathed me and he was Jeanette's great buddy. Forget the section – if I wanted to keep my job at all, I would have to get right back there and fight for it.

I was just dialling Ned's number, to get his take on it all, when Jay came loping round the corner, his beautiful face breaking into a broad smile when he saw me. I immediately put my phone down.

'I thought I'd find you here,' he said. 'Little Miss English Afternoon Tea. Having a little morsel of apple strudel, are we?'

I looked at him. So handsome, so suntanned, so relaxed and suddenly our glorious lazy days together seemed just that – lazy. If I could have got into a *Star Trek* transporter right there and rematerialized in the *Journal* office – preferably wearing something more than my bikini – I would have.

Jay sat down opposite and played footsie with me under the table.

'Did you have a nice nap?' I asked, a slight tension creeping into my voice, although I struggled to keep it out.

'It would have been nicer if I'd woken up to find you there,' he said. 'But it was pretty nice. So, what are you having?'

'Actually, Jay,' I said. 'I'm not having anything. I just came out for a walk and now something's happened I've got to tell you about.'

A cloud descended immediately across his face. We'd spent so much concentrated time together by then, we were acutely tuned into each other's moods and it was clear he knew immediately it wasn't good.

'Wassup?' he said.

'I just got some bad news from home,' I said.

'Not your family?' he asked, looking sincerely concerned.

'No, no, thank God. They're fine. No, it's about work.'

'Work?' said Jay, looking mystified. 'I thought you were

on holiday. Why are you even thinking about work?'

'Someone called me,' I said. 'Well, they texted me and I called them.'

'Bad move, isn't it?' he said. 'To call work, when you're on holiday . . .'

I sighed.

'I had to,' I said, shortly. 'Anyway, my editor-in-chief has been sacked – and I have to go home.'

He looked as though someone had thrown a bucket of iced water over his head.

'Go home? When?'

'As soon as possible.'

He looked at me completely uncomprehendingly.

'Why? Can you get your editor-in-chief his job back?'

'No,' I said, my voice rising.

He matched me. 'So why go home?'

'To hold on to *my* job,' I said, as though trying to explain something to a dense child.

He sank back in his seat, sighing and rolling his eyes.

'It's always the goddam job with you, isn't it? Don't you remember it was your beloved colleagues at the newspaper who shopped us to the tabloids right at the start and nearly split us up before we even began – and got you into all the trouble with your dad? Yet, still you cling on to this job. Why does it have such a hold on you?'

I just looked at him. I didn't know what to say.

He leaned forwards, speaking more softly and clearly trying to control his irritation.

'Don't you get it, Stella? If you're with me, you don't need a job. You don't have to work and put up with all the stress and crap that goes with it. And I want you to be with me, like this, all of the time – and I mean that, all of the time – and if you're with me, you don't need to work.'

'But I *want* to work, Jay,' I finally burst out. 'I love being here with you too, but this is a holiday, it's not real life. I love you, Jay, but I love my job too and I need it – to be me.'

I paused for a moment. 'It's been fun living like this for a few weeks, but I don't want to be some kind of a kept woman.'

He just looked at me, puzzled.

'I don't think you understand me, Stella,' he said quietly. 'How would it be if you were my wife? Would you be a kept woman then?'

I just stared back at him. Was he talking in general terms, or was he being specific? I certainly wasn't going to ask him to elucidate. He did anyway.

'Stella,' he said, 'I'm asking you to marry me.'

He took my hand in both of his and kissed it. 'I love you. Madly. I've never felt like this about anybody and I want to be with you. Always. Please marry me. Will you?'

My stomach felt like a tumble dryer. Had he said those words to me at any other moment in the previous five weeks, I would have spontaneously combusted with joy, but at this moment, I knew it wasn't right.

I swallowed and spoke very quietly.

'Could I still keep my job?' I said.

Jay slammed his hand down on to the little metal café table so hard it shook.

'No,' he said, letting his irritation show. 'If you're with me, you don't need some tinpot hack shit job. Being with me would be your job. Full pension benefits, medical insurance, and fifty-two weeks' holiday a year, on full pay. Don't you get it?'

'No,' I said.

We just looked at each other, across that yawning gulf between us, now wider than ever. Where I couldn't see how just being someone's wife – not even the wife of the man you loved more than anyone on earth – could possibly be enough, and where he couldn't imagine why anyone could feel defined by a job, rather than by the person they loved.

'It's the money, isn't it?' said Jay, eventually. 'Turns out, you're just like your dad, after all. Disgusted by inherited wealth. If I'd won it in a lottery would that be OK? Because, I did – a sperm lottery.'

'It's not the money, Jay,' I said quietly. 'The money's fun, I get that, it's fabulous – but it's not enough. Just spending money and lying around all day is not a life. Not for me. And you know what,' I said, standing up. 'Deep down inside, you know it's not enough for you either.'

'I don't do nothing, Stella,' he said, quietly. 'I've got the foundation . . .'

I didn't even let him finish.

'That's not a real job,' I snorted, contemptuously. 'That's just a money-bunny guilt charity – it's a play job. You don't know what a real job is, Jay, or you might have a bit more respect for mine.'

The words hung in the air, after I'd said them. I knew I'd gone too far – way too far – but I couldn't take them back and I couldn't apologize, because that's what I really believed. And, in that crystalline moment, I realized it had been festering inside me like a tumour.

For a couple of beats Jay just sat and looked up at me – in

shock, I think – almost like he was seeing me for the first time. I could see in that look just how much I had hurt him and there wasn't a thing I could do about it.

Then, he took hold of my hand, firmly, as though he was stopping me from walking away. Then he spoke very quietly.

'I've never asked anyone to marry me before, Stella,' he said. 'And, you have to understand, that for someone like me, it's a big deal, but after what you've just said, I take that as a no. But understand this – if you walk away from me now, that will be it. I've turned my soft belly to you and you've knifed me in it. If you go now, if you leave here, it's the end. I don't think I'll ever get over it, but that's the way it has to be.'

I knew he was serious. I looked back into those dark blue eyes, for what felt like an eternity, but was probably only a moment. I could hear my fate rushing in my ears as I let go of his hand and walked away.

I didn't even cry as I packed my bag. I was just numb with shock. I did wonder, for a moment, what the etiquette was about keeping all the stuff he'd bought for me, but decided it would be nastier to leave it behind than to take it.

I didn't even worry about how I was going to get home, I knew I just had to get away from Sveti Stefan and Jay, to somewhere else – anywhere – and then find a way to get back to London from there. I had my credit cards, there was a cash point in the hotel lobby, it wasn't complicated.

I called the concierge to order me a taxi to the nearest airport and to send someone up to get my bag. And then I wound my way through the labyrinthine streets down to

371

reception, with detours via the pool and the restaurant bar, for one last look at the views I had come to love.

When I got there the concierge called me over and handed me a large envelope.

'Mr Fisher left this for you,' he said.

I looked at him blankly for a moment. There were multiple ways to get anywhere on that funny little island and I realized that Jay must have been walking along different paths, but so close to me, back to the room and down to the lobby.

It was such a strange feeling and I realized that was how it would always be from then on. Jay and I both in the world, aware of each other, but travelling on parallel tracks. I felt tears starting to well up, as I opened the envelope. It contained a wad of $100 bills and a note.

'*You can still change your mind,*' it said. '*But if you don't, this is just to get you home. I will always love you, but I won't share you. J.*'

No kisses.

I handed it back to the concierge and left.

21

The next day, Ned and I were sitting in Gino's having lunch
– at Peter's table.

We had ordered what he always had – veal parmigiana
– and his usual bottle of Amarone. The only thing missing
was Peter. Because by the time I had got into the office, the
morning after leaving Sveti Stefan, he'd been sacked.

It turned out that just half an hour or so after I had
spoken to him on the Monday afternoon, Martin had called
him up to the editor-in-chief's office, where he was now
ensconced, like a poisonous spider at the centre of his web,
and told him he was being 'made redundant'.

What made it really sickening was that after forty-plus
years on the paper, Martin had told him to leave immediately
and not come back. He hadn't even given him a traditional
newsroom farewell.

'It's unbelievable, Stella,' Ned was saying. 'Martin told him
that he had to leave immediately because he represented a
competitive threat to the paper – because with his reputation he was bound to be snapped up by one of the *Journal*'s
competitors. He didn't even let him pack up his own desk, I
did it for him last night. Jesus, Stella, the man's barely a year
from his sixty-fifth birthday, and he's only ever worked here.
He's not getting a job anywhere.'

I pushed my veal around the plate. I had never felt less
hungry. I'd just walked out on the love of my life, and I'd

come back to this. Peter wasn't the only one who had been sacked. Far from it.

Doughnut's lovely PA, Sheila, had gone, and several of the long-standing reporters and section editors, who Martin clearly felt were Doughnut's men and women, had been summarily ousted. Some had resigned after being offered alternative jobs on the paper insultingly below their levels of experience and expertise.

The entire paper was in shock and when we got back from lunch the atmosphere in the office was positively toxic. Suspicion and paranoia filled the air and little clumps of people would gather to whisper and then disperse, before re-forming into new combinations. I couldn't help smiling sadly to myself as I looked at them. 'Clumping', Peter used to call it.

'Look, Stella,' he'd say, half standing at his desk, so he could see the rest of the office, peering over the partition. 'They're clumping. Something's going on. Go forth and seek intelligence, would you, my dear? Come back and tell me what's afoot.'

Misery is what I would have told him, if he'd been there to hear. But some people were happy. Jeanette had been promoted – she was now Deputy Editor, Features – and Rita was Chief Sub, Features. The two of them were positively strutting around the place.

Jeanette didn't even acknowledge me when she passed where I was sitting, back at my old desk. I know she'd seen me, though, because a small triumphant smile flickered at the edge of her mouth.

I rang Peter at home that night but his wife, Renee, said he had gone out and wouldn't be back until late. I could tell by her voice that she was lying – and hating having to do it – and after several more attempts to make contact over the ensuing days were met with the same response, I could only conclude that he was so wounded, he couldn't bear to speak to anyone from the paper.

In the end, I sent him a note, saying how much I missed him and how grateful I was for everything he had done for me in our time working together and how much I would like to see him. He didn't reply.

Jay was equally incommunicado. Finally shocked out of my state of numbness about him, I'd rung him the second night I was back, to see if there was any way we could salvage the situation, but his mobile number just rang out.

It didn't even go to message and I realized, with a sickening lurch, that he had probably already changed his number, just like Amy had told me he would when he didn't want to be found.

I took that as a clear statement that he had meant it when he said he would never see me again and, in that moment, I knew my entire world had collapsed in on me.

I cried until I fell into an exhausted sleep.

After that the days came and went in a kind of daze of unpleasantness. Work was some kind of hell and I hated being at home even more, because the whole place reminded me so cruelly of the happy times I had spent there with Jay. I missed him so much, I felt like one of my limbs had been torn off.

My little house was also uncomfortably close to Ham Central and, while I could hardly bear to admit it to myself, I knew if I saw him, I would not be able to keep up my wall of silence. I'd cave in the moment I saw his funny old face, so I just couldn't allow myself to make contact. My pride wouldn't let me.

Because what was I going to tell him? That Jay and I had split up because of the great overbearing colossus of his inherited wealth and his playboy attitude to life? I couldn't bear Ham to be right about that.

But while I couldn't bring myself to go up to the big house, I rang Chloe to tell her I was back, and she and Daisy would sneak down to see me quite often in the mornings. I think, in no small way, those visits got me through those dark days. Every time Daisy's little blonde head bounced into my room, it was like the sun coming out.

'Look, Stella,' she said, one morning. 'I can do a curtsy and I can walk like a princess.'

She demonstrated.

'Oh, very good, Daisy,' I said. 'That will be useful.'

'Yes,' said Daisy, nodding. 'I'm going to do it at your wedding. When I'm your bridesmaid. Can I have a white dress and flowers in my hair? Can I have sparkly shoes?'

Chloe pulled an embarrassed 'sorry' kind of face at me, but I didn't mind, it gave me something to laugh about.

Chloe was great. She didn't pry about what had happened with Jay, although it was pretty obvious she knew we'd been together and had guessed that we now weren't, and neither did she press me to make up with Ham. She was just there, and always willing to listen sympathetically while I told her what was going on at work. She really was a very good friend.

Most evenings I went straight from the office to several work-related events. My usual response to a crisis was to work harder and I didn't see how this one was any different

– it just happened to involve all three major foundations of my life at once: family, love and career.

And if my position was as insecure at the *Journal* as I felt it was, I needed to get my face out and about as much as possible. I might need to find a new job, at any moment.

The way I felt, it was very hard being upbeat and employable, but I did my best and it really helped having Ned around. Even though the section had now been formally cancelled, we continued to go to events together and although he was as unhappy as me about what was going on at the office, he could always find a joke to lighten a situation and somehow we had fun together, despite it all.

He didn't know I had a broken heart and a major family crisis going on as well as all the work drama, and it was a relief, as I could stop thinking about the other stuff when I was with him. I just blanked it out. It was only when I was alone that it all got to me, so I tried not to be on my own.

If there were no decent work parties to go to, Ned and I would see a film, and if we were feeling really restless, we'd go to two in one night, with a bowl of Vietnamese noodle soup in between.

Those were strange days.

Things finally reached a head at the office about four weeks after I had come back. A memo suddenly appeared in everyone's pigeonholes one morning from the *Journal*'s legal department about pension rights. I didn't even read it, and just stuffed it straight into a folder I kept for memos like that. The bin.

I was rewriting – for the fourth time, at Jeanette's insistence – a feature about the future of the Scottish cashmere industry, when I became aware of serious clumping going on around the office.

The desk next to me was still empty, but I did what Peter would have wanted and ventured out to find out what was going on.

I was on a spurious mission to the library, walking slowly, for maximum eavesdropping, when I ran into Ned.

'Stella,' he said, urgently. 'I was looking for you. You're not going to believe the latest. Meet me in the conference room in five.'

He meant the emergency stairwell, of course, a secret Tim and I had long ago let him in on. I walked once around the office, with my ears flapping, and then met him there.

'What's going on now?' I asked him, closing the fire door and leaning against it.

'You know how that shit Martin Ryan dressed Peter's sacking up as some kind of bogus redundancy?' said Ned, pacing restlessly on the concrete half landing.

I nodded. 'Yes, that's why the desk next to me is still very ostentatiously empty.'

'Well, through some kind of hideous small print in Peter's contract Martin has found a way of voiding most of his pension rights.'

I just stared at Ned.

'You're kidding,' I said.

Ned shook his head. He was holding a copy of the pensions memo in his hand, I realized. He held it up and shook it.

'That's what this piece of shit is all about, they're covering themselves so they can do it to anyone here.'

'Are you telling me that they have cancelled Peter's

pension when he is nearly sixty-five and has worked here for over forty years?'

'That's right.'

'That's despicable,' I said. 'Can they really do it?'

'It looks like they can, that's the terrible thing. We're on to the union, but most people here aren't members any more anyway. It will just be up to Peter, whether he takes them on or not. He'd have to pay his own legal fees out of the three months' redundancy money they gave him.'

Suddenly, my head felt clearer than it had for weeks.

'That's it,' I said, setting off down the thirty-one flights of concrete stairs to the ground floor. 'I'm done with this place. I'm going to resign. Right now.'

And I did.

I wasn't the only one. Even as I was composing my resignation letter, intraoffice messages kept flashing up on the screen, with the name of the latest person who had taken the plunge. I pressed 'Print' on my letter and then posted a message about my own resignation.

I didn't even wait for a response from Martin, after I'd dropped my letter with his new secretary, I just started packing up my things, ready to be sent on to me at home. Then I did a mass email to all the PRs I dealt with regularly, and got ready to leave. As I was writing that, an internal message flashed up announcing that Ned had resigned too. I smiled.

I was sitting at my desk, wondering if I should just get up and go, when Ned appeared to tell me that everyone who had resigned was going to walk out together, to make more of a point of it, and that we were to meet in the sports department as soon as possible.

The brains behind this protest was the *Journal*'s greyhound racing correspondent, Jim Flynn. I'd never really talked to him, but I knew who he was and that he'd worked at the paper for years.

Like Peter, he was one of the old guard of characters who'd come over to the new building from Fleet Street, and his racing tips – on the doggies and the ponies, as he called them – were legendary.

He was about five foot two, and sported a classic wide-boy trilby, and you'd see him outside the main doors, smoking like a squaddie, with the glowing ember turned into his palm.

By the time I got round to the sports department, Jim had several bottles of whisky, a bottle of gin and a bottle of Tia Maria on the go. It was strictly against *Journal* rules for any journalist to have alcohol on their desk, you could get sacked for it, but Jim had the bottles all lined up on his like a bar, and was serving the drinks in mugs.

'They can't sack me now for boozing,' he was saying. 'Because I'm already walking ... *Walking, after midnight*,' he sang cheerily. 'Allo, darling,' he said when he saw me. 'You coming out for Peter, are ya? Good girl, that's what I like to see – solidarity. Now what can I get you, young lady? A nice Tia?'

I had whisky – he filled the mug halfway to the top – and we had quite a little party. There were about ten of us, all up, which was pretty impressive, and would leave a satisfying hole in the *Journal*'s staff, especially as we came from such diverse parts of the paper.

One of the major leader writers was leaving, which was a big deal; as was the deputy-chief news sub; one of the main crime reporters; and the environmental correspondent. We were a rum crew, but we were united by our affection and respect for Peter, and a sense of disgust about the direction the paper's management was taking.

While our odd little wake was in full swing I heard my mobile phone beep; it was a text from Tim. He had just arrived back at Heathrow from somewhere and after hearing what was happening at the paper from the news subs, he had resigned too – and he wanted me to tell everyone. I stood on a chair to make the announcement and a huge cheer went up.

After about three-quarters of an hour things were getting a bit rowdy, and work had effectively stopped on the entire paper, with quite a lot of people who weren't leaving – mainly ones with large mortgages and small children – joining in to show their support.

I was having a great chat with Jim about the old days in Fleet Street and what a top geezer Peter had always been to him, when I realized the party had gone quiet. I looked round to see Jeanette standing in front of us, looking decidedly nervous – flanked by two security guards.

'The editor-in-chief has sent me to insist that you leave the building immediately,' she said, in a shaky voice. 'He accepts all your resignations with immediate effect. Your personal belongings will be sent on to you and you must leave now.'

'Getting you to do his dirty work already, is he, darling?' said Jim, chesting up to her, like a bantam cock.

She stepped back, looking terrified, and the security guards moved forwards towards Jim. Just for a moment, it looked like it could have turned really ugly, but then Jim swung round towards all of us and raised his arms in the air.

'Come on, comrades,' he said. 'We're off.'

And so we left – with Jim leading us in a rather shaky rendition of the Internationale, and the entire staff standing up to applaud us as we did one victory circuit of the news floor and then went out to the lifts.

Following Jim's lead again, as we walked out through reception we all threw our security passes on to the floor.

It was stirring stuff, but I did feel a little wobbly as I stepped out of the huge glass doors of the *Journal* building for the last time. We stood there, in a clump, for a while and then people started to peel off, until there was just me and Ned left.

He wanted us to go straight to The Groucho to drown our sorrows – or to celebrate our bold move, whichever it was – but although I was already a bit light-headed from Jim's whisky, I just couldn't raise any enthusiasm for it.

We craned our necks and looked up at the building together.

'There's the thirty-first floor,' he said. 'Will you miss it? It was over five years for you, Stella.'

I shook my head.

'No, I won't miss it. The *Journal* I loved doesn't exist any more. You?'

'Yes,' he said. 'I'll miss you.'

'Oh, Ned,' I said, giving him a quick hug. 'I'll miss you too, but we'll still be friends. We'll still be film buddies.'

'No, Stella,' he said, holding on to my arms, when I started to pull away. 'You don't understand – I'll really miss you.'

I looked up at him. He was gazing at me very intently and

before I knew what was happening, he had bent down and kissed me. Not a colleague's kiss on the cheek, but a proper kiss, on the mouth, involving his tongue.

I was so surprised, I didn't pull away immediately and as he put his arms around me and pressed that deep, broad chest against me, I felt a treacherous flicker in my groin. It was pure desire.

And without involving my conscious mind, my whisky-loosened tongue responded, sliding against his. Immediately, it was like we had both been set alight and we were kissing with an urgency I had almost forgotten in those numb weeks since I had left Jay. When we finally pulled back for air, we were panting like a pair of sprinters.

We just stood there, staring at each other, in a state of shock, but still I didn't pull away. It was such a crazy day, in such a crazy time, it didn't feel weird to be kissing Ned right outside the *Journal* building, with our former colleagues walking past us on both sides, to and from the main entrance. In fact, it felt absolutely right and I wasn't even bothered when a couple of them cheered and wolf-whistled us.

Then we were kissing again, even more passionately. His hands were behind my head, his fingers in my hair, pulling me closer, and mine were tearing aside his jacket, to get at the chest that had haunted the primal recesses of my mind ever since I had seen it in Ham's swimming pool.

As we pulled apart again, I could feel every nerve in my body snapping with lust for him. I felt as though the two of us would probably glow in the dark with it and we didn't need to say anything, it was clear we felt the same way. A cab came along, Ned hailed it and we got in and carried on where we had left off on the pavement.

I couldn't tell you how long we were in that cab, but when it stopped I could see we were somewhere grungy near Brick Lane. Ned took my hand and after paying the cabbie, opened the door of a house without ever letting go of me.

We pretty much ran up the stairs and into a bedroom I vaguely took in as painted white and fairly bare, with a simple bed on the floor. Then we tore each other's clothes off.

Ned's body was no disappointment – and neither was the part of him I had glimpsed inside his black undies that day at the pool. We rolled over each other, not even fully undressing, pressing our bodies against each other and just kissing and kissing, and it flashed through my mind that it was as though all the hours we had spent talking, sharing words, were now being replayed in a kind of heightened physical conversation.

There was no doubt about his skills as a lover, which I had heard whispered around the office. In what seemed like no time, he had me tuned up like a violin string.

Then, finally he moved, with his swimmer's elegance, to lie on top of me. Immediately my hips lifted to receive him, but then just as I could feel him at the very point of entering me, something clicked in my head.

'Stop!' I said.

Ned froze.

'Stop,' I said again, more quietly. 'I can't do this.'

He looked down at me, frozen, blinking with surprise.

'I'm really sorry, Ned,' I almost whispered. 'But I just can't do this. We're friends – and I really really value you as a friend – and if we do this, our friendship will never be the same again.'

Ned looked at me a moment longer and then rolled off. We just lay there, side by side, still panting a bit, staring at the ceiling, lost in our own thoughts.

I was thinking about Jay. I had spent the last few weeks exerting a Herculean effort not to think about him, to try and wean myself off the idea of him even, but just at the moment Ned was about to enter me, I had realized I couldn't bear anyone else but Jay to go there. In that moment I'd had such a potent physical memory of Jay, it was almost like he had been there with me.

I was as connected to him as I had ever been, I realized, even if he had pushed me away and I had tried to blank him out.

After a few moments, I reached out to find Ned's hand. I squeezed it and he turned his head to look at me.

'I'm sorry,' I said, again. 'I should never have let it go this far.'

'It's OK,' said Ned quietly. 'But can't we be more than friends, Stella? You weren't acting just now, I know you feel it, just like I do.'

I sighed deeply.

'You're a very attractive man, Ned,' I said eventually. 'In fact, you're one of the sexiest men I have ever met and well you know it, you're a shocking flirt – and I also adore you as a person, as a friend. But while the physical thing ran away with me just then, I can't combine the two with you, because I'm in love with someone else. Stupidly in love.'

'Is it Alex?' said Ned.

'No, it's not Alex,' I said, not knowing whether to laugh, or cry, at the suggestion. 'It's Jay Fisher.'

'Oh, shit,' said Ned, suddenly laughing. 'I give in, then.

Reckon I could take Alex on, but I can't beat a bloody billionaire. Especially not a handsome bastard, like him.'

He turned to look at me.

'So that was you in the *Daily Mail* with him then,' he said, his eyes starting up that familiar twinkle. 'You looked so shit in the picture, I thought it was someone else.'

I punched him on the shoulder and with the tension released, we got up, got dressed and sat drinking endless cups of tea – with whisky on the side – in Ned's messy kitchen.

He shared the house with three other people and it had very much the atmosphere of a student pad. And while it was warm and relaxed, with beaten-up old furniture, silly photos of them on the walls, great boxes of empty bottles and all the other detritus of the communal single life, I felt a very long way away from Jay's immaculate loft.

We laughed a lot and talked about Peter and the *Journal*, and all the funny things we had got up to there, but while we had a relentlessly jolly time, I knew we were both covering up a slight awkwardness over what had happened.

We'd been chatting and drinking for a couple of hours – and Ned had been hitting the whisky bottle more frequently than me – when he suddenly got a more serious look on his face.

'Stella,' he said quietly. 'Can you take another shock today?'

I just laughed.

'Bring it on,' I said, raising my glass to him. 'I can't imagine what else you can throw at me, but go ahead.'

'OK,' said Ned. 'Here goes – you know I said ages ago I'd try and find out why Jeanette hates you so much?'

I nodded.

'Well, I have.'

'Go on, then,' I said. 'Hit me.'

Ned looked uncomfortable, but clearly felt I needed to know.

'It was your dad,' he said.

'My dad?' I said.

'Well, it seems that a long time ago he – how can I put it – well, he rooted her. You know, shagged her? And he never called her after. She's been getting her own back on him through you, all this time.'

I really couldn't believe my ears – but then again, I totally could. I felt physically sick.

'Any idea how long ago?' I asked him, very quietly, trying to stop my voice catching.

'Quite a long time, I think,' said Ned. 'Before she got married. They met at some piss-up at the Labour Party conference – you know how wild those things can get – and she's never forgiven him. Hell hath no fury like a woman scorned, and all that . . .'

'God, he must have been drunk,' was all I could say. It was just too much. It was so appalling, I almost found it funny. Almost.

'But tell me, Ned,' I asked him. 'How on earth did you find that out?'

'Rita told me.'

'I didn't know you were that close to Rita,' I said.

He looked a tiny bit sheepish.

'I was for one night,' he said.

'You know what, Ned,' I said, suddenly feeling quite nauseated by the whole sordid business, by him and my dad and men in general, 'I think you and my father really have a lot in common – and not in a good way.'

And shortly afterwards, I left.

I got the Tube back to Notting Hill from Liverpool Street, relieved to have some anonymous neutral space just to exist in. The latest revelation about my dreadful father was just too much on top of everything else.

Hearing what he'd done to Jeanette just convinced me what an irretrievable shit he was when it came to women. I almost wondered, as I had a few times since it happened, whether I was doing the right thing, not telling Chloe what he was really like. Maybe, it would be better if she knew – but I couldn't take that on, I'd decided, not with everything else.

On top of all that, what had just happened between me and Ned had brought Jay to the front of my mind in a way I had been trying so hard to avoid. And just to finish it all off, while I sat there, staring into space in a whisky fug, it was just starting to sink in that I was unemployed.

I felt as though I was on some kind of nightmare fairground ride and as it turned around, the horrendous events of the past few weeks would present themselves to me over and over again, in turn.

I'd feel furious with my father – his behaviour was so bad I almost felt sympathetic with Jeanette. Then there'd be a moment of sick remorse about what I had just done – or nearly done – with Ned. That would lead me back to Jay and then I would remember all over again that I didn't have a job and that would take me back to my dad and his part in both those disasters. Whichever of the horrors I looked at, it led inexorably to another.

What had I been thinking when I left Jay behind on that island? I kept asking myself. I loved him, he loved me – he'd wanted to marry me – but I'd left all that behind for my job. A job which now seemed meaningless and unimportant – and which I no longer even had.

It seemed unbelievable now that I'd made that choice, but at the time, it had seemed the only possible course of action. That afternoon at Sveti Stefan, Jay's attitude had seemed unreasonable to me. Now I really didn't know what I thought any more.

All I knew was that now I had neither of them. No job and no Jay.

I was woken the next morning from a whisky-deadened sleep by my mobile ringing – I'd forgotten to turn it off when I slumped into bed – and it was the media reporter from the *Post*, wanting me to confirm that I had resigned from the *Journal*.

I told him that I had, but refused to be drawn into discussions about why I'd done it, just saying I'd been at the *Journal* for five years and had felt for a while it was time for me to move on.

I was still enough of a reporter to be ready for that question in the hope of avoiding getting a reputation as a bolshie troublemaker, but then he sprang another question on me, which took me completely off my guard.

'So,' he said. 'Have you got your next job lined up then? Presumably it will be something else in the luxury field . . .'

I recovered myself just enough to say that I was talking to various people and considering offers, but nothing was confirmed yet. All complete lies, but at least I wouldn't sound quite so much like an unemployed loser – I knew it was much harder to find a new job when you didn't have one.

But what really rattled me about his question was that I suddenly realized I didn't have a clue where I wanted to go and work next. I'd never really looked beyond the *Journal* and suddenly I had to.

Was this, I wondered, my big chance to break out of writing about twenty-carat diamonds and bespoke picnic sets and get into the more serious side of journalism I had always hankered after? Possibly. So why did I feel so unexcited about the prospect? Clearly, I needed to do some serious thinking.

In the meantime, though, I just wanted to be distracted so I rang Chloe to see if the coast was clear for me to come up to the big house to see her and Daisy.

I hadn't been up there for weeks, which was really odd, and after such a long break, I saw it again with fresh eyes. It was such a beautiful space, and the atmosphere really did have a special nurturing quality.

My father may have been a hypocritical, philandering bastard, but there was no doubt about his professional gifts.

Daisy was sitting in a big leather armchair watching television, and when I slid the glass door open, she ran down the room and threw herself at me, squealing with delight.

'Mummy! Mummy! It's Stella! Stella's come to play at our house!'

I swept her up and buried my head in her neck.

'Hello, crazy Daisy,' I said. 'How are you?'

'I'm a big girl,' said Daisy. 'I'm going to be a full sister.

You're my half-sister. So is Tabitha, but Alex isn't.'

I smiled down at her and ruffled her hair, then she put her head on one side and looked up at me, with her wide blue eyes.

'Daddy said you don't come here any more,' she said.

'Well, Daddy's wrong, isn't he?' I said.

Chloe came in, looking very pregnant, and gave me nearly as big a hug as Daisy had, reaching around her bump. I bent down to kiss it.

'Stella,' she said, 'it's so good to see you up here again at last. Daisy has really missed your bedtime stories, haven't you, sweetheart?'

Daisy nodded and put her little arms around my legs and hugged me. It was killing stuff.

We sat down on the stools at the kitchen counter and Chloe produced some of her famous brownies, along with a macchiato, just the way I liked it.

'How are you doing, Chloe?' I asked her, in full small-talk mode. 'How's your book coming along?'

'Me and the book are both doing well, thank you, Stella. Everything is fine, but how are you? If you don't mind me saying, you look a bit rough. Are you OK?'

I took a deep breath. I knew I couldn't cope with telling her the whole story. Obviously I had to leave the Ham part out and I knew I'd be a basket case if I had to tell anyone what had happened with Jay, so I gave Chloe an abridged version, just the work stuff.

'Well, you remember how my lovely editor was sacked a few weeks ago, along with a lot of other people?' I started. 'Well, it's all just blown up again and I've resigned in protest. Quite a few people have.'

'Gosh,' said Chloe, her eyes wide. 'That *is* dramatic. What are you going to do? Have you got another job?'

I just shook my head, and smiled ironically at her. It was the best reaction I could muster.

'Daisy, darling,' said Chloe, suddenly. 'Mummy is so silly – I've left my handbag upstairs. Would you be a darling and run up and get it for me?'

Daisy beamed – she loved helping – and ran out of the room. I could hear her racing up the stairs singing: 'Handbag, handbag, Mummy wants her handbag . . .'

Chloe looked at me with a serious expression on her face.

'Can I tell Henry about you leaving your job?' she said.

I shrugged.

'You can tell him whatever you want – it'll be all over the papers anyway.'

Chloe looked irritated, which was unusual for her.

'You know, Stella,' she said, 'I have made a real effort not to bring this up with you, but I can't keep quiet any more. Can you please just talk to your father about whatever it is you are so angry with him about? I presume it's still that Jay Fisher business – he won't talk to me about it, so I don't really know – but it's eating him alive. I've never seen him like this before and he's so bloody irritable and unpleasant to everybody, it's not that much fun for me actually. Or Daisy.'

She looked at me with real distress on her face.

'He made her cry the other day, he was so snappy with her,' she said quietly. 'So, while I love you dearly, in all honesty, Stella, I'm getting a bit pissed off with it. It's been weeks now, surely you've gone off the boil a bit? Couldn't you just sit and talk to him and try and work it out? You're both adults, Stella.'

I felt anger flash through me, like a lightning bolt. She was the bloody reason I'd fallen out with him – protecting her from his appalling behaviour. For a millisecond I felt like telling her what it was all about, and about Jeanette, for good measure, but sense stopped me.

'Is it still over that Jay Fisher business?' said Chloe, clearly determined to push me on it, but before I could speak, Daisy came running back into the kitchen with a sequinned evening bag.

'Here it is, Mummy, I've got your bag,' she was saying. 'It had lipstick in it. Can I have some lipstick?'

She was so clearly already wearing it – all over her face – my eyes met Chloe's and we dissolved into laughter. It was the perfect tension breaker.

'It's mainly that,' I said, when we'd recovered. 'But there's other stuff as well. It's really complicated. Oh, I don't know, Chloe. I'm sorry if he's been giving you a hard time, but I'm still finding it really hard to forgive him.'

'But weren't you staying with Jay Fisher in New York anyway?' she persisted. 'Henry showed me a picture of you with him, in the paper.'

'Yes, I was staying with him.'

'So, if you're not keeping that ridiculous promise Henry asked you to make all that time ago, why are you so angry with him? You've got your man and I think Henry is more than ready to make it up with you, if you'd just let him.'

'I haven't got my man,' I said, quickly. 'We broke up.'

I had to struggle to keep my composure. I wanted to burst into tears all over her, but I didn't dare start.

'Oh, I'm so sorry, Stella,' said Chloe, putting her hand on my arm. 'I'm really sorry. Forget everything I said. With that and what's happened with your job, I can see you're having a hard enough time without me laying a big guilt trip on you. So just forget what I said and do what you need to do to get through. You can't be having a very easy time.'

'Thanks, Chloe,' I said, holding it together by a thread. 'It is a bit crap, actually, but I'll survive.'

I bolted my coffee in one swig, told Chloe I had stuff to do and I'd see her later, but before I could get down from my stool, she put her hand on my arm again.

'Why don't you go down to Willow Barn for a while?' she said. 'Henry's in Chicago, so we won't be going down this weekend, or next. You can have some time to yourself down there.'

And as she spoke, I realized it was exactly what I needed to do.

22

Although there were reminders of my father in every inch of the place, Willow Barn seemed to work its magic on me from the moment I walked through the door.

Even though it was such a big house – the main living area was often described as 'cathedralic' by architecture writers – it was still a very comfortable space to be in on your own.

I slept in my favourite room in the kiddie corridor, had music playing night and day through the whole house, and spent my time reading, napping, walking in the garden and surrounding countryside, and exercising mindlessly.

Jay had taught me how to be busy doing nothing, I thought bitterly to myself, as I pedalled furiously on Ham's exercise bike, while watching *Brief Encounter* on cable TV.

The first time I used the pool, I had a strong flashback to the electrifying moment I had seen Ned there, glorious in his manhood, and felt sorry the way I had left things between us.

So when I got back into the house I called him – the sort of light-hearted, hello-how-are-you? do-you-want-to-meet-up-sometime? kind of call that you make to a friend, with no reference to what had happened that weird day – and I felt much better for it when I hung up.

The only thing that disturbed me about our conversation was that while I was kicking around at Willow Barn like I was on a mission to waste time, he was already having job interviews.

'I've been to see four papers, but I think it's going to be *The Observer*,' he had said excitedly. 'I had a really good meeting with them this morning and it was the stuff I did on the paper in Melbourne that they really liked – especially my series on youth gangs and organized crime – and it looks like they want to take me on as a junior investigative reporter. So I guess that means I won't be seeing you at any more key-ring launches, I'm afraid . . .'

My phone had been ringing too – the word had got round predictably quickly in my claustrophobic little world – but so far nothing had emerged I could even be bothered going up to town to follow up.

Becca had rung to tell me she could get me consulting work with Cartier anytime I wanted, and Tara Ryman had called to ask me if I wanted to join her company as a senior account director, with Huguenot as my major client.

The gossip columns of two mid-market tabloid newspapers had also offered me jobs – but they were clearly more interested in my connections with Jay and his crowd, plus my father's clients and political associates, than in my writing skills.

I diplomatically declined them all.

Then when Monday morning came around and there was a big report about the *Journal* resignations in *The Guardian* media section, I saw that there was a job going in newspapers that I was more than qualified for: Laura Birchwood had left the *Post* to take up my position on the *Journal*.

What really surprised me about it was that I didn't care. I didn't want my old job – or hers, any more – but I couldn't get excited about the idea of trying to kick-start a more challenging journalistic career either.

It was hard to admit it to myself, but if *The Observer* had called up offering me the kind of role they were signing Ned up for, I would have run a mile. Suddenly, it just all seemed too hard.

But as the days passed, in between working out and lazing about, I did have one pursuit to keep me seriously occupied down there. When I wasn't flicking through Ham's art books, snoozing through an old movie on cable – even CNN seemed too much effort – or torturing myself by listening to Van Morrison, and all the other music Jay loved, I put a lot of effort into trying to track him down.

At first I had been too shell-shocked even to try, but then something happened that shook me out of my torpor. I was idly flicking through the papers one morning when I came across a feature called 'From Crack House to Art House'.

It was about a young guy in LA who had been a hopeless crack addict, but who was now making a successful international career as a video artist, after being helped on his way by a charitable foundation which helped young drug addicts through rehab and mentored them into careers in the arts. He was having his first big London show at White Cube and everyone was very excited about him.

The piece went on at some length about the great work the foundation was doing and it was only then that it struck me: it was 'B & Me' – the charity Jay had set up in memory of his brother – yet nowhere in the article was he mentioned. He'd said he liked to keep a low profile about his involvement and now I could see he wasn't kidding.

The article said that the foundation was funded by 'anonymous benefactors' and that it was 'breaking new ground' in the rehabilitation of drug-addicted young people, with much greater success at keeping them away from substance abuse and the associated criminal lifestyle than most other post-rehab programmes.

I felt sick with shame for what I'd said that day on Sveti Stefan.

I could still see the way Jay had looked at me when I'd called the foundation 'a money-bunny guilt charity' and the shame prompted me into action: I had to get hold of him, just to apologize for that, if nothing else. I could still hear myself saying it was a 'play job'. I shuddered at the memory. How could I have been so nasty?

I also remembered all too well what he'd said about his last word being final – and I knew exactly how stubborn he was – so I didn't expect him to take me back or anything, but I had to say sorry for those awful things I'd said.

The fact that I no longer had any of his numbers did nothing to deter me. I kept trying his mobile, although I knew he would have changed it, and when I called his home number, there wasn't even an answering service on that any more either. I emailed him and it bounced back.

I rang international directory enquiries to try and find out his new home number – I had his address after all – but no dice. I knew it was hopeless, but I had to try. There must have been a bit of the dogged newspaper reporter left in me, after all, I realized.

One desperate afternoon I even called Zaria – I had her 'private' mobile number, which she had made a great show of giving me while I was in New York with Jay, so we could 'get together for girly lunches', as she had put it at the time.

I was quite surprised when she answered – in very friendly tones – it clearly was the really private number.

'Oh, hi, Zaria,' I stuttered out. 'It's Stella here – Stella Montecourt? Jay's, er, friend?'

But before I could even ask if she would give me his new mobile number, she had cut me off. I rang straight back – in case it was a transatlantic phone error – and it went straight to message bank. I didn't leave one. And when I tried the number again, a couple of days later – almost out of curiosity – I wasn't at all surprised when it just rang out.

But still I didn't give up. Even in my desperation I baulked at sending an email to the address I found on the B & Me website, so I wrote him a good old-fashioned letter and sent it off by snail mail to the New York apartment, desperately hoping it would get to him wherever he was and he would call me.

Then another line of enquiry occurred and I rang Amy at *Pratler*, to see if she had his new mobile number.

'Stella, darling,' she said. 'How great to hear from you – I was going to call you. We were talking about you in an ideas meeting the other day and Katie really wants you to write for the mag. Would you do a piece for us?'

Katie Wilde was the famously bright editor of *Pratler*, and writing for her was the first offer that had actually interested me. It might have been a society magazine, but it had really good features and was widely read. It could lead on to other interesting freelance work, I thought, maybe even *Vanity Fair*.

'That sounds interesting,' I said, feeling vaguely energized about work for the first time since I'd walked out of the *Journal*. 'What sort of thing have they got in mind?'

'Well,' said Amy. 'We want to do a major profile of Zaria Xydis. She won't give us an interview, but we've got hold of some great pictures of her from *Town and Country* and Katie thought perhaps you could ask her, because you know her so well through Jay Fisher. You saw a lot of her when you were in New York with him, didn't you?'

It was all I could do not to put the phone down on her, but I knew Amy wasn't nasty, she wasn't doing it to torture me, it was just her job. And there was no point denying any of it. Amy was kissy-kissy pals with all the people Jay and I had been hanging out with while I was in New York, she knew exactly what I'd been doing, where, when and with whom.

'Er, no, I don't think I really want to do that,' I said. 'It's a bit complicated and actually, Amy, that's why I rang you – I wondered if you can help me find Jay. I seem to have lost him again. Do you have his latest mobile number by any chance? Because the one I've got is kaput and he seems to have changed his home number too. And his email.'

'Oh, darling,' she said, sounding sincerely sorry – and more than a little disappointed. 'That is such a shame, I'd heard you two were quite the little couple, but it is how those boys operate, I'm afraid. Now, let me have a look . . .'

But the numbers she gave me were the ones I already had. I really had lost him – and that wasn't the end of it. When I opened the *Daily Mail* a couple of days later, my very worst fears were confirmed.

There was a picture of him leaving his building in SoHo with 'stunning Argentinian beef princess Patrizia

Fernandez'. Next to it was a story, quoting 'sources close to Fisher', who believed she would be the one 'finally to bag New York's most eligible bachelor' and that they were 'expecting an announcement any day'.

I studied that picture with the intensity of a scholar with a newly discovered medieval manuscript. She was beautiful, there was no denying that, and very chic. I thought back to the picture of me with him in my yoga gear, and cringed.

They weren't holding hands, that was one blessed relief, I think that would have killed me, but she was smiling, clearly very at ease in his company. I studied Jay's face. Did he look happy and in love? No, he didn't. His expression was blank, I couldn't read it at all. He could have been thinking about what he was going to have for breakfast.

When I felt strong, I told myself that maybe she had an apartment in the same building and they had just happened to be leaving at the same moment – although I'd never seen her there.

Then, if I really wanted to torture myself, I would imagine that they had been on their way round to Café Gitane for strong macchiatos, before heading off to a new exhibition and lunch at MoMA, or maybe a film at the Angelika in the afternoon, followed by dinner at Balthazar and late drinks at Bungalow 8.

Running through a scenario like that could leave me lying on the sofa sobbing for what felt like hours.

It was after one such crying jag that I decided I needed some fresh air. I went out through the back door and wandered around the garden for a while, admiring the last of the summer roses.

Then I strolled through the orchard pulling the seed

heads off the long grass and scattering them around, and checking the progress of the fruit. The plums were over, but the apples and pears were coming along nicely. They'd be ready in a couple of weeks or so.

I wouldn't be there for Ham's annual apple harvest picnic and barn dance that year, I thought sadly. It was always great fun, but I wasn't planning on taking part in any of his jolly family events anytime soon. They were just too bogus.

Without even thinking where I was going, I headed for the tree house. Its warm resinous woody smell was a comfort as soon as I climbed inside and I lay on my back on the floor, staring up at the knots in the ceiling planks and reflecting on the chain of events which had led me to be lying there in filthy old track pants and a stained T-shirt, my hair unwashed for days.

It was three o'clock on a Thursday afternoon. Had things been different, I reflected, I might just have been leaving a lunch at The Wolseley with the PR for Baume and Mercier, and wondering whether to go back to my desk at the *Journal*, before a six-thirty drinks party at the Burberry flagship store in Bond Street, to launch a new range of signature plaid iPod covers.

Alternatively, I might have been at the *Journal*, proofreading the final pages for my brilliantly successful luxury supplement, which would be coming out the next morning. Or just having a laugh in my office with Ned and Peter.

Or, I might have been sitting in Café Gitane with Jay, discussing US intervention in the internal political structures of foreign states, or the latest Ang Lee film. Or we might just have been in bed.

I rolled over on to my side and groaned. I'd fucked it all up, I thought. Even the parts of it that were within my control, I'd totally destroyed it all.

I was so wrapped up in my miserable thoughts, I didn't hear anyone climbing the steps up to the tree house and nearly died of fright when a face appeared at the door opposite me.

It was Ham.

'I thought I might find you here,' he was saying, as he struggled to get his large bulk through the small opening, and once he was inside he just took me in his arms and held me. I was so surprised I didn't protest. I sank my face into the intoxicatingly familiar smell of his shirt and wept.

'Oh, my poor baby,' he was saying. 'What have I done to you? I'm so sorry, my most beloved duckling. Please forgive me.'

I tried to speak, but I could only hiccup and splutter. It wasn't the kind of hysterical crying I'd been doing over Jay, it was more sobbing with relief. Because the moment I had seen that huge craggy head of his, I'd realized how very much I'd missed him.

'Oh, Ham,' I said, when I could finally speak. He offered me his shirt tail to blow my nose on and I did. 'I'm so sorry. I've been an idiot. I was furious with you, but I shouldn't have let it go on so long.'

'No, no,' he said. 'I'm the idiot. I've been an idiot all your life. I deserved to be told off. I don't know what I was doing with that woman, you were right, you caught me red-handed, but while I don't expect to be absolved from that, all I can tell you is that it was the first time I've strayed for years, Stella. Please believe me. And I won't do it again.'

He looked down at his hands for a moment and when he looked back up at me, there was real shame in his eyes.

'I've been looking hell in the face these past few weeks,' he said. 'Thinking what I'd do if you told Chloe and I lost her. I'll never do it again.'

'Do you promise?' I said. At least he was being honest about what he'd done at last. It was the pretending I couldn't stand.

'I promise. I really really promise. You made me realize what I was risking there. I'm not a young man any more, Stella. I may have small children, but I'm getting on. I think that's why I did it, really, the last desperate seduction of an ageing lothario, wanting to prove to himself he still has pulling power, but that's no excuse. Having small kids is all the more reason to behave like an adult myself.'

It was a fair and reasonable declaration and I decided to accept it at face value.

Sitting there with him, the air almost visibly starting to clear between us, I felt like I was able to breathe out again for the first time since I'd seen him on that terrible Friday – but then I remembered what Ned had told me about Jeanette. I had to ask him about it. I needed to know how low he was.

'Ham,' I said. 'Do you know a woman I work with – well, used to work with . . .'

He started to speak, but I stopped him.

'I'll tell you all about what happened at the *Journal* in a minute, but I need to ask you something first. I used to work with someone there called Jeanette Foster. Do you know her?'

'It's ringing a vague bell,' he said. 'What does she look like?'

'Harsh burgundy hair, weird teeth, terrible jewellery . . .'

'Oh, GOD,' said Ham. 'Not the one that ended up marrying that Lib Dem chap, what's his name . . . ?'

'Yes, that's her,' I said.

'Oh, she's the pits,' he was saying.

I said nothing, I wanted to see if he had anything to add. He did.

'Do you know, I had a terrible experience with her once. She used to be a Labour girl, and we were at the party conference in Bournemouth – years ago – and she wouldn't leave me alone. She kept trying to crack on to me, it got really embarrassing. She's got a terrible reputation, you know. She's what they call a Westminster Bicycle – she'll sleep with anyone with a seat.'

'Did you sleep with her?' I asked. I had to know.

Ham pulled a face.

'Are you mad? Have you seen what she looks like? Give me some credit, Stella, I may have been a shocking old tart in my time, but only with beautiful women.'

I couldn't help smiling. He was so appalling.

'But do you know what she did?' he was continuing. 'She just wouldn't give up, and in the middle of the night, after we'd all been at this big piss-up – I was out for the count – she came and knocked on my hotel-room door. I got up to answer it and she was standing there in this ridiculous trench coat, which she pulled open to reveal she was naked beneath, except for some ghastly cheap lingerie – stockings and suspenders, all that caper. I think I was supposed to be maddened with desire, but I'm afraid I just burst out laughing and went back to bed.'

I started to giggle, but he hadn't finished.

'And, you see, the thing is, I may have told a few people about it at breakfast the next morning and it rather got round the conference, the way these things do. She wasn't very pleased. In fact, I think that's when she went over to the Lib Dems . . .'

That was it. The laughter burst out of me like a dam breaking. I was howling with it and he joined in, until the two of us were rolling around in that tiny space. I could hardly breathe.

'Oh, my God, Ham,' I was spluttering. 'If you only knew . . .'

And then I was off again. We laughed until we had tears running down our cheeks and my stomach was aching from it. In the end we had to get out of the tree house, it was getting really claustrophobic in there with our limbs flailing around.

But Ham found it rather difficult to manoeuvre his large bulk in that tiny space, and from my vantage point behind him, with his head out of the door, his massive backside still inside, he reminded me so much of Winnie the Pooh getting stuck in Rabbit's burrow, I got even more hysterical.

In the end, we pretty much fell out and stumbled back to the house, stopping intermittently to crack up all over again, and by the time we sat down together at the round table, a bottle of champagne in front of us, I felt happier than I had for weeks.

Ham and I talked long into the night. We made dinner together – him cooking, me as a rather useless sous-chef, although Jay had taught me to chop an onion like a pro – ate it, cleared it away, and never stopped talking.

I had a lot to tell him and I realized I was soaking up his wise, inspired, measured responses to all that I had to say, like a downpour on a parched garden.

But, as we talked, I was aware that we were both skirting around what was, for me, the really big topic. In the end, it was Ham who broached it.

'So,' he said, finally. 'How are things between you and Jay Fisher?'

'They're not,' I said bluntly. 'Didn't Chloe tell you? It's all over.'

Ham looked surprised.

'No, she didn't tell me. I thought, after I'd seen that picture in the *Mail*, that you were practically living with him.'

'I suppose I was,' I said, the idea sinking in for the first time. Jay and I had been living together to all intents and purposes. I'd never done that before with anyone and I realized how much I'd loved it. That just made it all seem even worse, but I tried to make light of it.

'What can I say?' I said, shrugging casually. 'We broke up. I don't even know where he is now . . .'

It was the look on Ham's face that did it. He didn't look pleased, as I had expected him to – he looked really sad and sorry. And that's when the tears came again and, for the second time that day, I wept on my father's shoulder.

'Oh, my poor love,' Ham was saying. 'The first cut is the deepest and all that, and you've fallen in love for the first time so late in your life, it must be even harder for you.'

I just wept a bit more and let him talk. I wasn't about to remind him that I'd experienced my first love many years before and it had been Alex.

'I'm sorry about that terrible promise I forced you to make,' he was saying. 'I must have been deranged, but I'm afraid that is the effect his hideous family have on me and I just wanted to protect my most precious duckling from being hurt, when in fact, I just made it worse. If I hadn't interfered, you could have enjoyed your first love and events would have taken their natural course. And I feel terrible, because it's all my fault that you've found it so hard to surrender to those feelings in the first place. I do understand that.'

I blew my nose on his shirt again.

'Oh, don't go on about all that any more,' I said. 'What's done is done and at least I know what proper requited love is like now, even if it didn't last. And it wasn't your fault Jay and I split up, it was my fault – well, it was a bit his fault too – but if I could only turn back the clock, I'd still be with him. I brought it on myself. I was too attached to my bloody job.'

Ham looked at me, thoughtfully, for a moment.

'Tell me about him,' he said, eventually. 'I do admit that I liked him very much that day he came down here – even apart from that marvellous car, he seemed to be an engaging fellow. Good-looking too. I want to know about him. So tell me about it, right from the start.'

So I did, from the very first moment I had seen him in the garden at the Cap Mimosa. And my father being the man he was, I even told him about Jay's prodigious sexual appetites, which made him chuckle heartily.

'I knew he was a proper Alpha Male,' he said. 'I can always spot them. Takes one to know one, you know.'

He winked at me and I kicked him, lovingly, on the shin.

'Shut up, you old perve,' I said, realizing in that moment just how much I loved him.

I told him the whole story, right up to the very bitter end – rather enjoying Ham's amazed reaction when he heard what Jay had been studying at UCLA, before his father insisted he dropped out, after his brother's death.

That was a revelation to him.

'Well, blow me. I designed that whole bloody course. No wonder he was making such intelligent comments about this house,' he said, almost to himself. 'I was very impressed by that.'

'He'd presented a class paper on it,' I told him, with slightly spiteful relish. 'He knows more about it than I do.'

Ham shook his head and sighed.

'Sorry, duckling,' he said.

But he wasn't remotely surprised to hear about Jay's trials at the hands of his stepmother.

'Oh, my word, that woman is a hell monster,' he said, when I got to that part of the tale. 'She's even worse than his Uncle Edward, because she's not just nasty and neurotic, like him, she's stupid too. Stupid, but cunning, the most dangerous combination of all – and oh, that terrible son of hers. He's like a suet pudding on legs.'

He snorted with laughter, when I told him Jay called Todd the Hippo.

'Do you know,' he said, 'she was trying to get that hippo involved in the design of the institute at one point. I had to get Edward to see her off, which he rather enjoyed doing, I must say. I learned how to play them in the end, but they are a rum lot, Stella. How do you think your fellow has come out of it so relatively normal?'

'His mother, by the sound of it. She sounds really cool.'

Ham squinted at me thoughtfully.

'Hang on a minute – his mother . . . Now, something did occur to me about her. Obviously she didn't have anything to do with the building, and I thought I hadn't met her, but then after it all blew up I got to thinking that I might have known her once. Does she live in LA?'

'Used to. Topanga Canyon – like you.'

Ham snapped his fingers.

'Yes! I can place her now. Celia, that's her. We knew her back then. We were all part of the same gang up there.'

He glanced at me. He had a funny look on his face.

'Me and your mother – we knew her. Back in the seventies. Before you were born, of course, and before she met that terrible Robert Fisher. She was a great girl. Stunning-looking too . . .'

I couldn't stand it. I slumped down, my head in my hands. It was just too much.

It was a huge relief to be reunited with Ham, but I was still a mess. Job offers had continued to come in – all of them similar to my old gig, except not as good – but I just couldn't get excited about any of them. The thought of being on another luxury-brand press trip with Laura Birchwood and her ilk just held no appeal. But I had finally been forced to be truthful to myself about the Woodward and Bernstein thing too.

The whole notion of being a serious investigative reporter had never been more than a fantasy, I now accepted. An idea of the person I thought I'd wanted to be, but wasn't really. Not any more than Tim was truly a flighty fashion head.

I was really lucky, I kept telling myself like a mantra – I had my own place, so I didn't really need a job to survive – but the way I felt, I don't think I could have gone back into an office at that point, even had my life depended on it. I was still very vulnerable, as I discovered the morning the letter I had sent Jay came back unopened and with 'return to sender' on it. In his writing.

I was so wounded it put me in bed for a couple of days, until Daisy came and got me up, insisting I came and played with her myriad Sylvanian Families and their houses.

I found it strangely comforting, sitting on the floor with her, moving the small bits of furry plastic around. We made them change houses frequently, and various squirrel children would have to go and stay with the rabbits for the weekend, while mice and hedgehogs were despatched elsewhere.

'No, Stella,' Daisy said firmly, wrenching a baby badger from my hand. 'You know that baby badger doesn't like the daddy squirrel. He's going to stay with the rabbits this weekend. They're nice.'

It made total sense to both of us.

I don't know how long I might have drifted on like that, but eventually it was Ham who came up with the perfect solution to get me motivated again.

We'd just had dinner at the London house and he asked me to come through to his study, where he showed me the proposal he'd written for a new book his agent was in the process of selling around the world.

It was called *Willow Barn – the Story of a Family and a House*, and he asked me to co-write it with him.

'You know what it's like to live at Willow Barn better

than anyone, Stella,' he said. 'It has formed your family life, and ergo who you are, so who better? Plus, you are a marvellous writer. I'd love it if you would do it with me. I'd be honoured. And I think it would add another level of interest to the project if we worked on it together. Should get us loads of publicity.'

My answer was to throw my arms around him and give him my version of a double cheeseburger hug.

So, as it turned out, I would be going to the Willow Barn apple harvest picnic and barn dance that year, after all – in fact, I volunteered to organize it. I'd already swept out the old hay barn where the dancing took place, so I thought I might as well just do the whole thing.

Chloe normally did it all, but with only two months or so until the baby was due, it was a lot for her to take on, and as I was pretty much living down at Willow Barn full-time, working on the book, it seemed natural for me to take over.

I was quite excited about it. I'd spent the last five years going to lavish parties arranged by other people, as part of my job, so it was rather a lark to be organizing one myself.

I'd even had a look at some of Chloe's back issues of *Martha Stewart Living* to get some entertaining tips and I'd spent an evening discovering the joy of cookbooks for the first time, boning up on interesting ideas for barbecues. It was a whole new world for me, playing happy homemaker, and it was rather fun.

I'd just come off the phone from Chloe one evening, getting the low-down on the preferred butcher, the quantities of sausages to order, the numbers of glasses to hire, the phone number to book the ceilidh band and the rest of it, and was settling down for an orgy of list making, when the phone rang again. It was Ham.

'Darling,' he said. 'I've just been talking to Chloe and I

know you're being an angel helping her organize the apple harvest fest, but actually I'm going to make it rather different this year and I'm going to get caterers in.'

I felt so deflated, I couldn't think of anything to say.

'Don't be disappointed, Stella,' Ham said, reading my silence correctly. 'Because the thing is, we've got rather a lot of interest in our book. The American publisher wants to bring a major photographer he intends to use for the book over to see it, and there's a rather interesting film-maker who is talking about doing a feature-length documentary based on it, and he wants to visit too. So I thought they could all come to the apple harvest and experience a real Willow Barn family event. See the house as it's meant to be used.'

It was encouraging that there was a buzz starting up about the book, but I still wasn't very thrilled. I loved the hokey family and friends event the way it had always been and I'd been really rather stoked up about organizing it. I didn't want a load of Ham's architecture groupies there as well.

But he was clearly off on one, so I just let him drone on. When he was excited about something, he was an unstoppable force. My sausages on witty hazel-switch sticks would have to wait until next year.

'I've got a lot of people from the universities I teach at, who I need to entertain as well,' he was saying. 'And then there are all my students who are agitating to visit the house, so I thought we might as well have one big black-tie bash in a marquee and have them all at once.

'We'll have friends and family too, of course – the more of those, the better, for context – and we'll do the apple picking as normal and the lunchtime picnic and the barn-dance part. I just want the dinner to be more formal, but with an apple theme to the food. It will be a living example of my beliefs about the importance of formalized rituals in family life and creating fluid spaces for them to take place in . . .'

The marquee for this particular fluid yet formalized ritual was enormous, I soon discovered. It started going up several days before the event, while I was still the only one down there, and it wasn't just your bog-standard party marquee, it was a huge, circular, red and white stripy thing, like a circus tent.

'Ham,' I said, calling him on his mobile. 'Did you mean to order a big top for this dinner? It looks like Billy Smart's setting up on the lawn.'

He chuckled down the phone at me.

'Oh, excellent,' he said. 'That's just what I wanted. Has it got a large pennant flying from the central pole?'

I looked out of the window.

'Yes, with a picture of two apples on it . . .'

Ham chuckled some more and hung up on me.

Things got even weirder on the day of the big event. Chloe and the kids were all in residence and the VIPs who were staying in the Willow Barn guest wing were starting to arrive, but Ham hadn't even got down there yet.

I could hear some banging outside and when I went out to see what was going on, there were two men with lavish beards erecting a tall thin object in front of the big top.

'What on earth is that?' I asked the one with the longer beard.

He looked at me as though I were simple.

'It's a maypole,' he said.

'Did my father order that?' I asked him.

'If your father's called Henry Montecourt – yes,' said the beardy weirdy, and he went back to weaving long green, red and yellow ribbons around the pole.

'Funny time of year for one of those, isn't it?' I persisted, but he wasn't interested.

'Ask your father . . .' was all he said, and I didn't give it much more thought after that, because when Ham got going with one of his special events, anything was possible.

So, I just put it out of my mind – along with the large quantity of empty barrels which were just being delivered, out of which, I gathered, we were going to bob for apples; and the Druid priest and his attendants, who, Chloe had told me over breakfast, were coming to bless the trees and the harvest.

He loved a theme, did Ham.

Once it all kicked off and we actually got going with the apple harvest, I pretty much forgot about his more over-the-top details, it was so much fun.

The whole family was there, plus the much-loved add-ons. Archie was a permanent fixture with us now, and Alex came too, bringing Rose – and Monkey, of course.

I didn't know whether it was the looming presence of Ham's ridiculous stripy tent, the prospect of a proper black-tie rave-up, or just general high spirits, but they did all seem particularly excited.

We all loved a party down there, but Archie and Tabitha, in particular, seemed to be in a permanent state of near hysteria and Venezia kept changing her outfit into briefer and briefer ensembles, until so much of her midriff was on show, Ham sent her inside to put a shirt on.

At one point Daisy appeared in the orchard wearing a pair of terrible sparkly white shoes, like the ones little Mexican girls wear to get confirmed in, until Chloe quickly ushered her back to the house to change out of them.

I'd been spending so much time down there on my own, I decided I'd just forgotten what a bunch of nuts my collective family were.

As well as the academics and earnest-looking young people I assumed were Ham's students, who were taking photographs of us like we were some kind of anthropological display, friends arrived all through the afternoon and pitched in with the apple picking.

Ham had encouraged me to invite as many of my 'pals', as he called them, as possible, ranting on about it being an essential part of the mix to make the event work. I thought it was probably about time for me to entertain them, for once, so I'd invited Becca, Tim, Tara and Amy and they'd all come. Even Peter and his wife Renee showed up.

He'd finally rung me a few weeks before and I'd been delighted to find that he was back to his old self – and with good reason. He had a new job as a media commentator on Radio 4's *Today* programme, and from that position of strength, he had decided to take the *Journal* on over his pension entitlement – and the NUJ was going to pay his legal fees. They were making it a test case and it looked like the *Journal* were going to settle out of court, generously, in Peter's favour.

I'd already heard him on air with James Naughtie making much of the fact that he couldn't report on this particular item himself, because it concerned him, which only helped to hype it up into a much bigger story, written up in depth in all the newspapers, apart from the *Journal*.

To my particular delight, Martin and Jeanette had both come out of it all looking as scummy as they were. It had been a real 'trial by media' for both of them, which gave me intense satisfaction after what she'd done to me via the press.

To celebrate their humiliation I'd had a very funny dinner at The Groucho with Peter and Ned. And when I told them the full story about Jeanette and my father, they had laughed so much, I thought we might be asked to leave. Ned had been literally rolling around under the table spluttering.

I'd invited him to the harvest too, of course, and he was a great addition to the party, with his sense of fun – and his long swimmer's arms, which were excellent for reaching high branches.

Over time our friendship had settled back down into its old easy bantering companionship, although I was still conscious of not letting myself get too close to him physically. The spark was still there at a hormonal level, there was no denying it, whatever my brain and sense of propriety thought about it, but I knew it was just an animal reaction.

I watched him, sitting in a tree, fast-bowling cooking apples to Alex and Archie, who were fielding at far-flung points of the orchard, and I had to smile. The female architecture students seemed to find that scenario particularly photogenic, and so did a man with a camcorder, who I assumed was the documentary film-maker.

Alex was on fine form too. I'd hardly seen him for months, so it was great to catch up with him. He was always at his best down at Willow Barn, I thought, out in the open air, where he loved to be, fooling around, pink with exertion, and having a laugh. And I couldn't help noticing that he and Tara seemed to be getting on rather well too.

Ham just walked about the place beaming until I thought his face might split open. It was his idea of heaven: a classic Willow Barn family and friends event, with perfect Indian summer weather – and with lots of suitably informed people to watch us all being fabulously Willow Barn-y.

The only thing that seemed to be causing him any stress was his table plan. He'd mull for ages over how to seat 10 of us at a family dinner, so 240 people at 24 round tables was a huge deal for him; especially as he gave whole lectures on the topic, relating it back to 'further considerations of proximity and fluidity in the family home', as he put it.

This one was a major challenge, not only because of the sheer numbers – and the high proportion of guests who thought they were terribly important – but also because he was shamelessly showing off to his peers, fans and sycophants.

As a 'senior family member' and his co-author, I was hosting one of the key tables, he told me, and when I nipped into the big top for a quick snoop before dinner, after he'd put the place cards round, I was surprised to see that I had Alex sitting next to me.

I'd expected to have someone a little more germane to the success of the book project to look after and my heart sank as I realized Ham must be back to matchmaking between us again.

Despite those misgivings, I took special care with my appearance as I got ready for the dinner. I was excited about the book, after all, and wanted to do everything I could to help it along.

It felt really weird putting make-up on, though. I spent my time now pretty much permanently in my scruffiest clothes and I had to yank my mascara wand to get it out of the tube, it was so long since I had used it.

Mostly, I was quite happy to have left that pressured world of image behind, but for one night, I reckoned, I could turn it on again. Ham had given me a pair of beautiful Myla knickers for the occasion – chosen by Chloe – to get me in the mood, he'd said.

I couldn't imagine many women received that kind of underwear from their fathers, I thought, but from him, it just seemed normal.

As I slipped into them and then buckled on my gold Prada wedges, it was like stepping back into my former self, and when I looked in the mirror at the woman in the blue silk Lanvin dress, it was a little like looking at an old friend I hadn't seen for a while. I blew her a kiss.

As the dinner hour approached, I made sure I was at my table early to greet my guests. The film-maker was one of them, and he arrived with his camera rolling. He'd had the bloody thing going all day.

By ten minutes after the appointed time, everyone on my table had sat down apart from Alex.

I was just starting to wonder where the hell he was when he rushed over, looking gorgeous in his black tie, but even pinker in the cheeks than normal, and changed the name card on the place next to me.

'Last-minute change, Stella,' he said. 'Ham wants to put one of his students next to you, instead of me.'

I turned to speak to him, but he'd gone, so I glanced at the place card he'd put down to see who I was getting. I looked and blinked, wondering if I was seeing right. In immaculate black calligraphy, it said 'Jay Fisher'.

I was squinting at it, thinking that my eyes must be playing tricks on me, when Ham got up, clinking his glass with a spoon, to call everyone to attention so he could introduce the dinner.

As every head in the room turned to look at him, someone came and slid into the seat next to me.

It was Jay.

Jay, looking like a celestial being in black tie. Jay grinning at me, like it was the biggest lark in the world. Jay putting his arms round me and pulling me to him and kissing me, regardless of anyone else nearby. I noticed the film-maker had his camera pointed right at us, but I didn't care.

'So, are you pleased to see me?' he said.

I just nodded, like a moron.

'Well, are you going to say hello?' he asked, his eyes twinkling with mischievous delight.

'But Alex said it was going to be one of Dad's students . . .' I said, when I finally regained my powers of speech. I was still in shock.

'I am one of his students,' said Jay. 'I'm going back to college, Stella, in London – and your father has taken me on as an intern. I've done three years of architecture school already, remember.'

I closed my eyes and opened them again, just to make sure he was still there. He was.

After that we had to stop talking, because Ham was making his speech, although I noticed his eyes kept flicking over to me and Jay and he looked ready to burst with excitement.

'And so,' he was saying, 'I'm delighted to welcome you all to Willow Barn. Some of you are old friends, some are visiting for the first time – some for the second time . . .'

He looked over at us again, this time very deliberately. I leaned my head against Jay's shoulder and grinned back at him. Jay waved.

'And I hope you will all feel welcome in what is, above all other considerations, my family's home. All my family are here tonight to share it with you – every last one of them, which is saying something – and if anyone has any questions, there will be a short interactive session after the pudding, when you can ask me, or any of the family, anything you would like to know about the house and our lives here.'

The dinner was a complete blur for me. There may have been other people at the table, but I'm afraid I didn't speak to any of them. Jay and I might as well have been alone in that marquee.

'I tried to find you, Jay,' I told him. 'Not long after I left Sveti Stefan, I tried to find you, I knew I'd made a terrible mistake, and I felt so bad about what I said about your foundation. I really didn't understand how serious it was, and it was terrible what I said. I'm so sorry.'

My eyes filled up with tears and I thought I was going to lose it, but Jay just shook his head and kissed me tenderly on the lips.

'I couldn't get hold of you anywhere,' I continued. 'You'd changed all your numbers and then you sent my letter back. That's when I knew it was hopeless.'

'I'm sorry about that,' he said. 'That was brutal, but I was so hurt when you chose your job over me, and yes, the "toy

422

charity" thing did get to me, but it's OK, we all say dumb stuff in the heat of the moment and I hadn't told you about it properly anyway, so how were you supposed to know?'

We sat there for a moment, just looking at each other and breathing. It seemed such a miracle to be doing that in the same space again.

'And anyway, Stella,' he said eventually, entwining his fingers with mine, 'it wasn't just you that made me freak out that day. I was so confused about my dad and all that back then, I wasn't thinking straight at all. I so wanted to get back in touch with you, but I was just too ashamed of the way I'd behaved. And too stupidly stubborn . . .'

I bit him tenderly on the tip of his nose. Because I could.

'So where have you been all this time?' I asked him.

'I went back to New York first up, but I just couldn't hack being in the apartment without you . . .' He frowned a little. 'Did you see that paparazzi picture of me coming out of it with Patrizia, incidentally?'

I nodded, feeling a bit sick.

'I thought you would. She's just a friend, I've known her forever, and she's subletting the place from me, because I couldn't stand to be there without you. I'd been showing her round when they got that picture, the bastards. Anyway, I've been at my mom's ever since. I've been helping her with the grape harvest, and just hanging out, cooking, weeding the vegetable patch, swimming, sleeping, wasting my life, being a dumb "money bunny", as you call it, and thinking about you.'

Just what I'd been doing at Willow Barn, I thought. I shook my head, it was so nuts, I still couldn't take it in. All

423

those days of longing and loneliness and now he was really there. I kept touching him to make sure. Then I realized I hadn't asked him the obvious question.

'But how did you come to be here?'

Jay's eyes twinkled with mischief.

'Like I said, I'm your dad's student . . .'

'So how did you come to be his student, smartypants?' I said, poking him gently in his stomach, so he wriggled. I'd forgotten quite how nice that stomach was.

'Well, first he found me and invited me to this party . . .'

'OK, Jay Fisher,' I said. 'Enough of the mystery-man business, I've waited too long to see you – tell me exactly how you came to be here tonight. From the beginning.'

'Well, like I say, it was your dad. He's quite an operator. He called up Edward – you know, my heinous uncle, the one he did the museum with? – and got my mom's number on some pretext, and she took the call, because they knew each other back in the day, and she handed the phone to me. It was as simple as that.'

I just shook my head in amazement. Why didn't I think of that connection?

'But what did he say to you?'

'He said his most beloved firstborn daughter had a broken heart and that he felt responsible and that he was really sorry for intervening in our relationship and asked me if I would like to come to the Willow Barn apple harvest.'

'What did you say?' I asked.

'I said I would walk there from Santa Fe, barefoot, across broken glass, if I thought you would see me again. And then I asked him if he would consider taking me on as a student.'

424

'And he did?'

Jay laughed.

'No. He said that was an entirely different conversation and that I needed to send a formal application with my CV and all my college reports to his office. So I did – and he took me on, but I only found that bit out today.'

Then he kissed me a lot.

There was a bit of a break between the main course and the pudding, with people going to the loo and outside for ciggies, and I told Jay I was going over to thank Ham. He came with me. So did the film-maker, but I was getting used to him.

'Actually, Stella,' said Jay, as we walked across the marquee. 'There's someone on your father's table I really want you to meet.'

She'd been sitting with her back to me during the dinner, but as soon as she heard Jay's voice and turned round I knew straight away who it was – Celia, Jay's mother. She stood up and beamed at me, and then embraced me, like a long-lost friend.

'I know exactly who you are, honey,' she said to me. 'I am so happy to meet you, Stella. Jay has been wasting away on me, pining for you. I don't want you two to split up ever again. OK?'

'Neither do I,' I said, grinning back at her.

Ham came round to join us, beaming like a bright planet of delight. I hugged him with every ounce of hug I had in my body.

'Thank you, Ham,' I said. 'Thank you.'

There was nothing else to say.

Jay and I joined his table for the rest of the dinner and

it was the best fun. Every member of my mad mixed-up jigsaw of a family came over to kiss me and tease me and to tell me how they had known for ages that Jay was coming and how hard it had been not to let on. Especially when he had arrived a bit early and they'd had to hide him from me in the pool house.

Archie was hyper about the whole thing.

'I put him in the tree house first,' he said, between Butt-head sniggers. 'Then I thought – bad move – too obvious, Stella loves the tree house. So then I thought: pool house, yeah.' He clicked his fingers, like a jazz singer.

'Go on, Archie,' I said. 'Tell me the route.'

He beamed.

'Well, it was a hard call, because I had to avoid the barn and the house, so I went, tree house, paddock, drive, *behind* copse, lower garden, *behind* summer house, east side of lawn – we had to run that bit – guest-wing French windows, kitchen courtyard, kitchen garden, pool house. It was pretty risky – particularly the kitchen courtyard section – but I couldn't see any other way.'

I kissed his pimply cheek and, for once, he didn't flinch away.

'Mind you,' he said, 'I did have a sheet over his head as well.'

The question-and-answer session after the pudding was a little dull for those of us already well versed in Ham's theories, with the academics and students asking questions designed primarily to show how clever they were. I really just wanted to escape to be alone with Jay, but I knew I couldn't.

There was one moment of levity when Tabitha, clearly

goaded on by Rose and Alex, stood up and said she had a question for Ham.

She stood on her chair and said clearly to the whole room: 'Please can Daisy have a pug puppy for Christmas?'

He had to agree and everyone cheered.

After that the questioners returned to more earnest enquiries about the long-term emotional implications of the parental turret and the metaphorical meaning of the bamboo walk.

Then Jay stood up to ask a question. I thought he was being a bit keen as Ham's newest student, but at least it showed willing.

'I have a question for you, Henry,' he said, smiling broadly. 'Please can I have your permission to marry your eldest daughter?'

The room was silent for a moment, then everyone yelled and clapped and whistled their approval.

'I would be delighted, Jay,' Ham said. 'But you'll have to ask her – she's a very independent girl, as you know.'

Jay turned to me. I was dizzy from shock – first him turning up and now this.

'Will you marry me, Stella, baby?' he said.

A million thoughts raced across my brain in a nano-second as I stood there, everyone in the tent staring at me, my most intimate personal life on display as entertainment for the guests at Ham's party. A cute little footnote for future studies of the work of Lord Montecourt, I thought bitterly.

My first instinct was to flee from that marquee, pausing only to throw something heavy at my father's head. I felt a flash of pure white rage at him for orchestrating this outrageous situation and my head snapped round to give him a death-ray stare, but then I looked back at Jay's face and my anger immediately disappeared.

His expression was so loving and gentle, with a distinct hint of nerves in the eyes. And he had reason to be nervous – I'd never wanted to get married, he knew that. I stood there, silent, for another hearbeat, seriously considering my answer. But suddenly it was out of my mouth before I really knew it was happening. I loved this man. I wanted to spend the rest of my life with him. That was all that mattered.

'Yes,' I whispered.

'Louder!' shouted some wag from the back, who I had a strong feeling was Peter Wallington, so I said it again in my most ringing tones.

'Yes!'

There was a great roar of cheering and when it had all calmed down, Jay spoke again.

'Tonight?' he said.

I looked at him – then back at Ham, and suddenly it all made sense. The huge marquee. The filming. Daisy's sparkly shoes. The bloody maypole.

Ham threw back his head and roared with laughter. It was a total set-up. But this time I couldn't even be cross with him.

'Yes,' I said firmly. 'Yes, I will.'

I wasn't going to let Jay Fisher slip through my fingers again.

Of course, we couldn't actually get married there and then – there are forms to fill in, identities to prove, bans to be read and all that, before you can get legally hitched – but we had a symbolic wedding, conducted by the Druid priest, under a bower of fruit-laden apple branches in the centre of Ham's big top, with all my family and dearest friends there to share it with us.

I had to hand it to my father, I thought, as he walked me up what I could now see was the aisle – a straight gap from the top table to the bower – he might have been a shocking old control freak, but as Jay said, he was a hell of an operator. He'd got his big wedding without me having to get legally married. It was very clever and now I was stuck with it, I had to admit, all the details were perfect.

Darling Daisy was my bridesmaid, in her terrible sparkly shoes, Jay was resplendent in black tie, and I carried the floral centrepiece from Ham's table as my bouquet. Alex was Jay's best man and my ring was a free gift from one of Daisy's princess comics. Suited me.

I was even, I realized, wearing something old and blue – my dress, the one I'd had on the night I met Jay. Suddenly the new knickers made sense too, and Chloe insisting I borrowed her beautiful pearl drop earrings, to look my best 'To impress the film-maker', she'd said – and there he was again, I realized, happily filming as we made our vows. Nothing had been left to chance.

And that wasn't the end of it. When we left the big top to go over to the hay barn for the dancing, the two bearded men and several more of their ilk were skipping merrily around the maypole. I laughed so much I couldn't walk, so Jay picked me up and carried me.

The only aspect of the big fat bogus wedding Ham had thrust upon me that I refused to go along with was a bridal

429

waltz – carried away as I was with the lark of it all, I still had my limits.

Instead, I introduced Jay to the hectic delights of Strip the Willow and other exhausting reels and country dances – during which I was happy to notice that Alex and Tara seemed to be glued together, totally ignoring all the bits where you were supposed to change partners, and just dancing with each other.

Then, while everyone was caught up in the frenzy of the ceilidh, Jay and I quietly made our exit, and walked through the moonlit garden together, just savouring the moment.

I said nothing as he led me down across the orchard, round the pool, through the walled kitchen garden, into the house by the back door and out again through the glass doors at the front – clearly, he knew the plan of the place as well as I did – then past the marquee and down to the summer house at the end of the lawn.

I lay on the slatted wooden seat with my head in his lap, looking up at him and still marvelling that he was even there – let alone pretend-married to me.

'Hello, Mrs Non-Fisher,' he said, stroking my hair. Then he got a more serious look on his face.

'Er,' he continued, with unusual hesitance, 'you see, the thing is, Mrs Non-F – I've got one little thing I have to tell you. I hope you're not going to be mad I didn't do it before I got that plastic ring on your finger.'

I just smiled up at him and kissed the ring. What else could they possibly spring on me? I wondered, glancing around to see if there was a camera rolling.

'Will you mind being married to an impoverished architecture student?' he said.

'What do you mean?' I asked him.

'I quit,' he said. 'I'm not the heir any more. I had plenty of time to think about it while I was hiding out at my mom's place and she totally supports my decision. She encouraged me. I told my dad just before I came over here. The Hippo can have the lot, all the money and all the hassle. I mean, I should get to keep my trusts, although he could fight me for all of it, if he felt like it, and darling Jaclyn will certainly want him to, but I don't care. He can have it. I just want my own life – and you.'

I sat up and wrapped my arms around him. As unwedding presents go, it wasn't exactly conventional – but from Jay, it was the best I could have asked for.

'You're not disappointed, are you?' he asked me, sounding sincerely concerned.

I shook my head and smiled at him.

'Just as long as you understand that I'll have to get a job to support us . . .' I said.